# THE WITCH TREE
## By
## CEANE O'HANLON-LINCOLN

# THE WITCH TREE
## By
## CEANE O'HANLON-LINCOLN

A Sleuth Sisters Mystery
Book six in the bewitching series

A Magick Wand Production
"Thoughts are magick wands powerful enough to make anything happen– anything we choose!"

*This book is lovingly dedicated to time-travelers everywhere ~*
*And to my husband, Phillip R. Lincoln, who bought me my ticket.*

*Warm gratitude and blessings bright and beautiful to:*
*My husband Phillip,*

*And to my muses Beth Adams; Carrie Bartley; Janet Barvincak;*
*Sandy Bolish; William Colvin; Glen Gallentine; Nancy Hrabak;*
*Renowned psychic and High Priestess Kelly M. Kelleher;*
*Kathy Lincoln; Marie Lorah; Jean Minnick; Robin Moore;*
*Madeleine Stephenson;*
*And songstress, poet and author extraordinaire~*
*Rowena of the Glen~*

*For all the reasons they each know so well.*

A special, heartfelt thank-you to Rowena of the Glen/
Rowena Whaling
For the permission to use the lyrics to "Trance Dance"
(Parts 1 and 2)
From her magickal album *Book of Shadows*

iv

# THE WITCH TREE
### By
## Ceane O'Hanlon-Lincoln

## A Sleuth Sisters Mystery

## The Sleuth Sisters Mystery Series:
### ~By Ceane O'Hanlon-Lincoln~

In this paranormal-mystery series, Raine and Maggie McDonough and Aisling McDonough-Gwynn, first cousins, are the celebrated Sleuth Sisters from the rustically beautiful Pennsylvania town of Haleigh's Hamlet. With their magickal Time-Key, these winning white witches are able to unlock the door that will whisk them through yesteryear, but who knows what skeletons and dangers dangle in the closets their Key will open?

One thing is certain– magick, adventure, and surprise await them at the creak of every opening door and page-turn.

*The Witches' Time-Key*, book one of the *Sleuth Sisters Mystery Series*

*Fire Burn and Cauldron Bubble*, book two
*The Witch's Silent Scream*, book three
*Which Witch is Which?* book four
*Witch-Way*, book five
*The Witch Tree*, book six of the *Sleuth Sisters Mysteries*:
When their fellow sisters of the moon, the Keystone Coven, call upon the Sleuth Sisters to aid them in saving a 300-year-old plus, majestic oak tree from destruction at the hands of land developers, Raine, Maggie, and Aisling galvanize into action. The Witch Tree possesses a *mysterious* history, as well as the spirit of the powerful Colonial witch, Hester Duff. As the savvy Sisters struggle to save the tree, their efforts fire an already bubbling cauldron of mystery, mayhem and murder!

**Watch for *The Witch's Secret*, book seven in the bewitching series– coming soon!**
Amazon Books / www.amazon.com/amazon books

~~~

**Also by Ceane O'Hanlon-Lincoln:**

**In the mood for something different– something perhaps from another time and place?**

*Autumn Song* is a harmonious medley of short stories threaded and interwoven by their romantic destiny themes and autumnal settings.

Voodoo, ghostly lovers, and figures from the past– all interwoven into a collection of tales that will haunt you forever.

**Read the stories in the order the author presents them in the book for the most surprises.** *And the author hopes you like surprises!*

Each tale in this compelling anthology evokes its own special ambiance– and sensory impressions. *This book is a keeper you will re-visit often, as you do an old and cherished friend.*

O'Hanlon-Lincoln never judges her characters, several of whom resurface from tale to tale. These are honest portrayals, with meticulously researched historic backdrops, intrigue– *magick*– surprise endings– and thought-provoking twists.

For instance, in "A Matter of Time," on which side of the door is the main character when the story concludes?

From the first page of *Autumn Song*, the reader will take an active role in these fascinating stories, discovering all the electrifying threads that connect them.

How many will *you* find?

Available at Amazon Books / www.amazon.com/amazon books

~~~

*And*
**The award-winning history series:**

*County Chronicles*
*County Chronicles Volume II*
*County Chronicles Volume III*
*County Chronicles Volume IV*
*County Chronicles: There's No Place Like Home!*

"If you haven't read this author's **County Chronicles**, then you haven't discovered how *thrilling* history can be!  With meticulous research and her "state-of-the-heart" storytelling, Ceane O'Hanlon-Lincoln breathes life into historical figures and events with language that flows and captivates the senses." ~ Mechling Books / www.mechlingbooks.com

"I write history like a story, because that's what history is, a story– or rather, *layered* stories of the most significant events that ever unfolded!  Each volume of my *County Chronicles* is a spellbinding collection of *true* stories from Pennsylvania's exciting past."

~ Ceane O'Hanlon-Lincoln

~~~

# The Witch Tree
## ~ Cast of Characters ~

**Raine and Maggie McDonough, PhDs**– Sexy, savvy Sisters of the Craft, who *are* more like sisters than cousins. With sorcery in their glittering emerald eyes, these bewitching Pennsylvania history professors stir up a cauldron of action to save, in their neighboring town of Washingtonville, a haunted, majestic oak tree from destruction at the hands of land developers.

Will these "mystery magnets" be able to save the historic tree, solve its mystery *and* the mysteries connected to it?

**Aisling McDonough-Gwynn**– The blonde with the wand is the senior Sister in the magickal trio known, in Haleigh's Hamlet and beyond, as the "Sleuth Sisters." Aisling and her husband **Ian**, former police detectives, are partners in their successful Black Cat Detective Agency.

The Gwynns have a preteen daughter **Meredith (Merry) Fay**, who mirrors her magickal mother. Merry was named for the McDonough *grande dame*, who resides in the "Witch City" of Salem, Massachusetts.

**Aisling Tully McDonough**– The Sleuth Sisters' beloved **"Granny"** was the grand mistress of Tara, the Victorian mansion, where Raine and Maggie came of age, and where they yet reside. Born in Ireland, the departed Granny McDonough left her female heirs a very special gift– and at Tara, with its magickal mirrors, Granny is but a glance away.

**The Myrrdyn/ Merlin Cats**– Descendants of Granny McDonough's magickal feline Myrrdyn (the Celtic name for Merlin), these "Watchers" are the Sisters' closest companions. Wholly *familiar* with the Sleuth Sisters' powers, desires and needs, the Myrrdyn/ Merlin cats faithfully offer moral support, special knowledge– and timely messages.

**Cara**– The ancient spirit in the Sleuth Sisters' poppet continually proves– as the witched little doll's name suggests– to be a great friend to Raine, Maggie, and Aisling. But will Cara's magick prove strong enough against an especially unconscionable evil?

**Thaddeus Weatherby, PhD**– This absent-minded professor and head of Haleigh College's history department has an Einstein mind coupled with an uncontrollable childish curiosity that has been known to cause unadulterated mischief for the Sleuth Sisters. Thaddeus and Maggie are lovers and reunited kindred spirits.

**Beau Goodwin**– Raine's dashing **Beau**, soul mate, and next-door neighbor is a superior veterinarian with an extraordinary sixth sense. After all– his patients can't tell him what's wrong. Like Raine, this Starseed, too, is an empath and Old Soul, and he has a way about him that keeps his other half positively– *enchanted.*

**Hugh Goodwin**– Beau's semi-retired veterinary father– whose acute sixth sense matches his son's– has an avid appetite for mystery novels and an astonishing aptitude for solving them that the Sleuth Sisters find absolutely "wizard."

**Betty Donovan**– A retired librarian, Hugh's attractive companion shares his intense love of mysteries and is fast becoming his equal in solving them.

**Great-Aunt Meredith/ "Grantie Merry" McDonough**– A celebrated Salem witch and the McDonough *grande dame* who gifted Athena, the powerful, antique crystal ball, to the Sisters. Grantie's magick is wholly benign.

**Hannah Gilbert**– The Sleuth Sisters' loyal, protective housekeeper is a fountain of homespun wisdom. Her quirky purple sneakers and garish muumuus are indicative of her colorful personality– and like many snoopy servants before her, she continues to gather information that abets and serves the Sleuth Sisters in their quests.

**Eva Novak**– The Gypsy Tearoom proprietress' own special brew of "Tea-Time-Will-Tell" is not the *only* sustenance this charismatic woman delivers to the Sleuth Sisters.

**Kathy Wise**– Known throughout Haleigh's Hamlet as "Savvy Kathy," this receptionist at the Hamlet's Auto Doctor has been known to set the Sisters rolling on the path to discovery.

**Sophie Miller**– The owner of the charming Sal-San-Tries café-deli. Her delectable **sal**ads, **san**dwiches, and pas**tries** often fit the bill for the swamped, short-of-time Sleuth Sisters.

**Belle Christie**– Haleigh Hamlet's most popular beautician and its theatre's makeup artist frequently knows more than she tells. Belle's peels, concealers, and masks are *not* confined to her craft.

**Dr. Benjamin Wight**– Braddock County's supercilious coroner unexpectedly finds himself faced with the supernatural!

**Hester Duff/ "Dark Star"**– This powerful Colonial witch, whose name, Hester, is burned forever into the bark and essence of the Witch Tree, was destined to be burned into the collective memory of posterity too!

**Windwalker**– Hester's Delaware shaman friend, boon companion, and teacher. What magick did this wise "grandfather" perform for Mistress Duff?

**Will Granger**– The elderly farmer, who owns the property upon which the Witch Tree stands, is resolute in regard to the disposition of Witch-Tree Farm.

**Amanda Granger Woods**– Like her uncle, Will's niece seeks protection for the tree and Witch-Tree Farm, a legacy of the Granger family for over 100 years.

**Sam Woods**– Is Amanda's husband, the manager of the Washingtonville Lumber Company, a prime example of "Can't see the forest for the trees"?

**Gail Friday**– Will Granger's friend and neighbor whom he entrusts with a variety of tasks.

**Rex Chambers**– The "King of the Builders" and wealthy owner of Chambers Construction wants to purchase Witch-Tree Farm, fell the tree and build elite condos. The begging question is: Just how far is Chambers Construction willing to go to get what they want?

**Sirena Chambers**– Rex's daughter is being groomed to take over his thriving business, and like her father, she's used to getting what she wants. Sirena is rich, intelligent and beautiful. She's a siren– and she's harboring a dark secret.

**Derrick H. Mason**– The owner of DHM Construction Company and Rex Chambers' arch rival. He, too, wants to purchase Witch-Tree Farm, so he can remove the tree to put up a shopping center.

**Reggie Mason**– Derrick's playboy son is determined to prove himself and regain his father's approval! He has a wealth of ideas in his head– *but what is in his heart?*

**Etta Story**– A retired newspaper reporter and president of Washingtonville Historical Society, Etta is on a do-or-die quest to win Witch-Tree Farm for the society! And how far will *she* go to achieve this fervid goal?

**Mildred Grimm**– Fueled by political ambitions and her obstinate resolve to see a shopping center on the site of Witch-Tree Farm, the president of Washingtonville Town Council is spouting caustic opinions about the Witch Tree and the family connected to Witch-Tree Farm, the Sleuth Sisters, the Keystone Coven, and anyone else who gets in her way!

**Grace Seymour**– Just what did the nosy but "saving Grace" see at the Washingtonville Harvest Dance that ultimately helps the Sleuth Sisters in this baffling case?

**Teresa Moore**– Like the Sleuth Sisters, this Gypsy-at-heart descendant of Hester Duff travels to the beat of a different drum– and she has something *instrumental* in her possession that really strikes a chord with the Sleuth Sisters.

**Moonglow and Starlight**– These ardent sisters of the Keystone Coven, who live together in Washingtonville, have been *illuminating* the entire town that they'll stop at *nothing* to prevent destruction of the Witch Tree!

**High Priestess Robin and the Keystone Coven**– As they have in the past, the Keystone Coven joins forces with the Sleuth Sisters toward a unified aspiration that spells– *magick.*

**Chief Mann**– Known in his town as "The Man," Washingtonville's Chief of Police gets the word from Chief Fitzpatrick of Haleigh's Hamlet to trust the savvy Sleuth Sisters!

"I don't think you really want to know if I am a good witch
or a bad witch!
I'm not *just* a witch– I'm a storm with skin!"
~ Dr. Raine McDonough, PhD


"Evil comes to all us men of imagination,
wearing as its mask all the virtues."
~ W.B. Yeats


"Careful!  Careful what you *witch* for!"
~ Author Ceane O'Hanlon-Lincoln

"For all you know,
a witch might be living next door to you right now."
~ Roald Dahl

"I do believe in magick.
My heart is a thousand years old.  I am not like other people."
~ Author Ceane O'Hanlon-Lincoln


"Any time women come together with a collective intention, it's a
powerful thing …
when women come together with a collective intention–
*magick* happens."
~ Phylicia Rashad
~~~

# ~ Prologue ~

Known far and wide as the "Sleuth Sisters," raven-haired Raine and redheaded Maggie McDonough, cousins who shared the same surname, residence, and occupation, as well as a few other things in what could only be termed their *magickal* lives, were getting dressed for the day. It was a chilly, rainy Saturday morning in late October. As they dressed, their thoughts were on *mystery*, for they could keenly sense that another astonishing adventure was about to unfold in their extraordinary lives.

Last spring, they had no sooner returned from a thrilling mystery-solving sojourn that began in Scotland's remote Orkney Islands and concluded in the Witch City of Salem, Massachusetts, when they were asked to delve into the unsolved ax murders that had horrified their town of Haleigh's Hamlet in 1932. Though it took them several weeks to solve the nerve-jangling cold case, the "Sisters" were successful, proving yet again their merit as super-sleuths.

In her woodsy-themed bedroom with its large, green-marble fireplace, Raine slipped a lipstick, in her favorite shade of Gypsy Red, into her purse, a black shoulder bag with the Celtic Triquetra tooled into the leather. Turning partway round, she checked her appearance in the tall cheval glass. *I'll stop wearing black when they invent a darker color,* she laughed to herself. *Black is my happy color!*

The raven-haired Sister often donned Gothic attire, the style suiting her to the proverbial "T." Her Beau called her witchy chic "Raine gear." (Witches have always known that wearing black– like showering something, or someone, with water– neutralizes dark, negative energies.)

Today a favorite black Victorian blouse, with stand-up collar, coupled with a long riding skirt accentuated her trim figure. Raine loved witchy shoes and boots, and the vintage, high-button boots she sported today possessed all the witchy-woman wow she fancied. She smiled at the thought: *Women who wear black lead colorful lives.*

Down the hall in her bedroom, Maggie was just finishing her makeup. She stepped back from the bureau mirror to check her overall appearance. Taller than Raine and fuller-figured, Maggie, like her cousin and sister of the moon, enjoyed donning vintage clothing. But unlike Raine, the redheaded Maggie loved color, bright colors concordant with her passionate Scorpio nature. The green, Forties-style knit dress she chose for today skimmed her voluptuous curves, making her look quite fetching. Seeking the artsy scarf, splashed with autumn colors she'd set out earlier, her eyes scanned the room.

As spacious as Raine's bedchamber, this Sister's room, too, was graced with a substantial fireplace, though the marble here was dark red, the high-ceilinged room's palette the fiery hues of garnet and gold. Fall was Maggie's favorite time of year, and in her boudoir, it was forever autumn.

When Raine emerged from her room, she met Maggie in the upper corridor. "I've been thinking about our current challenge, and I feel quite confident we'll find a way to save the Witch Tree."

"Surely, our energies, combined with those of our dear sisters from Keystone Coven–" Maggie bobbed her head in an abrupt gesture, "Yes, we'll succeed in our quest."

It was the Sisters' custom to throw themselves into spirit-boosting pep talks when tackling a new mystery, for it quite bolstered their confidence. "In keeping with the Great Secret," Raine was fond of saying, "the *real* magick is believing in oneself!"

"I just hope," Maggie twirled a strand of her dark-red hair in a vague, pensive gesture, "there won't be any–"

"Fiddle-dee-dee!" Raine interposed with a wave of a bejeweled hand and typical Aries impetuosity. "People don't call us the 'Sleuth Sisters' for nothing!" She started briskly down the hall for the stairs.

"There are circumstances," Maggie began with raised brow, as she trailed after Raine, "with things of this nature that–"

"There always are," Raine said after a rapt moment, "but nothing *we* won't be able to handle."

Maggie grabbed Raine's arm, pausing her on the stairway landing. "What I'd started to say," Maggie cautioned, "is that greed and, or, some other evil could well be at the root of our tree problem; pun intended. And depending on how greedy the land developers are who're after Witch-Tree Farm, the situation could get sticky. Let's review what we know thus far through breakfast. Brainstorming always helps us unlock thought and reason, so we can connect the dots."

"Good idea," Raine returned.

Starting down the stairs, the Goth gal repeated thrice, more to the Universe than to her cousin and sister of the Craft, "We've bested evil before! We can do it again, and that's for sure!"

Raine was referring to their vanquishing of the ancient *Macbeth* curse from Whispering Shades, the Hamlet's "little theatre in the woods," that resulted in the most terrifying of battles. Besides ousting a bane of evil from their town and beloved theatre, they managed, in the bargain, to soothe Whispering Shades' resident ghost.

As the pair swept down the ornately carved staircase, they passed the framed oil painting, mounted on the stairwell wall, that Maggie had done of the famous Irish dolmen Poulnabrone, the prehistoric set of huge stones resembling a portal to the netherworld. A gifted photographer and artist, Maggie executed the oil painting from a photograph in which she'd captured the setting sun just as it flashed, star-like and centered, beneath the horizontal slab of the great standing stones.

Nearly three years prior, Raine and Maggie made the most significant journey of their lives– a trip to mystical Ireland, where they happened upon more than they had bargained for. There, they sought and found answers to the haunting questions connected to a very special quest of their own– and to a series of murders and legendary lost jewels at Barry Hall, a noble, old estate in County Clare. It was in Ireland where, after years of research, the pair ferreted out the magickal Time-Key, which, when properly activated, whisked them through the Tunnel of Time to yesteryear– to *any* year that they encoded.

Maggie's eyes drifted to the stair landing's tall stained-glass window that depicted the McDonough coat-of-arms with its fierce wild boar and lions *en passant*. She lingered to peer out a clear pane to the magnificent woods in their autumnal glory. "Autumn in our Hamlet is utterly enchanting!"

An enchanting place *any* time, Haleigh's Hamlet was a picturesque village– a historic southwestern Pennsylvania town that conferred countless glimpses of the past– with a charming cluster of Victorian, castle-like homes, replete with gingerbread and old money, all built during an era when help was cheap and plentiful, and the owners, coal and railroad barons (the life's blood of the village during its heyday), could well afford a bevy of servants.

To folks who lived elsewhere, the Hamlet's kingly mansions, each occupying a triple-sized wooded lot, were ever mysterious, bringing to mind secret rooms revealed with a touch to a certain "book" on a shelf and hidden staircases exposed by the twist of a latch disguised as a wall sconce. There was never any danger of anyone undesirable moving into one of the Hamlet's manors– the cost and upkeep warded off that problem.

A stately, turreted Queen Anne, Tara was Raine and Maggie's nineteenth-century Victorian home, located in the quaint, storied Hamlet on the edge of Haleigh's Wood. Anyone who visited Tara inevitably went away thinking that it was the right setting, the *perfect* setting, for the Sisters' personalities. Perfectionists by nature, they liked the atmosphere in their home to be flawless– and it was.

As the misty morning rain ceased, the sun, spilling rainbows through the Queen Anne's jewel-like stained-glass windows, splashed a cornucopia of color on the already vibrant collection of curious things the old mansion held within its sturdy walls, whilst the windowsills sparkled with rows of varicolored crystals– each charged with strong magick.

Among them were amber for vanquishing negativity, disease and dis-ease; amethyst for healing and inducing pleasant dreams; aquamarine for calming the nerves and lifting the spirits; citrine for cleansing; moonstone, "wolf's eye," for new beginnings and intuition; peridot for release from guilt; rose quartz for unconditional love and retaining youthfulness and beauty; tiger's eye and falcon's eye for protection; sapphire for insight and truth; emerald for bliss, loyalty, and wealth; and ruby for energy, passion, and vigor.

On the center sill of the dining room's trilogy of castle-themed stained-glass windows, a small smoky-glass bowl held Apache tears. To the Ancient Ones, these were frozen tears lost in the sands of time, the magickal stones proffering grounding, good luck and protection, as well as the ridding of negativity that held back realized dreams. Like amethyst and tiger's eye, Apache tears protected the Sisters against psychic attack– also known as the "Evil Eye."

Here too the Sisters kept a large Herkimer Diamond, which, despite the name, was not really a diamond at all but a powerful clear crystal. The Sisters understood that "Herkies," perfect conduits of the Universal Life Force, were exceptional healing crystals– the high-energy seekers of the crystal world that amplify the influence of other gemstones.

When the Sisters entered Tara's kitchen, the blue opalesque stained glass in the tall cabinet doors was shimmering with sunlight. It was a happy-feeling kitchen, and Maggie hummed merrily as she and Raine busied themselves with the breakfast things, including the proper brewing of their morning tea.

Introduced to them years before by their beloved Granny McDonough, teatime was something these steeped-in tradition ladies enjoyed whenever and wherever they could.

The spacious kitchen's focal point was the pretty, sky-blue, hooded stove, restored to its Victorian splendor, that had been their granny's pride and joy. The old house had most of the modern conveniences, but in the kitchen especially, Raine and Maggie preferred the Old Ways– trusted, tried and true.

Above them, bunches of dried herbs and flowers dangled from the dark, massive ceiling beams of abiding English oak. A small herb garden thrived year-round in the kitchen's bay window, and affixed to the brick chimney, a broom-riding Kitchen Witch warded off the bad and invited the good.

A besom-riding witch topped Tara's highest gable too. Celts have always been superstitious, as well as deeply spiritual. The tradition of the witch weather vane, imbued with Irish and Scottish folktales of enchanted old women flying over castle and field, casting spells and weaving magick, dates all the way back to the 1300s– or even earlier. Legend has it that if a passing witch saw such an effigy, she knew she could rest on the chimney top and consequently would cast no mischief upon the household.

Whilst the majestic manse's waterspouts channeled rainwater from Tara's slate roof and rust-colored brick walls, these conduits also served as watchful gargoyles, their mouths open in the silent shrieks that warded off evil.

Protective holly grew by every one of Tara's entrances and close to the rear gate leading into the garden, where, upon a faerie mound, spell-cast items were recharged under the full moon's energizing glow. Here, a garden plaque was engraved with a J.M. Wonderland quote: "The sun watches what I do, but the moon knows my secrets." At Tara's front entrance, a small, decorative sign near the holly bush read: *Magickal Black Cats Guard This Home!*

Like a bubbling cauldron, Tara– a grand old house, one of the Hamlet's great houses– *overflowed* with magick, casting its spell over anyone who set eyes upon it. Invisible to non-magick people, powerful energies encircled and protected the house and its occupants. In all honesty, it was not the most beautiful residence in the district but, unquestionably, it was the most unique– *as were its mistresses.*

Surrounded by a black, wrought-iron fence with fleur-de-lys finials, the turreted 1890s home was crowded with antiques, the cousins' vintage clothing, and a collection of *very special* jewelry, all of it enchanted, most of it heirloom and quite old.

The "McDonough Girls," as the Hamlet called them, had a charismatic flair, each for her own brand of fashion, each possessing the gift to *feel* the sensations cached away in their collected treasures, "As if," they were prone to say, "we are living history."

A long line of McDonough women possessed the gift for sensing, through proximity and touch, the layered stories and energies of those who previously owned the antique articles they acquired. Attired in their vintage clothing, these women were all gossamer and lace– but, make no mistake, they bore spines of cloaked steel.

Plainly put, the McDonoughs ran to women of passionate personalities– generation after generation. For the most part, they ignored convention, were headstrong and willful– with every intention of staying that way.

The family was an old one, full of tradition, mystique, and fire that dated back to the *Ard Ri* of Tara– the High Kings of Ireland.

The grand lady who named the house for Ireland's sacred Hill came, decades before, from County Meath, bequeathing her female heirs a special gift– and a great deal of magick.

McDonough women could make magick just by walking into a room. They had ages of it behind them, following in their wake like the long, fiery tail of a comet. *Samhain*– Hallowe'en– was their favorite holiday.

And then there were the cats– known in the world of the Craft as "Watchers," though some might say "Familiars," five at the moment, three of which, Black Jade and Black Jack O'Lantern and Panthèra, were descended from Granny McDonough's big tom, Myrrdyn, the Celtic name for Merlin. After all, it was a commodious old house– and it literally *purred* with love.

Back in the day, when Granny McDonough entered a room, the theatre, a shop, restaurant, or hall, whispers abruptly broke out like little hissing fires throughout the space. The villagers used to babble that Granny McDonough's "big ole black cat" assisted her with black magick. Black cats do that to some people, the un-magick anyway, rendering them shivery and illogical, while conjuring up all sorts of dark-night superstitions.

"Psychological poppycock! I have no patience with that sort of talk!" Granny used to cite– Granny whose magick was forever white. In response to those harsh muggle critics of the Craft who would say, "Magick is magick, and there is no such thing as *white* magick," Granny would smile sweetly and reply, "It all depends on *intent*, my dear. Magick is intended change, and *intention* creates the change." Her granddaughters would add– "Every intentional act is a magickal act."

Anyroad, tittle-tattle never bothered "The McDonough," as, in Irish custom, Granny was sometimes called. Mostly, she laughed it off, advocating, "Sure 'n ya might as well get th' benefit of it– gossip liberates you from convention."

But that's the way of any small town– people talked, and they always would; their tongues were never idle. Not to say that the folks of Haleigh's Hamlet didn't like the McDonoughs. They very much did, some even going so far as to flaunt pride for this longstanding Hamlet clan. Despite the whisperings of the townfolk, many were the times someone of them came knocking at the back door, under the veil of darkness, for a secret potion or a charm.

Maggie and Raine never forgot the advice, owing to small-town gossip, they overheard Granny give to one overwrought woman: "Mark me, lass, the greatest fear in th' world is the opinion of others. But the moment you aire unafraid of th' pack, you aire no longer a sheep. You become a *lion*," she enthused. "A great r-r-roar rises in yer heart– and that, my dear, is the roar of *freedom!*"

Over the long years, the McDonough family home gathered within its stout brick walls its fair share of arcane, esoteric, and cloak-and-dagger mysteries. Without the least bit of puffery or purple prose, Tara could be summarized as a house that embodied a *myriad* of veiled secrets– old and new.

The greatest secrets are hidden; the most significant, influential, things in the Universe unseen; and those who do not believe in *magick* will never experience it– will never uncover its mysteries.

Years before, at least three generations of the Hamlet's women found themselves drawn to Granny McDonough, wanting to confess *their* secrets to her in the shadows of her porch, where the sweet-smelling wisteria still grew thick in spring and summer, gracing the lattices with cascading, grape-like, pink and purple blooms.

And the Hamlet men, though they might scoff at such things, believed secretly, then and now, that on occasion a beautiful, young Aisling Tully McDonough, before she became known as "Granny," visited their dreams, igniting their carnal desires or whispering to them ways in which they might succeed in their careers.

The Hamlet learned that they could trust Granny McDonough with their secrets, and she conscientiously passed that torch on to her three granddaughters– to her namesake Aisling, to Maggie, and to Raine.

A solitary, eclectic witch, Granny shared her accumulated knowledge and wisdom with her granddaughters, teaching them well. Of course, Granny didn't confuse the two– knowledge and wisdom, that is. "Never mistake knowledge for wisdom," she said. "One helps you make a living; the other helps you make a life."

Forthright and candid, Granny had always looked straight into the eyes of anyone with whom she spoke. She was never one to sit on the fence or pussyfoot around, leaving "… that to the neighborhood cats, sugar-coatin' to the baker, and elegance to the tailor."

It was quoted far and wide that Granny McDonough was a wise woman and a healer– of many things. Hamlet folks had feared her, yet they sought her out, over time learning to love her, even going so far as to believe that if her long, black cloak brushed against them, as she passed on the street, its mere touch brought them good fortune for the remainder of their days.

Suffice it to say that the Celtic history of healing is a rich and powerful one, and *Celt* is synonymous with "free spirit."

Once when Raine was sent home from school for thrashing a fellow student, a boy much bigger than she, who had relentlessly teased her for being a witch, Granny sat her down and said, with a twinkle in her eyes, "Sure 'n didn't ya lar-rn Grandpa McDonough's KO punch better 'n Aisling or Maggie put t'gether!" (It had been the widowed Granny who'd taken the girls in hand, when they were pre-teens, to teach them how to defend themselves.)

"Now lar-rn this," Granny chided: "Be yerself, *a leanbh*, child," she reinforced in Gaelic. "An original is always better than a copy. And remember that you not only have th' *right* to be an individual, as a McDonough you have an *obligation* to be one."

When Raine, drying her tears, remarked that all she wanted was to be "normal," Granny pulled herself up to her full height to expound, "Me darlin' gurl, I'll tell ya true, here 'n now, that bein' 'normal,' as you call it, is utterly ordinary ... *commonplace!* And I'll tell ya flat out, lass– it rather denotes a lack iv courage."

*That's all it took.* The willful, ofttimes hoydenish, Raine was cured forever of wanting a "normal" life! Ever after, she delighted in quoting her adopted maxim: "Why be normal when you can be– *magickal?*"

After Grandpa McDonough passed on, Granny, who spoke to the end of her life with a brogue as thick as her good Irish stew, never wore anything but what the Hamlet referred to as her "widow's weeds."

With her shadowy cape billowing out behind her, she often walked her big, black tom on a leash after supper in the magickal owl light of evening. To the amazement of the villagers, the cat pranced– tail held high to form a question mark, neither twisting nor turning in any effort whatsoever to escape– at the end of a black velvet lead that was fastened to a fancy, jewel-studded collar around his neck, the other end wrapped several times round Granny's bejeweled hand. As self-important as you please, proudly and demurely did that tom swagger, with attitude and countenance that clearly avowed, "I am Granny McD's cat if you please– or if you don't please!"

Granny fathomed what most here in the New World of America did not– that gently stroking a black cat nine times, from head to tail, brought good fortune and luck in love (that went triple for *Samhain/* Hallowe'en). Treating cats kindly– with the respect they deserve– and warmly sharing one's home with cats of any color brought a multitude of blessings from the great Goddess. "You will always be lucky if you know how to make friends with cats," advocated "The McDonough" with the sagacity of a wise woman. "Cats possess charms a-plenty, and annyone who has iver owned a cat, if indaid one *can* own a cat, has fallen under Bastet's endurin' spell."

Granny taught her granddaughters many useful things about cats, including the fact that they love to curl up and nap within a circle. Indeed, they will intentionally remain inside a circle for long periods, sitting almost trancelike.

As one might expect, Granny McDonough's love of cats stayed with her all her life, just as the musical lilt of Ireland lingered on her tongue, and given that she raised Raine and Maggie, some of Granny's expressions and patterns of speech carried over and became part of them.

Cat tales abound in the McDonough and Tully clans, and Raine especially enjoyed spinning the colorful yarns– complete with Granny's brogue.

One year, for instance, when Mrs. Jenkins' brown tabby gave birth to kittens that everyone *knew* Myrrdyn had sired (when he darted out the door one brisk autumn night under the bewitching glow of the Hunter's Moon), it surprised the kibble out of a suddenly-younger-acting Gypsy and her owner. That tabby had thirteen years on her, if a day, and well past her kitten-bearing time was she. "The old fool!" Mrs. Jenkins had complained to anyone who would listen.

But there were kittens all right– *and what kittens!* The villagers took to calling them "faerie cats," and to be sure, there was something *magickal* about those glossy kittens, black as midnight each one, and shiny as patent leather, with bright pumpkin-colored eyes that seemed to bore clean through whomever they fixed with their mystical regard. Every child in town had fussed for one, and all these years later, Myrrdyn's charmed progeny still inhabit a few of the Hamlet's quaint old mansions. It's funny how things can stick in the mind over the mumbo jumbo of so many years– but that story has real sticking power.

Closer to the moment, Raine and Maggie were bustling about Tara's kitchen, where the former lit a thick, orange candle-in-a-jar labeled "Witches' Brew" that smelled suspiciously like pumpkin-pie spice, filling the space with a yummy aroma.

There was *magick* in candlelight. Its soft glow not only converted a room into an entrancing space, its illumination raised psychic awareness, and most significantly– a lit candle released energies. Raine just pulled the new candle from its box, and she wanted to light it straightaway, for Granny had taught that it was unlucky to keep a candle in the house that had never been lit.

Granny instilled many, what some might call, "flights of fantasy" or "old wives' tales" into her three granddaughters, such as a toppled chair upon standing was a bad omen. Spilled salt was too, unless you promptly tossed a pinch of it over your left shoulder to stave off the bad luck.

Remembering Granny, as she always did when she made tea, Maggie poured herself and Raine each a fragrant cup of the Irish breakfast brew. Nary a tea bag ever found its sorry way into Tara's traditional door! As was their habit, the pair used the eggshell-thin cups their granny had carefully carried, years before, from the "Old Country." At Tara, tea was never taken from a mug, or as Granny used to call it, a "beaker."

"I was just thinking of Granny's delicious soda bread," Raine mused, as she plucked their English muffins from the toaster. She sighed, looking across the room to the Boston rocker, where "The McDonough" had often sat by the kitchen window to read her arcane books. *We miss you, Granny.*

Following Raine's gaze, Maggie gave a knowing nod. Her eyes shone brilliant green as she finished buttering their muffins, setting the plate down on the table with a flourish of hand, her rings catching a beam from the sun that sparked a rainbow off a stained-glass window.

Through the window, the redheaded Sister could see Tara's small, cupola-crowned stable, home to their horses, Raine's ebony Tara's Pride and Maggie's cherry chestnut Isis. The stable's antique weathervane, a broom-riding witch, identical to the one atop Tara itself, told her there was a stiff wind out of the west.

Having arranged blackberry preserves and black currant jam with the muffins and their tea, Maggie took her seat at the kitchen's antique table– a heavy, round, claw-footed affair that matched the oak, pressed-back chairs around it. Immediately the stunning redhead began to trot through her mind the details of their current mystery; but reading her thoughts, it was the ever-more loquacious Raine who began.

"As I mentioned the other day, the Coven sisters," she stated, using the term in the Craft for female practitioners, "are absolutely livid over the prospect of losing the Witch Tree." Raine took a tentative sip of the hot tea. "And the more I think about it, the more I'm convinced that your feeling is dead-on. Greed, intense greed, resultant of a large sum of money, is at the root of this."

Maggie looked absorbed, reaching up to flick back the wave of fiery hair that frequently dipped over her eye. "Trouble often does boil down to money, but we'll find out soon enough. All I know for sure is that we can't let the Coven sisters down. We just can't fail them." Maggie's eyes met Raine's.

"We shan't," Raine remarked, aware that thoughts in the morning, positive or negative, frame the day. She rested her chin in her palms, elbows on the table, reflecting, "Though we aren't of the Coven, we've always aided and supported one another in just about everything. The sisters valiantly came to our rescue when we needed to rid our theatre of the *Macbeth* curse. And now, we need to reassure them that they can count on us to save the Witch Tree. It's empowering to have sisters who've got our backs; isn't it, Mags?"

"*Quite.*" Maggie dabbed at the corners of her mouth with a paper napkin. "Let's review what we know. You're the better *raconteur, darlin'.* You tell it."

Raine was quick to oblige. "When High Priestess Robin called to invite us to the Keystone Coven's *Samhain* fest at her home in Washingtonville, she told me she and the sisters were profoundly worried about the fate of the Witch Tree."

The Goth gal snapped her fingers in recollection. "By the bye, I rang Aisling right after I spoke with Robin, and she said *she'll* drive to the *Samhain* fête. She'll pick us up." Raine reached toward the center of the table for a napkin of her own from the holder, a hand-painted replica of their Tara. "Washingtonville's such a pretty spot, a yesteryear village, not unlike our own. Lots of rich history there too. And a big part of Washingtonville's appeal is the Witch Tree!

"When I talked to Robin, I didn't get all the particulars, but I do recall that she said there are some people, the worst sort of muggles apparently, who want to get hold of the land the Witch Tree is on to develop it for, I don't know, commercial or industrial use; and if they *get* that land, they'll cut down the Witch Tree also known, far and wide, as the Hester Tree!"

It was the second time Maggie was hearing those words from Raine, but nonetheless, her face went ghostly. "To fell a healthy– *majestic*– oak of 300-plus years with a rich history– it's **sacrilegious**?! I'm no botanist, but I know that's the type of oak that can live … five, six hundred years! I get so sick and tired of people who think what *they* think is the only way *to* think!"

"Don't get your knickers in a twist, Mags. We'll stop these unenlightened twits," Raine declared. "I have a witchy hunch that Robin will be ringing us today to propose a rendezvous so she can give us the nitty-gritties; and together, we can … **Craft** a plan of action." She bit into her muffin, swiping crumbs from her mouth with the napkin. "We could meet for lunch today or tomorrow." Raine picked up her tea, not wanting it to cool any further.

"Hmmmm," was all Maggie replied, for she was deep in thought. Like Raine, this history professor, too, was thinking about the rustically beautiful area where they lived.

The whole of Braddock County, Pennsylvania, was a treasure chest of legend and lore, possessing a rich history, a myriad of haunted sites and twilight superstitions. The rustic glen abounded with chronicles of great men from the French and Indian and Revolutionary war eras. Raine and Maggie recounted to their students that such tales thrive best in these sequestered, long-settled retreats.

After breathing its witching air, visitors, like the region's Celtic and German settlers, were captivated, for Washingtonville, as Haleigh's Hamlet, was an enchanting spot– a place to dream mysterious– cryptic– dreams, becoming all the more imaginative. That village, like the Sisters' own, attracted a variety of artsy people, as well as those interested in history– and, because of its legendary ghosts, a stream of cosmic seekers.

Feeling refreshed after sipping her tea, Raine acknowledged, "I can't explain it, except to say that I love the *feel* of a place like our Hamlet or Washingtonville."

"Yes, yes!" Maggie stirred approvingly. "I recall thinking that very same thing about our little corner of the commonwealth, when Thaddeus once took me for a sweeping, autumn helicopter ride." Her expression went dreamy. "Through the passage of time, this whole area has exuded a sleepy, bucolic ambiance that never seems to change, a sense of peace that radiates from every doorway, from each well-tended yard or farm, from every blossoming garden. I remind my students of that every term."

Raine lifted her cup in a toasting gesture. "Spot-on! There's a sense of reverence here for that which has gone before, a determination to preserve things as they were, perhaps even an unwillingness to acknowledge things as they are, as they have become. Some say it's because the place was bewitched centuries ago by an old Indian chief."

"Remember," Maggie interposed, "we always thought it was Nemacolin, who, though deprived of a tribe, emerged a powerful prophet."

"*You* thought that. I always said, if a bewitchment exists, it's more likely Shawnee or Seneca. Whatever," Raine concluded in a sub-rosa tone, "I think our Braddock County continues still under the sway of some *witching* power."

"I know one thing for sure. I always enjoy the scenic drive from our Hamlet to Washingtonville," Maggie went on after a pensive pause. She took a draught of tea, reflecting, "Especially in the autumn, when the trees are wearing their fall colors with just the right touches of green remaining; and the leaves dash at our windshield like the great Goddess' confetti. Oooh, there's nothing casual about the especial beauty of a Pennsylvania autumn. It's *visceral*, like the beauty of Ireland. *Mystical*." She brought a hand to her chest, with a thump to the heart, whispering– "*Magickal.*"

Raine concurred with a bow of her head; and as she bit into a jam-smeared muffin, she conjured happy images, her kitty-cat mouth turning up at the corners. "All along the route, from here to Washingtonville in the fall, pumpkins hauled in from the fields brighten roadside stands, together with big, rosy apples, jugs of golden apple cider, and jars of rich apple butter. I love seeing those neat little farms, as they prepare for another Pennsylvania winter, the smoky haze wafting over the cornfields, the captivating scarecrows standing watch, the cornstalks helter-skelter ..." her voice floated off with reminiscences– memories that quickly dissolved into other memories– like the autumn leaves drifting, at that very moment, past Tara's stained-glass windows, or skittering, with hushed whispering sounds, like cloaked, hurried faeries, along its brick driveway and walks.

"I was just thinking how our little corner of Pennsylvania has more than its share of spellbinding stories. *History* is a collection of those stories, *true* stories, and I love Washingtonville's as much as I do the Hamlet's," Raine rambled on. "Together, these neighboring little burgs have some *really* good ones." Her mind ran riot. "All the witching tales of old houses and woodlands flood back to clutch at me every time we take an autumn drive through the countryside: the legless figure in a long, black cloak, who searches the midnight roads for his lost love killed in the violence of a nor'easter over a century past; the White Lady of Haunted Rock, whose plaintive wails can be heard far and wide on the lonely, hollow wind; the reappearing faces in the mirrors at the manse of Fellowship Knoll; along with the misty, red-clad English soldiers, who cling to the old Braddock Road, perchance chained to earth and nightly wanderings due to their ghastly fates ... Ooooooo, when death wore feathers and garish paint on a long-ago day in 1755.

"The realms of heroes and villains from the past *spring* to life from fragments of history and myth– and, I daresay, from our own recited classroom tales of wonder," she dimpled. "In the eternal element of imagination, a symphony of phantom pioneers and dusky Native Americans– *all*– rise up to spook me. Bwahahahahahaha," she wiggled her fingers with their glittering rings and ebony-lacquered nails at Maggie, "and," she sizzled– "*I love it!*

"All along the route to Washingtonville, I can almost hear the bloodcurdling war cry of one of our county's legendary Senecas, a grotesquely painted shaman, his visage diabolically black, the eyes and nose edged in vermilion. Shrieking and wagging his head, covered with a panther pelt, he shakes his gourd rattle at me, chanting into my ear his spun-out curse!"

"But, of course, the best tale of all is the one connected to the Witch Tree! Tell it again, Raine, I love to hear *you* tell it," Maggie coaxed. She poured them both more tea from Granny's shamrock-sprinkled teapot, returning it to its green cozy, embroidered in swirly Edwardian script, with Granny's initials. Then she sat back in her chair to savor both the tea and Raine's telling of the ever-mysterious Hester legend.

"I just related this story to you about three weeks ago," the raven-haired Sister teased. Raine, however, never needed coaxing to spin a yarn. She was what the Irish call a *seanchaí*, a natural-born storyteller, and so she readily wove the tale again for her sister of the moon.

"Hester Duff was said to have been a striking woman, 'easy on the eyes,' folks back then would've been inclined to say. It was also said … *whispered* round about that Mistress Duff was a *witch*. According to legend, she had hair as black as midnight and eyes the deepest of blue, like a clear Scottish loch at sunset. Even her pet name was mysterious, 'Dark Star,' given to her by her Scottish parents, who arrived at what is now the Braddock County area with their remarkably pretty little girl sometime in the mid-to-late 1700s.

"The Duffs hankered after America's shores for the same reason so many left their homelands– to escape the old countries' class systems. For freedom and what the newcomers called 'elbow room.' On the precarious Pennsylvania frontier, though they would've had to fight Indians to hold every rod of land, these plucky pioneers were equal to their neighbors and free of any government boot on their necks.

"It's thought that when Hester's parents were killed by Indians, she was taken in by another frontier family. Farms, even small ones, could always use another pair of hands. 'Many hands make light work' was the frontier-farmer thinking. Whether Hester's surrogate parents passed away, were also killed by Indians, or she simply came of age and ventured out on her own, we can only speculate. All we know is that Hester lived alone in a simple log cabin deep in the woods here in Braddock County, in the vicinity of Washingtonville.

"There's no record as to what year Hester first showed up in this region. That's why I said mid-to-late 1700s. Probably, the Duffs' ship had docked in Philadelphia, and yearning for that sought-after elbow room, they made their way west, across Penn's Woods, here, to what was then the frontier. Like our Hamlet's mysterious hermit Rue Cameron, most of Hester's life was … *is* shrouded in mystery.

"Legend has it she kept to herself. In such a remote, isolated area of the frontier, the 'back country,' as it was known, folks became suspicious of Mistress Duff, as they were of all strangers, though they pretty much left her alone. That is, they left her alone in the beginning.

"By and by, as fear will do, it fired their imaginations to run wild, and they began to 'notice' that every time Hester appeared at the blockhouse, a misfortune befell them– a cow she touched went dry; a boy who taunted her suddenly took sick; a woman who gossiped about her, behind a hand, tripped and broke an arm or a leg; a man who made a snide remark was found scalped and mutilated in the forest." Raine leaned back in her chair, swinging one slim foot and narrowing her green eyes. "I've often wondered if the men who taunted Hester had been *rejected* by her. Anyroad, it soon became common practice to blame Mistress Duff for any and all misfortunes."

"Same ole, same ole– misunderstanding breeds fear … of witches especially." Maggie heaved a sigh. "It is what it is, Sister, what it has always been."

Raine held up a bejeweled hand. "If anyone were to ask me 'What is your religion?' I might answer, 'All paths that lead to the Light.'"

Maggie gave a thumbs-up. "And as eclectic witches, that would be, for us, a good response. The unenlightened have always feared witches."

The Goth gal lapsed into reverie. "Sometimes, when I'm out in public, I fix my gaze on an obvious muggle and think, 'What would you say if I told you I'm a witch?'"

"There are more of us than they think, darlin'," Maggie crooned.

"At any rate," Raine cleared her throat, coming out of her musing and picking up her tale, "Hester's neighbors' imaginings, along with their suspicions, might well have been unjustified– *likely were unjustified*– but rumors spread through the valley like wildfire, the gossip passing from mouth to mouth like a nasty disease. Still, no one lifted a hand against Hester Duff– that is until one particular autumn.

"Thought to have been the autumn of 1787, the incident occurred after Hester joined the neighboring settlers, whose small farms were scattered, the countryside round, at the centrally located blockhouse, when a war party of painted Shawnee had been sighted by local rangers. The poor woman was met with derision and nearly drummed out of the protective walls of the log fortress. Though the gathered settlers grudgingly permitted her to stay, Hester was shunned and humiliated. Three days hence, a violent storm destroyed the frontier farmers' entire harvest.

"That October, close to *Samhain* it was, just as it is now, an angry mob rushed Hester's cabin and, taking her captive, tied her to a sturdy oak in the forest. Mind, there were never any witch hunts or executions in Pennsylvania– nothing to speak of anyway– so what they intended to do to her is debatable; but they most certainly meant to frighten her enough to drive her out of the area.

"What I tend to think is that they were deciding what to do with her, shouting and arguing among themselves; when, in the time it would take to utter a curse, thunder and lightning began to rumble and crash. Hester looked skyward, uttering her oath; and in a literal flash, a violent bolt of lightning crashed into the tree, covering it, Hester, and the onlookers in thick smoke.

"Now this is powerful sorcery I'm talkin' here. Hester probably reached her tolerance level to craft a decision: 'Of conjuring a storm, you have accused me. Whad'ya think of this?! So mote it be!!'

"When the smoke cleared, the rope that had bound Hester to the tree was still there. I mean, it was still *tied* round the trunk; but Mistress Duff was *gone*, never to be seen or heard from again, *vanished* into the vapor– and a black hole of history!

"However, a sign that she existed remains to this day. By the power of the lightning bolt and that sister's strong magick, six letters were burned so deeply into that mighty oak, they are *still* visible– H-E-S-T-E-R! And so," Raine completed the legend with a lift of one ebony brow, "the prevailing wind that blows through the village of neighboring Washingtonville is one of *witchcraft* and *mystery*."

The Sisters heard a long, low whistle and, turning their heads, saw that it was coming from their poppet, Cara, who had materialized next to them on the kitchen counter.

"Merry Meet!" the Sisters voiced.

"Merry Meet," came the reedy reply. "Bleedin' good story, lass!"

"There's no force equal to that of a determined witch." Raine blew the ragdoll a kiss. "We'd like for you to house-and-cat sit today, Cara, if you please. I've a keen Irish feeling that High Priestess Robin will be ringing this morning to set up a meeting with us for lunch, and we'll likely be gone most of the afternoon." To Maggie, she said, "I doubt Aisling will be free to join us."

The redheaded Sister reflected a moment. "I doubt it too. She mentioned something about having an afternoon session today with a new client."

"I'm so proud of Aisling." Raine leaned back in her chair. "She and Ian have made a great success of their Black Cat Detective Agency."

"Iffin I kin git a wor-rd in, sure 'n I'll watch over tings t'day, puss!" the ragdoll retorted to Raine, its manner seeming to convey a wily simper. The witched little doll's speech was a lilting Irish brogue with shades of the Pennsylvania frontier whence it came.

Raine's pouty lips curved upward. "See you keep out of mischief, poppet!" She truly loved Cara and occasionally fretted about losing her. "But you're a wizard guardian; I'll say that for you. Wiz—zard!"

Before Cara could respond, Maggie, with head cocked in a reflective attitude, replied, "Your comment to Cara reminds me of our Hamlet's real Wizard." She thought for a long moment. *I wonder if we'll ever discover who the Keystone Coven's mystifying senior advisor really is?*

A kittenish moue manifested on Raine's face, as she wiped her hands on a napkin. "Never having met the Wizard in person, the *Coven* doesn't even know who he is! Now *there's* a mystery!" the raven-haired Sister exclaimed, having picked up her cousin and sister of the moon's thought. "That might be the one puzzle we *never* crack. Sometimes I think it's Thaddeus, other times Hugh, and then," her voice dropped, "there are ... *fervent* times, I'm convinced the Wizard is my Beau."

"Well, darlin'," Maggie responded with her favorite endearment, "if you ask me, Beau, Hugh, and Thaddeus are each suspect. You know what finely honed sixth senses Beau and Hugh possess, the pair of them. It's why they're excellent veterinarians. After all, their patients can't tell them what's wrong! As for Thaddeus," her Mona Lisa smile transformed her face to mysterious, "well … suffice it to say he's a *recurrent* wizard." *Every little thing he does is magick!* "The man's forever surprising me! I've never met anyone like him. But as Abraham Lincoln once said, 'Towering genius disdains a beaten path.'"

"All we and the Coven are certain of is that their senior advisor lives in our Hamlet. The sisters don't even know if the Wizard's a man or a woman. Just because, over the years, the Coven has referred to their enigmatic advisor as the 'Wizard,' doesn't necessarily mean it's a man. It could well be a *sister* of the Craft."

"True." Maggie got to her feet and rolled her shoulders. "I can image the joint head of our college's archaeology and anthropology departments as the Coven's covert advice-giver. With her long, signature cape and tall, forked staff, Dr. Yore– wise crone that she is– is betwixt and between an impish witch and a stern schoolmarm. And another thing," Maggie said abruptly, "the Coven sisters refer to this unknown entity as their *senior* advisor, due to the stream of wisdom he or she imparts, but none of us know for certain that the so-called Wizard is a person of golden years. For all we know–"

Raine opened her mouth to interject something when both Sisters were sharply silenced by their poppet.

**"Whist!"** the ragdoll shrieked, twisting partway round to face Raine, whence she was propped against the backsplash of the counter. "Some tings aire meant t' f'river remain a mystery!" She threw her little mitt-hands in the air. "Git over it!"

At a loss for words, Raine and Maggie exchanged looks, both Sisters trading the thought that Cara was what Granny would most certainly call a "corker."

*She's right, you know*, Maggie flashed telepathically to Raine. *Life itself is an unsolved mystery.*

"Right y' aire!" the poppet shouted, surprising the Sisters yet again.

The feisty Cara was bestowed on the Sleuth Sisters by another of their Hamlet's enigmas, an eighteenth-century hermit and fellow sister of the moon, whose violent murder the Sisters solved when they time-trekked, several months prior, to the perilous Pennsylvania frontier.

Approximately eleven inches tall, the haunted doll's head bore a mop of what used to be, over two centuries earlier, bright-red wool yarn for hair, faded now to a pale orangey hue. The rag-stuffed head and body were fashioned of a coarse, age-darkened muslin. Two faded, but still faintly visible, black ink dots represented the eyes; and the mouth, smeared undoubtedly by countless childish kisses over the tumbled years, was crooked, giving the evident impression of a *mischievous* grin.

A green vest, the design in the cambric long claimed by Time, was pinched in at the waist by a narrow, rope-like cord. The poppet's uneven skirt was pinked and somewhat tattered, the purple-ish color nearly gone the way of history; and though the doll sported no shoes, the ink-blackened feet were shaped as though it did, the soles turning up at the toes evoking the notion of a leprechaun.

An amused Raine stood, staring at the doll, hands on hips. "You are a corker," she pronounced, drawing on Granny's word and picking up the doll to hold it out in front of her. "Do you know that? But what a blessing to us and to Tara!"

The raven-haired Sister sat the witched poppet back down on the counter, then slid into her chair at table, facing Maggie. There was a little of the tea left, and tipping the teapot, she shared it.

Maggie lifted her cup, pausing it at her mouth. "By the Goddess' grace, we'll glean enough clues to solve Hester's mystery and the present-day mystery connected to it that, incidentally, I feel is *speeding* our way. I figure, at some point, we'll need to turn to our Time-Key. However, we must remain careful, *discriminating*, in how we utilize the Key. It's crucial we never *abuse* its sacred use."

Raine gave a brisk nod. "I'm certain Auntie Merry's powerful crystal ball will again prove to be a huge help to us, Mags."

"Speaking of *huge*, the *Witch Tree* is *huge*, and it will continue to grow even larger, ever and ever more majestic," Raine concluded, taking a quick sip of tea, after which she added, "if it's allowed to. That type of oak, as you said, can live hundreds of years. And some stupid muggles want to cut it down!" Her face dimmed from kitten to panther. "Not only would that be a damn shame and irreverent to Earth Mother, it would be downright *dangerous!*"

"You're right, of course. Some say Hester's *spirit* inhabits that tree! And I sense there'll be more behind this Hester predicament than will meet the eye."

"Always is," Raine laughed shortly. "I recall that Robin said something about having gone to the man, one of them anyway, who wants the land the tree is on, and entreating him to understand; but she said the coldness of his tone told her the 'frost is on the pumpkin.' And remember what I told you– Robin mentioned that several strange events have occurred, at Witch-Tree Farm, since our Tree problem began."

"Well, we've sorted out long-buried secrets before, even those taken to the grave. It won't be our first time at the rodeo, or more apropos, our first trip back to Colonial times," Maggie expressed after a moment.

"We'll take this latest challenge on, no matter what puzzles come attached to it, and *we'll solve the lot of them!*" Raine stated with fire, giving her sister of the moon an affable knock on the shoulder.

As the Sisters rose and began washing up the breakfast things, they chanted softly, "Still around the corner a new road doth wait. Just around the corner– another secret gate!"

A few minutes later, when the phone rang, as Raine predicted it would, it was Maggie who answered High Priestess Robin's call to set up a luncheon date. Raine had headed upstairs to the bathroom and was brushing her teeth before the mirror when the glass suddenly clouded, and the familiar image of Granny McDonough appeared in the mist.

"Don't be flyin' too high 'n mighty now, me darlin'," she chided firmly in her musical Irish brogue. The image smiled then.

*Granny*– the cloud of soft white hair in its loose bun; the unlined, pink-and-white face– angelically sweet and so profoundly loved by the surprised young woman poised before the mirror, the toothbrush in her hand.

Raine spit into the sink and hurriedly rinsed her mouth. "In peace and love I welcome you, Granny, but levitation, whatever do you mean?! You always tell us to have confidence, to believe in ourselves and in our powers."

"Aye, but you must balance that self-assurance with caution. I don't need t' manifest this warnin' to Maggie or Aisling, but sure 'n I need t' get the alert to *you!* Now heed me wor-rds, lass. Make use of every protection I taught ya, and I taught you well."

"But, Granny," Raine said in a pleading tone, "this is not really a dangerous endeavor we're delving into now, sticky and tricky perhaps, but not really danger–"

"*Och!*" Granny's voice took on a somber note. "Hitherto 'tisn't, but come I have t' warn ya that soon there will be more f'r you t' deal with than just the mysterious complexities of th' past, or the lobbyin' t' save an ancient oak."

"Great balls of fire! We really are 'mystery magnets'!" Raine was about to speak further, when–

Holding up a hand for silence, Granny's eyes softened benevolently, revealing a soul sated in wisdom and love. "Rest assured," she began with tender concern, "I shall be with you through the muddle. Always remember that the problems that lie in wait b'fore you are niver as strong as the ancestors who walk beside you."

Raine stared at Granny, uncharacteristically mute.

"Need I remind you, me darlin', that you– *the three of you*– have a sacred destiny?"

"Hecate yes … I mean *no*, no need to remind us, Granny. We know that, and *you* know how much I love a good mystery; but–" Raine broke off, and her face clouded. "*Levitation*," she repeated with zest, "Maggie and I were just talking about this! We sensed it coming! Once more, mystery and mayhem are about to land in our laps."

"F'r sar-tain, and I'm sorry t' add to the messy mix– **murder**." Granny's expression was stern. "But niver f'rget that you hold the sacred Power of Three, and if y' hold fast to the Great Secret an' keep control of yer fears– though in *your* case, a little fear cud be good– you will succeed in annythin' you set yer minds to. *Tré neart le chéile–* **together strong!** Just you mind that word **together**, lass! You have a habit of bein' far too impetuous at times. Saints 'n angels, ye'er yer Gran'fither McDonough over an' yet agin!"

And with that, Granny vanished from the mirror, after blowing a kiss, that reached a rather stunned Raine, in the sparkling form of gold and silver glitter that spun round and round her, making her feel all warm and fuzzy– *and loved.*

A few minutes later, Maggie appeared at the bathroom door. This Sister always seemed to glide across a floor, never making a sound and thus sometimes startling Raine, who whirled from the sink, surprised anew, when the redhead announced, "We're meeting Robin at The Gypsy Tearoom at noon. She said, since we would be driving to Washingtonville for their *Samhain* fest, that she'd drive here for our lunch rendezvous." Maggie raised one arched brow, crossing her arms over her ample chest. "So what did Granny have to say?"

The Goth gal's ebony brows rushed together. "How long have you been standing there?"

"I've only just come up, but I can *feel* Granny's presence. So give!"

After sharing most of what Granny said, Raine blew out her breath. "So there you have it." *Mystery, mayhem, and murder– again*, she thought, demanding silently of the Universe, *Why is there so much evil in this world?*

"I could give you several reasons, none of which, I daresay, would satisfy you. However, you can't really be surprised that another mystery, or in this case, *mysteries* have fallen into **our** laps," Maggie countered. "As Granny said, it's our destiny to solve crimes, come to the aid of innocents, and put things as right as we can. No negative thinking now, darlin'. We can't allow negative thinking to lead us. We don't want to program anything bad for ourselves or anyone else."

Raine jammed her hands into the pockets of her black riding skirt, wordless.

*Wordless*, however, was a rare condition for the verbose, brunette Sister. Often effusive, always bold, and ever more-than-ready for a new adventure, Raine was a sexy, somewhat naughty pixie who was destined to keep her looks and her youthful appearance. Pixies, after all, are enduring as well as endearing.

Whimsical Fate had ordained that Maggie, too, be blessed with a forever-youthful mien. In addition, the redheaded Sister was most enchantingly – *sensual*. Perchance it was her wittiness and vibrant sense of fun that helped retain her beauty and allure. Maggie loved to laugh, and she did so often. Her voice was musical, and she had an attractive, lilting expression of amusement.

The short laugh, however, she'd just pitched Raine, carried a hint of trepidation. "God and Goddess grant we don't encounter anything as risky as our last shock of quests. Stuff and nonsense!" Maggie rapidly amended. "We'll program our way."

Raine felt a flicker of concern but blew it off, not allowing it to take root.

Their ability to read each other's minds bonded Maggie and Raine; and though they sniped at one another on occasion, they were close– much more like sisters than first cousins.

For one thing, the magickal trio– Raine, Maggie, and Aisling– had identical eyes, arresting to anyone who looked upon them. The "McDonough eyes" the villagers called them– tip-tilted and vivid green, the color of Ireland itself, fringed with long, thick, inky lashes and blazing with insatiable life.

"God's fingers were sooty when he put in the eyes of my three lovely Irish granddaughters," Granny had been wont to say.

Like their blonde cousin Aisling, raven-haired Raine and redheaded Maggie accentuated their eyes with intense makeup, too theatrical for most– dramatically stunning and signature sexy for the Sleuth Sisters. And like their granny before them, all three McDonough lasses had beautiful complexions– rich cream, glowing and flawless.

Granny recognized, from birth, how extraordinary each of her granddaughters was– even for a Tully or a McDonough– predicting that they would be able to see what others, including their own kind, could not.

And from the moment each of the McDonough girls entered puberty– it was like bees to honey! Boys suddenly couldn't keep away from them. Just looking at them left most males so giddy, they acted like they'd had too much of old Buck Taylor's 'lectricfyin' applejack. Would-be suitors followed the McDonough gals home from high school and college, tied up their phones evenings, and fought with each other over who would escort them to dances and such.

Perhaps it was Granny's special olive-oil soap the threesome used that made their skin so luminous and turned their auras so bright that people– well, those who believed in magick, anyway– virtually saw them in dazzling, sparkly radiance, like the beautiful leaders of splendor and light they actually were. Or maybe it was simply the self-confidence Granny instilled in her granddaughters that made them shine so. Poise has an enchanting way of doing that. Granny always joked that "Sex appeal was fifty percent of what you've got, and fifty percent of what people think you've got." Whatever the reason, the McDonough lasses radiated something that was impossible to ignore.

Their artsy theatre friends summed them up by saying, "Raine, Maggie, and Aisling have that intangible *je ne sais quoi* that makes them unforgettable."

No one ever forgot a McDonough woman.

In all fairness, they did not collect hearts as one collects seashells or butterflies, and yet …

A few seconds ago, Raine, who was usually fearless about plunging into tomorrow, felt that fantastic McDonough confidence and optimism slip a notch. *Mystery, mayhem, and murder*. The harrowing thought, coupled with Granny's caveat, skimmed along her spine like cold, bony fingers, the disquiet making itself evident on her face.

Instinctively her hand flew to the antique talisman suspended on a thick silver chain around her neck. She brushed her ringed fingers across the large emerald embedded in the center of the amulet's broad silver-and-black-enameled surface. A colorful sprinkling of tiny, pinhead-size gems of moonstone, garnet, emerald, ruby, sapphire, amethyst, citrine, and various hues of quartz and topaz glittered in the treasured heirloom. For a long moment, Raine regarded the inspiring piece, as if seeing it for the first time. She looked to Maggie, the dimple in her cheek deepening. "Beau always ribs me that the mere mention of a mystery quickens my pulse." After a pensive few seconds, she said, "There's an Old English word, *Werifesteria*, that means 'To wander longingly through the forest in search of mystery.' It's *my* special word. Well, one of them anyway," she laughed. "Words cast spells. That's why it's called *spelling!*"

Maggie declined to respond, except to comment that the Merlin cats– Black Jade and Black Jack O'Lantern, with the more elusive Panthèra– perfectly aligned, were sitting before them, in the upstairs hallway, their combined steady purr growing louder.

Raine scrutinized their Watchers for a weighty moment. "They're telling us that this mystery will be unexpectedly alarming by dint of an especially unconscionable evil." The raven-haired Sister cocked her head. "You realize, Mags, that the unravelling of this soon-to-be-muddle just might hinge on our travel back in time to witness what exactly happened to Hester Duff."

Maggie responded with a nod, picking up Raine's train of thought, as the latter's mind sped on. "I don't know if the Witch Tree is protected by a Pennsylvania state historical marker or not. But gathering everything we can on Hester Duff, the tree and Witch-Tree Farm should help in obtaining a historical plaque that would, in turn, facilitate preservation of the tree. From under her clothing, she extracted the talisman she habitually wore on a strong silver chain around her neck.

Understandably, Maggie's heirloom piece matched Raine's exactly, save that the big center stone in hers was a blood-red ruby. Tracing a finger over the amulet's bejeweled Triquetra surface– or rather, her talisman's *third* of the Triquetra design– she said, imaging their accomplished Leo cousin Aisling, whose talisman hosted the center stone of sapphire, "There's indeed something to be said for the magick Power of Three. We'll prove ourselves yet again," Maggie managed to insert with quiet Scorpio force. "As Granny said, it's our destiny, and she left us more than just this house and a great trust fund. We were summoned to unlock a mystical portal, a gateway that unveils a world of ancient mysteries and hidden knowledge! To guard the Time-Key's secret and to use it for good."

A sudden surge of witchy-woman power fired Raine's Aries confidence, and she flashed her cousin and sister of the moon an understanding grin. *Woman In Total Control of Herself ... that's what it means to be a witch. And what a **delicious** word it is!* she reflected. "At a time like this, I can't help but be reminded of what Granny liked to quote from Abraham Lincoln: "The best way to predict the future is to create it!"

"That's our MO!"

"It's our credo ... or one of them. Come up to the tower room with me for a few minutes before we leave to meet Robin," Raine voiced to Maggie as the latter headed into the bathroom. "I want to research Pennsylvania state markers on the Internet and print it off to share with her."

"Splendid idea," Maggie said, picking up her toothbrush. "Go on, and I'll join you after I freshen up."

Out in the hall, Raine reached down and scooped up one of the black cats that on silent paws was shadowing her to Tara's tower room. Gazing into the depths of Black Jack O'Lantern's mesmerizing pumpkin-colored eyes, the raven-haired Sister recited her favorite tale, "Once upon a time, there were two pioneering college professors and one former police detective turned private eye– young but possessed of very old souls– from an unheard-of little hamlet in the backwoods of Pennsylvania. Nonetheless, the good works of this magickal trinity were widely noted, winning them the well-earned soubriquet the 'Sleuth Sisters.'"

Ten minutes later, Maggie joined Raine in the tower room in which the Sisters did their paperwork. From floor to ceiling, bookshelves encircled the high, round chamber, where the tall windows, crisscrossed with ecru lace curtains, let in plenty of light. The carpet and walls were a rich hunter green, and the woodwork, as throughout the manse, was a dark and durable English oak.

Raine perused the text on the computer screen, reading aloud. *"That's it.* It's all the info I could garner, thus far, on the Pennsylvania historical markers and on the Witch Tree." She printed off the pages, folded them, and slipped them into her shoulder bag that was hanging from the padded leather office chair.

With a wistful shrug, Maggie murmured, "We've had less of a start." She flicked her heavy, shoulder-length hair back from her face. The dark-red flame of her crowning glory, in certain luminosity such as here in the sunlit tower room, rippled blue lights through the thick waves. "Together, we'll figure out a way to save the tree. All we've got to do is keep to our path. That's how we ferreted out the Time-Key," she pondered, brushing a finger across the big Herkimer Diamond– the talisman of researchers– they kept on the claw-footed law table that held their computer, fax machine, and printer. "It's how we crafted our thesis on time-travel so that it was accepted by our fellow colleagues of letters, and how we defended it successfully to gain our doctorates. In addition, we solved a run of wicked murders in the past few years. And we did it *all* by keeping to the path of the Great Secret."

Tilting her dark head, Raine's fair cheeks took on a rosy tint. She ran her ringed fingers through her short, sassy asymmetric hair– as black and lustrous as their cats– the point-cut bangs dipping seductively over one eye. "Not to mention that we've safeguarded the secret of the Time-Key through, I might add, *five* nerve-jangling time-travel missions."

Some twenty minutes later, when Raine set her purse down next to Maggie's in the entrance hall near Tara's front door, Granny's parting words were replaying in her mind and heart– "Make use of every protection I taught you– and I taught you well."

Pulling a cake of soap, infused with the protective oils of frankincense and myrrh, from her pocket, she quickly pressed a corner of the bar to the English oak of their front door to draw a pentagram. She did this on *both* sides of the door. The symbol was invisible, but it was *there*, as extra protection for them and their home.

Raine glanced at her watch. Maggie had suggested leaving for their lunch date early, so they would have time, before Robin arrived, to visit for a spell with their good friend Eva Novak, the proprietress of The Gypsy Tearoom. They'd be departing in a few minutes.

While she waited for Maggie to come downstairs, the raven-haired Sister strode past the life-size knight-in-armor in the foyer to the pillared entry that led into Tara's parlor with its Victorian furnishings, green velvet drapes, and wall of books, the shelves crammed with leather-bound tomes spilling over with esoteric, arcane knowledge. Instantly her eyes locked with the pair, so like her own, of her grandmother whose fascinating portrait hung above the ornate fireplace.

The oil painting by Charles Dana Gibson captured Aisling Tully McDonough at the height of her beauty, the soft cloud of red hair, upswept in the famed Gibson-Girl coiffure of the era, graced the flawless oval of the face, the low-cut, off-the-shoulder, green velvet gown accentuating the hour-glass figure. Streaming down over one white shoulder, a long tendril of fiery red hair formed a perfect question mark. Gibson had entitled the captivating image *The Eternal Question*, and thus read the neat, brass plate at the base of the portrait.

There Raine lingered for a solemn moment, voicing her thought aloud, "Granny, it's *empowering* to know, from our past efforts, that we can travel down the Tunnel of Time, at will, to unlock the door that'll whisk us through the thrills and chills of yesteryear. Heady stuff! We need and welcome your continued guidance in making prudent choices."

The eyes in the portrait seemed to kindle, and a little cat smile lifted the corners of Raine's candy-apple-red mouth. "At risk of sounding boastful, I can't help my feeling that with each new adventure, Aisling, Maggie, and I advance to a whole new level of skill and achievement."

She dressed her normally husky voice with a thick coat of drama, "And as I always say— who knows what skeletons and dangers dangle in the closets our Time-Key will open? Along with those secreted perils— magick, adventure and surprise await us at the creak of every opening door." In her saucy manner, she finished with an eerie laugh.

Entering the room, Maggie said, "If and when we run into a snag, we'll make good and proper use of *all* our magickal tools, including our Time-Key. With it **and** the powerful crystal ball gifted us by Auntie Merry, we should be able to solve virtually *any* mystery that History has cloaked in shadow! One thing's certain— our lives are never boring. Again, we've some exciting days ahead."

"Danger and risk? Sure, but remember what Granny *always* told us— 'To be forewarned is to be forearmed.'" Raine shifted her gaze from the portrait to the redhead beside her, as her voice took on an even stronger element of anticipation, and her heart gave a leap. "Let's go. 'Time's a-wastin',' as 'The McDonough' used to say."

Maggie concurred with a nod, her eyes lifting to the riveting canvas. "Guide and guard us, Granny."

"So mote it be," Raine quickly ordained.

As the Sisters hastened out the door, Maggie, with her Mona Lisa smile and a witch's fiery passion, repeated the time-honored phrase— "So mote it be!"

Manifesting in a front window, the poppet Cara, watching the Sisters get into Raine's vintage MG, fortified the magickal mix with her own authoritative affirmation—

**"With the Power of Three— so mote it be!"**

"She was known as Dark Star, the Dark Witch, and her power
was great."

"It's OK to follow a different path,
so long as you always follow your heart."
~ Granny McDonough

## Chapter One

When Raine and Maggie entered The Gypsy Tearoom, at eleven-thirty that morning, a couple of tables and a booth were already occupied. The Tearoom was a popular eating place in and about the Hamlet, and it was a special favorite of the Sisters.

"I was hoping, since we're rather early for lunch, we'd be able to visit for a few minutes with Eva," Maggie whispered to Raine, as the pair stood in the doorway, waiting to be shown to a booth and allowing their eyes to adjust to the dim lighting.

"We will," Raine replied. Her gaze swept the room. "I love this place!"

The Gypsy Tearoom was a cozy café with romantic, flickering wall sconces and intimate seating. Located in the lowest level of what had once been the Hamlet's original armory– a 1907, red-brick, fortress-like structure built in the late Gothic Revival style– the comfy seating began life as horse stalls.

The historic building was purchased by Eva Novak when the new armory was built several years earlier. During renovation, the roomy box stalls were transformed into private booths, ideal for the readings that Eva's clientele often requested along with her special teas and the delectable Tearoom fare. Like her ancestors, Eva read tarot cards, palms, and tea leaves.

The ground floor was the banquet hall, reserved for groups and events. Eva used the third floor for her private quarters. Her living room occupied one of the building's twin turrets, her bedroom the other, making her feel, as she often said, like a queen in a castle tower.

*Renovation* of the edifice had been as the definition of the word affirms– cleaning, repairing, and reviving with as little actual remodeling as possible, for Eva was set on keeping the historic building's integrity.

In the Tearoom, wood table-and-bench seating filled each horse-stall-turned-booth. The walls of the cubicles were covered with dark-red, tufted leather, against which the occupants could comfortably rest their backs. Too, the booths' thick, padded walls provided additional privacy. Gothic-style tables and chairs occupied the center of the room. Miniature stained-glass lamps topped the tables, and on the opposite wall from the stalls was a magnificent stone fireplace. The ceiling flaunted the original walnut beams, the walls the same aged brick that was on the building's exterior. Massive, sliding barn doors, with medieval-looking, black hardware, separated the dining area from the kitchen.

No sooner had the Sisters arrived, when Eva, in colorful Gypsy attire– black, off-the-shoulder, low-cut blouse and flowing red skirt belted with a lacy black shawl– emerged from the adjacent kitchen to greet them. Snatching up a couple of menus, she sang out, "Welcome, my good friends, welcome! It's always a brighter day when I can share a part of it with you."

Each time Raine and Maggie looked into Eva's face, they saw her honest heart. "It's lovely to see you too," they chorused, returning the pleasant woman's warm embrace.

The proprietress showed the McDonoughs to their favorite booth, the Sisters sliding in to sit opposite one another.

Handing them the menus, Eva asked, "Shall I bring you my special brew?"

"Bring it on," Raine answered. "It'll do us good. We have someone joining us, so we won't order till she arrives. We'll enjoy the tea while we're waiting."

"*Soup du jour* is my very own Russian red borscht– seasonal vegetables in short-rib and bacon broth with potato and sour cream, cup or bowl. The bowl is a meal in itself. And today's special is caviar omelet crafted with sour cream and chives. Think about it," Eva flashed them a smile, "while I get your tea." As she turned on her heel and sailed off in the direction of the kitchen, her large gold hoop earrings winked in a beam of light from a flickering wall sconce.

Prompted by the glimmer, Raine quipped, "This is a matter that requires reflection." She opened the outsized menu, the cover of which bore a dreamy Gypsy daguerreotype of the proprietress' great-grandmother Anna. Every time the Sisters looked at a Tearoom menu, they thought how striking a resemblance Eva bore to Anna's ethereal likeness. "Hmmm, I'm hungrier than I thought."

"You're always hungry," Maggie retorted in response to her sister of the moon's comment.

A lascivious glint appeared in Raine's vivid green eyes. "For one thing or another," she answered in her throaty voice. "I've *healthy* appetites; and besides," her expression turned pouty, "in the realm of witches, passion is good, as we both know."

Slipping on her reading glasses to peruse the menu, Maggie replied with sexy overtone, "Passion is *indeed* good. Is Beau coming over to the house tonight?"

"If he doesn't get any farm calls, he'll come over early enough for us to eat dinner together, and if he does get called out, then he'll come over when he's through, to spend the night. Are you going to the cabin with Thaddeus?"

"Yes." Maggie's smart phone began to vibrate. "It's *him*," she said, pulling the cell from her purse. "Hello, darlin'," she purred. Listening, she smiled her mysterious smile, whispering aside to Raine after a moment, "He finished grading papers sooner than he thought. Would you mind if he joins us for lunch?"

"Not in the least." Raine scanned the bill of fare. "And I know Robin will be fine with it, because I mentioned to her that Thad might be joining us."

"We're at The Gypsy Tearoom," Maggie said into the phone. "Robin's not here yet, so we haven't ordered." Then after listening for a few seconds, she finished with, "Right. See you in a few."

Eva brought the tea things, setting them on the Sisters' table. "So what's new? I sense that you're hot on the trail of a new mystery." She lifted her brows. "Am I right?"

"You could say that," the Sisters responded in sync, as they were prone to do. They regarded their special friend as she leaned forward to pour the sweet-smelling tea.

Though in her fifties, Eva looked a good twenty years younger. Her hair, an enchanting blonde mix of silver and gold, was casual, the short soft waves and curls brushed back from her face. One little wisp of a curl fell forward to the center of her forehead, which always reminded the Sisters of Longfellow's rhyme about a little girl who could be both naughty and nice. Eva's skin was what used to be called "peaches and cream," unlined and glowing with health. Her almond-shaped, hazel eyes were the woman's most outstanding feature. These were the eyes of a leopard– *knowing and exotic*.

Eva had a soft voice and a natural-born womanliness that rendered her totally affable– both men and women liked "Sister Novak." Warm-hearted, vivacious and witty, Eva Novak made life a high joyous thing for anyone who spent time in her company.

"You always look happy, Eva," Raine commented.

Eva laughed. "Happiness is when you feel good about yourself without feeling the need for anyone else's approval." She lowered her voice, sinking down on the bench next to Raine, a look of expectation on her face. "Can you let me in on the gist of your new mystery, ladies? You lead such *fascinating* lives; I can't help but be curious. I've a few moments to listen," she said, peering out of the booth to see her waitress taking care of the early customers.

"Eva, keep this just between us," Maggie began, holding her voice to a whisper, "but we're going to aid the Keystone Coven in saving Washingtonville's Witch Tree from destruction."

"You mean the Hester Tree?"

The Sisters nodded, "Yes."

The proprietress' jaw dropped. "Why would anyone want to destroy the Hester Tree?" she questioned.

Raine shared what they knew thus far, which wasn't much.

"Eva, if you hear anything that might help us in this quest to save the tree, please, we entreat you, let us know," Maggie said in a pleading tone. "We know from experience we can count on you."

"I will do that; and yes, you can always count on me."

The Sisters exchanged pleased looks. "Great!" they answered.

"I wonder which of the big construction companies is after that land," Eva mused. "Derrick Mason used to come in here once in a while with his wife. After she had the heart attack that took her to the Summerland, I didn't see him for a long time, nearly two years I think it was. I could always tell they were close. It's only lately that I served him and his son. They've been in together a couple of times in the past three months."

"Do you know anything about him?" Raine asked *sotto voce*. "About the contractor, I mean."

Eva shook her head. "Not really. Only that he's well off. He looks a bit older since his wife passed and a lot sadder. It's hard to lose a mate you've been close with." Eva pulled a paper towel from her bra and began dabbing at her eyes. "Believe me, *I* know."

Sister Novak had been married four times. For some unknown reason, the woman had a penchant for the name "John," as well as for firemen. Raine and Maggie didn't know whether the husbands' given names were each John, or if Eva just blessed each with her favorite appellation. All the Sleuth Sisters knew is that all four of Eva's husbands had been called "John," and all four had been firemen. They knew for certain, too, that each husband, like Eva herself, had been of Hungarian extraction.

Eva was widowed twice and divorced twice. And never had the Sisters heard the woman speak unkindly of her former mates. Indeed, when any one of her husbands was ever mentioned, Eva habitually pulled a paper towel– as incongruous as it may seem– from the bra of the low-cut Gypsy blouse or dress she was sporting to wipe tearful eyes. The Sisters had never known their friend not to be prepared with her trusty paper towel. Sister Novak was one-of-a-kind; and now, they knew enough to wait until her grieving moment passed.

Presently, the older woman leaned forward to whisper, "You both know I'm not a gossip, but if this tidbit of info will help you, then here it is. I've heard that Derrick Mason's son– his *only* offspring– is totin' the rep of being a *player*."

The Sisters traded looks.

"Devilishly handsome, the son." Eva cocked her blonde head in thought. "'Course Derrick's good-lookin' too. That grey he got in his black hair looks distinguished. He could leave his shoes under my bed whenever!" she winked. "Anyway, it looked to me as though they were arguing the times they were in here, he and his boy. Not with rowdiness or anything like that, but arguing nonetheless."

"How old is the playboy son?" Raine queried.

"Couldn't say exactly, but he looks to be fresh outta college. I think I read in the paper a while back that he attended some fancy Ivy League university somewhere up in … New England?" Eva pursed her lips in thought. "Yeah, it was. Harvard. I'd guess he's in his twenties, and I'm guessin' he's no dummy if he graduated Harvard." Leaning forward again, she added, keeping her voice to a murmur, "For what it's worth, I'd say he's a *spoiled* young buck. Looks to be full of himself, if you know what I'm trying to say." She snapped her fingers as a fragment of memory hit her. "I heard the father say something about how he had to cut off the kid's credit cards when he was in college, and Reggie shot back with, 'Yeah, and I made my *own* money, didn't I?' I think the son said he earned the money designing web sites or something, something related to computers."

The proprietress peered out the booth to check on the customer situation. "I'd better get back to work; lunchtime can get hectic." Eva rose. "Do you need more menus?"

"Two," Maggie stated. "Thaddeus will be joining us as well."

"Then I'll bring another pot of my special brew with two more place settings." And with that, the colorful lady headed back to the kitchen.

No sooner had Eva hurried off, when Dr. Weatherby entered the Tearoom, his eyes, behind his specs, quickly locating the Sisters in their preferred booth. Swiftly did he remove his Indiana Jones hat and trench coat, moving with purpose toward the ladies.

"Hello, luv," he said to Maggie, bending to kiss her. "Got here as soon as I could. I had to change my shirt. Hello, Raine."

"Aren't you going to say you love me madly?" Maggie laughed, scooting over to let Thaddeus slide in next to her. Her green eyes skimmed his tweedy attire, and she said with slow deliberation, "You look good. I see you selected one of the Italian knit shirts we picked out together last weekend."

"You look good too," the professor replied. "Good enough to–" he completed the thought in her ear, causing her to respond with a sexy mien. "And yes, darling, I love you madly." He kissed her again, soundly on the cheek, his whiskers tickling her skin.

As the esteemed head of Haleigh College's history department, Dr. Thaddeus Weatherby had been the perfect advisor to Raine and Maggie when they were working toward their doctorates in history. His mentorship bonded him with the McDonoughs and aroused his fervent love for Maggie. As the Sisters came to discover, the inimitable Dr. Weatherby was well-versed in a wide range of subjects, and he possessed a colorful spectrum of talents. Not to suggest that he was a jack of all trades, but he most assuredly was a master of many.

Moreover– and to the point– Dr. Thaddeus Weatherby, PhD, was the textbook absent-minded professor with a brain like a steel trap. To put it another way, the highly respected Dr. Weatherby was a bona fide genius, and like most intellects, he had his quirks. For instance, he occasionally displayed a childlike nature, or more precisely what, owing to his passionate curiosity, colleagues *mistook* for a childlike nature that, at times, drove his fellows in the history department a tad crazy. But then, as those of the Craft know well, the secret of genius is to carry the riddle of the child into old age. One of the things Dr. Weatherby was fond of saying was, "You're never too old to enjoy a happy childhood. Take time every day to do something amusing!"

And one of the most special characteristics– *and there were several*– about the professor was that he possessed extraordinarily accurate and vivid recall, both visual and audial, an "eidetic memory" some might call it. The remarkable man's sharp Scorpio wit and courage, or as Hemingway penned it, "grace under pressure," served the Sleuth Sisters well on more than one close-call circumstance in the past.

A wiry and surprisingly muscular, middle-age man, Thaddeus' dark grey hair, thanks to Maggie's influence, was no longer reminiscent of Einstein's; rather it was professionally styled. "It doesn't look as if you comb your hair with firecrackers anymore," Raine teased when first she'd seen Thaddeus' new look.

His once careless manner of dress was now "country gentry," Irish tweeds replacing the rumpled, mismatched "Weatherby wear," a twist about which, once upon a time, his students did genially jest. However, he retained, regardless of what he was wearing, his signature, cherry-red bow tie. Due to his significant other's sway, nowadays the professor sported a neat van dyke mustache and beard, and though he wore his contacts more often than he used to, this afternoon his bright blue eyes peered from behind his workaday Harry Potter spectacles that adjusted to light.

"Let's get Thad up-to-date, and then, when Robin gets here, we can start formulating a plan," Raine suggested.

For the next several minutes, while they sipped the tea the proprietress brought them, the Sisters shared with Thaddeus what they had discussed with each other that morning, adding, at the end, what Eva told them.

Hearing a familiar voice, Raine looked toward the entrance. "Ah, here comes Robin now."

A stunning redhead, High Priestess Robin, whose witch name was Athena, resembled actress Nicole Kidman. As she followed Eva to the Sisters' booth, she looked a trifle harried, giving the impression that she rushed to make their rendezvous.

"Robin, this is our dear friend Eva Novak. Eva, this is another dear friend, Robin O'Malley," Raine pronounced, sliding over to allow room for the High Priestess to be seated next to her. "And you remember Dr. Weatherby, I'm sure."

- 42 -

"How could I forget Dr. Weatherby? How are you, Thaddeus?" Robin queried politely.

"Well, thank you. A very good afternoon to you, Robin," the professor remarked. Having risen, he settled back into the bench seat next to Maggie.

Eva laughed. "Robin and I need no introduction. We go back quite a way," she said, reaching out to squeeze the High Priestess' hand. "We met in Pittsburgh several years ago at a psychic fair."

"We did. You looked into your faithful crystal ball and told me you saw two different wedding bands, revealing that I'd have two marriages." Robin turned toward the Sisters and Thaddeus. "And she was right." Now it was the priestess' turn to laugh. "I only wish I would have consulted you *before* I married the first time. The old adage 'love is blind' is absolutely true. When I think back on it now, I don't know how I could have been so stupid."

Eva patted Robin's hand. "You weren't stupid, my dear, just young. Young, and, as you said, in love."

"*Infatuated*," Robin amended.

"Been there, done that," Eva reflected, pulling out the inevitable paper towel to dab at her eyes.

A few more customers entered the cozy room, prompting Sister Novak to say, "I'll leave you to think about the specials and glance over the menus. Enjoy the tea."

Thaddeus picked up the teapot to fill Robin's cup. "This will relax you," he asserted quietly. "It's called 'Tea-Time-Will-Tell,' Eva's special brew. Guaranteed to soothe and calm the nerves."

"Bless you. I *have* been stressed with worry over the fate of the Witch Tree," Robin admitted. "And I should know better. Worrying is like praying for what you don't want." She picked up her cup and took a long draught of the fragrant beverage. "That's better," she sighed, setting the cup in the saucer. "Now, let me begin by saying that I am deeply grateful; the *whole Coven* is grateful that you will be helping us with this … *situation*."

"We've got your backs," Raine put in with the grit of her warrior McDonough ancestors.

"And we have yours." Robin flashed the Sisters a quick smile. "Incidentally, it was our senior advisor from the Hamlet here, the mysterious unknown we refer to as the 'Wizard,' who prodded us to ask for your help."

The Sisters exchanged looks.

"You don't say?" Raine mused. She was about to add something, when–

Thaddeus cleared his throat and broke in. "Who owns the property the Witch Tree is on?"

"An elderly widower named Will Granger," Robin supplied, speaking in a hushed voice. "He's a good man, but it must be a great temptation to sell Witch-Tree Farm. Two different builders want to develop the land. I have it in the strictest confidence that each has offered the old fella a substantial sum of money."

"How *much* money; do you have any idea?" Maggie queried.

"I've heard each offer is in the neighborhood of three million dollars," Robin whispered.

"*Pricey* neighborhood," Raine commented, picking up her teacup.

Robin dipped her head in agreement. "As I'm certain you're aware, Washingtonville is ever-becoming a touristy town. We've lots of history, as well as more and more artsy things to do and see. Witch-Tree Farm is an especially beautiful parcel of land, about a hundred acres, close to town, so it's prime real estate."

"Location, location, location," Maggie chanted with understanding expression.

"The farm's been in Will's family for over a hundred years, so he doesn't really want to see it go to strangers. His wife passed on several years back. They had no children, but he does have a niece, Amanda Granger Woods, with whom he's always been close, *and* to whom he's promised to leave Witch-Tree Farm." Robin stole another hasty gulp of her tea. "However, he's been heard remarking that the offers from the builders are tempting, to say the least."

"What's the niece like?" Maggie asked, lifting her cup to sip the comforting drink.

Robin inclined her head, her long, straight fiery-red hair gleaming like silk in the glow from the wall sconces. "She's an elementary-school teacher, who's recently been down-sized by the district, so she's not working now; and I'd wager that hurts, because her husband looks to be the type who likes the best."

The High Priestess drained her cup, as she turned things over in her mind. "I shouldn't have said that. Just because a man drives a Mercedes doesn't mean he's a high-roller. Forgive me. That's not like me. I'm not a judgmental person. I'm just, as I said, *stressed.* At any rate, Amanda's husband, Sam, is an agreeable fellow, what Central Casting might call 'Leading-Man Handsome.' He's the overall manager of Washingtonville Lumber Company, and that's a big outfit, with three locations. He must be a hard worker, because he climbed the ladder from junior clerk to the head position in a few short years.

"Anyway, I think Amanda came into some money when her parents passed away, so the Woods probably have a nice savings." Several moments slipped by, after which Robin groaned, "This all sounds so gossipy, like tittle-tattle. I fear I'm relating it clumsily. Makes me feel guilty; you know, openly discussing people in such a personal manner. I would never want to besmirch anyone's good name."

"We take your meaning, Robin; but with all due respect, we need to know everything you can tell us about the people involved," Raine answered. "It will help us."

Thaddeus poured the High Priestess another cup of tea. "Wonder if Granger has a will? You said he promised to leave the farm to his niece. Did you say she's his only living relative?"

"I *think* she is. And I don't know if he ever made a will. Mr. Granger was overheard telling the waitress at our coffee shop, The Witch's Brew Café, that he always wanted the farm to go to Amanda. But to quote him, 'It's tempting to sell the place to one of those fancy-schmancy builders. And if I hadn't given my word to my niece that I'd leave the farm to her, I might just consider their offers and take a trip around the world.'" Robin's mouth tightened. "The lady who overheard his conversation with the waitress at the café was our town busybody, Gracie Seymour. She said Will seemed to be joking, not really serious, but you know the old saying, 'Money talks, and–'"

"Let's not think the worst," Maggie intervened. "Robin, what do you know about Will Granger personally?"

Robin thought for a speculative moment before answering. "Like I said, by all indication, he's a decent sort, hard-working. Always kept the farm up. I know he took really good care of his wife when she was dying of cancer. I've never heard a negative thing about him."

An instant later, Robin snapped her fingers, "Great Goddess, I don't want to forget to mention that as Will was leaving The Witch's Brew, I was just going in, and so we literally bumped into each other at the entrance. He seemed a bit shaken about the voices he said he's been hearing in the wind, when he's close to the tree, and sometimes even at night in his bed. When he and his dog take what he referred to as their 'daily constitution,' the dog's been refusing to walk near the Witch Tree. He said his dog barks at the tree, whimpers and whines, displaying fear, which never happened before. I told him the spirit in that ancient oak is Hester Duff, and it seems to me she is not at all happy that her tree is in jeopardy."

"What was his reaction to that?" Thaddeus rested his back against the tufted leather of the booth.

Robin wrinkled her forehead. "He answered that the tree was only in jeopardy if he sold his farm to one of those land developers, and at this point in time, that was not his intention."

"Was anything else said?" Dr. Weatherby questioned.

With an anxious look in her eyes, Robin bobbed her head in a brusque gesture. "I then told him I sensed that Hester was aware of the talk being battered around about felling her tree; but he cut me off, saying that was something Washingtonville always had a surplus of– *talk*." The High Priestess chortled. "He's right about that!"

"Has he been able to decipher what the voices in the wind are saying?" Raine asked, leaning forward with a witch's keen interest.

Robin shook her head. "He said not."

The Sisters traded nods of acknowledgment, with Raine remarking, "I'd really like to do some wind-listening at Witch-Tree Farm. Do you think Will Granger would mind? Would he grant me permission, do you think?"

"I think he would," Robin answered. "You're an expert at wind-listening, Sister. *Do* ask him. It just might help us in our quest to save the tree."

"I will." Raine's expression became sober. "Our granny used to take us for long walks in Haleigh's Wood, urging us to listen to the magick whispers of old trees."

"I can relate to that," Robin replied.

"Granger's niece? What do you think of *her* personally?" Maggie urged. "You told us she's a teacher, but what's she *like*?"

"She's a delicate little thing. Reminds me of a wood nymph. In my opinion, she's very sweet. I've never heard a negative phrase spoken about her. Like Will Granger, Amanda and her husband, Sam Woods, have always been respected residents of our town … good, upstanding citizens, all three." Robin picked up her menu, opening it and asking, "What do you recommend? I am *starving*. I've been rushed off my feet all morning, so I haven't had a thing to eat since early last evening."

"Anything you order here will be scrumptious," Maggie and Raine responded as one.

"I suggest we decide what we want, then we can resume our discussion," Thaddeus said, as his intense blue eyes started down the menu of savory choices.

A moment later, Eva took their orders, after which she said in low tones, "Couldn't help hearing the name *Woods* dropped a moment ago. If you mean the fella who runs the lumber yard over in Washingtonville, he and his wife come in here once in a while. Seem like a nice couple."

When they were again alone, Raine reopened their dialogue. "How about filling us in on the two builders who want the property the Witch Tree's on?"

"They aren't the only ones who want the property, nor are they the sole threats to the tree," the High Priestess delivered. Seeing the looks on her friends' faces, Robin quickly pulled up. "But first let me tell you what I know about each of the builders." She took another long swallow of the soothing tea and began.

"Rex Chambers is known as the 'King of the Builders' all across western Pennsylvania. Truth is he's built an empire for himself and his daughter. He's been married numerous times. Five, I think, but has only the one offspring, the daughter he's been grooming to take over for him when he's gone. Chambers is ostentatious and arrogant, but I couldn't find any evidence that he conducts shady business deals, though I've heard talk. The talk might be just that– mindless *gossip*."

"What about the daughter?" Maggie leaned back against the booth's red leather padding.

Robin rolled her eyes. "Sirena Chambers. Aptly named that one! A real siren. Rich, beautiful, and intelligent. I don't know about spoiled, because, like her father, the woman is a workaholic. She appears to want to learn everything she can from her dad while she can, in order to be even better than he at running Chambers Construction one day.

"Derrick Mason is the owner of the rival company, DHM Construction, that wants to get hands on Witch-Tree Farm. Again, I never heard any negative talk about him. He lost his wife not long ago, a couple years I think it's been; and he, too, has only one offspring, a son, Reggie, who, now that he's out of college, is being coached to carry on the business one day.

"The mother, I've gathered, indulged her handsome son in every way, as some parents do with an only child. Reggie was always in trouble in school. Nothing too terrible, though he's a born con man. I found out that his father had to make more than one trip to Harvard when the kid was in trouble up there. You know, to try and keep him *in* school. He was a party boy; but somehow, he got through college and graduated, though, not like his father, who graduated *cum laude*."

"Reggie Mason," Thaddeus rolled the name off his tongue. "Strikes a sour note. Let me hum a few bars," he quipped, stroking his beard as memories flooded back. "I hired him one summer to cut my lawn and trim shrubbery and hedges. Yes, it was about six years ago. He had just graduated from high school, so it was the summer before he left for college; and you're right, he *is* a born con. He told me I didn't have to pay him till the end of the season, and we agreed on a price; but he figured on cheating me out of more money, which I didn't allow him to do. He was clever, though, quite clever in the way he'd orchestrated it. Sorry, Robin, I didn't mean to interrupt you."

"You didn't. As Raine said, whatever we can garner about these people should help us. As I was saying, Reggie was, probably still is, a playboy." It was on the tip of the High Priestess' tongue to add, *As well as a person of questionable character*. However, she restrained herself, but not before Maggie nicked her thought.

"He always needed more money than his father's allowance provided," Robin continued, "which was why he was doing lawns the summer before he left for college. He was also working for his dad that summer. I found out Reggie goes through money like a buzz saw. Furthermore, I've nipped from the town grapevine– and you know how active the grapevine is in any small town– that the prodigal son is now frantically trying to *prove* himself to his father, who has cut him off from any money for a while, except what he actually *earns* working for him. I heard he even lifted Reggie's credit cards."

"Hmmm," Maggie pondered, "old sins have long shadows."

Robin dipped her head. "Yes, and in a small town, folks ferret out all the dark secrets hidden in those shadows– sooner or later."

"At any rate," Robin went on, "Chambers Construction wants to tear down the tree and build elite condos on the land, which Rex Chambers would call 'Hester Gardens.' That would mean razing the nineteenth-century farmhouse too, which is in good shape despite its age."

"I can understand, in a way, having to take the current house on the property down, but why couldn't they leave the historic tree where it is?" Raine blurted.

"As you know, that tree is over 300 years old, and it will keep getting bigger and bigger. That type of oak can live hundreds of years. The tree is about smack in the center of the property, and the root system is already far-reaching. In order to build his condos, Chambers would have to bring down the tree. He has offered to put a commemorative plaque and an elegant fountain on or near the spot where the tree is now, and his aim is to construct the fountain to look like a giant oak."

"What does Mason Construction ... 'r *DHM Construction* want to build on the Witch-Tree property?" Thaddeus inquired.

"To quote Derrick Mason– a 'unique shopping center.' His company's been doing some serious lobbying with the Washingtonville Town Council to talk Will Granger into selling to *them*, because DHM assures that the shopping center will create jobs for our residents *and* bring in more tourists."

"What does Derrick Mason mean by *unique*?" Raine wondered aloud.

"Unique to our area, our town, its interests and history," Robin supplied. "The shops he proposes would include a craft shop; a yogurt shop and café; an organic grocery, bakery and café combination; an upscale restaurant; a holistic center that offers classes in yoga and meditation; a gemstone and crystal shop; an art gallery, et cetera. He claims he has these vendors ... renters for the shops already lined up for his 'Enchanted Elements Emporium.' Washingtonville could use more eateries; and yes, those shops and generating more jobs would be nice, but– and this is a *big* but–"

"He'd have to fell the Witch Tree too," Maggie and Raine repeated together.

"Yes," Robin pronounced glumly. She drained her tea and nested the cup back in its saucer.

"You said something about the builders not being the only people who want to get hold of Witch-Tree Farm," Thaddeus reminded.

Before the High Priestess could respond, Eva brought their food.

"Two caviar omelets," she said, setting the plates before Maggie and Thaddeus. "Goat cheese organic green salad for you, Raine; and for Robin, the tea sandwich combo with a cup of my Russian red borscht." Eva put her hands on her hips to regard her patrons. "Now, can I bring you more tea?"

"Yes," chorused the table.

"And I hope you'll want dessert today, because the special is a plate of my mini tarts to share. My famous chocolate tarts, my lemon and all my fruit tarts, including my dark chocolate-dark berry tart, which is absolutely *divine*. They're so cute that I call the platter 'Tea For T'Arts.'"

"Oh, I am certain we'll want dessert, Eva!" Raine conveyed in robust voice, already dipping her fork into a wedge of warm *chèvre*.

"So, in addition to the two land developers, both the president of the town council *and* Washingtonville Historical Society's president have been badgering poor old Mr. Granger about his land." Robin leaned back away from the table. "That was delicious, but I can't eat another bite!" In actuality, that was about all she had left on her plate.

"I assume– which we don't make a practice of doing, but for the moment anyway– that the historical society would protect the tree?" Maggie said. It was more of a question than a statement. She put her fork down and dabbed at the corners of her mouth with a napkin.

"I believe they would," the High Priestess answered without hesitation. "Their president, Etta Story, is on a *mission* to stop Will Granger from selling to land developers. She'd rather he kept his promise to leave Witch-Tree Farm to his niece, Amanda, than to see the historic tree cut down by contractors; though, of course, she would *love it* if Granger left his land to the historical society."

"Has the society a plan for it? Sounds like it might," Thaddeus remarked. He poured everyone more tea.

"The historical society most definitely does have a plan," Robin replied. "A long-time dream really. They want to turn the farmhouse into a museum. That's where they'd have their meetings, their annual Christmas parties, and such. You see, the Washingtonville Historical Society doesn't have a building of its own. Since its beginnings, WHS rents a small upstairs room from the library. However, they have so many artifacts– Native American artifacts, old maps, vintage photographs, films, paintings, antique uniforms, an authentic Civil War drum, so many things, but nowhere to exhibit them. President Etta Story would love nothing better than to talk Will Granger into leaving the farm to the society. They'd convert the grounds into a nice park, where they'd hold their annual picnics and other outdoor affairs; and, of course, the Witch Tree would be saved. Etta said she'd get donations for a lightning rod for it, and a lot of the work for the farmhouse-turned-museum would be volunteer work, with donated time and materials. The same goes for the dream of a park on the grounds."

"If Will Granger leaves the place to his niece, would she and her husband preserve the tree, do you think?" Raine asked.

"Yes, I do," Robin stated. "Like her uncle, Amanda has always expressed her love for the tree and the family farm. And I'm reasonably certain, from all I've heard and gathered, that her husband, Sam, is a big help to Will at Witch-Tree, especially now that Will's 'getting up there,' as we say in these parts."

"How old *is* Will Granger? And is he in good health?" Thaddeus mused aloud.

Robin thought a moment, answering, "I think he's in his seventies, mid-or-late seventies. And as for his health, he seems to be in good shape. He's lived active years with plenty of fresh air and exercise. Farm life is a wholesome lifestyle."

"Really, Robin, the situation doesn't look as bleak as I was expecting," Maggie said, taking a sip of tea and tilting her head in thought. "There are several people who want to save and protect the tree, including the Coven, the historical society, Will Granger, his niece, and her husband."

"True. We know since Mr. Granger and his deceased wife never had any children, he has come to look upon Amanda– who lost her parents in a car accident when a drunk plowed into them several Christmases ago– as a daughter, and she thinks of him as a surrogate father." Changing her mind, Robin polished off the last couple bites of sandwich she'd left on her plate.

"And you said that Granger *promised* his niece he'd leave her Witch-Tree Farm, right?" Raine adjusted herself in her seat to a more comfortable position.

"Also true," the High Priestess sighed, "but have you ever heard the old saying, 'Money is the root of all evil'?"

"The world is full of magic things,
patiently waiting for our senses to grow sharper."
~ W.B. Yeats

# Chapter Two

The pentacle dangling from the miniature besom suspended from Raine's rearview mirror swayed to and fro, as the Sisters sped down the highway toward the not-too-distant village of Washingtonville.

"You better slow down," Maggie suggested. "It's easy to forget how fast we're going in this car on a dry, open road with virtually no traffic. We don't want to get a ticket, darlin'."

Raine checked the MG TD's speedometer. "Sorry about that," she said, immediately slowing the sports car to the speed limit.

Ever since her childhood, when she polished off Nancy Drew mysteries faster than Granny McDonough could supply them, Raine planned on having a vintage roadster of her own one day. When she was ready for the purchase, she searched everywhere for just the right vehicle, scanning the Internet and newspapers daily, round-about used-car dealerships weekly.

The crafty young woman knew, by then, *what* she wanted; thenceforward, just as Maggie had manifested her Land Rover, Raine needed to manifest her goal MG. Via research, she got a clear vision of *precisely* what she sought, intensifying the energy each and every time she visualized the 1953 model she desired. She was thoroughly and carefully *specific* with each and every detail, from the signature headlights to the wire-wheels– and she truly *believed* with all her heart and soul. Within a month, the MG of her dreams appeared in the classified ads of the *Hamlet Herald*– within the price range she had programmed into her meticulously woven spell.

The sports car's like-new red and black interior and grill were the Sisters' high school and college colors, and the pristine cream body was the perfect canvas for the wee magick wand Raine had detailed on the driver's door, with her initials in fancy script on the wand's grip. The MG's *pièce de résistance* was the license plate.

It read——— *BROOM.*

Dr. Raine McDonough, PhD, was resourceful as well as clever. "Every intention sets energy in motion, whether you're conscious of it or not," she liked to say.

Now what she was saying, as she drove that morning to Witch-Tree Farm was this: "Mags, I was pleasantly surprised by Will Granger's reaction to my telephone call last night."

"Why?" Maggie turned her head to study Raine's profile. "Nowadays, a lot of people know who we are."

"Yes, but our wish to pay him a visit was rather short notice, and today *is* Sunday. Many folks have plans for one thing or other on Sundays, even if it's just to rest. I was stunned by his comment that he would *welcome* a visit from us. It sounded like more than just a friendly thing to say. In fact, it struck me as bordering on distress." Raine expertly shifted gears and maneuvered the little car into the passing lane to overtake a slow-moving pickup truck. The elderly fellow behind the wheel was so short, she nearly gasped that a child was driving the beat-up old Ford.

"You mean because of the voices in the wind?" Maggie was asking.

"Right." Raine was quiet for a pensive moment before adding, "I asked him if I could wind-listen, alone, at the tree, and he readily agreed," she chortled, "as long as I promised to tell him what the message or messages are."

"And did you ... *promise*?" Maggie took a lipstick from her purse and glided the glossy red color over her full lips.

Raine was quick to reply. "Whatever Hester is whispering in the wind that blows over Witch-Tree farm– Will Granger has a right to know."

About a half-hour later, as Raine and Maggie motored up the scenic tree-lined lane to Witch-Tree Farm, each was silent, thinking about what they would say to Will Granger, what they would ask him about his intentions in regard to his property, which, in actuality, was none of their business.

When the farmhouse came into view, Maggie remarked, "Looks like the old saltbox style of architecture that originated in New England, circa 1650, I believe."

Raine shifted into low gear, slowing the MG, to enjoy the sight of the charming old homestead. "Spot on, Mags! I did a bit of research before we left, and that's *exactly* the style of the old Witch-Tree house. The man who built it hailed from Massachusetts. He was the captain of a whaling vessel, and his name was Nate Brewster. In the late 1890s, he came here, to accept a job as a riverboat captain when his wife demanded that he stop going out to sea for such long periods of time. Not to mention that whaling was super-dangerous work.

"Captain Brewster had his house built after the style of home he was used to in New England. When he passed on, the place went to his wife, then his son, who died late in 1911, the result of apoplexy … stroke. The first of the Grangers, Will's great-grandfather, took over the farm in 1912, purchasing it from Nate Brewster's daughter, who had married a banker and was residing in New York City."

Exiting the car, the Sisters started up the flagstone walkway to the house, when a large black and tan Airedale, that had been resting on the porch, came loping toward them, barking and looking as if he wanted to let the visitors know, in no uncertain terms, that he was in charge of guarding Witch-Tree Farm.

"Jasper, come!" a stentorian voice called from the doorway. "Come, Jasper! It's all right, fella; it's all right." Will Granger stepped out on the porch to receive the Sisters. He leaned down to pat the dog. "Good boy!"

The Airedale ceased its barking.

"Good-morning, Mr. Granger," the Sisters called in unison. "Thank you for agreeing to see us today."

Meanwhile, Jasper, drawn to Raine, was sniffing the hand she extended toward him. Almost immediately, he began emitting happy noises, standing upright, a paw on each of that Sister's shoulders, as he licked her face with delight.

"Well, I'll be!" Will exclaimed. "I've never seen him take so to a stranger. He seems to really like you, missy. Get down, Jasper! You'll muss her clothes!"

Raine glanced over at Granger– and liked him. She liked his gravity and his simplicity, and for some inexplicable reason, she felt sorry for him. "No worries," she smiled, playfully tugging the dog's mustaches. "I have a way with animals."

Will returned the smile, looking the magickal pair over with scrutinizing eyes. "So who would've thought? The famous Sleuth Sisters here at Witch-Tree Farm! I'd-a recognized you anywhere from your photos in the papers." For a moment, he appeared puzzled. "Always read there're *three* of you."

"There *are* three of us," the Sisters answered jointly, with Raine expounding, "Our cousin Aisling couldn't make it, sir. She's hosting her husband's parents for Sunday dinner today."

Again Granger gave the impression of bemusement. "Cousin? You're not all three sisters?"

Raine and Maggie traded looks with the thought *Oh, we're Sisters, all right!*

"We're first cousins, but we're so like sisters," Raine explained, "everyone calls us the Sleuth Sisters," the pair finished together.

Will nodded his understanding.

"*What* a good dog!" Raine bubbled, as she scratched behind the Airedale's ears, folded over into perfect triangles.

"My father raised Airedales, and I've always had one. Always had one named Jasper too. Come on inside," Granger said suddenly. "I've put a fresh pot of coffee on the stove. We can talk before we walk out to the tree." He flung open the back door, and they entered a cheerful kitchen.

The room was white, clean and cozy, with open shelves, in the old-fashioned farmhouse style, and an oval, wooden table with four spindle-back chairs, also painted white. A couple of quaint rag rugs splashed the hardwood floor with color. The sunny-yellow curtains and tablecloth matched, and the Sisters got a quick vision of Will's wife lovingly sewing them by hand. The bottom panels of the tiered curtains were pushed open; and through the window, the Sisters could see the rolling Pennsylvania countryside, the trees aflame with their autumn cloaks of vivid hues.

"Sit down," Will indicated, gesturing toward the table and chairs.

The welcoming aroma and sound of percolating coffee permeated the space, as the Sisters removed their black, hooded capes and took seats at the table, placing their wraps on the back of the chairs. For the next few moments, while he busied himself with the coffee, they studied the man before them.

Will Granger was tall and lanky, with dark brown hair frosted heavily with grey. His eyes, too, were brown. They were kind eyes, tired eyes, and the Sisters thought he looked somewhat drained from a lifetime of hard work. He wore a red plaid flannel shirt beneath bib overalls that hung on his frame, as *though he had lost weight, or*, Maggie thought, *he just likes his clothes loose and comfortable.*

"You're quite a fan of *National Geographic*, Mr. Granger," Raine said, having noted the stacks of the magazine in the kitchen and the adjoining parlor.

With an agreeing grunt, Will finished pouring the coffee, setting steaming mugs before Maggie and Raine, then bringing his own to the table, where he took a seat opposite the Sisters. "I got a whole house full-a them magazines. They go back years. Oh, do you take cream and sugar?" He stood.

"Just cream," they replied.

"Did you and your wife do much traveling?" Raine queried. "Thank you," she said, accepting the small carton of cream for her coffee.

Will gave a good-natured chuckle. "Farmers don't get to travel. You raise or buy five-hundred-pound calves in the spring, put 'em on pasture, toss 'em grain, and hope to sell thousand-pound steers for beef in the fall. No such thing as a retired farmer or farmer's wife. Nooo, ma'am, farmin's the original 24/7 job. There's always somethin' to mend, mow, clean, plant, or pick. The animals *and* the land are demanding. It's either plantin' time or hayin' time, or harvest. And ya can't hire anyone who wants to work nowadays. Hell, young folks today don't wanna work. *Work?* Huh! That's the one four-letter word missin' from their vocabulary. No," he shook his head in a musing gesture, "never ask a farmer if he's ever traveled. Waste of your time." He smiled a little sadly. "I'm just a wayfarin' stranger travelin' through this world of woe."

Raine lit up. "I know that old song!"

"Thought you'd be too young to know that song." Granger took a careful sip of the hot coffee.

"I like Bluegrass music," the Goth gal stated. "It touches my Celtic heart."

Will responded with a slight movement of his head, leading the Sisters to believe that music stirred him too. "Would you fancy a muffin with that?"

"No, thank you," the Sisters answered.

"We'd rather spend our time chatting with you," Maggie asserted in her serene manner.

"Contrarywise, ladies, I done a lot of what folks call *armchair travel* in my day. Still do." Granger's countenance bespoke reflection. "Been to every country in the world in that ole chair yonder." He pointed to an overstuffed armchair visible through the door to the parlor, where Jasper was lying before the fireplace, the crackling flames warming him.

"I suppose it is tempting to take that trip round the world now that you've been offered so much money by the land developers," the more daring Raine commented flatly. She made her tone sound casual.

Will guffawed. "So you've heard the gossip, huh? Scatty women in this here town! Well, I'll tell you the same thing I've told the two pushy contractors, the nervy president of the town council, the fanatical president of the historical society– which I sometimes think should be renamed the 'hysterical society'– and the good witch Robin. If I had no one to leave the farm to, you bet I'd be tempted. Who th' hell wouldn't be? But I *do* have someone to leave the place to– a niece; and she's like a daughter to me. T' boot, both she and her husband are a big help and comfort to me; so, as I promised Amanda, the farm will go to her."

His tone was not angry, but the Sisters could tell, he was getting a mite tired of answering the question Raine had put to him.

"I figure you're here because you're worried about the fate of the Hester Tree. And my figurin' is due to the fact that you and the Coven are likely in cahoots with one another on this thing …"

Raine and Maggie traded pointed looks.

"Not," Will went on, waving aside a negative interpretation, "that I blame you for it. So here's the scoop: This farm's been in my family for over a hundred years, and I want it to *stay* in the family. My niece Amanda and her husband Sam– who, by the way, love this place as much as I do and would protect the tree from harm– are planning to have children; so, for posterity's sake, there you have it. Enough said."

"Mr. Granger, if you don't mind our saying so, you should have a will in which you've made it crystal clear that you bequeath Witch-Tree Farm to your niece. If you're writing it yourself, it should be witnessed and notarized, in the parlance of the law, to make it legal and binding. Or you could have an attorney draw it up," Maggie suggested in a kind tone.

"I'm one step ahead of you. I just finished writin' my will. Didn't want all the whereases and whereforths the damn attorneys toss into the mix, so's no one can understand the confounded thing but them, and–" he halted briefly, his eyes widening in sudden realization, "who better to witness the notarizin' of my will than *you* two! Everyone knows your reputation– **yes**!" he slapped a calloused hand down on the table, giving Maggie a start. You're here, so why th' hell not?!"

"We'd be *happy* to witness your will, Mr. Granger," the redheaded Sister replied, "but it's Sunday. How–"

"*Not* a problem, ladies." The farmer took a quick sip of his coffee. "My neighbor is a notary public, used to be a paralegal, so she advised and assisted me with the will. All I have to do is give her a call to let her know we're comin' over, and she'll notarize it. She's a widow, and we sort of look out for one another. I had a wife, and she was the love of my life, so Gail and me are friends, nothin' more. She's a *good* friend, however, and I'm blessed to have her as a neighbor."

His declaration made the Sisters suspect that Gail, anyway, would like to see the friendship blossom, though Raine and Maggie both sensed that Will was content with the present status of their relationship.

He hoisted his mug to say, "When you're done with your coffee, we can drive over in my Jeep." He glanced out the window. "Won't get three of us in that sardine can you got. Then, when we come back, we can take a walk to the tree. Miss Raine can do her thing out there; and, Miss Maggie, you and I can come back to the house and enjoy a piece of Gail's apple pie. She told me on the phone last evenin' she was baking me one."

"Splendid!" the Sisters chimed.

A rosy-cheeked Gail Friday opened her kitchen door to Will and the Sisters with a cheerful smile and the cordial greeting, "Come on in," she hailed, wiping her hands on her apron. "You're just in time for a big piece of my deep-dish apple pie."

"First things first," Will answered. "These here are two of the famous Sleuth Sisters we've all heard so much about, Raine and Maggie McDonough. Ladies, this is my good friend Gail Friday, and I can tell ya true, she whips up a mean pie of any sort."

Salutations were exchanged after which Gail waved her visitors inside, out of the chill late-October wind, indicating they should be seated at her table, where she had her notary things ready at hand.

The widow Friday was a petite woman, though a bit stout, with short, snow-white hair styled in what used to be termed a "pixie cut." Her eyes were a dark blue, so dark that one might miss the fact that they *were* blue unless the woman was standing in light, which she was at the moment. Beneath her flower-patterned, indigo bib apron, her cotton dress, too, bore a floral print– small, multi-color, green-leafed flowers against a tan backdrop.

"Let's take care of the business at hand," Will suggested, extracting a large brown envelope from the inside of his jacket. "I got the papers right here. Gail, I read over every word, as you advised me to do, and it says what I want to say. I appreciate your typing it up and putting it together for me."

Gail took the envelope. "You fixed my kitchen sink last month, didn't you? Saved me getting a plumber. Can I pour you all some coffee first? It's fresh. I put the pot on when you telephoned."

When everyone decided to have the coffee later with the pie, Gail sat at the table with her guests. Without further preamble, she slipped on a pair of tortoise-shell reading glasses and began studying the document Will had handed her. "One last check," she said, adjusting her spectacles.

For the next several minutes, whilst the Sisters leafed through the magazines they picked up from a side table, Gail read silently, only nodding her head occasionally, or making a low sound of agreement. Finally, she leaned back in her chair, removed her glasses and, focusing her eyes on Granger, said, "It's clear; it's succinct; and it will be totally legal and binding as soon as it's witnessed and notarized, which we can do now."

"Will, speaking as a paralegal and your long-time friend, I just want to reiterate that I helped you execute this will for the reason that I didn't want your niece to have problems down the road with a sloppy-executed self-prepared will being either contested or thrown out in probate. Now," she sighed, "what we'll do here is have the testator … that's *you*, Will, sign before me, the notary, that you are fully aware of what is being signed; and then you ladies will sign, as disinterested witnesses– witnesses, of legal age and sound mind, who are not heirs under the will– witnessing the fact that the testator, Will Granger, did sign this document, his last will and testament, before *me*, a notary public.

"I'll need some ID, ladies, and we can conclude this business," Gail said, handing Will a pen.

While the Sisters fished in their bags for their driver's licenses, Granger carefully put his signature to his testament, followed by first Raine, then Maggie. Lastly, the notary stamped, dated, and signed the document. It was done.

*That's a load off our minds and hearts.* Raine zipped the thought to Maggie.

*Then why,* Maggie returned, her face puckered with doubt and anxiety, *do I feel there's still plenty of work to be done?*

When the Sisters and Will got back to Witch-Tree Farm, they piled out of Granger's Jeep to begin their tramp to the Hester Tree. Jasper, waiting patiently on the porch, jumped up and came forward, making certain to give Raine another of his wet kisses.

"I'm completely in the dark, so tell me again what you intend on doing at the tree," Will asked Raine, as they set out on the well-traveled trail, from the side of the house, that led to the Witch Tree, Jasper bouncing along with them.

"As a farmer, I'm certain you'd agree that nature is not mute. It is man who is ofttimes deaf. Wind-listening is an ancient form of divination that is best experienced on a *windy* day." Raine leaned her head back and breathed in the invigorating autumn air. "Today is perfect. Ideal sort of day for self-cleansing also. As Earth Mother's besom … broom, the wind sweeps away negativity, if you ask it to. But to answer your question, I will need to be alone when I wind-listen. What I'll do is lie down on the earth and *breathe*, taking deep breaths until I feel centered. I'll wholly relax, releasing all negativity, as I imagine the wind passing through me and carrying off all negativity clinging to me. All the while, I'll feel Earth Mother breathing beneath me.

"Once I feel in complete harmony with the tree and my surroundings, I'll begin to focus on the sound of the wind rustling through the leaves and branches above and around me. The voice or voices I will hear will be messages far beyond the conscious mind; and they will be, I am guessing– though it's an educated guess– relevant to the tree, the farm– and to *you*."

Seeing the look on Will's face, Raine added, "Not to worry. I will listen carefully, and though we might be surprised by the message or messages, we must never fear wind-listening. There's an old Native American proverb that says, 'Listen to the wind; it talks. Listen to the silence; it speaks. Listen to your heart– it *knows*.'"

"Well now, that old saying of my ma's proves true once again," Will succumbed. "You learn somethin' new every day."

Raine smiled, flinging out her hands, "Not all classrooms have four walls. I tell my students that all the time."

Maggie, meanwhile, was soaking up the beauty of their surroundings.

Witch-Tree Farm was nestled into a rolling, tree-sprinkled meadowland surrounded by rugged hills covered in deep woods. The autumn foliage, at its peak in a riot of color, delighted the eye, and the woodsy scent of the fallen leaves was invigorating. October's chill breath fluttered the Sisters' black wool capes out behind them, effecting a witchy image as they made their way to the Hester Tree.

A babbling creek meandered through the farm, on the lower south end, dancing over rocks that, if they could talk, would tell colorful tales of yesteryear's warriors whose moccasin-shod feet passed over those shining waters. In whatever direction the Sisters gazed, they were enraptured with the idyllic scenery.

"What a gorgeous farm this is!" Maggie exclaimed, her emerald gaze skimming the sparkling creek at the base of a dip in the adjacent forest, the gold, red, magenta and orange leaves reflecting brightly in the water.

Will looked pleased. "Thank you. This place is very dear to me." His tired eyes misted, and he looked quickly away, calling to Jasper who had run off, hot on the trail of a rabbit.

When there was no sign of the dog, Raine sent the errant canine a telepathic message to come back *at once* to his master. In the twinkling of an eye, Jasper came loping toward them from beyond the tree line.

"Was this ever a dairy farm, or did you always run beef cattle?" Raine queried, thinking that she knew what his answer would be due to their earlier conversation. She crouched down to praise Jasper, who replied with a single bark, licking her face.

"Always beef cattle. Black Angus," Will answered. "Sold them all last November. When I sold the bull, it was like partin' with a pet. Bruce was my buddy." Will looked wistful. "I miss not having any cows on the place, but I knew it was time to stop." He grew pensive.

"When I took my steers to the slaughter house, I always made sure the crew was on hand to butcher as soon as they were unloaded. I never wanted them standin' around, getting jumpy and fretful. Their meat is tough when they fret. I made it a habit to go with them to the slaughter house, to make certain their death was quick. I felt I owed my steers that. Anyhow, my beef was always wrapped and frozen by mid or late November, before deer season started. Never wanted my good Angus shakin' hands with wild deer meat at the processin' place." Again Will quieted.

Both Raine and Maggie noted the sadness in the man's voice.

*The farm was ... **is** his life; farming's in his blood.* Maggie sent the thought to Raine, who gave back with– *Yep, and he took great satisfaction in what he did.*

"I'd wager you still get up at daybreak, Mr. Granger," Maggie remarked.

"And you'd win that bet. Old habits are hard to break." Granger pointed yonder. "There's the Witch Tree, ladies!"

The Sisters paused on the trail to gaze in wonder at the majestic oak, ablaze in crimson autumn splendor.

"Wiz–zard!" Raine rasped, blinking. "She looks to be nearly a hundred feet tall!"

"That's about right," Granger answered with noted pride carried on his voice. "Lucky thing the tree is down in a dip of this rolling ground, or I'd be more worried about lightning than I am. Hester there's a white oak, but as you can readily see, the bark is actually a greyish color, and that's common. Not *un*common for this type of oak to be as wide as it is tall, and it can live to six hundred years. Yes, ma'am, ole Hester, in years to come, will grow taller and wider than she already is."

As they continued walking toward the tree, Jasper became more and more agitated, barking, whining and whimpering in turns.

"There he goes," Will said, stopping to stare at his dog. "He just started fussin' when we walk near to the tree … oh, 'bout three weeks now. Never did this before."

The Airedale's hair was standing on end, and he appeared to be afraid to make another move toward their objective.

"Jasper, you quit your fussin'." Raine knelt before the dog, taking its long face between her hands. "Mr. Granger, I'm going to try and let him know it's OK, that nothing will harm him. As I told you, I have a way with animals." She looked up to fix her witchy stare on the farmer, "And I can communicate with them. I send them images and thoughts telepathically. A lot of folks wouldn't believe that, but it's what I do. All I ask is your patience and the chance to try."

"I used to know a fella, years ago it was, who could talk to horses, so why wouldn't I believe you?" Granger replied. "Go ahead, try your luck. I like takin' our evenin' walks out this way, and lately Jasper has been a problem. I don't know what to do with 'im."

The raven-haired Sister looked the dog directly in the eyes to send him her message: *There's nothing to be afraid of, Jasper. Settle down now. The spirit in that tree is Hester Duff, who used to live here, and the tree is her home. This farm is her home, just as it is yours. She will not harm you. Truly, she has been protecting this farm and the people on it for many long years. Trust me, Jasper. Nothing or no one will harm you.*

The dog tilted his head to the left, listening intently. Then he tipped his long, mustached face to the right, the triangular folds of his ears twitching.

*Just like you watch over your master and this farm, the spirit in that tree is watching over your master, Jasper, and over you. It's a **good** thing. Really it is.*

Within a few moments, the large Airedale was completely calm and, as he did before, he swiped his tongue over Raine's face, sending her a quick happy bark.

"I think he'll accompany us to the tree now, Mr. Granger." Raine stood, patting the dog on the head. "Let's see if he will." She dusted off her knees and took a couple of steps onward.

For a brief moment, Jasper hesitated, then he leaped forward to continue in the direction the others were going.

"Don't know how you did what ya did, but I sure am glad you did it!" The elderly farmer shook his head. "Whadja tell 'im?"

Raine related the thoughts she had sent Jasper, concluding with, "I've been doing this most of my life. A lot of people would laugh at me if I told them I tele-communicate with animals."

Will rubbed the back of his neck with a rough, calloused hand. "If folks are laughin' at you behind your back, then they're in a dang good position to kiss your ass."

The Sisters giggled merrily.

"I really like you, Will Granger!" Raine pronounced with hearty sincerity, slapping him on the back. "You're what our granny would call a 'good ole boy'!"

"Well, I like you too, Miss Raine. You know, I never once believed that Hester Duff was a bad person. I always felt she was misunderstood– just the way the ladies of the Keystone Coven are misunderstood by some of the townspeople around here. I know the Keystone ladies do a lot of good in these parts, and folks ought-a remember that, rather than makin' up crazy stories about 'em– like they do sacrifices and worship the Devil. Figure mebbe it was the same for ole Hester in her day."

The Sisters signaled one another how much they liked Will Granger.

"There's no devil in the Craft, Mr. Granger, and I assure you, neither we nor the Keystone Coven conduct sacrifices," Maggie asserted in her soft-spoken manner.

"Nor do we eat babies or drink blood," Raine added, rolling her green eyes skyward. "Great Goddess!"

Having arrived at the tree, they stood, staring up, through its lofty red blaze of leaves and grey network of branches, to cerulean blue patches of clear October sky.

Raine breathed out slowly. "You've known Robin O'Malley for many years, I take it; and you've heard and read about us and the things we do, so–"

"No need to go on. I'm an old man," Will cut in, "and I've lived long enough to learn a thing or two. Doesn't matter what color someone is, how they worship, or who their ancestors were. Naw, the only thing that matters is what's in here," he patted his chest, "in a person's heart."

Maggie, who had been rather quiet since they started for the tree, commented, "Witches have always gotten bad press; but what a lot of people don't realize is that a witch is a healer, a teacher, and a protector of all things. Not to mention a seeker of knowledge, wisdom– and Truth. That definition honestly describes High Priestess Robin and the Keystone Coven, and I have a witchy feeling it would accurately describe Hester Duff as well."

"Whatever the case may be, when ya got more yesterd'ys than tomorras, you don't like t' label anyone, dead or alive, as black or white," Granger chortled, "since most of us are what I'd call 'grey.'"

Raine grinned. "Varying shades of grey. Like the Hester Tree."

"Have you any Hester stories you could share with us, Mr. Granger?" Maggie asked.

Granger pointed to the green, lacy wrought-iron bench beneath the tree. "Let's take a load off, and I'll do that."

Once they seated themselves on the bench, with a calm, settled Jasper stretched out on the ground at their feet, the farmer began. "According to a story passed down in my family, Hester, as you brung to mind a moment ago, was a healer, what they called in olden times a 'midwife.' She delivered babies, brewed up herb remedies and poultices for the sick and infirm, human and animal alike; and legend tells us she cooked up potions too. Unfortunately, when someone like Hester lost a patient, gossip took root and ran rampant. People die, it's part of livin', and when it's your time, there ain't no arguin' about it– *you go home!* But human bein's like to point fingers, and that's one thing that's never changed in hundreds of years.

"Someone died," Granger picked up where he left off. "Storms destroyed crops. No matter what sad or bad things occurred, natural or otherwise, more and more the settlers here in our neck of Penn's Woods blamed Hester. What eventually happened, I've always believed, is that those folks plumb forgot the *good* Hester done. How she brought their babies into this world, cured them of their ailments, patched them up when they was hurt, and fixed up their livestock t' boot. I tend t' think Hester made just as many friends as she had enemies, and by 'enemies' I mean those who were either jealous of her or scared of 'er. I always thought, when she disappeared, that she run off with a friend or friends, perhaps with someone she'd healed or helped in some way, to escape those pointin' fingers I mentioned."

Maggie bobbed her head, "That could well be, Mr. Granger. Raine and I have said the same thing."

"Just a damn shame not much is known about poor Hester," the farmer sighed. He thought for a moment, seemingly remembering something. "I got this bench for my wife. Bonnie used to love to sit out here and say her prayers, think problems through, or read in the summers, after she finished her chores. It was always cool here under the Hester Tree and, as Bonnie used to say, '*comfortin'*.'"

"Nature's hush can be quite healing. I *feel* the magick here," Raine said, tilting her head back to gaze up, into the tree's cathedral canopy of bright autumn. "It's *strong*."

Maggie closed her eyes. Powerful energies were at work there, and she felt a tad dizzy. "Magick is all around us. You just have to believe."

Granger lapsed into silence, while the Sisters picked up his thoughts about his beloved wife. He was imaging the day, on their thirtieth wedding anniversary, when he'd walked her out to the Witch Tree, a red bandana over her eyes, to surprise her with the bench.

Will gave the redheaded Sister a sudden smile and, slapping his hands down on his thighs, rose. "Well, Miss Maggie, how's about we leave Miss Raine to do her listenin', and you and me go back to the house for some coffee and pie." He looked to Raine. "I hope you can decipher what Hester is strivin' to tell me. She's even been whisperin' at night when I'm tryin' t' sleep; but for the life of me, I can never make out what she's sayin'. It's all gibberish to me!"

As soon as Raine was alone, she drew a circle of protection around herself and the tree with her finger, making a wide, sweeping gesture. She chanted a protective mantra, then lowered herself to the ground and stretched out on the opposite side of the tree from the bench. Breathing in deeply, she let her breath out slowly several times before she felt completely centered. Closing her eyes, she petitioned Hester Duff to speak to her via the wind. Then she lay quite still, listening to the tree, as its branches swayed, and its leaves began revealing secrets.

It wasn't long before the voice for which she was waiting whispered to her.

When the raven-haired Sister reentered the farmhouse, she discovered that Maggie and Will were joined at the kitchen table by a comely young woman and a clean-cut, attractive man. They were all drinking coffee from Granger's thick, white mugs.

"Raine," Granger stood to pour that Sister a mug of coffee, "this is my niece, Amanda, and her husband, Sam Woods. Sam's the manager of the Washingtonville Lumber Company. Amanda's my deceased brother's girl. She's a school teacher," he stated with unabashed pride. "Amanda and Sam, this is Raine McDonough, one of the famous Sleuth Sisters from Haleigh's Hamlet."

Amanda was a fay of a girl, petite and wistful with big brown eyes and long, straight, honey-blonde hair. Sam was medium height with the muscular physique of a man who worked out and was conscious of his looks. His styled blond hair was lighter than his wife's, his thick, neatly trimmed mustache several shades darker than the hair on his head. The Woods made a beautiful couple.

For a few moments, small talk circled the table, with Will concluding, "Amanda and Sam have been such a comfort to me since my wife passed. Amanda makes sure I'm fed, and Sam cuts my grass and helps me with one thing 'r other around the place. They're the daughter and son Bonnie and I never had."

"Thank you, Will," Sam replied, standing and rubbing the back of his hand along his square jaw. "I think the weather report said we might have showers later on today. I'd better start on that grass." He sent the Sisters a smile. "It was nice meeting you."

"Uncle Will told you I make sure he's fed, but lately, he hasn't had his usual appetite." Amanda's tone and the look she exhibited to Granger carried admonishment.

"I don't work like I used to, gal, so I no longer have a workaday appetite!" Will scoffed. Abruptly remembering why Raine had been out at the tree, he asked, "Any luck out there?"

"Hester's message was loud and clear," Raine replied, sinking down into one of the spindle-back chairs at the kitchen table. She told me she's protected the tree, this farm, and the people on it for many years. She said she's always protected the Grangers, and now it's time for the Grangers to protect her tree, *with*," she sent Maggie a pointed look, "*our* help and the help of fellow sisters of the moon, the Keystone Coven."

"H'ain't that exactly what we're doin'?!" Will exclaimed. He considered, tilting his head and narrowing his eyes. "What else did she say?"

Maggie sent Raine an anxious flash: *You're holding something back. Spill it. As you said yourself, Will Granger should know—* **whatever** *it is.*

Raine bit her lip, glancing over at Maggie before answering. "Hester said to beware and to be wary and watchful."

"Beware?!" Will blurted, "of who, of what?"

Raine's usual Aries-ram air turned sheepish. "That was the one thing I could not decipher— what to beware of. Truthfully, I don't think she even said of what or of whom to beware. She just said, "Beware. Be wary and watchful.""

\*\*\*

"OK, darlin', what did Hester *really* say?" Maggie asked, as soon as they were alone in the MG.

Behind the wheel, Raine looked a bit disgruntled. "Just what I told Will. I didn't keep anything from him. That's what Hester said, 'Beware; be wary and watchful.'"

Maggie digested this for a moment, commenting, "Well, it's pretty much what Granny said too."

As Witch-Tree Farm receded in the MG's rearview mirror, Raine glanced over at Maggie and remarked, "You look worried, why? We'll keep on top of the situation. And we'll keep a weathered eye on those land developers, though I don't think we have to worry about who will get that property now. Mr. Granger's will is a private matter, which we'll keep to ourselves; but I do think we should let Robin know that he made a will, leaving the farm to his like-minded niece and her husband. She'll respect Will's privacy. After meeting the niece and her husband, I don't think we need to wor–"

Maggie broke in on her hasty sister of the moon. "It's not *the* will I'm worried about; it's *Will*," she stated.

"A spell in rhyme works every time."
~ Witches throughout the ages

# Chapter Three

With Aisling behind the wheel of her black SUV, the trio of Sleuth Sisters were on the road, headed for the *Samhain* fest at High Priestess Robin O'Malley's home in Washingtonville.

The senior Sleuth Sister, Aisling McDonough-Gwynn was, succinctly put, the archetypical tall, cool blonde. Aisling was cool in the sense that she kept her head in even the most dangerous situations; however, she had a warm heart. A spot-on Leo, the blonde with the wand was a versatile woman, skilled in many aspects of the Craft. This was the Sister most likely to take control of a situation, and she was usually the first to take the initiative to help those in need.

Now, as she drove down the scenic highway from Haleigh's Hamlet to the *Samhain* meet, she listened intently to what Raine and Maggie had, thus far, garnered about their current challenge. Like her cousins, she had dressed for the occasion, sporting a black witchy gown under a long, black, hooded cape. A trinity of enchanting, black witch hats, each decorated in a different manner, rested on the backseat. Raine's was bedecked with a funky swirl of forest-green netting that sparkled with silver and gold glitter and was pinned at the crown with a huge shooting-star brooch cast with a spell for enticing laughter and fun. Maggie's bore a glittering, wide purple ribbon, and Aisling's a glitzy silver and gold band, each pinned with a bewitched moon-and-stars brooch that was sure to draw only good and an abundance of good from the Universe.

"Be careful not to tilt that colcannon, Raine," Aisling chided, glancing quickly over at the raven-haired Sister, whose attention was focused on the passing autumn-dressed scenery. "I'm sorry you have to hold that plate on your lap, but I don't want it to spill. Ian and I followed Granny's authentic Irish recipe, using thick, lean bacon rather than ham. Nothing better than rashers, cabbage and leeks over buttery mashed potatoes. My favorite *Samhain* dish!"

"The ultimate comfort food. What all are *we* bringing to the food table?" Maggie asked.

"In addition to the Irish colcannon," Aisling began, "Ian whipped up Granny's cheesy potatoes. So with your spice faerie cakes, pumpk—"

"I much prefer the term 'faerie cakes' to 'cup cakes,' don't you?!" Raine cut in.

"Hecate yes!" came the Sisters' joint reply.

"To continue," Aisling went on, "with your pumpkin bread, Granny's autumn butter, and her chocolate apples– that's our combined offering. By the bye, what did you two put into Granny's autumn butter recipe? I've forgotten what goes in it."

Maggie smiled in her mysterious way. "Mmmm, we mixed brown sugar, pumpkin pie spice, whipping cream and softened Irish butter together, blending it well. That was the *trick* Granny always said, the *blending*; and her autumn butter is sure to *treat!*"

"With just a smidgen of extra cinnamon," Raine reminded. "That's another word I like to say– *smidgen*. Anyway, on both the pumpkin bread and the spice faerie cakes, Granny's autumn butter is delectable," she raved. "Ooooooh, I love *everything* about autumn, including its harvest foods!"

"You love food, period," Maggie taunted, her eyes twinkling at Raine's enthusiasm. "I wish I could eat as much as you do. If I did, I'd be as big as Sister Luna. Honestly, I don't know how you do it!"

Raine deepened the dimple in her left cheek, whilst she whispered the word *"magick!"* Their talk was making her hungry, and she breathed in the savory smells escaping the colcannon. "I can't wait to see what the other sisters made. It's such fun sampling everything!"

"I know that Robin made *Samhain* soul cakes with black currants," Maggie replied, gazing out the side window at the rustic farmland. "Ah, and I remember her mentioning she made oven hash, the old-fashioned way her gr-auntie Allesandra made it, as well as harvest scalloped corn and her acclaimed almond-and-dark-chocolate-harvest-moon cookies. And there's yet another utterance for your treasure chest of words, darlin'," she directed at Raine, "the *gr-auntie* moniker for great-aunt."

"Hmmmm," Raine murmured in reverie, picturing the food table as she remembered it from past festivals in Robin's yard. "What did you say? Yes, *gr-auntie* … we should call Auntie Merry that from now on; I love it! Suits her too!"

"Wouldn't it be nice if, one day, the Wizard would make a surprise appearance, at one of the Coven's meets, to reveal his, or *her* identity?" Maggie commented. She was enjoying the ride, as she always did, through the vivid autumn Pennsylvania countryside.

"I doubt that will ever happen," the pragmatic Aisling countered.

"Hmmm," Raine repeated, "I wonder ..."

"Oh, look at that scarecrow!" Aisling pointed, keeping her eyes on the road. "It's the best I've seen thus far!"

The straw man's jack-o'-lantern head was carved so that the nefarious-looking eyes slanted upward at the outer corners, and the jagged mouth grinned a scary snarl. Its long coat, billowing out in the late-October wind, had long, voluminous sleeves, from which poked gnarled branches that looked as if the effigy might lunge forward to grab hold of anyone who came within its wicked reach.

All along their route, the Sisters enjoyed the rolling landscape, with its patchwork of farms and woods, the houses decorated for Hallowe'en, the windows glowing golden in the October twilight. There was no question that, the turning wheel of the seasons, this was their favorite time o' year.

"Listen, the wind is rising, and the air is wild with leaves!" Raine sang gaily. "We love our autumn evenings, especially October's evenings– and now for *Samhain's* eve!"

When they came to the turn-off, Aisling drove slowly up the lane that led to Robin's unique house the latter had christened "Moonstone Manor." Aisling loved the faerie-tale home of the Keystone Coven's High Priestess, and she wanted to savor its charming image.

Though the Gothic grey-stone residence looked small from the front, it was actually much larger than it first appeared. Topped by a peaked roof, the scarlet-red, hobbit-style front door bore antique, black hardware, and the entrance's round, leaded-glass window was crafted as a spider web. To the right of the door was a round turret capped with a roof that looked very much like a black witch's hat. A trilogy of tall stone chimneys soared gracefully above the main roof. All in all, it was a house straight from the pages of a Grimm storybook.

"Robin did a fantastic job with the decorations!" Raine exclaimed. "The house looks *magickal!*"

Lighted jack-o'-lanterns lined the cobblestone walk leading to the house, whilst several graced the stoop on either side of the front door.

Inside, all the window sills bore electric jack-o'-lanterns, and the trees scattered about the neat, pastoral setting were aglow with tiny orange lights. There were several cars in the circular drive at the rear of the house, and that is where Aisling parked the SUV.

When the Sisters exited the vehicle to walk round to the front door, they could hear music playing. They instantly recognized Rowena of the Glen's album *Book of Shadows.* Rowena Whaling was a favorite artist of not only the Sleuth Sisters but the Keystone Coven as well. There was a reason for that– Rowena's music was *transporting.*

High Priestess Robin stepped through the opened door dressed in flowing robes of black and orange, the colors of *Samhain.* A wreath of bright fall leaves topped her fiery red hair, long and curled, that cascaded prettily over her shoulders. A braided section at each temple fastened at the back of the head with a large, gold barrette in the shape of a leaf.

"Merry Meet, dear Sisters! Welcome!" She gestured with a gracious wave of her arm, "Come in! Everyone's here, and we're all … *over the moon* to share this night with you!"

The Sisters returned the salutation, as they filed into the kitchen to lend a hand, carrying their food contributions, each Sister holding an open box out in front of her like a ritual offering. For the next several minutes, the sisters of the Coven welcomed the Sleuth Sisters, with everyone embracing and exchanging warm greetings.

"Let's leave the food here in the kitchen till we're ready for it," Robin said. "I've crammed what needs to be kept cool in the fridge, and Moonglow and Starlight have volunteered to come in, after our prayers, and warm anything that needs to be heated. The chafing dishes, with lighted candles beneath, will keep the hot foods warm, then, afterward.

"My hubby was going to help out," Robin went on, as she checked a few last-minute things in the kitchen, "but I gave him the night off, so he's playing poker with some of his buddies. We can all pitch in later to carry the food outside to the two picnic tables." She smiled. "Everything's in readiness out there, so shall we adjourn to the side yard? *Samhain* should be enjoyed outside, under the beautiful, golden Hunter's Moon with which we've been so wondrously blessed this hallowed night! Come, dear sisters, let us go and cast our sacred circle!"

The mesmerizing magick of Rowena of the Glen drifted over the clear, cool October night, as her *Book of Shadows* album played on.

When the gathering of sisters trooped outside, they were met with the twinkling orange lights that illuminated the trees sprinkled throughout Robin's charming property. In addition, pumpkin lights outlining the back door flashed off and on, whilst across the side of the house, under a motion light, a giant silhouette of a besom-riding witch took sudden form. In lieu of a bonfire, there was a central fire pit surrounded by carved, candle-lit jack-o'-lanterns, each different, all captivating.

"Oh, I love the witch stirring her cauldron in *that* pumpkin!" Raine indicated, as excited as a child at the prospect of a party.

"My husband and his cousin did all the pumpkin carving," Robin replied. "Didn't they do a fantastic job?"

Everyone wholeheartedly agreed.

"Wiz–zard!" Raine pronounced, resorting to her favorite expression. "Absolutely wizard!"

On one side of the centrally located fire pit, a safe distance from the flames, Robin's life-size straw man, an ancient symbol of *Samhain,* stood sentry over the scene; and the Sleuth Sisters could not help thinking that he was almost identical to the riveting jack-o'-lantern scarecrow they had seen en route to the High Priestess' house.

However, it was the life-size witch, on the opposite side of the fire pit, that captured the Sisters' full attention. This figure was nothing short of *chilling*. Like the straw man, its head, too, was a jack-o'-lantern, the sinister grin effecting a startling snarl, the slanted eyes glowing orange. A black witch's hat, banded with purple, topped the carved pumpkin head, whilst an old ritual robe covered the body, the black, tattered fabric dripping from the arms and over the unseen feet. Claw-like hands poked out of the wide sleeves, one holding an old-fashioned lantern that sent flickering light and shadow across the menacing visage, giving rise to the illusion the sinister figure was alive. Dangling chains lent the eerie impression that the creature had just broken free from centuries of restraint on the dark side of the veil, unleased and ready now to cause mayhem!

"*That*," Maggie pointed, whispering to Aisling, "just sent a chill down my spine."

"It's," the silvery-blonde Sister hesitated, groping for a word, and finding none, settled on, "*chilling*, all right."

"It's purrrr-fect." Raine leaned toward her cousins to rumble in her deep voice, **"Bwahahahahahahahahahahaaa!"**

The Goth gal stood staring at the straw-witch for a long moment, adding, "As the ancient druids intended those many centuries ago with their own scary effigies and costumes, *that* thing should frighten off any evil spirits who might attempt to come through the veil."

In the fire pit, the flames danced and crackled cheerily, and on a table topped with a bright orange cloth, an attractive altar had been readied.

"We invite you to place mementoes and photos of your ancestors on our *Samhain* altar, of loved ones, as well as beloved pets and familiars, who have crossed over to the Summerland. Come," Robin beckoned with outstretched hand, the sleeve of her witchy black dress flowing from her extended arm.

With that, the Sleuth Sisters drew, from the satchels they carried, sepia images, as well as black-and-white and color photographs, some framed, others not, placing them on the altar.

With the help of the Coven, Robin– all the while chanting a protection mantra– set about lighting all the candles in the dozens of jack-o'-lanterns surrounding their circle– the entire side yard, an extensive area for their sacred space.  Lastly, they touched fire to the candles on the outdoor altar.

*The result was literally dazzling!*

In a twinkling, Robin switched off the music, to be turned back on after the opening prayers.  Now, the *Samhain* ritual could officially begin.

The gathering of sisters formed a circle, from whence Aisling and High Priestess Robin moved to the center.  After surrounding their space with a ring of sea salt, they lit four special white candles on the altar, one at each compass point, then "drew" with their athames the circle of protection around the sacred space, beginning, as one, to chant: "By all the power in us and all the power of the Universe, we cast this circle.  May it protect us from unwanted energies and draw to us only energies that resonate with Love and Light.  All other energies– **begone!**  So mote it be!  Blessed be!"

"Blessed be!" echoed the assembly of sisters.

Then starting in the northeastern corner of the circle, Aisling and Robin, using blessed besoms, began sweeping widdershins (counterclockwise) to rid any nasty energy that might still be lurking about.  "With these brooms we sweep away all negativity that comes our way!

"Negative energy may not stay!  We release it and send it on its way!  Negative energy, we banish thee!  Our final words– *so mote it be!*"

"Let us clear our minds of all unwanted thoughts and worries," High Priestess Robin directed.

The vast Hunter Moon's powerful energies sparked a blaze of light from the High Priestess' rings on her raised hand.  With signaled sanction from both Aisling and Robin, several of the Keystone sisters spread out then, lighting bundles of white sage in glass dishes and fanning, with large feathers, the smoking essence to permeate throughout the circle as they chanted, "We smudge this area completely free of all evil and all negativity!  Fill this space with joy and love; send your blessings from above!  So mote it be! Blessed be!"

Now it was time, on this one night of the year when the physical and spirit worlds are separated by the most delicate of curtains, to call forth the ancestors and those loved ones, human and animal, who have crossed to the Summerland.

"This is the night when the veil between our world and the spirit world is the thinnest," Robin began. "Tonight is the night to call on those who came before. Tonight we honor our ancestors." The High Priestess raised her arms skyward. "Spirits of our fathers and mothers, we call to you and welcome you to join us on this sacred night! You watch over us always, guarding and guiding, and tonight we thank you! Your blood runs in our veins. Your spirits are in our hearts. Your memories are in our souls." Robin tilted her head back and closed her eyes for a long, silent moment.

"With the gift of remembrance," she continued, "we lovingly remember all of you. Though you are in the Summerland, you will never be forgotten. You live on within us and within those who will come after us." The High Priestess opened her eyes to send Aisling a nod.

Raising their arms in invocation, Robin and Aisling chanted loudly, "Forest misty dark and deep, the door between the worlds release! Loved ones, family, favored pets, join us in this evening's fête! Darksome night and Hunter's Moon, harken to the witches' rune! Those of you who've gone before, speak to us from Crossroads' Door! Whisper words of love and care. Let us know that you are here!"

When Aisling and Robin repeated the chant, the assembly of sisters all joined in, reciting it thrice. All the sisters present could feel, through the tall peaks of their black witch hats, the conjured energies rising to form the familiar cone of brightness– *and power.*

Joining hands, the witches' circle waited. With bated breaths, they waited in hopeful silence.

Of a sudden, the wind kicked up, and colorful autumn leaves whirled and swirled all about them. The evening's gentle breath increased with a swift cold intensity, whilst the whispered voices in the *Samhain* wind, beset with ancient secrets, reached the ears of the entire gathering. Candles flickered energetically on the altar; and in the multitude of glaring jack-o'-lanterns, the trembling candles wakened the carved faces.

In the surrounding trees, the lighted branches swayed and stirred; and the straw man and witch, their black, tattered arms flailing frightfully, their glowing jack-o'-lantern faces grimacing forcefully in the darkness of that magick-filled night, seemed to come ever more alive.

"The magick is working," Raine whispered, more to herself than anyone. "I *feel* it."

"It is *powerful*," Maggie breathed, "more so than I ever recall from past *Samhains*."

Subsequent to those chilling moments, the night was again calm as dozens of shimmering white orbs appeared, singularly and in groups, within and throughout the sacred circle, bringing forth from the gathered witches varied expressions of gratitude.

*The dead of night*, Raine quipped, zipping the thought to Maggie. "I sense the wisdom of the ancestors– and Granny's smile."

"Praise the God-Goddess!  Blessed be!" Aisling and Robin cried out.

"We thank you for this wondrous reunion with those with whom we have the unbroken bond of love, for *love*, like spirit, like the soul itself, is indestructible– *eternal!*" the High Priestess proclaimed.

"As Granny reminded us, love is the *only* thing we take with us when we pass over," Maggie whispered in an aside to Raine.

"We entreat you," Robin chanted, "revered ancestors and loved ones, stay with us this sacred night.  Join us in our *Samhain* delight! Tonight we invite you into our dreams.  Resume your visit on silver moonbeams!  So mote it be.  Blessed be!"

Amidst a blend of happy sounds, the night– the sisters' sacred space– was now replete with orbs, some brighter than others, but all clearly visible.  They danced and bounced and floated to their living relatives and descendants among the merry meet of sisters.

As on past *Samhains*, one large– especially bright– orb hovered directly above Aisling.  It gradually lowered itself to rest on her shoulder, bringing a whispered reply from the blonde Sister's parted, upturned lips, "Granny, we love and miss you!"

The orb seemed to shimmer, as it traveled to Raine and Maggie, bobbing from one blissful Sister to the other, then back again to Aisling.

After several minutes of joyful reunions, everyone took out the printed sheet given to each sister upon arrival at Robin's home. In unison, the circle of witches chanted: "All hail! *Samhain* is here, our favorite sabbat, the witches' New Year! How crisp the air! What drama is here! The autumn leaves, the pumpkins, the great Hunter's Moon! We know the long, frosty nights will be here soon! Beloved spirits, we honor your presence at our special fest– and this makes *Samhain* the year's very best! We celebrate reunion of living and dead, for as witches we know there is nothing to dread! Dance the dance of ancestors in our blessed circle of love. The great Goddess smiles on us from moon 'n stars above."

The gathering of sisters raised their arms skyward, calling out, "Ancestors and spirits join us in our dance around the fire! Join us please, for 'tis our true hearts' desire! Beget the *Samhain* magick with all of its lore! Bring us love, health, and prosperity– now and forevermore!"

With the conclusion of the initial prayers, Robin switched the selected *Samhain* music back on, and the witches began to dance to Rowena of the Glen's "Trance Dance Part 1" from her powerful album, *Book of Shadows.* In a great animated circle, they danced, frolicking round and round the large fire pit's blaze of flames. Amid the watching, glowing jack-o-lanterns and straw figures, each sister expressed appreciation and remembrance for her ancestors and spirit loved ones in her own way, the opening chant of Rowena's song enhancing the sacred space:

"Air, Fire, Water, and Earth … you're what we're made of … you're what gives us worth!" Rowena's distinctive voice rang out, infusing the sisters with intense emotion.

"Calling all of spirit to the fire … to the trance … let your soul fly– ***and Dance!!***"

Dance they did, the evocative music utterly enrapturing, as the witches rose higher and higher on wings of devotion and appreciation! Dancing to the beat of the music! Dancing to the beat of their hearts!

"Whoa, whoa, Trance Dance … Whoa, whoa, Trance Dance … Whoa, whoa, Trance Dance.

"Cerridwen's cauldron, Hecate's keys, Ishtar's dragons, Inanna's bees … What will be, will be, will be … What will be, will be, will be … What will be, will be, will be …"

The sisters continued to dance under the Hunter Moon's energizing brilliance, basking in the rhythm of Rowena's *Book of Shadows*, its magick sending them into a pleasant haze. Her earthy voice and soul-stirring music evoked memories and deep-seated feelings, sending forth a bubbling cauldron of magick that wove a strong, pulsating spell round and round the cavorting witches– a spell that was poignant, empowering and– *hauntingly beautiful.*

Beneath the great golden moon and within the fire-lit circle, the gathering of sisters sat enjoying the hot mulled wine and cider, as well as the bounty of harvest foods at the tables in Robin's yard. Laughter and happy conversation floated on the brisk air.

There were so many goodies to choose from, in addition to the dishes contributed by the Sleuth Sisters– hot, creamy Indian corn chowder; rich, thick butternut-squash soup; savory shepherd's pie; hearty vegetable stew; spicy Scottish meat pies; apple, pumpkin, and fruit-of-the-forest pies; apple cake rich with nuts and raisins; and the special *Samhain* fortune-telling bread the Irish call *barmbrack* chockfull of dried fruits, nuts, spices, and the charms that bespoke the fortunes.

"Careful of the charms in the *barmbrack*, sisters!" Robin cautioned, setting the special treat– warm and fragrant from the oven– on one of the long tables in the moonlit yard. "I don't want anyone to break a tooth! But inside each slice of my fortune-telling bread is a charm. Everyone choose your own slice, and the charm inside will be meant for you. What each of your charms will indicate will be *true* magick– I promise you!" she announced in a clear voice.

"Our granny's autumn butter will be delicious on the *barmbrack*," Maggie suggested.

The sisters all hastened to the table where Robin had set the Irish fortune bread that, in reality, was much like a tasty teacake.

Two of the Coven sisters, Autumn and Raven, found heart charms in their slices of *barmbrack*, indicating that they would draw more love in the coming year. A welcome blessing to both, for each had suffered lost love in the preceding months. Silver and Undine got four-leaf clovers, indicating good luck, a boon, for both those sisters had faced difficult challenges in the past year. Morgana's slice held a purse charm, so she knew she could expect more money this New Year, which thrilled her, for she had programmed a better-paying job. Glinda was even more thrilled to find a baby charm, for she so wanted to become pregnant. High Priestess Robin told her to be careful, because her slice held *two* charms. The second amulet the good witch Glinda was to give to her husband.

Hecate's charm was a wee suitcase, hence she knew she'd be taking that trip to Europe she was planning in the coming months, Karma she richly deserved. Sister Marie's find was a horseshoe, rendering her immediately grateful for the forthcoming good luck. Sea Witch's charm was a book, and that told her she was on the right path, for she had been planning to go back to school to get a higher degree. When Old Soul Witch discovered a drama mask, she knew she would win the dramatic role she coveted in the community theatre's spring production of *Camelot*.

Moonglow and Starlight discovered, in their *barmbrack* slices, identical stop-sign charms that they correctly translated to mean they should stop being so overzealous.

Each sister's charm so befitted her needs and desires; but when Verity got a songbird charm, she cried out with the thrill, for she knew she would land the lead role in the musical for which she'd auditioned at the Pittsburgh Playhouse. The charm that brought the most joy, however, was the one discovered by Minerva. It was a cat charm, and that sister knew her lost kitten would be found. Robin whispered that Cupid would be on the back porch waiting for her upon her return home that evening.

The only sister who got a charm that gave her pause was Astra, who received a caduceus, the medical symbol with snake and staff. Robin came round behind her and whispered into her ear.

"Go to the doctor's and have that test, dear sister. You will see that the results will be negative, and it will give you peace. Your usual psychic gifts are not working due to your anxiety, your fears. But you will see; it will be all right," the High Priestess reassured with a warm hug.

The flames were yet crackling and leaping in the fire pit; and the candles, lanterns, and orange Hallowe'en lights, as well as the vast scattering of jack-o'-lanterns still glowed brightly.

Everyone seemed to be thoroughly enjoying themselves, as laughter and merriment rang out in the crisp night air, harmonizing pleasantly with Rowena of the Glen's music issuing from the CD player on the side steps.

While the sisters chatted, ate, and drank of the hot mulled wine and spiced cider, many of them took advantage of the gathering to trade rune or tarot readings, as well as enchanted items.

"Come, sisters, let us toss our stones into the fire pit!" Robin suggested, since it was by now approaching midnight. "I've marked the stones with our names; there's one for each of us. The pebbles are over there, in a basket, by the fire pit. This, as you know, is an ancient *Samhain* tradition, so before you cast your stone into the fire, hold it in your hands, close your eyes, and make a heartfelt wish. Visualize your wish coming true. *Believe* with all your essence, and *thank* as if you already have whatever it is you want."

The High Priestess brought her hands together. "Now, everyone find your proper stone. I printed the names *clearly* on each."

"What will you wish for?" Maggie asked Raine, as they cued up to ferret out their stones from the basket.

"Same thing you're about to wish for, Mags– that we'll be successful in saving the Witch Tree." Raine bent to find her stone in the pretty, leaf-decorated basket. "Found mine!" she said, moving to the side and rubbing it between her hands. As Robin had suggested, she closed her eyes and ardently made her wish. Then she tossed the pebble into the fire. "I've let the Universe hear my wish," she concluded. "And now, I'm keyed-up and eager to see what magick is about to unfold! So mote it be," she resolved. "Blessed be!"

Maggie and Aisling followed suit, with Aisling whispering to her cousins, "I'd lay a wager everyone of us made the same wish this *Samhain*." After a beat, she added, "Actually, if we have all made the *same* wish, *that* would be a blessing in itself."

As Raine swayed to the music of Rowena of the Glen's "The Creature," the excitement of the sabbat throbbing passionately in her magickal Celtic blood, she happened to glance toward the life-size witch. Without warning, its sinister jack-o'-lantern face, illuminated by the flames from the fire pit, sprang unexpectedly to life. Instantly, Raine drew in her breath, at the same time grasping Maggie and Aisling each by an arm. "Sisters, **look!**" she gasped.

In a sudden gust of icy wind, the effigy's purple-banded witch hat blew off, whilst its tattered black robes billowed wildly, rattling the dangling chains. Chillingly, the jack-o'-lantern face grimaced, the eyes narrowing, as the thing began to speak in a voice that was deep and booming, though hollow-sounding, as if it were coming from afar.

To the gathered sisters, it was nothing short of jarring, as all eyes stayed riveted to the straw-witch figure: "Through this jack-o'-lantern I speak. Heed my words; they be not f'r the weak! Beware of one who pretends and lies. Be wary of those who seek the prize. Be ever vigilant of my tree! **YOU**," the specter pointed a claw-like finger at the Sleuth Sisters, "must clear my name to lift my blame, for only *that* will efface my shame! In fine, I swear on my sacred tree that ***death doth come– the death of three!***"

This last was louder than the preceding words, and their effect was evident on each and every one of the stunned sisters that unforgettable *Samhain* at High Priestess Robin's fest.

For several moments, the gathering of witches was hushed– at some point, the music had stopped– as each sister tried to grasp the meaning of the words that had been hurled at them.

The Sleuth Sisters rushed forth, calling, "Hester!"

"She tried to talk to me when I wind-listened at her tree; but now, on *Samhain*, when the veil between the worlds has been lifted, and we've invited the dead to speak, her voice is clear– loud and clear!"

Breaking off, Raine ran forth, to stand before the spellbinding form. "Hester, fellow sister of the moon, tell us more! Who is the liar we must be wary of?!" And hers was a wide, green-eyed gaze.

The tattered black robes continued to blow in the chill wind, that was calmer now– but no longer did the witch image speak.

Standing about, the Coven sisters were astounded, a few gripping one another in shock. Sister Undine withdrew even further into the hood of her long black robe, like a turtle in its shell, unable to prevent an apprehensive shiver.

"Be not afraid!" Robin called out, walking with purpose among her flock. "*Samhain* is the most auspicious time to make contact with the dead. It is a double magickal portal, a betwixt and between time– the point between *both* the new season *and* the witches' New Year. Plus, sisters, we are at midnight, the point betwixt and between day and night. 'Tis no wonder, powerful magick is afoot! The message was given us as a heads-up, and we must be grateful and acknowledge the messenger."

The High Priestess raised her arms skyward, throwing her head back. "We are grateful, dear Sister Hester, for your wise counsel." Robin smiled. "You certainly captured our attention! Rest assured we will take what you've told us to heart, and we will be vigilant."

The assembly of witches cried out in unison, "So mote it be!"

Recovering her balance, Maggie whispered to Raine and Aisling, "Takes me back to what Granny used to say about Wild Woman Magick. 'The Wild Woman's magick is old. The Wild Woman's magick is strong. Together with Mother Nature, she sings of the ancestors in song!'"

"Fear not, Sister Hester!" shouted the buxom, Coven sister Moonglow, her long, curly, red-gold hair blowing about her face in a sudden gust of wind.

"Fear not!" echoed her partner, the petite, dark and lithe Starlight.

"We will protect your tree **at all cost! At all cost!! So mote it be!**" the pair finished together.

**"So mote it be!"** the remaining sisters shouted–

While, at the same time, Aisling whispered to Maggie and Raine, "Speaking of Wild Woman Magick!"

After a moment, Maggie repeated Hester's dire words; but when she spoke, the voice that flowed from her was not her own. 'Twas the passionate Irish expression of Granny McDonough: "In fine, in summary, I caution thee– ***Death doth come, the death of three!***"

**"Granny!"** the trio of Sleuth Sisters exclaimed, trading wide-eyed looks with one another.

"'Tis the night for ancestors," Maggie whispered, her personal voice restored.

"I wish Sister Hester had told us more," Aisling rejoined, shaking her head.

"We will clear Hester's name," Raine stated firmly. "Both she and our granny have summoned us to do so, and we can hardly ignore those summons, especially not on *Samhain*. Besides, my witch's intuition is that clearing Hester's name will unveil whatever else we'll need to clean up what will soon be a messy mystery."

"I have the same feeling," Maggie and Aisling voiced in near unison.

"Have you, indeed?" said Robin. "*So do I.*"

The High Priestess eased the McDonoughs to a benched picnic table in a far corner of the yard where they could talk privately. She seized a large, wooden bowl of apples, to relocate it further down the tabletop. Two of the red orbs rolled off and stopped, as though obeying the command of a witch's wand, on the lawn at Aisling's feet.

Picking up the apples, the blonde Sister replaced one to the bowl and, swiping the other over her sleeve, bit heartily into it. "Crisp and tart. Perfect for Snap-Apple Night."

Once they were seated, Robin said, "We're all going to have to be especially vigilant, as Hester advised."

"Our Granny told us that, in advance of tonight's event," Raine replied.

"I wonder why Hester waited till the end of the night to make an appearance?" Maggie mused aloud.

"I don't think she wanted to throw a damper on our fest," Aisling answered, munching away at her apple. "As a sister of the Craft, she would have the highest regard for *Samhain*."

"*Death doth come, the death of three?*" Robin whispered, leaning closer to the Sleuth Sisters. "I sure didn't like the sound of that!"

Ever-the-detective, Aisling uttered quietly, "This really doesn't surprise us. Where there's that much money involved, there's bound to be greed, and greed often breeds violence. Hester has given us a heads-up, as you said, and now it will be up to us to do whatever we can to protect the innocents in what will unfold."

"In addition to protecting the Witch Tree," Moonglow and Starlight reiterated, as they traipsed past the table. Slowing to turn around, they stated with a passion that was readable on their faces. **"At all costs, we must protect that tree!"**

There was something furtive and ethereal about the pair in the moonlight– like two ghosts. Restless ghosts, at that.

When they were again alone at their table, Robin said in low tones, "Great Goddess protect us! I worry about those two. They are extraordinary women with exceptional powers, but they can get carried away sometimes. 'Course their zealous behavior has facilitated their business ventures. They've become successful computer tutors and web designers." The High Priestess watched the couple for a moment, seeming to *drag* her thoughts back to the situation at hand. "I ran into old Mr. Granger this morning in town, when I went to pick up a few last-minute food items for our fest. He told me he's still being pestered about selling his land."

The Sleuth Sisters exchanged looks, and Maggie's lips parted to speak, when–

Robin interjected, "I know you witnessed the will. He told me. That gives me some relief, to know that Mr. Granger's wishes are now legally set in stone, but I have a feeling that the tree is still not safe, that this whole mess is just beginning."

Again the Sisters swapped looks, with Maggie and Raine trading the thought that they were relieved Farmer Granger had told Robin himself about the will.

"I can tell you share that sentiment with me," Robin determined correctly, in regard to the whole mess just beginning. "I just hate seeing Will Granger tormented like this. He said reps from the two construction companies were still after him to sell, as well as the pushy president of the town council." The High Priestess shook her head sadly. "Those types are what Sister Marie calls 'Energy Vampires.' The poor man looked sapped, almost sickly."

Robin tipped even closer toward the Sleuth Sisters to whisper more of what Will had communicated to her. "Even the president of the historical society is still goading him to *donate* the land to them, promising they will oversee it better than anyone, and that both the farmhouse and the tree will be ever protected and looked-after." Ducking her head, Robin disclosed, "I like Etta Story, but she can be too persistent at times. I mean, she's like a hungry dog with a piece of red meat when she sets her mind on something. Mr. Granger said *she's* worse than the land developers! I tell you enough is enough!"

It was quiet for a moment, as the four sisters sipped their hot drinks and listened to the wind, the nocturnal birds, a distant neighbor's barking dog, as well as the crackling flames in the fire pit, those night sounds punctuated with snips of sisterly conversation and laughter.

Finally, Aisling asked, "Did Will Granger tell you anything else this morning?"

Robin nodded emphatically. "Actually, he did. He said he told every single one of the 'confounded pests'– as he called them– that he had just completed his will, that it was all done and legal, and it wouldn't do anyone of them any good to keep on pressuring him. He told them the land, as he had vowed, would go to his niece and her husband; and if for whatever reason, they did not take possession of Witch-Tree Farm within a year's time, it would pass to the Washingtonville Historical Society. It would also pass to the society in the event something happened to both Amanda and Sam Woods, if at that point in time, the Woods had no children to inherit."

Yet again, the Sleuth Sisters looked to one another to exchange thoughts.

"What's wrong?" Robin probed. "You seem troubled by something I said."

"Not by something *you* said." Aisling's face clouded. "But by something Will Granger said." She wrapped her apple core in a napkin to discard in one of the scattered dustbins.

The foursome continued to talk for the next several minutes, at which time, the High Priestess bade the McDonoughs, "I've tried reasoning with the people who are bent on dogging poor old Mr. Granger, but to no avail. You three would have more clout. Would you mind speaking with those people to see if you can get them to lay off?"

"We'll do it," the McDonoughs answered. "You can count on that."

"And you can count on our clearing Hester's name too," Raine affirmed.

Once more, the High Priestess leaned toward the Sleuth Sisters with ardent expression, fixing them with her witchy stare. "Watch your backs, Sisters, and let me repeat that as fervently as I can. *Watch your backs*, for– 'By the pricking of my thumbs, something *wicked* this way comes.'"

Sometime later, the haunting words of the High Priestess resounded in their essences as Rowena of the Glen's "Trance Dance Part 2" assisted them in closing the circle to end their *Samhain* fest–

"Air, Earth, Water, and Fire, you've satisfied our hungers, rekindled our desires … And to you of Spirit, who hold us in your hands, thank you one and all … for the dance!

"Whoa, whoa, Trance Dance … Whoa, whoa, Trance Dance … Whoa, whoa, Trance Dance.

"Cerridwen's cauldron, Hecate's keys, Ishtar's dragons, Inanna's bees … What will be, will be, will be … What will be, will be, will be …

*"What will be, will be, will be …"*

*"Lord, what fools these mortals be!"*
~ William Shakespeare, *A Midsummer Night's Dream*,
Act I, Scene I

# Chapter Four

About the time when the *Samhain* fest at Moonstone Manor would have just been getting under way, Sam Woods dropped in at Witch-Tree Farm.

Shadowed by Jasper, who had been asleep on the back porch, he sauntered through the kitchen door, calling out, "Will, it's me! I got your mail and the paper. You upstairs?!"

At the old, roll-top, pigeon-hole desk in the corner, where he was about to leave the mail, Sam noticed some papers that captured his attention. The small, green-shade lamp that Will burned dusk to dawn in the kitchen spilled light on the scatter of bills, mail, and the like spread out on the desk's open writing table.

Picking up what had caught his eye, Sam began scanning the first sheet, acquainting himself with its contents, when a loud creak on the stairs in the adjacent room told him Will was coming down from the top floor. Sam had been so engrossed in what he was reading that he almost didn't hear the creaking steps.

Quickly, he set the papers back down on the desk where he'd found them and moved lightly across the room to the kitchen table, where he placed Will's mail and newspaper. Then he shifted to the old-fashioned range, grabbing the coffeepot to fill the mug he'd lifted from the sink. Will was just entering the room.

"Thanks for bringing up my mail and paper, Sam. You're a good man. Where's my beautiful niece this evening? Didn't she come with you?" Will took the proffered mug from his nephew-in-law's hands, dropping down into one of the chairs at table.

"Amanda's at the library, gathering information for where to send her résumé for a teaching position." He drained the pot into a mug for himself. "She misses teaching, but she doesn't want to drive too far. You know Amanda's always been a nervous winter driver. I told her not to bother sending out applications, that likely she'll be called back to work in a year or so, when the district gets back on its feet; but she said, 'What harm can sending out résumés do?' Told me to tell you she'll be over tomorrow with a few goodies."

"Tell her to take care of what she needs to do for herself, Sam. I'm fine, and she needn't feel she has to send me something every day. If Amanda and Gail next door had their way, I'd be as plump as a partridge. I've never been a big eater, and now that I don't have as much work around the place, well … ." Taking a sip of the strong coffee, Will let the thought melt away, shrugged, and set the mug down on the table at his usual place. He sat, looking up at Sam, who took a seat across from him.

"Will, I've been meaning to talk to you for some time now."

"Sounds serious," Granger said in a somewhat joking tone.

"It *is* serious," Sam answered. "Every time I come into his house, I see those heaps," he motioned toward the magazine rack next to the rocker by the window, "of *National Geographic,* and I'm reminded of how much you've enjoyed your armchair travel over the years."

Will cocked his greying head. "What are you gettin' at, son?"

Sam leaned forward, holding the older man with his gaze. "Why not travel for real, to all the places you've read about, *dreamed about*, over the years when you couldn't even leave the farm to take a day trip somewhere? You could do it now, if you sold the farm, and you could do it in style … first class all the way. You've *earned* it."

Will started to respond, but Sam held up a hand and hurried on.

"Hear me out. You do *not* have an obligation to leave this place to Amanda and me. I make good money, and Amanda has her teaching degree. We have money in the bank, a nice cushion, and we've no debts to speak of. We're fine. You don't owe us anything. But you *do* owe it to yourself to do what you've always dreamed of. You worked hard all your life, and now you should reward yourself. It's what Amanda and I want for you."

A look of sadness settled over Will's features. "You're talkin' as if you don't want the farm. I was always under the impression that you *both* loved this place as much as I do, as Bonnie did till the day she died."

Sam reached across the table and patted Will's arm. "We do love the farm, but we love you more." After a moment, he asked, concern in his voice, "You don't look well today. Are you feeling all right?"

The old farmer pursed his mouth, raising a calloused hand to brush away his nephew-in-law's uneasiness. "A touch of indigestion is all. Comes with age." Will's expression turned wistful. "You know, I used to dread gettin' older, because I thought I wouldn't be able to do all the things I wanted to do, but I'll tell you a secret. Now that I am older, I find I don't *want* to do them."

"You're just saying that. Anyway—"

"Listen," Will cut in, "I was going to wait to tell you Sunday, at dinner, when you're here together, but I'll tell you now; and you can let Amanda know. I've made my will. It's notarized— *done!* I want this farm to stay in the family. One day, you two will have kids of your own, and you'll pass it on to them. It's what I want, and I thought it was what you both wanted." His tone bespoke hurt feelings.

Sam stood, carrying his mug to the sink, where he rinsed it. Turning, he said, "Will, what we want is for you to be happy, to reap the rewards of your years of hard work. All I'm saying is this— *think about it.*

"If you sold the farm to Derrick Mason," Sam reasoned, "you'd not only be helping yourself, you'd be helping the whole town, because he wants to build a shopping center, which would create needed jobs, and God knows this town could use another restaurant or two. Most people drive over to Haleigh's Hamlet to eat, because all we have here is the Witch's Brew Café, a couple lousy fast-food joints, a pizzeria, and the Chinese restaurant. Washingtonville is growing. We need more eateries, and we need more shops for the tourists this whole area is attracting.

"If you sold to Rex Chambers, you'd be giving the town more housing, and Washingtonville can use that too. In reality, I'd say with the way the town's growing, those condos Chambers wants to put up are even *more* essential. Plus, for what it's worth, I think you'd get a better deal from Chambers." Laying a hand on Will's thin shoulders, Sam's voice took on emotion. "Amanda and I think of you as a father. We don't want you bound to a promise we both think is not in your best interest." He patted the shoulder. "Like I said, *think* about it."

When Sam got back to the townhouse apartment that he and Amanda rented, he shared his visit at Witch-Tree Farm with his wife.

"I wish *you* would talk to Will," he concluded, washing up to lend her a hand with dinner. He poured them each a glass of red wine to go with the lasagna she made.

Amanda suspended her salad preparation to sip the Chianti. "I don't want to hurt his feelings, Sam. He'll take it to mean we don't want the farm, that we don't appreciate his generosity. I *know* my uncle."

"You and I both know that's not true. Unk could *never* think ill of you. He worships the ground you walk on; but in his heart of hearts, I have a feeling Will has been entertaining the idea of selling. Look, we have to at least *try* to convince him that we are not *holding* him to a vow that the land developers' offers … well, their proposals *changed* things. Frankly, those builders have altered the whole situation. Will should know how we feel, that we *want* him to be able to make the most of his golden years with the money they're offering. I feel *sorry* for him, honey. I really do. He's like a lost soul since your Aunt Bonnie died. Let's release him from this pledge he feels he has to keep to us, and allow him to enjoy life now. He's *earned* it!"

Leaning back against the kitchen counter and sipping her wine, Amanda thought for a long, private moment. "I refuse to contest this with him. I'll not be as those others; but I agree, we should both talk to him on Sunday. As much as I love Witch-Tree Farm and the Witch Tree, I don't want to rob Uncle Will of his dreams."

"Another thing is all the work that farm demands, even without the cows, and even with me helping out. When I stopped over there today, he looked beat. I told him not to do all that weed-whacking and leaf-raking in the yard around the house, but he did it anyway. He also repaired that fence I told him I'd take care of this weekend, but he couldn't wait until tomorrow. All Will does is work; it's what he's used to, and it's all he knows. We're never going to get him to kick back as long as he has the farm."

Sam took a swallow of his wine, keeping his gaze on Amanda. "We have a spare room. He could move in here with us after he sells the farm. I think that would be a good thing for him and for you." He gave a nod. "And I sure wouldn't mind having him to talk to. Will has a way about him. He's the father I never had. But first, we gotta talk him *into* selling so he can realize his dreams. It's really up to us, isn't it?"

"You're right," she answered after another quiet moment, the troubled look vanishing from her expressive brown eyes. "If anyone deserves a great retirement, it's Uncle Will."

The day following the *Samhain* fest was a Saturday. Thus, Raine and Maggie were free from their teaching duties at the college. Though they had reached home late the night before, they rose early and met in Tara's kitchen, where they were planning their day over a light breakfast.

"I woke thinking about our current mystery, Mags, and I think we should use today to speak with the two land developers, in addition to the presidents of Washingtonville's town council and historical society," Raine put forth, as she poured their tea. She handed a steaming cup to Maggie, joining her at table, where the latter was buttering the warmed *barmbrack* High Priestess Robin had given them to take home.

The night before, they discovered their fortune charms in the *barmbrack* they enjoyed at the fête. All three Sleuth Sisters got *wand* charms, which made them think their powers would be boosted in the coming months. True to their natures, they didn't make a production of it at the gathering, keeping the charms and related thoughts to themselves.

"I propose we just pop into the construction companies' offices and the historical society and hope to catch those people," Maggie replied in reference to Raine's mention of Will Granger's tormentors.

"Robin said that Mildred Grimm, the president of the town council, is always in the library on Saturdays. Since the historical society's office is upstairs in the library, we can kill two birds with one stone," Raine quipped.

"From what we've been hearing about Mildred Grimm," Maggie recollected, "I'm kind of surprised to learn she's a book worm. Doesn't seem the type who reads, if you ask me. Robin overhead her spout in the Witch's Brew Café the other day, and I quote, 'If it weren't for Granger's confounded niece, the old goat would sell his farm to Derrick Mason, and we'd get our shopping center! *Amanda*'s the thorn in the restorative ointment for our ailing town!'"

Raine held up a finger for "One moment," as she finished chewing. "Baa! Washingtonville's not ailing; it's growing! At any rate, Robin said Mildred Grimm works all week. Manages the Style Shoppe, a ladies' clothing store in Washingtonville, though Robin also mentioned that their town council president has some pretty lofty political ambitions. Anyway, the only day Grimm can haunt the library is Saturday. Seems she's a mystery buff. Likes to scan the shelves for whodunits on the weekends when she's off."

Maggie cocked her head. "Manages the *Style* Shoppe?! You'd never know it, at least not from the pictures I've seen of her!"

"Humph," Raine shrugged, "Robin said the woman was, and I quote, 'Downright *spooky*.'"

"Did Robin say what time of day Grimm's apt to be in the library?" Maggie cut another slice of the warm *barmbrack* and began spreading it with Granny's autumn butter.

"She did," Raine answered. "Usually right after lunch." She darted a glance at the antique railroad clock on the kitchen wall. "Let's not tarry. If we get to Washingtonville this morning round ten, we can drop in on the land developers first, then stop at the library to speak with both Mildred Grimm and Etta Story."

The Sisters were at the kitchen sink, washing up the few breakfast things, when the house phone rang. Picking it up, Maggie discovered the caller to be High Priestess Robin O'Malley, who sounded as though she'd been struck with fear.

"Moonglow and Starlight's stones are missing!" she cried out, anxiety thick on her voice. "No one here last night at our fest would have filched those stones. And you know what missing ritual stones on the morrow mean– *bad luck*. I've told those two repeatedly not to go about crowing that they'd do anything to save the Witch Tree, that they'd stop at nothing! It's the *way* they say it, too," she rattled on, "that always gives me concern. I worry that their words and intentions might be misunderstood; and now, I fear the worst. I absolutely fear the worst!"

It was ten after ten, that morning, when Raine swung into the parking lot of Chambers Construction. She switched the MG's ignition off and turned to glance at Maggie in the passenger seat. "Ready?"

"Do you have any idea what we're going to say?" the redheaded Sister asked. "Nothing we tossed back and forth, on the way over here, sounded quite right to me."

"That's because we were trying to camouflage what we intend. Let's just be upfront about this, Mags. We'll say …"

"Mr. Chambers, we're friends of Will Granger, and though he would never ask us to speak in his behalf– in fact, he doesn't even know we're here– nonetheless, we're concerned that you seem to be pressing him to sell you his farm." Raine paused to take a needed breath.

Rex Chamber's expensive leather chair creaked when he leaned back in it, and a faint but superior smile played at his lips. "And you want me to stop."

"We do," the Sisters replied at once.

Rex Chambers was a tall man who bulked large from eating rich foods and drinking too much alcohol to wrap business deals that made him a lot of money. On the wall was a bigger-than-life oil painting of himself sporting a crown, under which an engraved brass plaque bore the portrait title: *Rex Chambers, King of the Builders*. The remaining wall space was covered with awards and accolades he had won over the years as a local business man and successful entrepreneur.

"And how does this concern you?" Rex put to the Sisters in a sarcastic tone. His fleshy face exhibited a high color that looked as though he might have a health issue.

"I just told you," Raine answered evenly. "Will is our friend." *What an egotistical jackass!*

"Then act like friends!" Rex fired back. "I'm offering Granger a damn good price for his land. He could enjoy his retirement in style, not tied to a farm to babysit a bunch of cows."

"Will sold his cows," Maggie interjected, "and that farm's been in his family over a hundred years. He wants to *keep* it in the family." She softened her expression and her tone. "Look, there must be a hundred other sites around here on which you could build those condos. Can't we entreat you to lay off Will Granger? This whole matter seems to be draining him."

"With all your accomplishments," Raine gestured to the wall of plaques, "certainly you don't want to be the cause of the poor man losing his health, do you?"

"I haven't done anything to jeopardize old man Granger's health!" Rex retorted, his face heavy and truculent, as it took on even more color. "And I highly resent your insinuating that I have. Why don't you two–"

His message was cut short when a striking young woman quickly stepped into the office from the adjacent space. "Now Dad, remember what the doctor said about your blood pressure. These ladies are only looking out for their friend." The attractive brunette smiled at the Sisters, advancing toward them with extended hand. "I'm Sirena Chambers." She shook hands with both Sisters, saying, "You're the famous Sleuth Sisters, aren't you? From neighboring Haleigh's Hamlet?"

"People call us that, yes." A grin tickled the corners of Raine's pouty mouth.

Maggie was studying Rex's daughter. Of medium height with a curvy figure and jet-black hair, the woman's eyes were an enrapturing violet-blue, her complexion fair. Maggie pitched the thought to Raine– *Looks like a young Liz Taylor.*

Meantime, Sirena was scrutinizing the Sisters. "You mentioned other sites for the condos; but you see, ladies, Witch-Tree Farm happens to be in a prime location for the particular homes we want to build. We've offered Mr. Granger a price well above what the property should sell for simply because we think it would make a lovely setting for the superior homes for which we are known. Our offer is generous, and our intentions above board; I assure you. Moreover, I must clarify– *never* have we pressed or, in any way, harassed the man."

"We're not the only land developers who want to purchase that farm!" Rex shouted. "Why don't you pay a visit to Derrick Mason? Though I doubt *he* would do any real pushing, that no-account son of his surely would."

Sirena pitched her father a look to stop his ranting. "Dad, we don't know that Reggie's been hassling Mr. Granger." She turned her exquisite regard on the Sisters. "But Dad's right. DHM Construction is also interested in making a deal with Will Granger. As a matter of fact, they've been seducing the Washingtonville Town Council to their corner. *If* anyone's been putting the pressure on– note I said '*If*'– it would be them and the president of the town council, not us. In addition, I've heard the Washingtonville Historical Society's been pushing Mr. Granger to *donate* his land to them."

"We'll be making our plea to those folks too," Raine replied.

"Wait a minute. Wa——it a minute!" Rex exploded, snapping his fat fingers. "The Sleuth Sisters! Aren't you psychics or somethin'?" he hurled in captious question. "I'll bet you're in some sort of sneaky alliance with that Keystone bunch, the 'Ditzy Druids' some of us call 'em! They're the ones lobbying to save that Witch Tree! One of 'em stopped in here a few days ago to try and talk me outta buying Witch-Tree Farm. You've got a lotta nerve tellin' me to stop tendering offers to old man Granger! You're probably cookin' up a scheme to get hold of that land yourselves!"

The Sisters rose to take their leave.

"Hardly that, Mr. Chambers," Raine reacted with as much dignity as she could muster. *The man is obnoxious!* she thought, struggling to keep her poise. *Would I love to wave my wand over his fat ass! Not to worry, I always practice safe hex. **A toad?*** she flung to Maggie.

*Cake! He already looks like one!* the redheaded Sister volleyed in return.

Sirena, in the interim, had sped her father an even spikier look, and turning to the Sisters, she said in a professional tone, "You must forgive my father's outburst. He's a business man not a diplomat. I respect the work you've done with crime solving; but, ladies, no crime has been committed by Chambers Construction. We only want–"

"*Please,*" Maggie interposed in her smooth, soft voice, "we know you're not the only ones after that land, but please refrain from asking Will Granger again to sell to you. His ardent wish is to keep the farm in his family; hence we *entreat* you, *respect* that, and leave him alone."

But the last word was not to be the Sisters'. Heaving himself from his chair, his face a scarlet red, Rex pointed to the portrait of himself and shouted, "I'll tell you the same thing I told the ditzy druid– 'The King of the Builders never lets anything, *or anyone*, get in his way! Never lets anyone or anything foil a plan formulated for a Chambers' project!' You'd do well to *remember* that!"

Raine sent Maggie a look with the thought, *Ooooh, he can be assured– we will remember!*

***

When Raine pulled the MG into a parking space in front of DHM Construction Company, she said to her sister of the moon, "Mags, I hope this interview goes better than the last one."

"The last one didn't go so badly, darlin'. We conveyed our message succinctly and clearly. For now, anyway, that's all we can do."

As the pair walked to the front door of the long, buff-brick structure, they became privy to the heated dialogue being spewed by a young man reaming out a male employee on the side of the building. Both men were wearing work clothes and hard hats.

"We require each crew to meet every morning, to sit down and discuss what activities are on the list for the day! You *know* this! This has *always* been our policy; it's nothing new! We insist crews go over whatever hazards are associated with daily agendas. Am I right?! You know this is a *must* with this company! *Am. I. Right?!* Don't just stand there, gawking at me, *answer me!"*

The employee shoved fisted hands into his pockets and stuttered out a response. "Y-yes, sir."

"Then why-in-*the*-hell weren't **YOU** present for your crew's morning meeting two days in a row?!" Before the employee had a chance to reply, the boss vented on, his voice booming, "If a crew knows *exactly* what they're going to be doing and *how* it's to be done, that results in a *safer* operation. Planning is *key* to our success here! **Got that?!** No more missed morning meetings! I don't care what your excuse is! If I have to tell you again, you're through here! *Got it?!"*

"Yes, sir, I do."

"Then take your sorry ass back to your crew and get to work!"

The Sisters were about to enter the building, when the man who had been shouting hurried up behind them to hold the door, his hard hat tucked under his arm. "Thank you," they spoke in unison.

"Is there something I can do for you?" he asked, his expert gaze scanning the attractive pair.

*So this is the famous playboy Reggie!* Raine shot to Maggie, who fired back–

*In the flesh.* Clearly, the redheaded Sister was savoring the view.

*Sleuthing can be more than a bit of enjoyment.* Aloud the Goth gal said, "We'd like to speak to the owner, Derrick Mason. It's a personal matter."

Amusement kindled in the young man's hot blue eyes, his countenance a mingled air of fun and arrogance. "Personal huh? *Well* now," again his eyes raked their figures in the curve-hugging black knit dresses they were sporting, their capes flung over their arms, "perhaps *I* can help you. I'm Derrick's son, Reggie."

Introductions were made, wherein Reggie recognized Raine and Maggie as two of the Sleuth Sisters. Then, gesturing ahead of him, he beckoned, "This way, ladies."

Trading quick looks, the Sisters allowed themselves to be ushered to Reggie boy's office.

*We've nothing to lose*, Maggie rocketed to Raine.

*And we just might discover something interesting,* the raven-haired Sister chortled back.

Inside the plush office, the Sisters sat opposite Reggie's chair at his large, ornate desk, where he plonked the hard hat to run fingers through his tousled hair.

"Now," he said, lowering himself into his seat, repartee dancing in his eyes, "what can I do for you?"

*Wouldn't he just?* Maggie flung to Raine, one dark-red brow raised with salacious humor.

"We're friends of Will Granger, the owner of Witch-Tree Farm," Raine began. "First, let me preface what we're about to say with this– Mr. Granger does *not* know we've come to speak with you, nor would he ever ask us to speak in his behalf. However, in light of what's been happening, we feel we must."

Reggie Mason was less impressive than his office, but he did his best. "Then why don't you stop beating around the bush," he leaned back in the padded leather chair, "and just say what you've come here to say?" His query rang of incivility.

*OK, buster, here it is with both barrels.* Raine looked keenly into Reggie's eyes. "Please stop asking Will Granger to sell his land to you, to DHM Construction. Will's set on keeping the farm in his family, to be passed down from one generation to the next. He's a strong-minded, *resolute* individual. As he told you himself, his will's made. *Fait accompli.* You won't budge him; so please stop hounding the poor man!"

"If you call trying to make a good deal 'hounding,'" Reggie uttered, tilting his dark head, the blue eyes unflinching.

The Sisters fixed their emerald gazes on the bold bloke. He was, as they had heard, wickedly handsome– tall, dark and handsome– as cinema portrays its leading men. And his physique in the tight jeans and tee he was wearing was every girl's dream.

"A good deal for whom?" Maggie put forth quietly. "Mr. Granger doesn't wish to sell, and likely he's too much of a gentleman to tell you straight up to lay off, though I think he's getting to the saturation point with your company *and* Chambers Construction."

"Oh please," Reggie retorted with visible scorn, "Will's a big boy who can speak for himself! And let me remind you that *I* have every right to talk to him about his property! *You*, on the other hand, have *no* right coming in here to order me to do or not do anything!"

"Like we told Mr. Chambers, there are probably a hundred other sites on which you could build. You'll have no trouble finding another location for your shopping center, so please stop bedeviling Will Granger," Raine urged, determined not to let Reggie's barb get under her skin.

"What's this about Will Granger?" asked a distinguished older man with slightly greying dark hair, who was peering into the office from the hall.

"Dad, these are friends of Granger's, Raine and Maggie McDonough, better known in these parts as the Sleuth Sisters."

A light went on in Derrick's blue eyes. "Ah, the famous crime-solving psychics from Haleigh's Hamlet! I've read about you several times in the newspapers. To what do we owe this pleasure?"

"As we were saying," Maggie said, "we've come to plead with you to stop asking our friend, Will Granger, to sell his farm to your company. He doesn't wish to sell to anyone. As he told you or your son himself, he's leaving Witch-Tree Farm to his niece and her husband. The farm's been in his family for over a century, and he's steadfast about *keeping* it in the family."

"We're concerned that he's being pressured, even badgered, and we've come to ask you, in a respectful, affable manner, to please stop," Raine finished sensibly.

Though he was answering the Sisters, having now stepped inside the office, Derrick sent his son a prickly look. "I was not aware that Will Granger was being badgered." His voice carried a hint of admonition. Redirecting his gaze to Raine and Maggie, the CEO immediately softened his tone. "The shopping center we proposed would be a great boon to the whole of Washingtonville, ladies; and, assuredly, we offered the owner of Witch-Tree Farm a more-than-fair price for his land; but most certainly our company will respect Mr. Granger's wishes. We have always been a highly respected organization that has given back to the area many times over. We've reaped many rewards and awards, and we would never do anything to tarnish our sterling reputation. Would we, Reggie?" The last was more a warning than a question.

"No, sir," the young man replied, looking decidedly uncomfortable.

The Sisters rose, moving toward the door, where Derrick Mason shook each of their hands. Both Raine and Maggie took notice that Mason, senior, had a firm handshake.

"I'm glad you stopped in today," he said with noted sincerity. "Truly, it's been a privilege meeting you. I've always admired the good you accomplish."

As the Sisters drove away, on the road to Washingtonville's Abbott Library, Raine said, "Mags, I bet you there's another reaming going on right now at DHM Construction, and this time, I'd wager Reggie boy is the recipient!"

"I'd have to agree," Maggie laughed. "Oh, would that I were a fly on the wall in Reggie's office right now!"

"Well, hopefully, we did some good there," Raine commented.

"Dishy young chap though, wouldn't you say?" Maggie winked.

*Ever the cougar!* Raine sniped.

Both Maggie and Raine were looking forward to stopping by the one-of-a-kind Abbott Library– that boasted three resident cats, one on each floor.

Built in 1901, Washingtonville's unique library had been a private residence until the last of the wealthy Abbotts passed on in 1967, and the noble mansion was willed to the town. The integrity of the old manse was retained with renovation, and the result was a warm and welcoming public library of which the historic town was duly proud.

Four years earlier, Professors Raine and Maggie McDonough had given a talk on local history at "The Abbott," and they were delighted that one of the resident cats attended. About five minutes before the lecture began, the big brown tabby strolled into the room, announcing himself with an economy of kitty words. As self-important as you please, he leaped into one of the easy chairs in the front row, and chin on outstretched paws, was ever attentive during the Sisters' entire presentation. As soon as the talk ended, Dickens— that was the cat's name— got up, stretched and, on silent paws, exited the room, tail in the air, giving new meaning to the phrase, "Cute as the Dickens."

"I wonder if Dickens is still here," Maggie mused, as they climbed the steps leading to the library's front porch and main entrance.

"We'll soon find out," Raine grinned. "What were the names of the other two library cats? I can't recall."

Maggie reflected. "Agatha and Hemingway."

Inside, the Sisters glanced quickly round. The main-floor library cat, the calico Agatha, was curled up on a cozy easy chair before one of the fireplaces, where a cheery fire burned brightly.

"Let's mosey over to the mystery section and look for Mildred Grimm," Raine whispered.

No sooner had the pair arrived at the special display this library provided for its mystery addicts, when they spotted the president of the Washingtonville Town Council surfing the whodunit shelves.

"That's Mildred," Maggie breathed into Raine's ear. "I recognize her from her pictures in the paper. There's *no* mistaking that old tabby!"

Grimm's bony face looked out on the world with shrewd appraisal. She had the necessary long, hooked nose and prominent chin that, in profile, nearly met, stamping her Hallowe'en's quintessential wicked witch. But the vilest feature was her cruel pencil line of a mouth bestowed upon her, brooded Maggie, by the hostile faeries who'd presided over her birth.

Raine sent her sister of the moon a thought, holding up a curled thumb and forefinger in the "OK" gesture. She jerked her head in the direction where Grimm was standing, indicating that Maggie should point her feet that way too.

"Mrs. Grimm?" the Goth gal inquired.

"Yes," the somber, sixty-ish woman answered, bemused. "Do I know you?"

"You possibly know *of* us," Raine replied, introducing herself and Maggie.

Mildred appraised the Sisters over the rim of her reading glasses. "And what, pray, would the Sleuth Sisters want to discuss with me?" The watery, silvery-blue eyes narrowed, and the practiced, slippery voice came off with definite sinister undertones.

Grimm's whole demeanor was frosty; and grey, the color of her hair, sweater and skirt, seemed apropos for the tall, ungainly councilwoman.

*I don't like to poke fun at anyone's looks, but "old tabby" she is not. Looks more like the Wicked Witch of the West,* Raine pitched to Maggie.

*Cackle-cackle! Complete with the attitude,* the redheaded Sister shot back. *All that's missing are the foul, doggerel rhymes to spawn black magick!*

*Lest we forget the flying monkeys!* Aloud, the raven-haired Sister said, "Could we have a few moments of your time?" She gestured to the adjacent library café. "We'd like to talk to you about something, over a cup of tea or coffee perhaps?"

*Careful,* Maggie cautioned Raine. *Don't be too quick to dismiss my "old tabby" verdict. She gives the distinct impression of one who would pounce, swift and sharp, like a cat upon a mouse.*

Mildred Grimm, in the intervening time, had given an exasperated sigh. "I think I can guess what you want to talk to me about, and if I were you, I'd–"

"Ah, but you're not," Raine cut in, ignoring Maggie's counsel. Noting the return of the baffled look on the woman's face, she clarified, "*Me*. You're *not* me." Again she motioned toward the quaint in-house café. "C'mon, let's talk over a cup of tea. We won't keep you from your Saturday errands, we promise."

"So what do you think gives you the right to ask me to stop pushing Will Granger to do what's right for this town? You're not from here; you're from Haleigh's Hamlet!" This last was uttered as if Grimm were accusing the Sisters of hailing from the dark depths of Hades.

"We told you. We're friends of Will's. It worries us that he is being pressured. It's starting to get to him–" Raine thought for a moment, trying a whole new approach. "Oscar Wilde once said that you don't love someone for their looks, for their clothes, or their fancy car; but because they sing a song only you can hear. As friends of Will, we understand how he feels about his farm," she delivered with an Irishman's love of the land. "He wants to keep it in his family, pass it on to Amanda, and to her children. It's a heritage, a part of himself, he can leave behind to them."

"Sentimental hogwash!" Mildred shrieked in true wicked-witch style, picking up her teacup to drain it as she gazed at the Sisters with unconcealed annoyance. Then, in the blink of an eye she stood, indicating their talk was over. "What I need to do is start working on the niece and her husband. I agree with you on one thing– that old goat Granger is probably not going to budge."

Grimm cocked her grey head, and her face screwed in concentration. "It's just occurred to me that you two–" her eyes narrowed. "Aren't there supposed to be *three* of you? *Whatever*," she waved aside what the Sisters were about to say. "It's just dawned on me that you are doubtless in league with that gang of meddlesome witches trying to protect the Witch Tree! Of course, why didn't I see through the dribbling nonsense you were spewing sooner?! No wonder you don't want to see progress in this town! You've got a *double* reason– Haleigh's Hamlet is our rival, and you're in cahoots with the damn druids! *Now you listen to me–*" the insufferable woman pointed a bony, claw-like finger at Raine and Maggie.

"Don't point that at us. It has a nail on it," Raine retorted blithely, cutting her off whilst lightly directing the finger out of their faces.

"Washingtonville needs that shopping mall," Grimm blustered on. "What we don't need– or want– is any more meddling magick in our town! Do I make myself clear?!"

It was on the tip of Raine's tongue to say, *If you can't open your mind, then shut your stupid mouth!* when–

Maggie's thought struck her like a thunderbolt. *Great Goddess, what a crank!*

And, simultaneously, Mildred decided to add, "I'm not the only one who feels this way, you know. That coven of witches is making enemies in this town by sticking their noses into things that are none of their– or *your*– business!"

"Protecting innocent people and heading off or righting wrongs is always our business," the feisty Goth gal replied smoothly. Raine attributed her smoothness to Granny. Maggie's use of the word *crank* reminded her of their wise grandmother, bequeathing a calming moment. Granny liked to apply *crank* to especially annoying muggles.

Almost as if she had read the Sisters' thoughts, Mildred guffawed, her expression condescending. "More foolish sentiment! You think you've been blessed with so much power, eh?"

Raine looked hard at the woman. "Power is no blessing in itself, Mrs. Grimm, except when it is used to protect the innocent."

Maggie, meanwhile, had turned her attention to the mystery novels, on the empty chair between them, that the town council president had checked out. She fixed the titles, *Murder on the Road* and *Murder is Simple*, in her head. Somehow, with her sharp-edged intuition, the redheaded Sister felt that bit of information might prove useful in the very near future.

Just before Mildred Grimm left the Sisters in the library café, she turned and glanced back at them. There was something in that black look that startled the empathic pair. It was loaded with stabbing malice, along with a curious intimate knowledge that was almost chilling.

As the Sisters climbed the stairs to the library's second floor, Maggie whispered to Raine. "I doubt very much our talks with Will's tormentors will help Mr. Granger whatsoever."

"Perhaps not; but, at least, we're meeting the pushy culprits, and that might help us down the road if and when we have to deal with them." Of a sudden, Raine scoffed, "Hostile faeries my ass, Mags! Grimm was kissed on the lips by a vulture at birth!"

The first thing Raine and Maggie noticed when they arrived at the top of the stairs was the large brown tabby Dickens curled up asleep on a cushioned, sunny window seat, tail wrapped around him.

"Oh, let's go over and say hello," Raine suggested happily.

When the pair reached down to stroke the cat, he stretched and opened his golden eyes to peer at them with a touch of inquiry.

"I wonder if he recognizes us," Maggie said, looking to Raine.

"I'll ask him." The raven-haired Sister sent the cat the query.

"Well?"

Raine let out a sigh. "He doesn't, but he mentioned that there was something familiar about me."

The sound of Maggie's laugh was like wind chimes. "Blessed are the familiars," she whispered.

Raine pointed to a small, neatly lettered sign on the wall that read **Office of Washingtonville Historical Society** →

"This way," said she, giving Maggie's arm a tug.

The office door was closed, but an OPEN sign hung from the brass doorknob. Raine and Maggie entered to find a petite, middle-aged woman sitting at the desk, working at a computer.

"Good-morning," the Sisters crooned.

"Good-morning," the woman answered pleasantly, looking up from her keyboard. "Whew! I've always considered myself a computer whiz, but this new program is taking some getting used to. May I help you?"

Raine smiled. "Might you be Etta Story, President of the Washingtonville Historical Society?"

"Guilty as charged," she joked, returning the smile.

Etta's short, casual hair was a rich brown with gold streaks that lit up her complexion and hazel eyes. Her brown skirt was topped by a tan sweater and fringed shawl-scarf in an eye-catching, autumn-leaves pattern that quite suited her.

*Classy lady*, Raine spun to Maggie.

Since no one else was in the office, after introducing themselves, Raine launched into her plea for Etta to cease bedeviling Will Granger to donate his land to the society.

With a sigh, Etta lifted a perfectly manicured hand, the nails garnet red, to shift her reading glasses to the top of her head. "Look around," she signaled with a sweep of hand. "This is the *only* space we have. The society needs a place of our own." Rising, she moved to a cupboard from which she drew an album. "This is only one book cataloging our artifacts and antiques, wonderful things we'd love to be able to share with the public; but we've nowhere to display them. They're all in storage, and it's a shame. These things need a home, a place where people can come and look at them, *learn* from them." She handed the book to Raine, who transmitted the thought to Maggie that *Etta Story was certainly an efficient woman.*

"We've always hoped and prayed that one day Will Granger would leave his farm to us. I mean, with his wife gone and no children …" Etta let the thought trail off, unfinished, adding after a brief respite, "Oh, what we could do with that place! We'd keep the integrity of the old farmhouse, of course, though we'd need to change a few things about it," she bubbled with excitement. "But I know, I **know**, I could get most of what we'd need in supplies and labor donated. Plus, we've a nice sum in our treasury we could dip into for some of that. You see, we sell theme-decorated Christmas trees every year, among other fund-raising projects, so–" she stopped short, enthusiasm flashing in her eyes. "Oh, wouldn't Witch-Tree Farm be a *wonderland* decorated for Christmas?! Imagine all the lights and a big, old-fashioned tree in the farmhouse's front window!"

"We understand how you feel, certainly, but hasn't Mr. Granger told you that he's already made out his will, leaving Witch-Tree Farm to his niece and her husband?" Maggie queried kindly.

"Yes," Etta replied with a more audible exhalation, after which her expression seemed to darken. In a moment, her face softened again, and she went on, putting her thoughts deftly into words, as if Farmer Granger's land was still a possibility. "The Washingtonville Historical Society does a lot of good, you know. We especially work with young people, instilling in them the importance of history.

"The main goal of our society has always been to stimulate pride and appreciation in our area's rich, layered history and to spark further interest in our past. Greater minds than mine have distinguished history as the *most* important subject in school. Dear me! An *un*awareness of history is akin to planting cut flowers! History not only gives us roots, it teaches us valuable lessons. I always tell my young audiences that history teaches us what we stand for, and even more importantly what we should be willing to stand up for!" Etta caught herself, stopping abruptly. "Forgive me. I didn't mean to preach."

Raine reached out to touch the older woman's shoulder. "Don't ever apologize for the fire within you– it's *magick!*"

"But you're preaching to the choir when you're talking to us," Maggie inserted. "We teach history at Haleigh College."

"Your words resonate with our own lectures," Raine said with hint of a grin. "I often remind my classes of the vast wealth of history embedded in Pennsylvania's lush, rolling hills and valleys, majestic mountains, and ever-mysterious deep woods."

Etta's face lit up, as her hands met in a beseeching gesture. "Of course, of course!" she exclaimed, "Raine and Maggie McDonough, professors of history and archeology at Haleigh College. Why, you're the famous Sleuth Sisters! How silly of me! PhDs in history, both of you." She let out another huge sigh, and this time, it was one of relief. "Then you empathize. Surely you do! You can appreciate the importance of what our society does. This would be a valuable, *invaluable*, legacy that Will Granger would be leaving behind for posterity's sake."

When both Maggie and Raine started to say something, Etta raised her pointer finger for them to hear her out. "Understand, I'm not worried about Amanda and Sam protecting the Witch Tree and taking care of the historic farm and farmhouse, but who's to say what their children will one day do? Seems like each new generation has less and less respect for the past. Can't Will Granger see that he's *gambling* when he's leaving Witch-Tree Farm to his niece and nephew? Whereas, if he left the farm to the Washingtonville Historical Society, it would *always* be protected, kept up and intact.

"For one thing," she talked on, "we'd get a lightning rod to protect the Hester Tree, and we'd persuade Penn State to come over to evaluate what it needed, you know, to enrich the soil around the tree and so forth. In addition, we'd get a Pennsylvania historical marker that would aid us in protecting that tree for all time. Oh, I just wish we knew more about Hester Duff that would help us secure a historical marker!"

Etta's tone and face were set in determined lines. "Granger needs to think about this less emotionally and more rationally!"

The Sisters traded pointed looks.

"Oh," Etta lamented, "if *only* Will Granger would think more about this; if only he– why, we could draw something up that he leaves the farm to us under the provision that the society never sell it, that we never break up the lots, that we keep Witch-Tree Farm intact, and that we–"

Maggie reached out to capture both of Etta's hands between her own, stating in her silky voice, "Will's mind is made up, my dear. *It's done.*"


When the Sisters exited the library, they did not initially realize that someone was watching them from a copse of trees on the property. However, as they were about to get into the MG, they both turned to look over their shoulders at the small wood, to the right of the library, on the hillside. A chill wind blowing a whirl of leaves carried a resounding message.

*Watch your backs*, the High Priestess had cautioned them, for–
*Something wicked this way comes.*

# Chapter Five

That evening, Raine and Maggie made their way, over the well-worn path through the woods, to the adjacent Goodwin residence. Raine led, carrying the lighted antique railroad lantern the pair used to traverse their property in the dark. Maggie toted a bottle of wine. It had been a cloudy day and evening, and darkness settled early.

Hugh Goodwin, a semi-retired veterinarian and his son Beau, a full-time vet and Raine's "other half," lived next door to Tara. The Goodwin Veterinary Clinic was attached to Hugh's Colonial ranch house. It was a ten-minute walk for the Sisters, through the woods. Hugh kept the connecting path, along with the trails, cleared for Raine and Maggie, who enjoyed riding their horses through the serenity of the forest whenever time permitted.

"It was nice of Hugh to invite us to dinner tonight," Maggie stated. "I really didn't feel like fixing us anything after the day we've had. I can't shake this vexing feeling of imminent danger. Anyway, Hugh said on the phone that Betty came over to help him prepare a nice harvest supper. Comfort foods among boon companions on a chilly November night will be delightful– just what the doctor ordered," she quipped.

"I'm glad too. I figured we'd just pop into Sal-San-Tries for one of Sophie's special take-outs. The café-deli has great food, but this'll be so much better. Our whole sleuthing set will be there, and we can get everyone up-to-date on our latest challenge. Not that we have a crime to solve, but–" she broke off, clarifying, "your feeling matches Robin's when she said– 'Something wicked this way comes.'" Raine lowered the lantern to take a closer look at something on the trail. "Whew!" she breathed out. "Thought it was a snake. Just a stick. Rattlers and copperheads should be hibernating by now. Guess I'm a tad jumpy too." She started onward. "What time will Thaddeus be joining us?"

The redhead released a little sigh. "He said he'd meet us at the Goodwins' around seven. I hope he's on time; you know how forgetful he can be. Oh, I meant to tell you. I'll be leaving afterward with him. We're going to spend the night and tomorrow at the mountain cabin."

An owl hooted.

"Listen," Maggie said, pausing brusquely on the path. "Did you hear that?" She cocked her head, straining her ears and waiting for what seemed like a long time.

Raine, who also froze in her tracks, answered soberly, "I heard it. It's a warning."

In all, the owl hooted thrice.

Maggie's heart gave a sudden leap, the foreboding in her mind and heart mounting. "*Death*," she whispered, remembering what else they had heard at the *Samhain* gathering. "Death doth come– the death of three."


When the Sisters arrived at the Goodwin home, they knocked, announcing themselves, then opened the back door and entered the warm, rustic kitchen. "God and Goddess bless this house!"

Instantly, Hugh's sibling German shepherds, Nero and Wolfe, came loping toward them, barking their own excited greetings.

Raine sent the pair a telepathic message to *Settle down!* "Good boys!" she praised, giving each the treat she faithfully remembered to bring them.

"Come in! Dinner's almost ready," Betty called out, always in high spirits to spend time with the sleuthing set.

Maggie set the wine on the counter. "Fruit of the vine," she pronounced.

"Thank you," Hugh and Betty replied, with Betty adding, "You're so thoughtful."

"Thoughtful and sweet. Let me have your wraps," Hugh offered, lifting the Sisters' black, hooded capes from their extended hands.

Stretching on tiptoes to brush his cheek with a kiss, Raine murmured, "Bright blessings attend you both." Hugs were exchanged, with the raven-haired Sister patting Hugh on the stomach. "Your cooking agrees with him, Betty."

Betty Donovan and Hugh Goodwin became enamored with one another almost from the moment they met, opening their hearts again to love. When Betty posed the question, how much was due to Raine's magickal finagling, the Goth gal answered, "Oh, it was magick all right! Who's to say what love is?"

Hugh and Betty had just seemed so right for one another: both widowed, both animal lovers, and both ardent mystery buffs. Within a short time, Betty's Irish setter, Boru– practically impossible for her to manage after her husband passed away three years earlier– heeled perfectly when they walked with Hugh and his two shepherds, Nero and Wolfe; and Betty and Hugh both slept better nights after companionable sessions of reading aloud followed by lively discussion of whatever whodunit they were currently sorting out. Under the Sleuth Sisters' enchantment, Betty quickly became a believer in the maxim that "Nothing is impossible." As Raine told her, "The word itself says, 'I'm possible.'"

A retired librarian, Betty was an attractive woman with short, casual, salt-and-pepper hair and eyes like polished turquoise. She had a penchant for artsy Southwestern fashions and bold silver-and-turquoise jewelry that suited both her coloring and her adventurous Sagittarian personality.

Tall and robust like his son and their Highlander ancestors, the senior Goodwin's once-ebony hair was now an ennobling silver, as was his full, what-used-to-be-called "cavalry mustache." Indeed, the dear man habitually carried himself in a smart, soldierly manner.

Under wiry, expressive brows, the deep blue of Hugh's eyes had faded some with age, but the years had not diminished his zest for life, not perceivably anyway. In truth, Time had been gracious to Hugh Goodwin; and there were those ladies in Haleigh's Hamlet who considered him handsomer now than when he was young, and they'd all vied for his attention. But women have always been attracted to men with cavalry mustaches and soulful "bedroom eyes."

A virile, inventive Aquarius, Hugh was a good, upright man, a lover of life and all living things. If he had a fault, it was that he sometimes spoke gruffly– and those times he would huff his salty words into his mustache with the fire of his fierce Celtic ancestors– but he was never deliberately unkind, and his words carried truth.

They carried truth now when, turning to Betty, he remarked, in response to Raine's comment that something sure smelled *yummy*, "Looks like another of our sleuthing-set suppers is about to be a success." He bent to her height to kiss her cheek, rosy from the heat of the kitchen.

Betty laid a gentle hand on Hugh's noble face. "We make a good team."

"What *is* for dinner? I'm starved!" Raine exclaimed, moving to the table to snatch a stuffed mushroom from a plate of tempting hors d'oeuvres.

"As Hugh told you– tonight a *harvest* supper," Betty touted, opening the oven door. "*Harvest Home*," she added for the benefit of the witchy Sisters. Using pot holders, she pulled out a baking dish, its essence a savory element of the rich smells permeating the kitchen.

"What's that?!" Raine blurted, eyeing, with little-concealed zeal, the casserole's crusty brown top.

"Squash Gratin, like my mother used to make." Betty spooned a tiny morsel of the steaming concoction from the glass baking dish, holding it out, a hand under the spoon, for the raven-haired Sister to sample. "Butternut squash under a cozy blanket of breadcrumbs, parsley, and cheesy goodness."

Blowing on the proffered spoon, Raine's face lit up with happy expression. "Ambrosia! What else is there?" she pressed, peering into the open oven, as Betty lifted out more dishes.

"Breaded, stuffed pork chops, baked apples, Waldorf salad; and Hugh and I found a great apple dessert called 'Harvest Dance Pie.'" Betty laughed, and her face took on more color. "It was fun to make." She flashed Hugh a coy air, giving Raine the impression that the food preparation wasn't the only fun the two of them shared before their guests arrived.

Another knock sounded at the back door, through which trod Aisling and Ian, carrying a couple of covered dishes of their own.

"Hello the house!" Ian hailed, setting the foil-protected dish on the stove top. "Garlic mashed potatoes."

"Thank you, Ian, but you really didn't have to bring anything. We've plenty," Betty said, rushing forward to receive the two new arrivals.

"However, your garlic potatoes are always welcome in this house!" Hugh was quick to add.

"Brought some of Granny's sweet potato biscuits too," Aisling said, handing the sealed plastic container over to Betty, whose reaction included a huge hug.

"Oh, honey, these are my favorites!"

Aisling's husband, Ian, was a burly ex-cop with a mellow Leo personality that harmonized well with his wife's feline persona; and though he could be fanciful at times, like Aisling, he had no wishbone where a backbone ought to be. In fact, he liked to emphasize that, "To succeed in life, you need three things– a backbone, a wishbone, and a funny bone." There *were* times when Ian roared, though never at his wife or young daughter, who each had a talent for making him purr.

Ian's coloring was entirely red-gold. Thick, wavy reddish-gold hair covered his leonine head, whilst his hazel eyes flashed bright gold glints. Even his weathered skin gleamed golden, though it could instantly flame red with stirred emotion.

Aisling and Ian met on the Pittsburgh police force, several years prior, where they'd worked together as detectives, the stepping stone to their current career. The Gwynns' Black Cat Detective Agency was a successful operation; and all in all, these master sleuths were a well-matched, lionhearted couple. Aisling often said that she and Ian were true soul mates, and anyone seeing them together recognized the bond and the love they shared with one another, as well as with their precocious Fay of a daughter. The preteen Merry Fay mirrored her magickal mother– in more than just her charming looks.

"Where is Merry Fay?" Betty, who had truly connected with the child, asked, peering behind Aisling and Ian and through the door.

"At a friend's sleep-over," Aisling answered, or she'd have come with us. But she instructed me to tell you that she baked the sweet potato biscuits herself, and they're her thank-you gift to you, Betty, for making her Hallowe'en costume this year."

Betty looked pleased. "I enjoyed it. She made an adorable witch. Very ... *believable*," she thought to add with a girlish giggle.

"Evening, everyone!" Beau called out, as he entered the kitchen from the hall, where a connecting door led to the veterinary clinic. "Finished for the day; so barring any farm calls, I'm a free man." He directed this last to Raine, moving to her side to kiss her. "Mmmm, when you love a witch– magick happens," he pronounced, pulling her close.

"Come home with me after dinner," she whispered, brushing her lips tantalizing against his ear. "We'll have the house to ourselves. Play your cards right, and you'll think Yule came early this year."

His response was to kiss her again, this time with passion– and *promise.*

Tall and powerfully built, Beau Goodwin was blessed with the thick, wavy, jet-black hair and scorching blue eyes of a long line of Scottish and Scotch-Irish ancestors. In his thirties, his body was all lean muscle– muscle that moved with the kind of intensity and power that comes to men who get plenty of exercise a good deal of the time outdoors. His relentless farm calls afforded him continuous bodybuilding workouts; and like Raine, Beau enjoyed spending his free time, the turning wheel of the seasons, in Nature's rejuvenating company.

There was something, simply put– *special*– about Dr. Beau Goodwin that people– and above all, animals– noticed straightaway. Perhaps it was that *special something* that peered from his eyes, a soulful softness that revealed a good and pure heart. Animals reap a "knowing" when a human possesses empathy and kindness through the vibrations the human emits, and this provides the "fur, fin, and feather people" with a feeling of safety in the company of that human.

Beau was a healer, and like the Sisters, he was an Old Soul and an empath. (Most empaths are Old Souls.)

Raine often experienced an acute Celtic knowing, just as he frequently did of her, that he had come from somewhere else– somewhere not of this earth. At times, each felt homesick for a place they weren't even sure existed. "A place," Raine said, "where my heart is full, my body loved, and my soul understood."

*Beau understood.* To be sure, each half of this remarkable couple created magick in a singular way, and together these two Star Children enkindled an utterly magickal *Raine-Beau.*

Like all Starseeds, who are intrinsically programmed to find others like themselves, both preferred to work in fields that allowed them to use their innate but heightened talents– healing, imparting knowledge and truth– and searching for their own truths. "Truths beyond the ken of men," Beau was wont to philosophize on the rare occasion when he could relax with a tall glass of the imported beer he favored.

Raine had a saying of her own regarding their relationship. "It's said some lives are linked across time, connected by an ancient calling that echoes down the ages. We're like magnets, Beau and I, with each incarnation, reaching out and leaping across space to reunite. We cross oceans of time to find one another."

*Magick calls to magick.*

The couple shared several common denominators, and though there had been others in each of their lives, this was *why*, after so many years, Raine and Beau were still mutually enchanted.

Only a few things triggered Dr. Beau Goodwin's temper, causing him to lose his Leo chivalry– animal cruelty (he did *not* tolerate animal cruelty in the least) and, at times, Raine's too-daring, impetuous Aries disposition, along with her unwavering outlook on the woes of marriage, conventional muggle marriage, at any rate.

*Beau's different of late,* she was telling herself after his kiss. *He's trying hard to accept my sleuthing, every aspect of it, including the time it takes me away from him **and** the dangers involved, particularly the risky time-travel! But I can't help wondering what he's up to. It's not really like Beau to acquiesce to anything.*

The rare times Raine had dated someone else, she could not squelch the memories of Beau's scorching kisses, and those reminiscences alone could send a multitude of thrills coursing through her.

*There's no denying he has power over me*, she was thinking, as she always did when she gazed into his piercing eyes, eyes that held the color, wisdom and truth of lapis. *Much more than I let him know. Will **ever** let him know.* Her eyelids fluttered and fell before his intense regard. *There've been times, times like this, when I'm almost convinced my Beau is the–*

"Wiz-zard!" she exclaimed when she saw the two tickets peeking out of his shirt pocket. "You got them!"

"Yep, two tickets to the Harvest Dance at the Washingtonville Grange. Dad's going to cover for me at the clinic, so we know we'll be able to attend."

Through the kitchen window, the pair spied Thaddeus' 1950, maroon, bullet-nose Studebaker crunching the gravel as it motored up the lane. The vintage car resembled a missile, and that perchance was why the inimitable Dr. Weatherby habitually advised his students, prior to weekends and holidays, to be careful in their "missiles."

***

"So that's everything," Raine finished, leaning back in her chair at table with her glass of dessert port. She had completed her account, concluding with the trilogy of caveats given them, first by Granny and, more recently, at the fest, by the *Samhain* spirit of Hester Duff and High Priestess Robin.

"How about providing Hugh and me with the names of those mysteries Mildred Grimm checked out of the library?" Betty requested. "If you have a witch's feeling they may prove significant, then Hugh and I had better read and discuss them. That's right up our alley."

"Let's hope it won't lead to a dead-end alley," Maggie replied. "*Murder on the Road* and *Murder is Simple*," the redheaded Sister complied, relating the book titles. "Both by I. M. Cagey."

Betty jotted the info down on a small reminder pad she'd pulled from the deep pocket of her artsy skirt. "We're familiar with that author's work. She's a regular Agatha Christie, that one."

"I think," Maggie suggested, setting her fork on her emptied plate, "we should pay another visit to Will Granger." She sent Raine a questioning look. "One day this week, huh? Do you think you could go with us, Aisling?"

The blonde with the wand gave speedy consideration to the matter. "How about tomorrow? It's Sunday, and we're all off. I could pick you both up in the afternoon after lunch. Would that work for you?"

Maggie looked to Thaddeus. "We planned on spending tonight and tomorrow at the mountain cabin."

"Don't change your plans," Aisling said. "Raine and I can go."

Now it was the raven-haired Sister's turn to look to her "other half." They, too, had planned to spend the day alone together.

"Go on," Beau replied to her glance. Just ring me when you get back, and—"

"Oh no!" Aisling cut in. "I just remembered that I have a new client coming to the house tomorrow. It's the only time she can meet with me. I'm sorry."

"No problem," Beau voiced smoothly, surprising everyone. "Raine and I will go. I share her concerns for the Witch Tree, and the drive to Washingtonville is an enjoyable one, especially at this time of year."

*Either I'm punch drunk on theories or Hell has frozen over*, the Goth gal thought, all but choking on her wine. "Wiz-zard!" It was all she could think to say aloud.

***

Later that night, when Raine and Beau were walking the path through the connecting woods to Tara, she stopped and, setting the old railroad lantern on the ground, pulled him toward her, standing on tiptoes to kiss his lips, his thick mustache playing the familiar sensory game with her skin. For a dizzying, spun-out moment, he towered over her. Usually, she didn't give that a thought, but for some reason tonight, she felt his strength, his power, in addition to the bristle of whiskers against her cheek.

"What was that for?" he asked in his sexy drawl, referencing the kiss.

"For being more and more accepting of who I am and what I do." The words rolled from deep in her throat, and her voice sounded breathy. She couldn't help herself– she kissed him again.

Or rather, he returned the kiss, pushing her back against a stout tree, as his tongue plunged into her mouth, swirling round, tasting her, and causing the thoughts whirling in her head to nose-dive to a velvet silence.

Her hands clutched his lush, black hair, and she pulled him even closer, his mouth crushing hers.

Fueled all evening by exchanged looks and caresses, they had both been craving and anticipating this moment. Now it was difficult to stop after a couple of kisses. He needed to feel the press of her firm breasts against his chest, as he wedged a hard-muscled thigh between her legs, and tore open his coat and shirt.

In the lantern's flickering light, Raine caught the drawing of the Witch Tree on his chest. It took her by surprise, and reaching out a hand, she touched it, sucking in her breath. Their gazes locked, and a knowing look leaped into her cat eyes, inciting Beau to give her an abrupt nod. In a flash, his hands flung open her long, black cape to slip under her sweater and cup her breasts, as the need to touch and be touched overwhelmed the pair of them.

*He's so damn sexy. He can burn me up alive. And he can do it in the time it takes to wave a wand. Every little thing he does is magick.* Longing rushed through Raine like a tidal wave. She couldn't get close enough to him, as she strained against his hard body, breathing in the scent of the handmade Irish soap she bought him, the mélange of ylang-ylang and sweet orange sensual and stimulating. Raine had joked that the soap smelled "… like a really good-lookin' guy."

With a groan, he pushed her sweater up and, undoing her bra, bared her breasts to his mouth. She arched her back, letting out a moan, while he nipped first one, then the other. It was delicious torture; and she sighed as his hands roamed her body, traveling over her curves and under her skirt. Lifting it, he tore away the lacey black thong, causing her to utter a little cry.

"Yes," she mewed, "let's do it. Right here, right now." The hot blood pounded in her veins like a hard, driving rain on a tin roof.

In answer, he sent her a look of mock surprise, one expressive black brow raised. The touch of his hands was warm on her bare skin, sending even more heat to her core. There was fire there, intense heat, *need*, and it leaped from her to surge through him like a strike of the boldest lightning.

Grasping her shoulders, he kissed her again, long and passionately; and, for a timeless time– a magickal moment– their bodies seemed to melt and fuse together, her eyes closing with the explosion of golden-white light that went off simultaneously in both mind and heart.

"Beau," she rasped, her voice hoarse with emotion, as his hand slipped between her thighs.

She twitched, spreading her legs and swiveling her hips. "Please," she answered in a half-sob. "*Please.*"

Whilst his hands continued to work their magick, she opened her eyes to watch his face in the glimmering light from the lantern at their feet.

"How does that feel?" he breathed into her ear. "Hmmmm? Tell me."

Her eyes fluttered shut in the sweet euphoria of the moment. "Sooooooooo good. Don't stop. Pleeeeease, don't stop."

He made a guttural sound. "You like that, do you?"

It felt too gratifying to speak. *Ooooh, I'm lovin' this,* she thought, holding back what she was feeling. *Sooooooo good ...*

He stared at her, his scorching regard scanning her from head to foot, an errant lock of black hair falling over his forehead. She could feel his eyes, and when she reopened hers, she was staggered at how powerful he looked at that instant. She was amazed, too, at how he was orchestrating each exquisite moment.

"*Tell me,*" he pressed with an especially crafty flick of hand. "Tell me how it feels."

Her husky voice was breathless, and a look of pure rapture spread over her face. "It feels ... *extraordinary.* Ooooooooooh, *amazing!* Yes, yes! Y-yeeeeeeeeees!"

"That's a good girl," he whispered, several seconds later, against her temple, breathing in the pleasant fragrance from her midnight hair. For several moments longer, he resumed his fondling; then, gripping her tight little bottom, he lifted and pulled her onto his aching hardness, making her gasp as she wrapped her legs tight around him and clung to his shoulders as if she were drowning. "Now, my little witch, how does *that* feel?"

"Mmmmmmmm," she moaned, speechless, virtually mindless.

They moved together, the pair of them emitting blissful sounds.

"More," she exhaled, her sweet breath in the chill of the night warming his face.

"I have *so much* more for you, baby," he said with another thrust that took her breath.

Their love-making was always hot with bubbling passion, and they never failed to satisfy one another in every way. Theirs was a love that took no notice of time, for each and every time Raine and Beau made love, it was, in a way, like their first.

"Deeper," she whimpered. "Mmmmmmm …"

He pounded further into her, taking his lips from hers so he could see her face again in the lantern's flickering glow. "You want more, do you?"

"Yes," she gasped. "Oooooh, yes!" *What is happening to me?* she asked herself. *I used to be the one in charge. And I will be again; but for now, Great Goddess, this is just toooo good to stop and analyze.*

"Let yourself go," he whispered. "Give yourself up to it." Beau mumbled something then, and in her highly aroused state, the fragment Raine caught rang out like a language she was powerless to recognize. When he reached up to brush her wispy ebony bangs from her eye, she saw, in the teasing light from the lantern, as she had in the past– via the Sight or former-life memory, she knew not which– the entwined blue serpents of Avalon, symbolizing wisdom, that braceleted his wrist.

*Empowerment. Enlightenment*, she fathomed in her sweet, frenzied confusion.

As they had on other occasions, the serpents seemed to writhe, and when they did, Raine felt something beyond description flood her entire being. She drew in her breath, startled, for tonight she felt, quite literally– captivated. *Beau, what are you doing to me?*

Though she had seen and experienced the Avalon serpents before during their closest moments, nonetheless, it was always a bit unsettling, as well as unbearably exciting. In all their years of intimacy– and there had been volumes of shared sensuality between them– she had never experienced anything quite as erotic as Beau's sizzling lovemaking this night.

As if reading her thoughts, he said with something akin to gruffness on his voice, "You will never forget this night … *never!*"

*Oh, great Goddess*, she thought, *how? How is it possible? But it just keeps getting better.*

Provocatively, he pulled out, *slowly*, the anticipation nearly driving her wild, before driving in again, hard and fast, and making her cry out, her voice echoing through the night-veiled forest. It was electrifying, and it made her whole body shiver, inside and out.

With a quick, sudden movement, he turned her round, forcing her to grip the tree for support. Bending, she pushed back, toward him, and he entered her again, his strong, muscular legs possessing the power to give her the impact she desired. One hand held her, whilst the other reached under her to work its special magick.

"Take me, Beau!" She squirmed, wriggling her bottom against him. "Take me!"

"I'll take you!" he muttered. "How do you like this, my little witch?" he questioned low in his throat. "Tell me!!" he ordered.

"I love it!" she panted, her words weak with yearning. "*Love* it."

A short laugh, from deep in his throat, fell from his lips. "I asked you how it *feels*?" he said roughly with a thrust to match.

"It feels … sooooooo good, soooooooooo … oh, Beau, yes, yes, yes! Y-Y-E-E-E-E-E-S!"

In the dazzle from the old railroad lantern, the Witch Tree on his chest seemed to brighten and glow, as he whispered into her ear, and together, at once and at the supreme moment, they instinctively shot to the matrix of the Universe their unified goal.

For Maggie and Thaddeus, it was always a pleasure to spend time alone at his mountain cabin.

"Pour us some wine, darlin', while I freshen up," she said, heading into the rustic bath.

Thaddeus switched on a CD, a medley of their favorite music he had recorded to play at their retreat, then walked into the kitchen to open a bottle of wine. Having poured two large goblets, he reentered the living area, set the wine on a tray atop the cougar coffee table, lit a fire in the fireplace, and settled down on the couch to wait for Maggie. Whilst he did, he pulled a pen and notepad from his pocket to jot down a few notes.

Surrounded by a Colonial-style rail fence, the charming log cabin, Wood Haven, was situated above Haleigh's Hamlet, in a forest clearing of the Laurel Highlands. Inside, in the living room, small, stained-glass lamps topped log end tables on either side of a saddle-brown leather couch. The yawning fieldstone fireplace, beamed ceilings and stout log walls created the perfect setting for solitude and relaxation. A pair of antique snowshoes embellished the wall opposite the hearth. The third wall was lined with shelves holding a colorful assortment of books interspersed with various, small antiques and artifacts. A leaded-diamond window on the back wall looked out onto the wooded stream that tumbled merrily over the river rocks in a mini-waterfall. And outside, a myriad of wind chimes clinked and tinkled in delightful melody on the mountain breezes.

Wood Haven had electricity and water, a cozy loft bedroom, and a relaxing bathroom with a jetted Jacuzzi tub faced by logs, rendering it and everything else in the dwelling in perfect harmony with its forest setting. Antler chandeliers provided the main lighting, augmented by candle-like wall sconces that flickered to mimic actual candlelight. The cabin had everything, including a country kitchen with a pearl-grey, Victorian-style stove similar to Granny's blue one at Tara– everything, that is, except phone and Internet; and *that*, Thaddeus and Maggie both avowed, their getaway would never have.

Relaxing to the sensual music, Thaddeus sipped his wine, returning the goblet to the tray on the glass-top coffee table, the base of which was a realistic, life-size sculpture of a mountain lion. It was his house-warming gift to Maggie when he purchased the cabin several weeks before. Pausing in his scribblings, Dr. Weatherby's eyes traveled to the wall where he had recently hung a pleasing pastoral plaque that read: *Taking time to do nothing often brings everything into perspective.*

Presently, Maggie emerged from the bathroom, looking like the goddess she was. She wore a long, diaphanous purple dressing gown, that he could read through, and nothing else, other than lip gloss.

"You take my breath away. And you know it, don't you?"

"That was my plan," she purred, switching off the chandelier, to reduce the illumination to flickering candle sconces and hearth fire. Picking up her wine glass, Maggie sipped the good French Beaujolais he had purchased to please her. Taking a seat on the couch next to him, she nestled into the curve of his arm, releasing a sigh and enjoying the peacefulness of the moment– the soft music, the splash of the stream and waterfall, the tinkling of the wind chimes in the surrounding trees.

"I feel kind of guilty taking our getaway and forcing Raine to go to Witch-Tree Farm alone tomorrow," she said after a few moments of gazing into the fire. Especially since I'm the one who suggested the visit."

"She won't be alone. Beau's going with her." Thaddeus began to massage the back of her neck.

"That feels wonderful." She closed her eyes, enjoying the pressure of his strong fingers on her tense muscles. "I've noticed that Beau is changing his attitude about Raine's sleuthing, haven't you?"

"He worries about her. Raine can be far too daring, as we all know." His hands slithered down her back, and she leaned forward to accommodate him.

"That's lovely. Your hands are vanquishing all my stress, darlin'." Reaching for her glass, she sipped the red wine, thoroughly enjoying the massage. "Of course he worries. He always will, about the sleuthing, the time-travel; but he's certainly making an effort to– oh, yes, please keep going."

"Oooh, I intend to." His hands reached round to her full breasts, and she completely forgot what she started to say.

She set the goblet down on the tray, next to his glass. "Tell me, professor, what is on your agenda for tonight?" Maggie had always been a lusty witch, and she looked forward to the harmless sexual games they sometimes played, harmless but powerful in bringing about the results of goals they wished to attain. At this instant, she was thrilled by the twinkle of response she noted in his vivid blue eyes.

Reaching inside his shirt pocket, Thaddeus produced a folded sheet of paper. Without a word, he handed it to her, patiently awaiting her reaction. "As you will see, I have kept our telos– the ultimate end– succinct and simple, so that we'll be able to hold on to it at … *our* ultimate end."

*I've taught him well*, she thought, remembering the first time they had swirled their sensual skills together in sexual sorcery. She could feel herself hurtling back, past the months in time, as bright memories flashed and lingered in her essence with aching intensity.

Maggie had ignited the fires first that night. At Thaddeus' quaint English-Tudor home, where the fanciful redhead asked her lover to join her in casting a spell for success in solving a particularly alarming mystery that involved time-trekking back to the Colonial era, to the perilous Pennsylvania frontier. "All ritual spells, such as I am proposing with you tonight, that incorporate lovemaking, *consensual* acts of lovemaking, with magickal intent shared and released by the lovers, are blessed and celebrated by the God-Goddess," she had whispered to him. "And there is no stronger magick."

Now she told herself, *My professor has learned so well he has become the instructor.*

With her Mona Lisa smile, Maggie unfolded the single sheet, her emerald eyes, in the flickering light, perusing the list. In a trice, her laughter chimed like silver bells. "I heartily approve of your lesson plan, but I do have a question. Will I be graded on this, Doctor Weatherby?"

"I trust you are cognizant of the fact that I have a very unique grading system, my dear. We shall go over that in a bit; but first, I think we need to explore what tools we have to accomplish our goal."

Again the enigmatic smile curved her glossy, full lips, whilst she stretched, face up and cat-like, across his lap. "Ye—e—s—s—s, I believe this to be an advantageous proposal, for each of us and our unified goal– and I am more than agreeable."

He leaned down, lifted her head, and kissed her deeply, his tongue slithering inside her open mouth. "Shall we begin then?"

"Mmmmm, yes," she stretched out her arm and hand like a cat's paw, and he heard her voice " ... **purr**-fectly willing to let you assume the role of master. A good teacher is always learning."

"For all that I've enjoyed our little fire-side chat, I must say," he began, slipping easily into his role, "that your attire," his gaze raked her magnificent body sheathed in the see-through purple veil, "is certainly not in accordance with the academy's dress code. What is the meaning of this?" His fingers lightly circled her nipples through the dressing gown's thin fabric.

Maggie loved his teasing, and she expressed her amusement, but this time her laugh was lower in timbre. "I suppose I wanted to capture your attention, professor."

"Well, if you wanted my attention, you most certainly have it." With feather touch, he parted the see-through gown, circling each breast with a single finger. "I think, however, that these will be … just what the doctor ordered for what I have in mind."

"Then, please, make every use of them," she replied, nearly breathless.

"I want to be certain. It is very important that we both be extremely thorough in our exploration." He massaged and nipped for several minutes, while he watched her face. "We should always keep in mind that we are not only physical beings on a spiritual path, but spiritual beings on a physical path."

"Oooooh, I agree." Her eyes were closed, and her breath was coming in little gasps. "I *definitely* … agree."

"Have you decided on your next course of action, Doctor?" she queried after several enchanting moments had spun her onward.

"Don't rush me, my dear. Normally, you are a very good student. But know this– I shan't tolerate naughtiness."

"Oh no? Then you must know I can be very naughty," she breathed. "Very, *very* naughty."

"Then I shall have to deal with that, but first–" One hand held her firmly in place, as the other traveled lower and lower, slowly, ever so slowly, seductively, until she was literally squirming under his touch. She arched her back.

"Oh, you *can* be a naughty girl," he said in his best professor voice. "In point of fact, I was thinking that you might make up for it with extra credit work. But we shan't discuss that now. At the present, I want to finish my own research. Projects like this one require careful examination and analysis."

His hands busied themselves, pleasuring her as no one else had ever done. Maggie's professor was quite skilled in the art of love. He had to be, for Maggie could ofttimes be insatiable.

"Oooooooo, professor, I think you are every bit as naughty as I," she croaked a quivering groan in Eros's intensifying grip.

"You are impertinent, my dear, and you shall pay for it, when I finish my work here."

"Oh?" She strove to keep her voice level as another thrill jetted through her. "And what will you do to me?"

"I shall have to spank you," he said pointblank. "You've been begging for it for some time now, and I've restrained myself quite long enough. Keep in mind, however, that what I will administer will heighten the intense feelings that we will both need to achieve our telos– the objective we wish to bring about."

He found his mark, giving her all the benefits of his genius and talent. "If you are enjoying this, I have more for you. *Much more. Are* you enjoying it?"

"Y-e-e-e-e-e-e-e-e-s," she managed, her half-closed eyes on his face. "Give me what I want, and I'll purrrr like a hearth cat and be absolutely charming to you."

In a moment, their eyes locked, and he flicked and circled like a powerful cyclone as Maggie moaned and ground her hips to his rhythm, marveling all the while at his endless skills. "Is this what you want?"

Maggie gasped. "Oh, Doctor Weatherby, I– Oooooooooooooooh!" she cried out as the exquisite pleasance he was delivering overtook her in waves, and she abandoned herself to it.

He lightly ran his fingers down the inside of her arm and across her stomach whilst the ripples of gratification flowed from her body. "You were saying, my dear?" He continued his feather-light touching, knowing full well he would bring her to the threshold soon again.

Breathing hard with anticipation, she managed, "I ... ooooh ... have always gotten," she swallowed, "straight A's, and ... oh Goddess, yes, yes, yes," she uttered, gripping the couch at his renewed agenda, "I have always been a model student."

"This is true, and I will take that into consideration." His intense blue eyes looked deeply into hers, and she actually shivered.

Her whole body tingled. "Please, professor, carry on with your exploration. It is not my wish to interrupt your important ... *fieldwork.*"

His hands stilled as he stared at her.

"Carry on!" she ordered.

"As I said, I need to be thorough; but again, you dare to be," he reached under her and grabbed her derrière, "*cheeky*; and I warn you," he teased, "I will deal with your impertinence, though I must admit there's nothing sexier than a woman who knows how to misbehave."

"Mmmmm, as we both know, well-behaved women seldom make history." In a matter of moments, Maggie's body heated anew with the professor's ministrations. As she writhed and moved her hips to his pace, a flood of sensory satisfaction surged through her.

"Ahhhhhhhhhhhhhhhhhhhhhhhhh! Oh, Great Goddess, that was good," she gasped, completely breathless, her tip-tilted emerald eyes closing in the aftereffects of the professor's artful attention. "I so … needed that. You … you just keep getting … better 'n … better."

Dr. Weatherby looked pleased, suddenly surprising her by adroitly flipping her over, across his lap.

"Professor!!" Maggie yelped, clutching the couch for balance.

"It surprises you very much, does it? It shouldn't. You've been needing **this** for quite a while, my dear." With maddening slowness, he lifted her gown, one hand holding her in place, the other gently caressing her bare bottom. "*Bewitching*," he whispered.

In a moment, his hand came thrice down on the firm, round globes, after which he squeezed the blushing cheeks, as Maggie squealed and squirmed with desire. "Oooooooh, Doctor Weatherby, I think you're absolutely wicked. *Wicked!!*"

"I see you have not learned your lessons very well, and I *may* have to spank you a second, or even a third time." His hand kneaded and excited, causing her, again, to draw in her breath.

"Really, professor!" Maggie's tone was shrill with faux indignation. "You should have discovered by now that it's futile to argue with a redhead!"

"Now I *know* I shall have to spank you again. You leave me no choice. I take a dim view of insolence, and you would do well to remember that!" He could readily see that his provocative game had fully aroused her. "Have you nothing to say for yourself?"

"Ooooooh, I think I've been a *very* bad girl. *I can't help it.* It's in my nature to be naughty, so if you think I *need* another spanking, then a spanking is, indeed, in order. After all, I want to be able to … *graduate*," she purred in a voice heavy with sensuality that let him know she was close again to the goal.

In quick succession, he smacked her rosy tush another three times, as she murmured–

"Oooooooh, wicked! *Wicked!*"

"Now then, I think you've been duly …" he chortled, "shall we say 'warmed up,' and I believe you're more than ready for graduation; though we will most definitely want to finish our prevailing project first." He gave her glowing rump a final smack and rub, before he reached under her to transfer his massage elsewhere– until she screamed in rapture.

"A final word of warning, my dear. You'll need to watch your step in future."

"Yes … sir," she responded in her breathy voice. "Y-y-e-e-s-s-s, indeed I will."

"Come with me." He stood her on unsteady legs and led her to the large fur rug before the fireplace, where he slipped the thin gown from her shoulders, letting it fall to her feet in a misty purple puddle.

Positioning her where and how he wanted her on the rug, he began a few new fiery preparations of his own recent invention, pleasantly surprising her. "Is this what you want, my little redbird? To earn your degree, you must tell me precisely what you want, including cause and effect."

Maggie raised her head to whisper her most secret longings into his ear, kissing him passionately in conclusion.

"Yes, I think I can manage that. Why don't *you* start the proceedings while I ready myself."

"What a *magickal* idea," she breathed, her hand sliding down her stomach as her eyes closed.

Thaddeus stood and undressed, his gaze never leaving her. Then, lowering himself to Maggie's lush body, he ardently renewed their lovemaking before the warmth and glow of the crackling flames.

"Ahhhhhh, the Viking rune *Sowilo*," she said, reaching up to trace, on his chest, the painted zigzag, S-like symbol for success. "How I look forward to basking in your infinite wisdom," she whispered, her breath coming in little gasps.

"Not as much as I look forward to," he ground his hips, "*giving it to you.*"

"Harder!" she insisted after several minutes of their coupling, blowing a trilogy of hot words into his ear.

He thrust deeper, picking up his pace to give her more of what she wanted. Leaning in, he kissed her mouth hard and urgently, as she moaned against his lips.

"Y-e-sssssssss. Oooooooooooh, great Goddess ... **NOW!**"

Then they were lost, lost in a mystic rhapsody they both wished could last forever. As per their plan, they jointly held in mind and heart their telos, imaging it and shouting it aloud, together, in the throes of ecstasy, in perfect harmony with each other and the Universe.

It was written in the stars that night– for all three Sleuth Sisters were basking in the dual clutch of desire and passion.

Aisling and Ian were enjoying an evening alone in their forest abode, the rustic stone house that served as home and business for the pair of them. The senior Sister inherited the charming property, along with the means to start the Black Cat Detective Agency, from Granny McDonough, who had purchased it for Grandad McDonough as a hunting lodge.

Tonight, as it sometimes did, incense hung heavy in the air, along with the scent of candle wax.

Sitting up in bed, reading, the couple was so in tune with one another that they often picked up each other's thoughts.

"Are you thinking what I'm thinking?" Ian asked, setting his book on the nightstand, his gaze holding his wife.

Aisling did the same with her book, sending her husband a sultry look that answered his query, whilst she ran her fingers through his golden hair, pulling him close. "Come here," she said. "Some days I feel extra witchy."

"Mmmmm." His kiss was deep. "I thought our shower romp was it for tonight, but apparently, you have other plans, huh?" he mumbled against her mouth.

Her response rolled from her throat in a quiet purr, "I do. *Big* plans," she appended, reaching for him and breathing into his ear her erotic proposal.

"Well, then I think we need to remove any barriers," he said, pulling her nightgown up and off her raised arms, "so we can get to it."

"I was just about to suggest that. And this time, let's take it nice and slow." She stretched out on the bed, flinging the covers aside, arching her back when he glided a hand down her nude body. "We have *allllll* night."

Ian yanked off his shorts and knelt over her, his face breaking into a mischievous grin. "Do you realize what you just suggested? Hmmm?" Nestling his neck into hers, he began trailing kisses. "As slow as you like," he whispered, as he continued south. "Slow and intense, as you like it."

"That's how I like it," she answered huskily.

Though they had made love less than an hour before, Aisling's body began tingling with renewed need, for she was loving the feel of her husband's lips, tongue, and hands skimming over her.

"You can always do it to me, Ian," she said, with quickening breath.

"What's that, baby? What is it I do for you?" His lips were setting her aflame, making her feel as if she were tipsy.

"Turn me into a shameless wanton."

"Well then, let's release her, m' lady."

"Not yet," she whispered, lightly touching her fingers to his lips. "Let's draw it out to build the power. Hmmmmm, yes. Don't stop. That's exactly what I like. Yes, y-e-sss … ooooooh, that feels sooooo nice."

Ian was happy to resume his caressing. "You smell like gardenias … and you taste like honey." His low laugh made her shudder as more of his hot kisses traveled over her.

After several intensely delightful minutes, he tried again. "Release the lioness," he rasped.

Aisling ran her little tongue across her upper lip, laughing deep in her throat. "You sure? You know what that means, and there's no turning back. Are you up for it?" she teased.

"Take a look for yourself." In a moment, he slid his tongue into her mouth, swirling it round, twisting and turning until–

She moaned as desire pooled low in her belly. "Mmmmmmm, you were always a fantastic kisser."

Knowing that she would soon turn into the big-cat she really was, he sustained kissing her as his large hands enhanced the magick. Aisling relished the delicious sensations coursing through her. It was a liquid pleasure, and her breath caught in her throat as a thousand lights exploded behind her closed eyes. When his lips returned to her soft, warm mouth, he murmured–

"Is the lioness ready to pounce?" he queried playfully, his lips again finding hers. This time the kiss was long and lingering, leaving her breathless, dizzy– and close to ready for more.

"Soon," she whispered into his ear, a hiss of excitement escaping her. "I have every intention of giving you everything you want. But, for now, take a deep breath. Oooooh yeah, let's lux-u-ri-ate in what we're creating … make it last … make it *powerful*."

Ian fixed her with a look. "Oh, it's going to be powerful, all right." He grabbed her round the waist.

"Grrrrrrrrrrrrrr," she growled, rolling them on the bed, so that she was now on top.

"Come on," he urged, lifting her to accommodate him.

Aisling's full lips parted, and running her hands up his chest, she threw her head back. "Oh, y-e-e-s-s-s, you can always do it to me," she repeated, her voice hitched with lust. She was right on the edge, but she held back for the intensity she sought with the goal she envisioned, her husband her willing partner. She purposefully kept their telos simple, so that they could hold on to it at the supreme moment.

"And you are always so smokin' hot," he said, his hands sliding down her hips to find their true destination. There, he expertly performed all the little tricks she had taught him over the years.

Her heart fluttered at the amatory expression in his hazel eyes. "You married a witch, what did you expect?" she winked, a naughty smile playing at her lips. "Ooooooooooooh, Ian, yes, yes, yes! Keep going, baby. You know what to do … and you know what it does to me."

"As much as you like," he growled.

The smile remained on Aisling's lips– and she looked every bit the part of the wild lioness, with her shimmering blonde mane obscuring one eye. When Ian reached up to caress her full breasts, she hummed with the voluptuousness he was inciting. He lowered his hands to her bottom, as they continued to move in perfect harmony with one another, falling into an easy, delectable, rhythm.

Aisling had anticipated this night for a week, and now, it was absolutely incredible. Again and again, her pleasure peaked, whilst rivers of excitement rushed through her.

Now it was her turn to plead, because he was taking her higher than they had ever soared. "Ooh, Ian, yes!! I've … been thinking about this for days, and … mmmm, you are good … soooo good!"

"I had a good teacher," he whispered.

"But you've a *natural* talent. Don't stop … don't stop … don't stop!"

Nothing else in the Universe existed, and Aisling strove to rein the magick in. It was not the first time the blonde with the wand made a wish upon a star that came true. And the stars were in perfect placement for this especial desire.

"Let go, Ash. Let it go, and let me carry you through it!"

"Ooooooooooh, *give it to me, baby!* Now! **NOOOOOOOOOW!!"** she screamed as, together, they went spinning toward their goal, the pair of them soaring to new heights. The cry of ecstasy that escaped her caught her by surprise. Never had their love-making been so wildly intense!

Overcome with the significance of it all, they both struggled to catch their breath for a moment, after which Aisling let out a little bubble of laughter.

The elite life-energy produced by the trio of Sisters' love-making that star-fated night sped their unified telos out into the Universe. Via the power-of-three magnitude and momentum, with intention and emotion acting as hammer and chisel, they created a "magickal childe"– *a bundle of powerful energies*– that would serve and aid them in the challenging days to come.

# Chapter Six

Beau was behind the wheel of Raine's MG, as the couple motored down the highway from Tara to Witch-Tree Farm. Every once in a while, with unconcealed adoration, Raine turned her glittering green eyes on the object of her affection, who traded her regard for a studying one of his own.

*Every time I look at him now, butterflies fill my stomach, and– Great Goddess' nightgown! It's as if I'm a teenager again, in love for the very first time!* She placed a hand on his muscular thigh.

"What're you thinking? I can *feel* those wily wheels of yours turning," he joked, keeping his eyes on the highway. It was beginning to drizzle, more like descending mist than rain, but the roads were wet from a previous shower.

She swallowed. "I was thinking how much I love you," she said softly, utterly surprising herself. Rarely was she the serious one in their relationship.

A twinkle sparked in his lapis-blue eyes. "Were you now?" He reached over to slide a hand up her leg, under the black skirt she was sporting, the action causing her to draw in her breath.

"Ooh, Beau ..." Her green eyes fluttered closed, and she moved the hand on his thigh a tad upward. *I need to get back in control,* she told herself firmly. *He hasn't mentioned the M word for a while, but I'd better be careful. I might ... might agree to a handfasting ceremony, the old way. That way, if we're both not totally blissed out at the end of a year's time, we have an out. But only if he'd agree to live at Tara.* Then after a moment, she weighed in. *No, no! I'm still not ready for even that!*

"Stop," he said, "or I'll have to pull this car over."

The Goth gal laughed, removing her hand.

"Did you remember to telephone Will Granger to let him know we're stopping by?"

"Yes," she answered, her thoughts fused to the night before, when he had sent her to the moon multiple times, again and again, on rocketing rapture that transformed their lovemaking to a spiritual level.

"Good girl," he uttered in his deep voice, the words flashing her a memory, from their recent intimacy in the woods, that rushed through her like a runaway train. *Great Goddess*, she thought, turning her head to study the passing rural scenery.

When they arrived at Witch-Tree Farm, they could hear Jasper barking. Within a moment of their pulling up to the back of the house, the door opened, and the Airedale came bounding toward them, still sounding his warning that he was the farm's guardian.

"Hush now, Jasper. You know Miss Raine," Will said, coming out onto the porch.

Immediately the dog quieted, as the raven-haired Sister reached down to stroke him. "Hello, big boy! How you doin' today, huh?"

Jasper stood up, a paw on each of Raine's shoulders, as he commenced to lick her face. He not only remembered her, he seemed extremely happy to see her.

"Jasper, get down!" Will managed to croak out. He appeared wan and downright ill.

Raine was stunned by how different he looked from the last time she had seen him– only a few days before. "I should put the same question to you, Mr. Granger," she said after a moment. "How are *you*?" Before he could respond, she added, "You don't look well."

Her green gaze scanned him, and again she was struck by his sickly appearance. The old man had lost even more weight, and the bib overalls and plaid flannel shirt he was wearing hung loose on his gaunt frame.

"I'm takin' one day at a time. It's what ya do at my age," he returned, shifting his tired-looking eyes to Beau.

"Oh, forgive me," Raine said quickly. "This is my … other half," she said, finding it impossible today to use the more casual word *boyfriend*. Beau Goodwin. Beau, this is Will Granger."

The men shook hands, exchanging greetings, after which Raine, whose eyes had never left Farmer Granger, questioned, "Are you OK?"

"I've been better," he answered. "Let's go inside. Cold and wet out here. C'mon, Jasper," he called. The dog was sniffing the ground, on the trail of a critter that had passed that way earlier. "Jasper, come!"

Once they were all inside the cozy kitchen, Raine asked, "Will, might I fix you something to eat?"

Granger seemed to recoil. "No. I've food a-plenty that my niece has been sendin' over. No way I kin eat it all. A couple days ago, I telephoned t' tell her to stop." He convulsed, seemingly seized by pain. "Couldn't eat all week."

Raine and Beau exchanged looks, then sat down at the table, where Will indicated they should sit.

"Can I put some coffee on for you?" the farmer inquired, still standing, but looking as though he might collapse at any moment.

"No, thank you," the couple answered, with Beau saying, "Mr. Granger, I'm a veterinarian not a physician, but I can clearly see you've got a jaundice look ... yellowing of the skin and the whites of your eyes. You look quite ill. May we take you to the emergency room?"

"No," he answered, dropping down into the nearest chair. "T'wouldn't do no good. I know what's wrong with me, and there's no help for it."

Raine leaped up to put a hand on the farmer's shoulder. She was shocked at how bony it felt. It was as though her fingers had touched a skeleton. "Tell us what's wrong. Maybe we can help," she persisted.

"Can't nobody help me. Not even God," came the quiet response. Noting the looks on their faces, he said, "I learned this a long time ago. Expectin' life to treat you well 'cause you live a good life is kinda like expectin' an angry bull not t' charge a vegetarian." He attempted a smile that fell short to a grimace of pain.

"Let me get you some water." Raine stood to open the refrigerator, only to find it crammed with untouched plates of food that Amanda had sent to her uncle. Seeing no water jug, she closed the door and, spying a glass on the sink, let the water run to allow it to get cooler. After filling the glass half-way, she handed it to Will.

One sip, and he set the tumbler down on the table. "I'll tell you what it is." His face seemed to go grey. "'Cuse me," he said, rushing from the room as swiftly as his feeble legs could take him.

Raine's eyes found Beau's, her face mirroring the emotion churning inside her. "Cancer?" she mouthed quietly.

He patted her hand, and his grieved expression told the tale.

A few minutes later, when Will reentered the kitchen, he looked even worse than when his guests had arrived. "Damn heaves and vomitin'!"

"Mr. Granger," Beau said in a concerned voice, "are you certain you don't want us to take you to the hospital? They could make you more comfortable."

Granger sagged heavily into the chair he had vacated earlier, waving the offer aside. "Hell no, son!" he choked out. "When I go, I want to die at home. I'm glad you're here. I've a couple things I want you to do for me, but the damn hospital's not one of 'em." With that, he unbuttoned his cuff and raised his sleeve to reveal a patch on his upper arm. "For the pain," he stated. "I'm dyin'. Pancreatic cancer," he pronounced drily.

"Oh, Will! I'm so terribly sorry. What can we do for you?" Raine asked, reaching out to take his hand between her own.

"You and your sisters ... cousins–" pain interrupted him, and he grasped himself round the middle, holding up a calloused hand for Raine and Beau to leave him alone. "I'm askin' you to do whatever you can to protect Witch-Tree Farm and the tree."

Raine started to speak, but again Will raised a quivering hand, this time for silence.

"If," he went on, "for whatever reason my niece 'n her husband can't take possession of the place, then make sure it goes to the historical society, just as I've stipulated in my will. You and Miss Maggie were witnesses, so you know," he winced again in sudden pain, "you know what I want."

"You can count on us," she said, as tears filled her eyes. "Does Amanda know?"

Will shook his head as another pain knifed his stomach, traveling round to his back and just about doubling him over. He waited till it passed to speak, during which time, involuntarily, Raine's hand flew to her mouth. As empaths, both she and Beau could feel Will's suffering, and it was not an easy thing to perceive.

The Airedale moved across the room and laid his whiskered head on Granger's knees with a whimper.

"Jasper knows." With a wan smile, Will scratched behind the dog's ears. "He knows it's my time. He's been stuck to me like glue all week."

Keeping his head on Will's knees, Jasper lifted his eyes to soulfully regard his master.

"I've kept th' truth from Amanda, tellin' her m' nerves are shot due to the naggin' pests after my farm." Will's face darkened a bit. "Partly true anyhow. She don't know the real ... the whole truth. Neither does Sam. Don't want them troubled by this, especially not Amanda. She's not strong." The old man appeared to be reaching back in memory for something.

Finally, he said, "Remember when you and Miss Maggie mentioned that marker the Commonwealth of Pennsylvania grants to historic sites?"

Raine bobbed her head, not trusting her voice.

"Well, see if you three Sleuth Sisters can get one for my farm– for the Witch Tree. That should help to protect it in years to come. Can you do that for me?"

"We're thinking the same thing, and we'll sure try our best to accomplish it. It'll mean doing research, learning who Hester Duff really was, what she did in her life, but *we'll do it*, Will. We'll find out everything we can about her, and we'll prove that she was a good person. Why," she pointed in the direction of the tree, "the scientific phenomenon alone should merit a marker! My stars, her name is burned into the tree for all time!" She gave a curt nod, as a determined look spread over her face. "We'll get that historic plaque, and we'll protect your tree and your farm. Don't you fret about it." She looked to Beau, and seeing the compassion in his deep blue eyes, she directed her question to Granger, "Do you want us to stay with you today?" She already knew what he would say.

The old man coughed out a response, "This week's been ... *bad*. Don't think it'll be long now. Yes, if you kin stay, I'd be grateful." He paused, fighting down the nausea. "I'm glad you came over. You can do a couple more things for me. Can you feed Jasper? And son, can you help me upstairs to my bed?"

"You got it," Beau answered, standing to wash the dog's bowl and freshen his water. A hefty bag of dogfood was setting in plain view near the back door.

"Why don't you let us get you upstairs to your bed first, where you can lie down?" Raine asked. "Beau will stay with you, while I feed Jasper."

"No, I want to be sure Jasper's fed. *After*, make sure my neighbor, Gail, takes him till Amanda and Sam move in here. Ask Amanda to move in as … soon as she can, because Jasper's a handful, and Gail ain't no … spring chicken. I've already talked to Gail about Jasper. Make sure she takes his food. Her number is by the phone. So is Amanda's. But don't call them now. *After*," he finished, breathless, as more pain gripped him, and he strove not to retch.

"Mr. Granger, did your doctor give you anything else for the pain besides the patch?" Beau asked.

"These tablets," Will answered, picking up a bottle from the counter near the sink.

Beau read the label on the bottle. "When did you last take this medication?"

Granger glanced at the kitchen wall clock. "Time for it now," he said, moving to the sink, where Beau handed him a glass of water and a pill.

Raine finished washing the dog's dishes, replenishing the water bowl, while Beau filled the food dish. Then, he and Raine, each taking an arm, helped Will upstairs to his bedroom.

"Beau, why don't you help Will into a pair of pajamas? I'll wait out in the hall," she said.

"I'm glad you're here," the old man repeated for the third time that afternoon. "No one wants to die alone."

"No one ever dies alone," Raine answered softly. She squeezed the large, rough hand she was holding. "Are you certain you don't want us to telephone Amanda and Sam? They would want to be with you."

Granger's face took on a wild look. "*No!* She lost her parents … to … drunk driver years ago. Both killed. Poor gal … went through hell. Don't want her to see me … like this. She'll know soon enough … but at least … I kin … spare her this."

The racking pain had gotten progressively worse, and there were times, in the past three hours, when Raine and Beau both thought Will Granger had passed over. The sun had long set. Mercifully, the old man had drifted in and out of sleep all day. Taking Raine aside, at one point, Beau told her the end would come soon.

"If only," he whispered, "we could make human deaths as painless as we do animals'.""

Will's wrinkled, sunken eyes opened slowly. His breathing had been labored, but now, of a sudden, it seemed to ease. The pained expression in his yellowed eyes softened, as they traveled to a corner of the room, beyond the two people sitting at his bedside. He smiled, prompting Raine and Beau to turn, to see what he was looking at. All they saw was a faded green chair. "You're here," he whispered.

Raine pressed the calloused hand again. "We're here, Will. Don't worry; we're not going to leave you."

Still, the old man was not looking at Raine or Beau. He continued staring beyond them, with his unwavering smile, at the corner and the chair. "No," he answered, more alert than he had been all day. It's my Bonnie. She's come for me."

Raine turned partway round to again glance at the chair.

On the opposite side of the bed, Beau leaned forward to touch Will's thin shoulder. "Yes, Will, she *has* come for you. It's OK; you can let go now. She's here to take you *home*."

"J–" Will labored for breath, "an' it's m' brother Jeff! I never thought I'd see Jeff again. And my … my mother!" He tried to sit up, but couldn't, fastening his eyes on Raine. "Can you see them?"

"I *sense* their presence, Will," she answered. "They've come to guide you through the tunnel to the Light." She enfolded his hand in both of hers. "They're waiting for you, Will. It's OK. We'll take care of things here."

"Jasper," he uttered, when the dog, lying next to him on the bed, whimpered, staring fixedly into the corner.

"Don't worry about Jasper," Beau and Raine said at once.

"Amanda, Sam, 'n Jasper …"

"Yes," Raine replied, squeezing the dying man's hand. "We'll make sure they take care of Jasper."

"Take Bonnie's hand, Will," Beau said softly, his own hand still resting on the old man's shoulder.

Will gave a half-nod. "They're waiting … f'r me … have to go. It's– *beautiful*." He closed his eyes, and the smile relaxed on his lips, as he released a long, final, breath.

Beau felt for a pulse. "He's gone, Raine."

***

"Are you all right?" Beau asked, as they drove home later that night.

"Yes. I hope we made all the proper calls and did everything we should do."

"We did. Was the niece angry that you didn't telephone her sooner?"

"I don't think so, but she sounded inconsolable. I'm glad Will's neighbor, Gail, dropped in when she did. She'll take care of Jasper till Amanda and Sam move to the farm."

Beau cast Raine a quick glance, before returning his eyes to the road. "It was a good thing you were able to communicate to the dog, baby. We might've had trouble getting him to go with the neighbor. He didn't want to go. What did you tell Jasper?"

"I told him that Will *wants* him to guard Gail now; and then, when Amanda and Sam move in, in a few days, that Will wants him to carry on as the guardian at the farm, just as he always has. I–" her voice caught, and she waited a beat before continuing. "I also told him that he'd be with Will again one day, and then they'd be together forever, that this was a *temporary* separation; but for now, Will was really counting on him to carry on as the family guardian."

Raine stared out the window in silence for several moments, gathering herself before going on. "Amanda said on the phone, they couldn't take Jasper to their apartment, but she was going to ask the landlord if he would excuse them from the last two months of their lease. That way, they could move into Witch-Tree Farm soon and take Jasper with them. Right now, she's only thinking of the loss of her uncle and the funeral arrangements."

After a moment, Raine remembered she hadn't telephoned High Priestess Robin, Maggie or Aisling. She decided to call Robin first, then Aisling. She wasn't sure if Maggie was still at the cabin, where she wouldn't be able to contact her. There was no land phone at the cabin, and both Maggie and Thaddeus would have turned off their cells, if they were still there. She foraged for her phone amidst the clutter in her purse and speed-dialed the High Priestess. Within a couple of rings, Robin answered. Trying not to cry, Raine related that Will Granger had passed away.

"Oh no! No!" Robin exclaimed. "How? How did he die?"

"With a sigh of relief," Raine stated softly, suddenly realizing that was exactly what Will's last breath had been.

What the Sister did not realize was that someone had been watching her and Beau as they drove away from Witch-Tree Farm.

Meanwhile, Raine and Beau weren't the only ones being watched. At the mountain cabin where they were abed, Maggie and Thaddeus, too, were being stalked.

"What's the matter?" the redheaded Sister questioned, sitting up in bed.

Thaddeus was peering out the window, through a chink in the curtain. "Shhh, someone's out there."

"What?!" She started to get up.

"Stay down and quiet!" He stared out, into the night, for several moments, saying, "I'm going out the back door to find out who and what we have here."

A look of concern clouded Maggie's face. "You be careful," she answered, sending him a strong protective light, as, step by step, he edged down the loft ladder to the floor below, his clothes flung over his shoulder.

Both were holding their voices to a whisper.

Maggie crept out of bed, keeping low, to shadow Thaddeus down the ladder. In the living room, she hid behind the drape to peer through the window. When she looked out, she saw a dark figure, then another, skulking around the side of the cabin.

She wasn't too worried, for, incongruous with his scholarly appearance, Dr. Weatherby held a black belt in Karate. However, she did take a moment to implore, "Divine Mother, Mother Divine, show me the way, give me a sign."

Pulling on his khakis, Thaddeus said softly, "Keep quiet; stay low and away from the windows. Don't turn on any lights. I'll be back directly." He exited the room on silent feet and slipped outside.

When the professor started round the corner of the cabin, someone grabbed him from behind. "Where you goin', old man?!" a youthful male voice jeered. Thaddeus broke loose with a powerful roundhouse kick to the groin.

"Aaaaaaaaauuuuugh!" the attacker fell to the ground, when–

A second attacker, brandishing a crowbar, came at Thaddeus from the front, only to be met with a snap kick to his groin, followed by an elbow smash to the face. He instantly dropped the weapon to clutch his jewels. "Ooooooooooooooooooooooooow!" he yelled as he too went down.

Standing over the pair, who looked to be in their late teens or early twenties, Dr. Weatherby said in a stentorian voice, "You two are lucky I'm here, or else you'd have tripped the silent alarm. The police would be arresting you by now, and you'd be facing charges. You still might!"

Lolling on the ground, the intruders groaned.

"We weren't going to steal anything. We just wanted a place to crash for the night," the one rasped.

"Yeah, let us go. I give you my word, we won't be back," the second one pleaded.

"Your word, huh? How very comforting. Just to make sure," Maggie said, appearing in Thaddeus' hastily donned trench coat, her smart phone in hand, "we want something to remember you by." She quickly captured a photo of each of them. Looking at the images on her phone, she said, "Well now, you each take a nice picture. Very nice, indeed."

Roughly grabbing the first assailant, Thaddeus jerked him around to yank his wallet from his pants. "Here, Maggie, get a nice clear shot of their driver's licenses too."

When the second young man attempted to stand for a getaway, Dr. Weatherby expertly collared him and, snatching his wallet, held it out for Maggie to capture a photograph of it.

"Now," Thaddeus thundered, "you two better hope and pray no one ever breaks in here, because the police will be coming after *you*. And you have *our* word on that."

"You can't do this. It's blackmail!" the one who had wielded the crowbar hollered.

"No, it's insurance, *our* insurance you'll never come back here. If you do, then you *will* pay," he retorted with a grunt. "Like I said, you'll be the ones arrested. And can't you freakin' read?!" Thaddeus gave the nearest man a thump alongside his head, pointing to the No Trespassing sign posted on a nearby tree, where a light shone on it. You're breaking the law just by being on my property." He hurled the wallets at the two prowlers. "Now pick 'em up and get the hell outta here before I *really* lose my temper."

***

Once everyone attending the graveside service was seated in the folding chairs under the tent-like shelter, the Reverend John Summers began to speak.

"We are gathered together today to commit William Elijah Granger to his final resting place beside his one true love, Bonnie McFadden Granger. We gather to comfort each other in grief and to honor the life that Will led– a life that was filled with hope, happiness, laughter and love in the good times, as well as the bad.

"Three days ago, Washingtonville lost a fine man. I knew Will Granger personally, as his pastor and his friend, for many years. He was a devoted husband and uncle, and he was an honest, hard-working man with integrity …"

Since their classes were cancelled due to a heating problem at the college– it was turning out to be an especially frigid November– Maggie and Raine were able to attend Will Granger's funeral service. Aisling, however, could not attend. She and Ian were called away to Pittsburgh for the day to deal with a current case.

Upon leaving the small Greenridge Methodist church, family and friends had driven to the cemetery. The Sleuth Sisters were seated next to one another, off to themselves, in the back of the tent-like shelter, and to the side, where they could observe the actions and reactions of everyone. It was their way.

Leaning toward Maggie, Raine whispered into her ear, "I'm surprised to see Mildred Grimm here, not to mention Reggie Mason and Sirena Chambers ... even Etta Story for that matter."

Maggie turned her head to give a moment of concentration to the fore-mentioned attendees. Then, leaning in, she whispered to her sister of the moon, "Could be they want to make a good impression, so they can start working on Amanda and Sam for what they each want."

Raine dipped her head in subtle agreement. *Coven's all here.* Her green gaze traveled over the assembly. *That's Gail Friday sitting next to Amanda and Sam. The others must be friends from the Grange and the church Will belonged to.*

The minister carried on. "Though Bonnie and Will had no children together, they were very special mentors in so many folks' lives ..."

The Sleuth Sisters noted that many of those present were nodding their agreement, and a sob rose from Amanda, as her husband tightened his arm around her.

It had dawned cold and turned colder; and now, large, fat flakes began to descend with the area's first snowfall of the season.

"Will was like a father to Amanda and Sam Woods ..."

Again, the reverend's words brought a sob from the deceased's devastated niece.

"Will loved his wife, his niece and nephew-in-law, and he loved his farm and his animals. He was a friend to everyone ..."

As the minister talked on, the Sleuth Sisters' observant gaze continued to peruse the gathering. One person in particular caught their attention. Their sharp eyes noted that this individual constantly stared at a single attendee– and that one only. For now, they filed this observation away, to be discussed later.

Moonglow and Starlight were glaring, unabashedly, at Mildred Grimm and the two land developers, Reggie Mason and Sirena Chambers, who were all sitting across the aisle from the Coven sisters. Gail and Sam, flanking Amanda, were constantly endeavoring to comfort her, as she wept throughout the service.

"To signify Will's promise to his very special niece, I invite all of you who wish to, to come forward and take a small amount of this soil from Will Granger's farm to bless his final resting place." Reverend Summers indicated the large bowl of earth from Witch-Tree Farm, as most of those present rose to queue up for the soil. The minister began the invocation, then, from the *Book of Common Prayer*, "Ashes to ashes, dust to dust …"

Music began to play softly from a recorder, an *Amazing Grace* instrumental. The Sleuth Sisters went forth to each scoop a handful of Witch-Tree Farm's soil, whispering a blessing of their own before letting the earth drop onto the casket, which was suspended over the grave on the straps of the lowering device. Raine and Maggie had both taken special notice of those present who did not participate in the soil rite.

Amanda waited to the last before letting her handful of earth from Witch-Tree Farm sift through her fingers onto her uncle's casket. She remained contemplative, whence she whispered, "Rest in peace, Uncle Will. I'll never give up the beautiful legacy you left Sam and me. *Never.*"

"And be gracious unto him and give him peace. Amen." Within a few moments, the minister closed the prayer book he held to announce, "Thank you all for coming. We shall all hold William Granger in our hearts from this day forward, remembering him for his good and loving heart, his hard work, his selfless ways, and his generosity. Here ends the ceremony. Here begins Will Granger's new life. Amen."

The recorder keened with the beautiful old Christian hymn *Going Home*.

"Going home, going home … I'm just going home …"

*Oooooh*, Maggie thought, *music is what feelings sound like.*

Reverend Summers moved from the head of the coffin, at graveside, to Amanda and Sam, putting a hand on each of their shoulders. He whispered something inaudible to them, then stepped discreetly away so that friends might exchange words with the couple, before they headed to their cars.

"Work all done, cares laid by ... going to fear no more ..."

As Mildred Grimm was leaving, she paused before the grief-stricken Amanda to say, "I'm sorry for your loss, Amanda, but perhaps now you'll think seriously about –"

Amanda cut her off with a curt wave of her hand. It was clear, by her expression, that anger was fast bubbling to the surface, and though she did her best to keep her voice low, the intensity carried on it was clearly heard by everyone lingering at the graveside gathering, where the tension was palpable.

"We just put my uncle to rest," she began in a terse voice, "and now let us put this nagging to rest once and for all. I will *never* part with the farm. Do you understand? And you are *not* going to browbeat me the way you did my poor uncle. I'm *appalled* you have the nerve to show up here today." Amanda turned her swollen eyes to Reggie, Sirena, and Etta, and her voice came out with an edge of hard resentment. "Do you *all* hear me?! I will never sell! *I will never part with the farm!*"

Sam had started to add something of his own, but instead, chose to focus on Amanda. He was trying his best to hush and comfort his wife, pulling her, in a protective gesture, close to his chest and soothing her with soft words. For a moment, Amanda wept quietly in her husband's embrace, allowing herself to relax; then, catching sight of Mildred Grimm still looming menacingly before her, looking for all the world as her surname, the sobbing young woman sniffled, "Go away and leave us in peace!"

The town council president turned and started walking toward her vehicle, where she was joined by Reggie Mason, who pulled her aside. With their heads together, the pair continued talking through whispered exchanges, as the gathering began breaking up, and *Going Home* played on–

"Momma's there expecting me ... papa's waiting too ..."

It was snowing hard now, and a biting wind snapped at the remaining people at the graveside.

When Raine and Maggie approached Amanda, Raine especially was unsure of how Will's niece would react. However, she broke from her husband's arms to heartily hug the raven-haired Sister. "Thank you," she whispered tearfully, "for making sure my uncle didn't die alone. I appreciate what you did for him."

"I so wanted to telephone you, but, Amanda, he flat-out refused. He wanted to spare you whatever grief he could." Raine returned the embrace.

"He's in the Summerland now, darlin', a Shining Land," Maggie whispered, reaching out to take Amanda in her arms. "Where there is no pain, only Love, Light, and Joy."

"Yes," the grief-stricken woman replied. It was not her word for the afterlife, but she was in tune with Maggie's message.

"Our Irish granny used to say that Death leaves a heartache no one can fill, but Love leaves a memory no one can steal." When Maggie released her, Amanda kissed her cheek.

"Tell me, Raine, did he suffer? Tell me the truth, please, I need to know."

The music played on. "All the friends I knew ..."

Raine considered, answering after a careful moment, "He was tired, Amanda, very tired. He was ready to go." She took the young woman's hand and led her to the nearest chair, sitting down beside her. Then, still holding the hand between her own, she poured out what Will had seen during his last moments– his beloved Bonnie, his brother and his mother who had departed before him. Lastly, she shared with Amanda how peaceful her uncle had gone, with a soft smile and the words "It's beautiful" on his lips.

"Going home ... going home ... I'm just going home ..."

Amanda hugged the raven-haired Sister again. "Thank you. That is most comforting. You've been uncommonly good to us." She thought for a long moment, remembering, the Sisters supposed, something about her uncle. "I just can't believe he's gone, Raine. Unk was my hero, and heroes *never* die. Sam and I just spoke with him the evening before. He talked about his will, how he–" She shook her head, as two tears streamed slowly down her face. "Forgive me; this is difficult."

"Go ahead and cry," Maggie uttered softly. "Cry all you want. A person who doesn't know how to weep with the whole heart doesn't know how to laugh either."

Amanda attempted a thin smile, indicating her husband with a tilt of her head. "We'll be moving to the farm in a few days. When I asked him, our landlord released us from the final two months of our lease. Sam and I both want to get moved as soon as we can. For one thing, we want to take Jasper." She turned her head to regard Gail conversing with Sam a few steps away. "Gail's been so kind, but we don't want to take advantage of her."

As if she heard those words spoken of her, Gail Friday turned her head to send Amanda Woods a consoling smile.

When Raine and Maggie started for the redheaded Sister's green Land Rover, they were struck by the glowering looks both Mildred and Reggie were directing at Amanda and Sam. In addition, they noticed that Etta Story, standing at the top of the swell of land, next to the road with its line of parked cars, was observing everyone, studying the little groups that had formed. The look on her face was almost calculating, as though she were planning something. As the Sisters watched, Moonglow and Starlight joined the historical society president, and the three began talking quietly, close together, for several minutes.

Breaking away from a cluster of her Coven sisters, High Priestess Robin linked arms with Raine and Maggie, walking between them toward their vehicles. As they passed by Mildred Grimm, they heard her grumble to Reggie, "What are all these … *heathens* doing here today?!" She darted the sisters a glance of reproach, after which she screwed her face into a sneer and made a sound that came off as a hiss, rendering her, more than ever, the archetypal wicked witch.

Raine returned the look with one of sharp rebuke. *Ignorant, pompous ass.*

*Insufferable dolt* were the words that leaped into Maggie's mind.

The Sisters had taken an immediate dislike to Mildred Grimm, and now the feeling tripled in intensity. They watched as the town council president and Reggie Mason again put their heads together for whispered dialogue. When they broke away, Grimm's face, as she cast a final glance at Amanda and Sam at graveside, registered a surly expression. Trading looks with Robin, Raine and Maggie kept their opinions to themselves.

Essentially, they had been concentrating on picking up as many thoughts as they could garner from those present at the service. Thought-harvesting from others, rather than from one another, was not an easy task for the Sisters to accomplish; nevertheless, when circumstances were right, it could be done.

"Amanda's going to really need Sam's support now, more than ever," an elderly man remarked before opening the car door for his wife.

Looking back at the couple, as they stood hand-in-hand, alone now, over the casket, the Sisters saw that the woebegone Amanda's lips moved in silent prayer.

"That's one thing I don't think we need to fret about," Robin commented to Raine and Maggie. "From what I hear, he's always worshiped the ground she walks on."

"A single dream is more powerful than a thousand realities."
~ Granny McDonough

## Chapter Seven

When Tara's phone rang the next evening, Maggie was somewhat surprised to hear Eva Novak's pleasant voice.

"You asked me to keep my eyes and ears open for anything that I thought might help you in your current quest," the Tearoom proprietress began. "Well, I think I have a piece of information you should know. Can you stop in tomorrow after your classes are done? I'm on my cell, and I really don't want to discuss this over the phone."

Maggie thought for a second, "Tomorrow's Thursday. Yes, Eva, Raine and I will stop in for an early dinner tomorrow, sometime after four-thirty. Thaddeus may be with us."

"Great. See you then."

"Thank you, Eva. Bless you!"

Once Raine, Maggie and Thaddeus were seated at The Gypsy Tearoom, Eva found a few free minutes to scoot into their booth, next to Raine, so she could speak to them.

"You will never believe who was in here yesterday, nice and cozy, in one of my booths!" she said breathlessly, leaning forward, toward Maggie and Thaddeus, to keep their conversation as private as possible.

"Who?" came the united reply.

When the proprietress voiced the two names, Raine and Maggie exchanged the thought–

*No! Surely not!* Then they turned their shocked expressions on Eva.

"I was pretty sure who they were. They've both been in here before– though not together, and I think that's what threw me. I wasn't a hundred percent certain of their identities. So later, after they left, and I had a breather in my customer flow, I looked them up on the Internet. You know, to find out if I was right– *and I was.* You see, after we talked about all this the first time, I looked everyone up on the Internet. Anyway, they sat in my most private booth, opposite one another, but I saw them holding hands across the table a couple-a times. And the way they were gazing into one another's eyes," Eva wagged her blonde head, "well, they looked to have more than a nodding acquaintance between them, as the saying goes."

"Levitation!" Raine exclaimed. "Did you pick up any of their conversation?"

"Only fragments, I'm afraid. They were whispering, and every time I approached their booth, they got as quiet as a bird with the red-tailed hawk overhead. I pretended to do all sorts of things near that booth; but, as I said, they clammed up every time I got close." Eva reflected for a moment. "I did catch one thing the man said. He asked her to hold someone off from doing something. At least, I *think* that's how he worded it. It looked as though he was trying to talk her into something, or that he was trying to talk her into getting someone else to either do something, or not do it. I also caught the phrase, 'No matter what I have to do!' *That* was louder than anything else the man said, so I had *no* trouble hearing it, and … you know what I'm tryin' to say; it was spoken with more emotion, so I remember it verbatim."

Eva gave a huge sigh. "I'm sorry I didn't get a-hold of more. My booths are designed for privacy, and," she shrugged, spreading her hands, palms up, "that's how it is. This is probably not much help to you, but I just felt you should know what little I could tell you. It didn't look– what's the word?" She lifted her shoulders again in a shrug, settling for "*Right*. It just didn't look right to me. I've no proof, mind. It could've been a perfectly innocent lunch with a friend or acquaintance, but it didn't look … or *feel* that way to me. Do you know what I mean?"

The Sisters looked to one another, answering, "We do."

"And– oh, here's the best part, and I pert near forgot to tell you– I heard *your* names mentioned. 'The Sleuth Sisters.' But again, I couldn't hear what they said. I only heard one word after your names were spoken. *Watched*." Noting the looks on all three of her patrons' faces, Eva thought to repeat, "That's what I caught– *watched*." She pursed her lips, raising her expressive blonde brows. "What do you make of *that?*"

*\*\**

The turning wheel of the year, each season has its own glory for witches, for Nature is their church, their place of healing, where the wise go to rejuvenate, to listen to the trees, the wind, the rush of the water of ocean, river, or stream; but *autumn* was Raine and Maggie's favorite time.

That fall, the leaves of southwestern Pennsylvania had exploded with color– red, yellow, gold, maroon, purple, and ochre; and the surrounding forests seemed to glow with jewel-like intensity. The foliage began to change around the second week of October, and by the third and fourth weeks, it was magnificent. Now, at mid-November, most of the leaves had fallen. Still, it was autumn, and here and there, wee splashes of color remained.

There is a peacefulness, a drowsiness, about a Pennsylvania autumn, with a luster to the sky that doesn't exist at any other season. Raine, Maggie, and Aisling always held that there was something indefinable about this colorful time of year– something *magickal*– about the clear, brisk days of October and November especially. *They could feel the spirit of autumn.*

Though it carries a punch of yearning, the Sisters advocated that this was the season when emotions overflow, a whole realm of emotions, and the starry-eyed Maggie said she could sense romance everywhere.

Early in the season, the first sight of the Canadian geese in the sky, honking and flying in their V formation as they pass through on their way south; the first frost; the first smell and sounds of the furnace kicking on; the leaves drifting by Tara's windows, flurrying down and along the ground before the wind that plays a wistful tune, misty and melancholy like a piece of music in a minor key; a carved jack-o'-lantern sitting in a window with toothless grin or scowling frown; the soft, comforting glow of candlelight or hearth fire; the crackling sounds of a fire or fallen leaves beneath the feet; the last leaves in November that, having clung so tenaciously, now drift from the withered trees to the ground to welcome the repose of winter– to the Sisters, a Pennsylvania autumn was always dreamlike and enchanting.

"I never stop dreaming in the fall," Maggie often said.

"Perfect weather for solving a mystery," Raine was prone to say.

This year, right after *Samhain*, a good hard frost came swiftly in the night– a sly, stealthy visit from Jack Frost, the winter sprite, who turned Tara's windows lacy white. An unseasonably cold spell followed; but now, all of a sudden, capricious Indian summer, all mellow and soft, was passing through in one of its surprise sojourns.

Carrying her tea out to the screened-in back porch that evening to enjoy the faerie lights in and around their fountain, Maggie said, "When Indian summer graces us with her presence, as she almost always does here in Pennsylvania, nothing indoors seems important." The redhead let out a long sigh. "Of course, the wind can change overnight, and with a wave of Jack Frost's wand, we wake up to winter." Her gaze traversed the cozy area. "We need to put our porch fountain and furniture to bed for the season. Let's do it Saturday morning, and then we'll take a nice leisurely ride. Except for the paddock, the horses haven't been exercised for three weeks. We owe them and ourselves an outing." She sipped her tea, after which she said to Raine, who had decided to pick up her own cup and follow Maggie to the porch, "So, darlin', what do you make of Eva's scandalous tidings?"

"Know what? A nice ride through the woods and a gallop over the fields will help to cleanse our auras. As for the scandalous tidings, well, you know what Granny used to say." Raine laughed, amending, "Granny and Edgar Allan Poe, that is– 'Believe only half of what you see and nothing that you hear.'"

Maggie suddenly remembered something. "You know what some folks deem is the cure for a broken heart, don't you?"

"What?"

"Money."

"Who th' devil said that?" the Goth gal blurted. "Surely not Granny."

Maggie sent her sister of the moon what the latter often referred to as the *Look*. "My ex-husband," she replied in answer to the question put so smartly to her.

Raine downed a quick swallow of tea, guffawing, "Your ex-husband! He's been married, what? Five, six times?!"

"True, but the logic is still sound."

"Maggie, this doesn't sound at all like you," Raine refuted.

"That's because it isn't me. Allow me to explain ..."

"Although ..." Maggie oscillated several minutes later, "it *could* have been an innocent lunch. Perhaps an offering of peace and sympathy, or, as it were, tea and sympathy. Maybe they just ran into each other at the Tearoom, started talking and decided to share a booth." She tilted her head. "But you and I know, in our cores, it *wasn't* an innocent lunch; and, too, *Eva* had a feeling that it was more. *Much* more. She's not only a good friend, she's a really good psychic."

Raine concurred with a brisk movement of her head. "True. Granny taught us to always trust our instincts. They are messages from the soul. I'm thinking this is a case of 'We're all like the bright moon– *we still have our dark, or as the case may be, darker side.*'"

"And that *phrase* Eva heard the man speak! 'No matter what I have to do!' *That* really bothers me." Maggie looked through the screen to the starry night sky. "I think Eva's spot-on with her hunch. There's something not right here. I've often thought– and we've learned this lesson the hard way– *some people are difficult to read.* Practiced evil-doers can *veil* their wickedness– and quite nicely too– appearing in stolen light. To paraphrase the Bard from *Macbeth*, the innocent flower could well have the serpent beneath!"

"I say! You're right about that!" Raine bellowed. "*That* sort damn near got us killed solving our last mystery!"

"And now, we just might've stumbled onto another example of a wolf in sheep's clothing. *The innocent flower with the serpent beneath,*" she repeated to herself, brooding. "For *now*, darlin', the Eva info is something we file away, to be used later." Maggie copped a swig of tea. "And my witch's intuition is that we *will* be making use of this sticky-wicket file– sooner than later."

"There are no accidents in life," Raine pronounced. "We asked Eva to keep her eyes and ears open, and consequently she saw what she did *for a reason.* Y-y-yes, I agree," the Sister ruminated with a bob of her head. "We'll be making use of this information before too long."

"The word *watched* troubles me in connection with *our* names. I told you what happened to Thad and me at the cabin. Just a couple of punks, but I wonder. I wonder …" She paused to polish off her tea whilst she puzzled over the matter.

Raine looked a bit shamefaced. "I never said anything to you before, but there've been times in the past few days when I felt watching eyes."

Maggie instantly came out of her reverie. "Watching eyes?! Where?"

"The day you and I talked to Mildred Grimm and Etta Story at the library in Washingtonville and the evening Will passed over, when Beau and I were leaving Witch-Tree Farm."

"Well that settles it then," Maggie said firmly, setting her teacup down in its saucer. "*We* better start watching too. And we start by watching our backs!"

\*\*\*

From their small stable, Raine and Maggie headed into the woods on horseback, following the trails that Hugh and Beau graciously kept clear for them. The stable was situated far to the rear of the house, on Tara's triple-size lot. Its cupola was topped with a witch weathervane like the one on the house's highest gable. Before Beau attached either to the rooftops, the Sisters infused the witchy guardians with strong blessings of protection.

Full of mettle and mischief like his owner, Raine's jet-black Arabian, Tara's Pride, was a feisty gelding that always appeared to be in a hurry. Even his walk was hurried, if one could actually call it a walk; and today, though Indian summer lingered, a brisk wind and the fact that, other than the paddock, he hadn't been out, rendered him, as his mistress was apt to say, "Rarin' to go!" The Goth gal maintained a tight rein until they could get to a clearing.

"You're a real beauty." Maggie patted the sleek neck of her chestnut mare. "You know," she directed to Raine, "I was thinking of changing her name due to all the craziness in the world; well, I changed my mind instead," she finished, interrupting herself. "Isis is named for the Egyptian goddess of magick and life. It suits her, and I'll not change it."

"Nor should you." Raine leaned forward in the Spanish saddle to smooth Tara's ebony mane. "Who was that on the phone earlier? When I came in from getting the paper, you were just hanging up. I meant to ask you then, but remembered I had to go upstairs for something, and afterward it slipped my mind."

"Oh, sorry, darlin'. We got in a rush to get down to the stable, and I forgot to tell you that Robin rang to say she'd run into Amanda at the grocery store yesterday. The will's been officially read, and Amanda told Robin that if, for any reason, she and Sam don't, can't or whatever, take over or hold on to Witch-Tree Farm, it will go to the Washingtonville Historical Society."

"As Will told us himself," Raine reflected with a nod. "Did she say anything else?"

"She said she and Sam would be moving in a few days. In fact, right after the Washingtonville Harvest Dance. Since she was on the food committee way before her uncle died, she's still going to bake apple treats to bring to the affair, though she doesn't feel in any way like celebrating. She told Robin she and Sam aren't planning on staying, but are only going to drop off her offerings."

Raine squeezed her thighs, and her mount's quick walk instantly became a stately trot, Maggie's mare, with soft whinny, moving easily into the new rhythm, the Sisters posting.

After several minutes, the brunette patted her horse's neck, reining in to slow to a walk. "Easy now, big boy. We'll be at the meadow before too long, and I'll let you have a nice gallop to release that pent-up energy." To Maggie, she said, "How *is* Amanda? I mean, how is she *really*?" She posed the question with a raised brow, turning partway round in the saddle to face Maggie on the trail behind her.

"Robin said she sounded *melancholy*; that's the word she used. Said Amanda was looking forward, however, to the move and to picking up Jasper. By the bye, are you and Beau still going to the Harvest Dance?"

"You bet! I've always wanted to go to Washingtonville's Harvest Dance; but, until this year, Beau was never free to take me. Thank the great Goddess for Hugh, huh?"

"Wasn't the Harvest Dance always in October before? It should be anyway," Maggie asked of a sudden.

"It *is* in October; but this year, it had to be moved to November, due to work being done on the Washingtonville Grange. Robin said it's an old building, a former barn, that needed renovation," Raine answered. "The work was supposed to be done by mid-October, but Reggie Mason, of DHM Construction, didn't deliver on his promise, so they had to reschedule the Harvest Dance for November."

"*Reggie*," Maggie mused, "I've been thinking about him, and you know what …"

The pair discussed Maggie's thought until a cardinal flew to a nearby branch, emitting little chirps, whilst the wind whispered secrets through the boughs, the sound reminding Raine of the wind-listening she had experienced several days past at the Witch Tree.

The redheaded Sister, too, was enjoying the commune with Nature. "The winter birds have settled in. We'll have to make time to keep up with our birdfeeders. Not good to start them and then quit." She gazed up, through the tree branches. "We see more sky now, and it's as soft as a dove's breast. Oh, look, there's a grinny out and about on this Indian summer day! Busy little rascal!"

When the chipmunk scurried off, Maggie's crystal laugh zapped Raine out of her meditation.

The cardinal resumed its chirping, as it flew from branch to branch, paralleling the Sisters' progress.

*When a cardinal appears, it's a loved one visiting from the Other Side*, Raine thought. "All right, Granny! Maggie," she said louder, "let's ring Aisling when we get back to the house to ask her to come over here tomorrow. It's Sunday, and with any luck, she'll be free. It's time the three of us consulted Grantie Merry's crystal ball Athena for whatever she can tell us about Hester Duff. We especially need the *date* when the incident at the Witch Tree took place, when Hester burned her name into the tree. That way, we can go back in time and witness everything that happened. But first, we need the exact date in order to program our Time-Key!"

"Yes, we promised Will. We want to *keep* our promise, so we better get started!" Maggie reasoned. "Raine, I've been thinking. After we get the date from our crystal oracle, why don't we program our Time-Key for the day *before* the incident at the tree? Then we can plan to meet Hester, have a heart-to-heart with her, and speak perhaps with others in the area *about* her. That MO has worked for us in the past."

"First-rate proposal, Mags! That's exactly what we'll do. Do you think Thaddeus will want to accompany us?" she teased, knowing full well what Maggie's, or for that matter, Thaddeus' response would be to that query.

"Need you ask?!" Maggie replied, matching Raine's impish tone. "Hey, did you realize you said *Grantie*, rather than *Auntie* Merry?"

Raine giggled. "I did. That's my new name for her. I'm spelling it g-r-a-n-t-i-e and slurring it together à la French *liaison*. Think about it. She's our great-aunt, and she's granted us so many blessings of wisdom and gifts, including the very special crystal ball Athena."

"*I like it. Grantie* Merry it is! Athena has already proven to be a *great* blessing– the purrrr-fect companion tool to our Time-Key."

They rode in silence for a while, save for the sounds of the horses or the occasional bird. After several minutes, Maggie spoke wistfully, "In the fall, I sort of miss the long summer twilights, when days seem to linger indefinitely, and we can take our evening tea on the back porch. The days are shutting down early now. But I love the frosty cobweb mornings! They have a crystalline sparkle, don't they, darlin'?" Without waiting for an answer, she said, "And I love seeing the shadow of Tara, silvered by the great Goddess' frost, when sun has melted the crystals on the lawn."

"Hmmmm," Raine replied, thinking aloud, "next week we should take the screens off. The storm windows are in the garage, newly painted and ready to be put on. I'll ask Beau. I had a feeling we were in for a fickle Pennsylvania Indian summer, so I hesitated asking him to do it sooner." She drew rein.

They had come to the meadow. Exiting the woods, the Goth gal whooped. As Tara's Pride broke into a full gallop and into the open field, she delighted in the horse's smooth stretching and the rush of the wind in her ears. "Last one across is a mutton-headed muggle!"

\*\*\*

The following day, Sunday, the trio of Sleuth Sisters trooped up the attic stairs to Tara's top floor, where they habitually wove their spells and performed other feats of their magick. On their heels, as they always were when magick was afoot, trailed the three Merlin cats– Black Jade and Black Jack O'Lantern and Panthèra. The two other cats– Tiger, the brown tabby, and Madame Woo, the Siamese– were exactly the opposite. They preferred one of Tara's warm radiators or comfy, sun-splashed window seats to spellcasting.

Leading the way, Maggie carried the battery-operated lantern they kept on the bottom attic step. True to her musings, evening descended early in November. It was dark, and they needed the extra illumination, in addition to the night-light in the stairwell.

At the top of the stairs, the redheaded Sister paused on the landing with the lantern. Raine pulled on the creaking attic door, holding it open, as Aisling and the cats, then Maggie, with lantern in one hand and the poppet Cara in the other, all filed in. There, the women took down the black ritual robes hanging from pegs at the entrance to Tara's uppermost room.

Once the Sisters slipped into their robes, they reached beneath the bodices to lift out their talismans, each suspended from a chain round the neck. Raine scooped up Black Jack to walk the circumference of the attic room with her deosil, clockwise; whilst Maggie went, with lighted lantern, to the wooden bookstand that held their ultra-thick *Book of Shadows.*

The huge tome's black leather cover was embossed in gold gilt with full-blown Triquetra, the ancient Celtic knot symbolizing all trinities– *and infinite power*. Above it, from a thick oak beam jutted a hook; and that's where Maggie hung the lantern, splashing the colorful, hodgepodge room with the soft glow of light and the mystery of shadow.

Supporting their granny's grimoire and occupying a place of honor before three grand stained-glass windows, the vintage bookstand had been prized by Granny McDonough because it was the lectern used by the celebrated orator William Jennings Bryan when, at the turn of the last century, he had come to speak at the Hamlet's Addison McKenzie Library.

A former maid's quarters, Tara's attic was dominated by its trilogy of stained-glass windows, the tall center one the largest, displaying the symbol and soul of Ireland– a golden harp. The two smaller, flanking, stained-glass windows each depicted a bright-green shamrock, another symbol of Ireland, and one of the supreme Trinity.

There were two stairways, the "front" and the "back" (the back being the "servants' stairs"), leading to this attic room, the Sisters' sacred ritual room, that they referred to as the "Heavens." It seemed a fitting name since it was the place where they did most of their spellcasting, weaving powerful magick; and it was here they conjured their dear granny. Today, however, they would be conducting another ritual– the ancient ritual of scrying.

The spacious attic room's furniture was an assortment of odds and ends, touched by Time and not fitting enough for the rest of the manse, but too steeped in memories to cast away, such as a green velvet couch and two somewhat lumpy, but still handsome, easy chairs in a rich claret shade of a fabric that had come from *Belle Époque* Paris. An antique spinning wheel stood in one corner, and in another was a stack of curious old hat boxes, a couple from Edwardian London that held cunning little hats with veils. Maggie, especially, enjoyed sporting those witchy hats for the added mystery their veils afforded her.

Atop two cabriole end tables rested a pair of porcelain lamps. Chipped from decades of use, the glowing lamps' bases depicted romantic scenes of eighteenth-century lovers engaged in a waltz. Once, after a particularly strong conjuring session, Raine reported to Maggie that she'd actually seen *and heard* the dancing couples swirling in a spin-two-three Viennese waltz!

On each end of the attic room, two domed trunks occupied places under the eaves; whilst the center of the scarred-wood floor was graced by a threadbare French carpet, its floral design faded by Time, sun, and the treading of countless feet.

Whenever they regarded that carpet, Raine and Maggie recalled Granny's musical brogue: "So many waltzin' feet have tripped th' light fantastic over this rug! Sure 'n it holds so many magickal memories an' energies, I cannot bear to part with it, though it's as old as the hills."

One piece of furniture in Tara's attic room was not chipped, faded, worn or shabby, though it was most certainly old.

This was the tall cheval glass that had accompanied Aisling Tully McDonough, "Granny," as the Sisters called her, on her fateful journey from Ireland to America. The antique mirror was likely worth a fortune, so ornate was it in carved giltwood with Irish symbols and heroes from the Emerald Isle's turbulent past. Bestowed on her by a favorite uncle when she was quite young, it had been Granny's most cherished keepsake from the Old Country. The Sisters wanted to preserve as much of Granny's essence with that mirror as possible; and so they kept it in their sacred attic room, draped, when not in use, with a protective ghostly sheet. Hence, no one else ever handled (confused the energies of) this treasured family heirloom.

On one side of the mirror hung Granny's Irish knit shawl; from the opposite side dangled a favorite necklace, a long, thick rope of pure silver from which hung two round, silver Gypsy bells. Granny had purchased the charmed necklace years before in Ireland, "… from an especially talented tinker." She always declared that the bells' delightful tinkling soothed away her troubles and brought to mind the shell chimes she remembered hanging in the windows of the Old Sod's seaside cottages. The shawl, in a spider-web design, and black as jet, sparkled with dozens of tiny aurora borealis crystals. Granny's widow's weeds had enfolded style, as well as a great deal of magick!

Raine always made it a point to choose something of Granny's to hold in her hand from a small treasure box of things that rested on one of the cabriole end tables. Today 'twas a pair of pearl earrings. Then, as was her custom, she stood for a few quiet moments at the tranquil trilogy of stained-glass windows, peering out the clear portions to the faerie-tale Hamlet below. In a mysterious way, did a mist oft hover over the beautiful but contrary Youghiogheny River.

To center herself, the Sister drew a deep breath, releasing it slowly. The sight of the curving ribbon of river never failed to relax her, freeing her mind of unwanted thoughts and anxieties. Once in a while she would hear the lonely, nostalgic sound of a horn from one of the boats, as it navigated the fog pockets. In the fog, sounds carried a long distance, seeming ofttimes to echo. It was a curious thing, that. Sometimes, Raine even imagined she heard voices in the fog.

Perhaps she did.

After having set their poppet down on the chair where she would be sitting, Maggie used her wand to draw a second circle of protection around the attic room, calling upon the God-Goddess, their angel and spirit guides, as well as the guardians of the watchtowers– the spirits of the four elements– to secure their sacred space.

Aisling busied herself with the lighting of four white, beeswax candles, whilst Raine was touching her lighter to a frankincense-and-myrrh incense cone in its burner. With the aid of a large, purple feather, the Goth gal fanned the smoke, allowing the aromatic fragrances to permeate the entire area before setting it down on a stand.

Successively, Maggie lit three small bundles of white sage, each in a big, fan-shaped seashell; after which, she handed them to her sisters of the moon, keeping one for herself. Carrying the smoking sage in a clockwise motion, the Sisters cleansed the room of negativity, all the while chanting a smudging mantra.

"Negativity that invades our sacred place, we banish you with the light of our grace. You have no hold or power here. We stand and face you with no fear. Be you gone forever, for now we say– this is *our* sacred space, and you will obey!"

"Let us, all three, walk the room one last time, together," Aisling advised, beginning another cleansing chant, "We cleanse this area completely free of any and all negativity."

The Sisters walked deosil thrice, chanting and cleansing in perfect accord, as Tara's attic room took on the pleasing mingled aromas of burning white sage, candle wax, and "frank and myrrh."

At that, Maggie swished across the attic room, her black robe fluttering behind her, to switch off the lantern hanging above their lectern-held *Book of Shadows*. Before she did, however, she opened the grimoire and checked something on a ribboned page.

Having properly smudged their sacred space, the three Sleuth Sisters seated themselves about a small round table from which they temporarily removed a lamp. The lit lamp, now the attic's only illumination, rested on a trunk positioned behind the colossal, amethyst crystal ball that their Great-Aunt Merry of Salem had christened "Athena."

"Just a reminder: Grantie told us we must always address our crystal oracle by her name," Raine recapped, looking across the table at Aisling, to whom she had explained their mentor's new title the evening before on the phone. "Maggie and I gave Athena a nice cleansing just before you got here. As per Grantie Merry's instructions, we bathed her with a soft cloth in tepid water and a mild, good-smelling dishwashing soap."

"Perfect," Aisling replied, conjuring the visit, the past spring, with their beloved great-aunt at the Witch City of Salem, in faraway Massachusetts. "We must keep her physically clean. It will cleanse her energies as well." The senior Sister placed her hands lovingly on each side of the ball, whilst she spoke quietly. "Before we program Athena today, we'll also have to smudge *her* with white sage, as Aunt– Grantie taught. Remember, we'll need to smudge her, *before* and *after, each* session, so no negative energies will ever do her *or us* any harm.

"Now," Aisling sighed, "when we begin, the leader will do *some* talking, while the others remain silent and focused. I hardly need remind you that it's a difficult discipline to master, talking and focusing when scrying. Auntie–" she looked to Raine, tossing her a grin. "No worries, I'll get used to it. *Grantie* has been doing it for many decades, so it's no problem for her."

Aisling looked thoughtful. "I'm thinking *Maggie* should be the one to lead this scrying session rather than me. She is the most gifted with a crystal ball. More than you and I," she said to Raine.

"You did a fine job of it last time, Maggie, and I have confidence you'll do so again. Yes," Aisling decided, getting an agreeing nod from Raine, "*you* lead us, Maggie. **You** had the vision that time of Grantie and Granny handing *you* the ball. And none of us can deny the power of a vision. Have you and Raine read over Grantie Merry's instructions, that you transferred to our *Book of Shadows*, so we can be certain of hitting all the steps?"

Raine and Maggie answered concurrently, "We have, Sister."

"All right then. As before, let's begin by making physical contact with Athena," Aisling directed. "Stroking the ball, before using it, energizes the crystal and strengthens our psychic bond with our oracle. We need to do this now– the three of us together."

For several moments, simultaneously, the Sisters caressed the amethyst crystal ball, gently passing their hands over the cool, smooth– and quite lovely– purple surface. Athena was so large, this action was effortlessly accomplished.

Finally, Maggie, balancing their poppet Cara on her lap, reached deep into the pocket of her ritual robe for the Lemuria oil she had remembered to put there earlier. Glancing at Aisling, she held the vial out to receive an assenting look from the firstborn Sister.

Maggie dabbed a bit of the oil on the third-eye area of her forehead, passing the ampoule round to Aisling and Raine. The redheaded Sister, thenceforth, began a deep breathing pattern, allowing all the stress and negative energies to flow completely out of her body as she exhaled. During the meditation, her two sisters of the moon followed suit, breathing deeply, each at her own rhythm: *Healing energies in ... negative energies out. Healing energies in ... negative energies out ...*

"Healing energies in ... negative energies out," Cara repeated in her tiny voice.

There was a silence as the magickal threesome, with their poppet, applied themselves to the task. It was always at this juncture of the ritual when Raine remembered feeling, last spring at Grantie's cottage, like a child waiting, with eager anticipation, for the white rabbit to be whisked from the enchanted depths of a wizard's top hat. Quickly, she did her utmost to tame her excitement. It would *not* do to be expectant, not for crystal-ball scrying!

After several minutes, Maggie opened her eyes and began focusing on an area of the ball to which she felt expressly drawn. "Focus," she pronounced in her silky voice, "focus on an area of Athena's crystal depths that draws each of you in."

Several quiet, peaceful moments lapsed, after which Maggie began to chant softly, "Athena, as we go into a trance/ Bestow on us the magick glance/ Take us back in time today/ Reveal what happened come what may/ Back in time two centuries twenty-nine/ When Washingtonville was in its prime/ Whence Hester Duff burned her name into her tree/ We ask the date; this is our plea/ Take us to her little shack, for all the images and the clack/ For long-kept secrets to be unlocked/ Within the hours of the clock/ That you have chosen for us to learn/ *The date!/ The facts!/* For *that*, we now return!"

As the colossal crystal ball's powerful energy commenced to flow, the seated, black-robed Sisters imaged their vibratory levels rising to harmonize with the antique sphere, henceforth to craft the needed psychic connection.

*The magick was working! All three witches could now **feel** Athena's super power coursing around them and through them like an electric shock!*

"People who create their own hurtful drama,
get their own very special Karma."
~ Author Ceane O'Hanlon-Lincoln

# Chapter Eight

Within a few minutes, each of the Sisters began to experience a strange tingling sensation. Maggie and Aisling felt a surge of heat, whilst Raine felt suddenly cooler. The Sisters were adjusting to the ball's vibration– each in her own way, through the same sensations they'd experienced during previous scrying sessions with Athena.

"Remember, expectation is *not* helpful," Maggie reminded softly, keeping within the trance. "We know from experience now, we must clear away any and all expectations. We will see what Athena wants us to see– nothing more, nothing less.

"Let us allow our minds to become as clear as the crystal. *Relax ... relax* and look into the ball's deep crystal cavern. Hold your gazes, Sisters. Grantie counseled that sometimes making connection with Athena takes what seems like eons, other times not. We *know* we can do this. We've done it successfully before. Yes, we ..."

"Shall see what we shall see," the poppet, swaying slowly from side to side, crooned from her position on Maggie's lap, blending her voice with the Sister's.

Keeping their regards on the ball, not blinking an eye or moving an inch, all three Sisters smiled inwardly as, within a few ticks of the clock and the big crystal ball's mystical amethyst depths, a ghostly mist appeared.

"Ahhhhhhh, our connection with Athena has been made," Maggie drawled softly. "The door is opening. Keep your focus. Let Athena's mists draw us in. That's it," she droned. *"Good."*

*"Ver-ry, ver-ry good,"* Cara warbled quietly.

Inside the amethyst ball, the ethereal mist swirled, slowly at first, then faster, then slowly again, before the crystal began to clear.

"Hmmmm," Maggie hummed serenely, "now let us drift. Light as feathers, let us drift inside Athena's crystal cave ... for like Merlin's, it will show only Truth. Soon now, the light and sound images, indestructible and eternal to the Universe, will reveal to us what we seek–"

"At what Athena lets us peek," chimed the poppet in her tiny voice.

*"Whatever* will be..." Maggie whispered.

"Whativer we see …" Cara interjected, anticipating the redheaded Sister's next words.

"Remain calm," Maggie finished her thought, "*calm*, so not to break the trance with emotions."

As the mists cleared, Maggie recalled something significant about which Grantie Merry had warned. Careful not to raise her voice, she cautioned softly, "We might see and hear what we do not anticipate. Often, this is so, but Athena knows best what we need to know," she rhymed smoothly.

"A spell in rhyme works every time," Cara trilled.

"Indeed it does. Again, I hark back to Grantie's directive. Allow Athena to take us where she will. *What we need to know she'll show us* … that's the drill." Maggie's full lips were open slightly, as she sighed softly, endeavoring to keep her own serenity. "Do not try and make sense of anything till everything has faded away, for attempting to sort out will only break our spell and our bond with Athena today.

"Simply *allow* the scenes, one into the next, to flow. *Calm and centered as we go.* That's it, Sisters, keep feelings at bay. When the magickal movie ends, everything will fade away." Maggie drew in another breath, slowly releasing it, as she kept her focus and her gaze.

Her fellow sisters of the moon and their poppet did likewise. It was easier this time from earlier sessions with Athena. Within the Sisters' sacred circle of protection, even the Merlin cats appeared wholly sedate, sitting in purring contentment with half-closed eyes, sending out, each of them, what Raine referred to as their comforting Number-Three Purr.

Meanwhile, out of the evaporating mists inside the crystal ball, an image of a humble Colonial log cabin was gradually taking form.

A clearing encircled the cabin and, beyond, as far as the Sisters' eyes could discern, dark forest. Though it was night, the Sisters could see an assembly of frontiersmen walking into view from the tree line. Several were holding lit lanterns and flaming torches. All carried Pennsylvania long rifles. And in the dazzle from the lamps, the Sisters could clearly recognize anger stamped darkly upon their grim faces.

Increasingly, the magickal trio and Cara were drawn deeper inside the ball's crystal depths, there to witness exactly what had unfolded that mysterious night, over two centuries past, when Hester Duff's name was linked for all eternity to what became known as the Witch Tree.

Irrespective of their experiences thus far with Athena, Aisling, and most especially the impetuous Raine, grew evermore eager, so much so they could scarcely draw breath. The Colonial image inside the ball fluttered, close to disappearing, as the Sisters strove to control their emotions.

Forthwith, all three skilled witches heard the distinct pounding at Hester's cabin door, after which angry shouts rose from the mob.

"Open the door, Mistress Duff! We know you to be t' home!"

"Come out, witch, and face your accusers!"

"You cursed our harvest, and now you'll pay for what you did!"

"We'll make you pay for the evil you've done!"

*Thus far, seems like the legend matches what happened,* Raine told herself.

The heavy cabin door groaned opened to reveal a woman of medium stature with hair as black as pitch and eyes a deep, intense blue; and though those eyes sparked in the blaze from the lit lanterns and torches of her irate neighbors, Hester Duff looked to be a– **W**oman **I**n **T**otal **C**ontrol of **H**erself.

She wore a long black dress topped with a clean, white apron. Her glossy, black hair cascaded over her shoulders in loose waves, as though she had recently freed it from a braid. Standing her ground, Hester calmly faced the shouting men. She spoke not a word, but, rather, stared fixedly with her intense witch's gaze at her accusers.

"Let us bind her arms and legs 'n toss her into Moon Lake. We'll *see* if she be witch or no!" a burly frontiersman in the front yelled.

"Bah, we know she's a witch. I say **hang her!**" a man within the angry swarm shouted. "She destroyed our crops. Our families will starve! An eye for an eye! **Hang her**! 'Tis what she deserves!"

Another quickly rose to the bait, shouting with rage, "I vote with Dan'el! **Hang the witch!**"

"**NO**!! Be not so hasty and so rash!" a stentorian shout exploded over the din of voices, a Scottish burr thick on his words. With swift strides, he pushed and threaded his way through the pack. "Hark you, man! Have ya a padlock on yer arse that you shite through yer teeth! We want to banish her, dr-rive her away, *far-r* away, from 'r settlement, but lest we f'r-r-git we aire Christians here!"

Raine and Aisling drew in their breaths, making certain to keep their own emotions in check. Remarkably, the passionate Maggie was having an easier time of it. "Relax, Sisters, *relax* … Athena will show us what she will," she repeated softly.

"Aye," the poppet murmured, "steady on now."

Hester took a step forward, visibly squaring her shoulders and coming into full view of the enraged frontier farmers, as well as the Sleuth Sisters, who, with bated breath, were gazing with focus into the huge crystal ball.

"'An eye for an eye' you say!" Mistress Duff cast her witchy glare over the irate men, and her look was sated in scorn. "You know not yer own Book, neighbors! Those words be not a blessing for revenge, but a caveat. If you take an eye, an eye will be taken from *you!* Does not the God you pray to advocate 'Vengeance is Mine'? I have heard you preachify it often enough!"

Again her deep-blue stare traveled over the crowd of what appeared to be about fifteen men. "Do you never cease from accusin' me? 'Twas a storm took yer harvest. I have done nothing wrong. Quite the reverse, I have never forsaken man or beast that waire in pain. If truth be told here this night, I bestowed succor upon th' lot of you– **you ungrateful varlets** gathered here to do *me* harm. Will ya never cease yer bullyin'?!" Her beautiful eyes skimmed the crowd, who hushed to hear what she would further say.

"**You**," she pointed an accusing finger of her own, "Tom Baker! I delivered yer babe. Your wife would have died iffen I had not, for the babe was turned in her womb." Again Hester's eyes swept the crowd, who pressed forward either to better hear her words or do her imminent injury.

"**You**," she pointed at another, "John Chandler! I nursed you back to health when you raged with misery from the fever!" Her gaze fell upon the man next to him. "James Cox! Have **you** forgot how I saved yer sorry hide when you were bit by that rattler? Has the serpent's bite turned *you* into a snake, f'r 'tis venom that flows from yer mouth this night!"

"And **you**, Daniel Thatcher! Didya f'rgit how I sewed you up after that bear attacked ya last spring?! Iffin I had not come upon you in th' forest and got ya back to me cabin, y'd not be standin' here this night, roarin', like th' drunken sod ye aire, t' hang me from the nearest tree!"

The frontiersmen looked to one another. A few appeared ill at ease after Hester's scathing remarks. None responded directly, though inaudible mutterings erupted within the press of disgruntled men, now mere inches from Mistress Duff, who continued to stand her ground, facing her accusers with dignity and courage.

"Ah, I see Wiley Edwards hidin' in yer midst. Have you, Edwards, f'rgot how I mended yer horse that went lame so's you could put in yer crop last April? And, indeed, how I mended yer boy when he tore open *his* leg last winter? You sought me out then, for ya knew I was the *only* one who could save th' young master from the vile poison that got inta his blood!"

Hester stared at the men for a long, smoldering moment, finishing. "You've short memories in these parts."

"Nay, we remember, witch! We remember how you cursed our crops! How do you expect us to survive this winter with our harvest gone?! An' all th' signs foretell a long, hard winter a-comin'!" a farmer shouted over the mutterings of the torch-bearing horde.

"'Twas not my doin'. I have *not* cursed yer crops. 'Tis guilt makes ya think in this twisted, sick way! You see others as yerselves– bitter, thankless, and fault-findin'! But I am **not** like you, nor wud I want t' be! If there be wrong doin' here, it is *you* who bear the guilt of that! *You* who are filled with hate. You hate because you fear, and you fear what you do not understand. 'Tis cowards y' aire! Weak as water– every man jack of you!" Hester hurled at the men, who were stirring to new anger. She shook her head in utter aggravation. "Your world is *dark*, bereft of all Light, as if you want for sun, moon and stars!"

"Enough of this jawin'!" a man in the rear shouted. **"Seize her!!"**

With that, several of the rabble rushed forward to take violent hold of Hester, who began to thrash against their rough hands. "Release me, you who call yerselves Christians, lest you be treated as you treat me! Ya preach one thing, and you practice yet another! *Humbugs*, the lot iv ya! **Humbugs 'n cowards!"**

"No more of yer trouble-brewin', witch! May ya choke on yer evil curses! Take her to that stout tree, yonder!" the man who seemed to be the leader called over the clamor of raised voices. "And tie her there whilst we decide her lot!"

As the Sisters watched, the men dragged the struggling Hester to what would become known, ever after, as the Witch Tree. There, amidst the mad shouting, they secured her to the trunk with a strong rope.

Then, just as the Sisters had always envisioned, Mistress Duff looked to the stars. Her lips began to move, and her eyes closed. Within a matter of moments, a wild wind roared in, an awesome reminder of Nature's power; even as dark clouds raced, like a runaway horse and trap, to veil the moon and stars. A great fork of lightning rent the black night sky, and thunder rolled over the watchers like a rumbling dirge of doom.

"How now! Storm's a-blowin' in fast!" a young, portly farmer in the front hollered. He wet a finger to hold it up. "A nor'easter. Let's hurry 'n fire her cabin with everything in it! That will force her to go and take her evil curses with her!"

"Nay, y' puppy! Aire y' daft?! Wind's too strong f'r that!" interposed another.

More thunder could be heard in the distance, though, strangely, there was no accompanying rain. Suddenly, the men, as well as the watching Sisters, realized that it was not only thunder and loud cracks of lightning they were hearing– but gunshots.

From out of the darkness, the sound of Indian scalphullos reached the mob, who stampeded across the clearing to take refuge inside the cabin, leaving their bound prisoner behind to her fate. Her midnight hair blowing wildly in the fierce wind, Hester again looked skyward, uttering her petition.

"Let the Injuns solve 'r problem f'r us!" one of the men shouted, as he ran, with the others, for the log shelter. "Kill an' scalp th' witch!" he bellowed to the veiled forest foe before ducking quickly inside.

At once, shots were exchanged between the frontier farmers and the unseen Native Americans– lurking somewhere in the dark, mysterious cover of the surrounding woods. It was impossible for the frontiersmen to tell how many Indians were out there, just as it was impossible to get a bead on any of the attackers. In addition to the pall of night, smoke was heavy in the air from the flintlocks going off, one by one.

For the next several minutes, the wind continued as boisterous as the shrouded Natives, whose feral shrieks rang out from one segment of the forest to another, giving the impression there were more in the war party than the watching history professors reckoned there to be. It was an old Indian trick– the moving to and fro, hither and thither, amidst thick forest cover, to give the impression of a large force.

Still no rain fell. The wind seemed to be dying down; when, in a literal flash– and louder than any shot fired– an ear-shattering crack of lightning crashed against the tree, felling a huge limb and startling the frontiersmen as well as the focused, ball-gazing Sisters.

Smoke covered the area, veiling the forsaken, tree-bound Hester from sight.

After getting off a few more scattered shots, accompanied by their bloodcurdling yells and shrieks, the Native Americans grew unexpectedly quiet.

Realizing the Indians had ceased firing, the gunfire from the cabin also ended.

Some minutes passed in near silence– a lull that to the watching Sisters and their poppet seemed like an eternity– before a couple of Hester's persecutors crept stealthily from her log dwelling.

By then, the smoke had all but cleared, and though the wind had calmed considerably, the thunderstorm had not blown itself out. The curious thought struck the Sisters that a dry thunderstorm in autumn with no heat and humidity was highly unusual. As professors of history, Maggie and Raine reasoned that the two men emerging from the cabin were likely rangers, who would scout a wide radius to make certain the Indians had left the area.

Keeping low, the men ventured first to the tree, where they had secured Mistress Duff. What they found there astounded them, inciting the younger of the two to momentarily forget his ranger training.

Instinctively, he called to the others, who remained either inside or close to the shelter of the cabin, "She's gone! The rope is yet tied, but th' witch has–!"

His words froze on his lips when another great bolt of lightning forked the sky, lighting up the area with the great burst of its energy. A faction of the remaining men rushed forth from the cabin to see, at that express moment, in the bright flash, the name H-E-S-T-E-R burned deeply into the greyish-white bark of the tree's rough trunk.

"On this day, 31 October 1787," one of the frontiersmen proclaimed in a somewhat quaking voice, "we have witnessed something *not of this earth*! ***God protect us!!***"

All three Sisters got so excited then that the images and sounds blurred, faded, and vanished in the crystal ball's swirling grey mists. The witches knew, then and there, that their current session with Athena was over.

"Bloody hell!" Raine exclaimed in exasperation. "We didn't get to see *how* Hester accomplished her disappearing act and where she disappeared *to!*"

"To quote Scarlett O'Hara, darlin', 'Tomorrow is another day,' and to cite both Granny and Grantie Merry, 'Every day holds new magick, and gratitude today can transform our tomorrows!'" Maggie's voice carried more than a trace of the dissatisfaction she was feeling toward the Goth gal for allowing her Aries impetuosity to get the better of her.

Raine stuck out her tongue at her sister of the moon in a fine Scarlett imitation. "Fiddle-dee-dee! I want to know **now**! I hate *waiting* for anything!" And she stamped her foot, emphasizing her words.

"Aw, stop yer messin'!" Shaking her little head with its faded yarn hair, Cara released the traditional trilogy of tsks.

However, to the Sisters' surprise, from the ball's eddying mists, nearly gone now, surfaced a familiar face– a sweet and beloved countenance, smiling at them to impart comforting words–

"Merry meet! 'Tis Grantie here, my dear girls, Cara," the image in the ball announced cheerily.

Without speaking, the poppet gave a wee bow of acknowledgment, whilst the Sisters traded surprised looks, with Raine blurting, "*Grantie?!* How did you know we've started calling you that?"

"I have my ways!" the *grande dame* of the magickal McDonough clan laughed in a way that reminded the Sisters how their great-aunt had received her nickname.

Meredith "Merry" McDonough was an average size woman. That is, she was of medium height with a slight build, but her physique was absolutely the *only* average thing about her.

A cloud of white hair, which she wore in a loose bun, softly framed her once cameo-pretty face. In point of fact, Merry was still comely, even as a centenarian.

The previous April, the Sisters had helped their great-aunt celebrate her hundredth birthday, when they visited her in Salem, and Grantie informed that, when she left this world, her 300-year-old seaside cottage with most of the things in it would go to them. Cognizant of the Sisters' time-travel, and knowing– as she did many things– what an asset Athena would be to them, Grantie decided to allow her great-nieces to take her antique crystal ball back to Haleigh's Hamlet when they left the Witch City.

Captivated once more by Athena's strong magick, the Sisters regarded Grantie's benevolent visage. Hers was an intelligent, sensitive face, with grey eyes of a peculiar and searching intensity. Her features were what many would term "classical," and for most of her life Merry used nothing but a soft-pink lip color and a light dusting of powder on her surprisingly unlined skin.

To look upon this pink-and-white confection, one, if not familiar with Merry McDonough, would think of her as a "sweet little old lady," but Grantie Merry was anything but. Indeed, she would have *cringed* at that description. Not to say that she was unkind and hard-hearted, but she was certainly not made of sugar candy.

"My," she was saying from the huge ball's crystal depths, "you're beginning to have great success with Athena, as I knew you would, of course! Aisling, you are wise to appoint Maggie, yet again, to lead." Merry grinned, repeating something the Sisters had heard from their great-aunt on an earlier occasion. "Maggie's super-sensual nature is purrrrrr-fect for directing your scrying sessions. It's prudent to have your poppet and familiars with you too. Well now, that's enough for today, my dears. When we finish chatting here, conclude your ritual, and be certain to follow the proper steps.

"Raine, my impetuous little pixie, Maggie is right. Give it another go in the days to come, if you three find you need to scry more information on this new quest of yours." She inclined her snowy white head to one side, lending her the appearance of an amiable cockatoo. "Raine, don't pout. It's impossible to tame the spirit of one who has magick in his or her veins, but you could use more self-discipline in your life, dear girl. I've been telling you that since you were three!"

Before Raine could respond, Grantie said, "I hope you'll all be coming up to Salem for your cousin Emerald's wedding. If … *when* you do, I've another surprise that I prefer to give you in person. You're doing so well with Athena that I've decided to let you have something else I know will make a great supplement to your Time-Key.

"But getting back to Emerald," Grantie chortled, "you know our Emerald," she expressed with a roll of her eyes. "She's changed the wedding date thrice. At the moment, she's planning a traditional, Old-Way handfast at Beltane. 'Twas your cousin Sean who presented her with that idea; and, to be sure, it's an admirable one, but we shall see. I'll keep you informed, my darlings. I daresay Emerald's rolling along her road of enlightenment quite nicely. She's much better than she used to be; but, as I said, she's still our fanciful, flawed but many faceted, one-of-a-kind Emerald.

"Now," their great-aunt declared, bringing her bejeweled hands together in pure delight, "the *real* reason for my appearance today at the close of your session with Athena: I happen to know that Hester Duff has a direct descendant who lives ... well, not terribly far from Haleigh's Hamlet. You'll have a bit of a drive, but Hester's successor has something in her possession that will answer several of your questions and will aid you emphatically in clearing Sister Hester's good name. I have the contact information right here, so if you'll write it all down ..."

After giving the Sisters the information about Hester's descendant, Grantie Merry's benevolent image seemed to fragment, snap, and vanish as rapidly as she had appeared, her parting words echoing in the shadowy attic room, "Bles——sed beeeeeeeeeeee, dear————ies!"

Grantie's merry laugh, however, lingered all around the Sisters, like the silvery shimmer of stardust after a meteor shower.

"**Blessed be!**" they chorused joyously.

"Blessed be!" the poppet restated, lifting her little arms in emphasis.

Then, as per their great-aunt's teachings, they stroked the colossal amethyst ball, side by side thanking the God-Goddess for helping them via the magnificent crystal oracle.

"May the circle be open yet unbroken," they finished a few minutes later, releasing the energies they had summoned.

The happy witches ended by smudging Athena with more of their white sage. Covering the crystal ball with a black velvet cloth and settling her comfortably back inside her protective case, Raine restored Athena to the built-in cabinet, they kept locked at all times, in their sacred attic space.

In addition to the cleansing and smudging, Athena was to be stored, covered, in a *dark* place, where no sunlight could lessen her ability to perform, and no other hands, save the Sisters', would ever come in contact with her.

"Now blink," Maggie advised. "Blink your eyes several times and breathe deeply, so we can allow our minds to return to the physical plane. A cold glass of water and a light snack will help to ground us, as we gradually reconnect to the Earth's energies."

"As well we know from our time-travels," Raine avowed with zeal. "After all, this, too, is time-trekking."

"Aye, 'tis," Cara agreed from Maggie's vacated chair.

"I'm dying for a bracing cup of tea," Maggie sighed. "Scrying can be rather draining."

Aisling exhaled slowly and stretched. "Sisters, crystal ball gazing, scrying of all sorts, takes a lot of practice and patience. Maggie, you did a first-rate job." The blonde with the wand cast a gentle glance to Raine, who was undoing the snaps of her ritual robe. "She does it better than we do, and I'm beginning to think she always will. Though, in time, we'll all three become more adapt and skilled with Athena, I'm convinced this is Maggie's special gift. Plus, she's the one of us who had the vision. She should lead us at *each* session."

Aisling slipped out of the black robe that covered her ebony sweater and jeans. "The Universe is filled with neutral potential, and magick is sculpting and charging that promise *with* and *to* our will. Witchcraft, as we know, is spiritual artistry."

Maggie smiled in her enigmatic way. "Grantie told us to be patient with Athena when she bequeathed her to us. She asked only that we treat her with the utmost respect; and she, in turn, will serve us well in the good works we attempt to do." The striking redhead pulled off her robe, revealing the green, form-fitting Fifties-style pencil skirt and sweater she was wearing beneath. "I appreciate your faith in me, Aisling, and I accept your bid; but let us never forget that *together* we possess the Power of Three." The redheaded Sister reached down and picked up their poppet, cradling the ragdoll in her arms.

Raine and Aisling simultaneously embraced Maggie– spurring a squashed Cara to shriek – "*Och!* Steady on now!"– after which the Sisters restored their robes to the wall pegs at the top of the attic stairs.

"It was so nice chatting with Grantie Merry," Raine said, as she skipped down the attic steps with Maggie, Cara, and Aisling en route to Tara's kitchen for their refreshment, the Merlin cats shadowing them. "I wonder what the surprise is that Grantie wants to give us when we go up to Salem for Emerald's wedding?"

"A supplement to our Time-Key," Aisling repeated. "Though I have a feeling it's destined to be much more than that."

"Bang on!" Cara giggled in Maggie's embrace.

"Grantie won't tell us till she's good and ready; that's for sure," Aisling asserted. "So don't you two trouble her over it."

"We won't," Maggie replied, glancing over at Raine, who suddenly looked like the cat who swallowed the canary. "We mustn't forget to telephone Grantie after we contact Hester's descendant."

"I'll always prefer the Athena way!" Raine giggled. "**Hec**-a-te yes! It's quite better than Skype!"

\*\*\*

As the Sisters grounded themselves with food and drink, they were making ready to stir up even more of their magick. Raine especially was chomping at the bit to contact Hester's successor.

"Allow me to review the facts that Grantie Merry shared with us," Raine said excitedly, as she sipped a cup of Eva Novak's special tea. The brew never failed to relax and restore her. "Teresa Moore, a lifetime practicing witch and healer, known throughout the area where she lives as 'Mother Teresa,' has something, in her possession, that Grantie says will aid us in clearing Hester's name."

"What could it be?" Maggie asked no one in particular. She broke off a piece of teacake and popped the morsel into her mouth, savoring the rich texture and taste. "A diary perhaps?"

"Time will tell," Cara parroted that Sister's captured thought, as she breathed in her own bit of teacake and small cup of tea laced with the good Irish whiskey she favored. The poppet didn't physically eat or drink. Rather, she seemed to *sense* food and drink, breathing in the essence of each.

"Grantie wants to make *sure* we contact Teresa," Aisling said, "so she refrained from mentioning that bit of information." The blonde Sister reflected for a moment. "Where exactly is the Mohican River area of Ohio? Have you a map around here?"

"Hold on," Raine answered, jumping up and heading for the basement. "I think we have an atlas down cellar," she tossed over her shoulder as she disappeared through the kitchen door that led downstairs.

In a trice she was back, plopping a large book of maps down on the table. It smelled slightly musty as the Sisters flipped through the pages, soon locating what they needed.

"Grantie Merry said Teresa lives on the Mohican River near Loudonville, Ohio," Raine said, pointing to an area of the map. She traced her ebony-lacquered fingernail along the glossy page. "Here's Loudonville. Ah, and there's the village of Brinkhaven, where Grantie said Teresa lives."

"East-central Ohio," Aisling mumbled. "Not too, too far. Let's see ... looks to be a little over a hundred miles, less than a hundred twenty. That should take us two and a half to three hours by car, depending on the roads and traffic."

"I think we should try and go on a weekday," Maggie said. "Look Aisling, Raine and I have a break from our college teaching schedule coming up at Thanksgiving. If you could take a day then– perhaps the day after the holiday– we could all three go together."

"Oh, Aising, *do* try," Raine implored with kitten expression, and she had such a pleading look in her feline eyes that Aisling gave her a loving embrace.

Raine grinned in satisfaction. "That will give us plenty of time to telephone Teresa and set something up with her."

The contented Cara glanced up from her whiskey-tea. "Afore y' ask– aye, I'll house-'n-cat sit here at Tara whilst y'er gone."

"Thank you," Raine and Maggie replied in harmony.

Setting her teacup down with resolve, Aisling said, "I'll arrange my schedule, and I'll drive. I think, too, we should all three go." The blonde Sister looked speculatively to her cousins. "Do you think you'll even **need** to time-trek on this endeavor?"

Raine and Maggie gaped at Aisling, exclaiming with unified determination, "**Yes!** It'll be the *only* way we can actually *meet* Hester Duff and talk with her!"

"Talk to those who knew her too," Raine added quickly. "And I think it'll be the only way we'll find out how she actually did what she did, and where she vanished. We know she used her strong magick to conjure the lightning to burn her name for all time into the Witch Tree, but how did she *vanish*? Was that part of her magick, or did she have help?"

Aisling joined the tips of her fingers in a pensive gesture. "That Indian attack at the time she disappeared ... I'm thinking it was a diversion."

Maggie and Raine looked to one another, with the pair of them answering, "We're thinking the same thing, Sister."

"And did you notice there was no rain with the conjured storm? It had to have been Hester's doing, that storm. Think about it. A *dry* thunderstorm at the end of a Pennsylvania October! Hey, 1787 was *wa–ay* before global warming. Quite possibly Hester schemed not to bring rain with her conjured storm, so the Native Americans who staged that diversion could keep their powder dry to fire their weapons." Raine's dark brows came together in a grimace. "We've always thought that Hester was a healer, and by the evidence revealed to us by Athena, we were right. However," Raine's grimace became a scowl, "it looks as though she helped a lot of ungrateful muggles."

"Well, *frightened* muggles anyway," Aisling stated. "Mmmm, our Hannah bakes a great Irish teacake, doesn't she?"

Raine gave an abstracted nod. "So, let's plan on doing our time-travel the night of the next full moon– that's less than two weeks– now that we have the correct date, 31 October 1787, with which to program our Time-Key. Bless my wand, what a magickal *Samhain that* was!

"Anyroad, we'll program the Key, as Maggie suggested to me yesterday, for the *day before*, so that we might talk with Hester and to people who knew her. Agreed?" the Goth gal urged, her heart giving a leap over the prospect of actually meeting Hester Duff.

Maggie and Aisling replied nearly simultaneously in the affirmative, with the poppet chiming in, "Aye, brilliant!"

"*That's* settled then," Raine hurried on, organizing her thoughts aloud, "a few days later, *subsequent* to our time-trek, we'll set off the day after Thanksgiving to confer with Hester's descendant. In the meantime, Amanda and Sam ... *and* Jasper will be moving into Witch-Tree Farm this coming week, and Beau and I will be going to the Harvest Dance over in Washingtonville, where *I* plan to do a bit of sleuthing, just to see what the confounded pests might be up to. I sure hope they won't be harrying Amanda and Sam like they did poor Will!"

"Why don't we drive over to Witch-Tree Farm with a house-warming gift?" Maggie suggested. "Something we could bless with a strong protection spell for their home ... for Witch-Tree Farm and its famous tree."

"Wiz-zard, Mags!" Raine sat back in the kitchen chair, looking like a cat that just polished off a nice bowl of cream. "At any rate, everything seems to be falling into place." She brushed crumbs from the black tunic she was sporting over leggings that bore the signs of the zodiac.

It was then the memory of Robin at the *Samhain* fest rose up to haunt all three Sisters: The High Priestess had leaned toward them with fervid expression, her words couched in strong terms, "Watch your backs, Sisters. Watch your backs–

*"Something wicked this way comes!"*

# Chapter Nine

When Raine and Maggie pulled up to the house at Witch-Tree Farm early the next evening, they immediately heard Jasper barking. The large Airedale came bounding down the back-porch steps to greet them when Amanda opened the door to peer out at who was coming up the lane.

Exiting the MG and starting forward, Raine laughed aloud, as the dog stood on its hind legs, a paw on each of her shoulders, to lick her face.

"Jasper! Get down!" Amanda scolded in a firm voice.

"Oh, he's not hurting anything!" Raine replied, taking Jasper's long face between her hands to plant a kiss on his wiry forehead. "How are you, old boy?" She looked to Amanda, "How's he been adjusting?"

"OK, I guess. He misses Uncle Will; that's for certain. I catch him in my uncle's chair sometimes, and he looks at me with such sad eyes. I've started taking him for a daily walk, like Unk used to do. When we get to the Witch Tree, he goes to the bench and just lies there, on the ground, with his head on his paws, looking so forlorn that it makes me cry.

"The other day, I got the idea to take him with me to the cemetery, and you won't believe this. He actually stretched out on the grave with his head on his paws and whimpered, *like he knew.* It's kind of hard to believe, isn't it? I mean, Jasper wasn't at the funeral with us when we buried Uncle Will."

Raine's emerald gaze returned to the dog for a private moment before turning back to Amanda. "He does know. What you described is rather common, in fact. Your uncle's energies are there, and Jasper senses that. Don't you, boy?" She rubbed his head.

"Sorry we didn't call first," Maggie said, coming up behind Raine, after having lifted a box from the MG's trunk. "We wanted to drop off a house-warming gift," she smiled, proffering the big, gift-wrapped package she cradled in her arms.

"How thoughtful of you!" Amanda replied, hugging first Raine, then Maggie. "Do come in and have a cup of tea or coffee with us; but I warn you, there're boxes everywhere."

"Let me take that," Sam offered, lifting the gaily wrapped present from Maggie and holding the door open for the Sisters to go inside.

As they entered the kitchen, with Jasper trailing after them, Raine and Maggie recited jointly, "Bless this house, God-Goddess."

Raine shoved the gift that Sam had set on the kitchen table toward Amanda, saying, "Open it. I doubt you have one," she giggled.

"You really didn't have to do this; it's very sweet." Amanda removed the sparkly silver ribbon and began tearing off the glitter-sprinkled white paper. When she unsealed the box, her eyes widened, and her mouth opened, but no words came forth.

"Here, let me help you," Raine offered, pulling the foot-high statue from its box.

Still, Amanda appeared speechless. "I ... it's ... it's ..."

"A *gargoyle*," Maggie finished for her. "Oh, we know it's not pretty and girly like you, but it's *purposeful*."

"Yes, we've cast him with a strong protection spell for Witch-Tree Farm and the Witch Tree." Raine patted the gargoyle's scaly, horned head, the gesture similar to the one she'd bestowed on Jasper.

Still Amanda looked doubtful as her eyes took in the fearsome creature.

"If you're not comfortable with the word *spell*, then think of it as energies or blessings. When we cast the gargoyle, we infused him with protective energies for your home and property," Maggie stated in her soothing voice. "It's all right; really it is. Surely you know that gargoyles have warded off evil from houses of worship for centuries, my dear."

Finding her voice, Amanda uttered with sincerity, "Thank you. I was just a bit taken aback by his appearance, I suppose." She stepped forward to embrace both Sisters. "We appreciate your thoughtfulness."

Sam echoed his wife's sentiment. "You're most kind."

"Be sure to place your house gargoyle in an east window. That way, he'll get the rising sun, which will keep him cleansed of negativity, and the rising moon, which will keep him charged," Raine advised. She reached into the box and lifted out a large chunk of raw citrine along with a velvety-smooth stick of selenite, handing both to Amanda. "This citrine will aid in zapping negativity, and this wand of selenite will help keep our protection spell super strong, so place them in the same east window, one on each side of the statuette. We figure you don't know about smudging, so—"

"What's that?" Amanda broke in, inducing Maggie to explain.

"In a word– *cleansing.*" She gestured toward the gargoyle. "His resin body makes him indoor or outdoor, so you could set him out in the rain once in a while, then let him dry in direct sunlight to super-cleanse him, before placing him back in the east window," the redheaded Sister suggested.

"I will," Amanda replied with a nod. "I will do everything you suggest. Should I give him a name?" Her normally soulful brown eyes danced with mischief.

The Sisters traded looks, answering together, "If you like."

Amanda thought for a long moment. "He's big, and you say he's powerful, so I'm thinking *Hercules.*"

"Quite fitting!" the Sisters laughed.

Raine glanced curiously round the kitchen and adjoining living-dining space to see the piles of unpacked boxes standing about. "I love what you haven't done to the place," she said in a jocular manner.

"I know. I know. You probably thought we'd be all unpacked and completely settled in by now, but we first had to make way for our things by clearing out all of Unk's closets and drawers. He was not, as you may have suspected, a materialistic person, but there were still things to give away, pack away; and," her eyes became moist, "well, that was difficult for me."

Sam moved to his wife's side to slide an arm around her slender waist. "But we're getting through it. Goodness, where're our manners?! First we let you standing out on the porch in the chill, and now this! Sit down, why don't you?"

The Sisters pulled off their wool capes and sat at the table, placing their wraps on the backs of their chairs.

"May I make you a cup of tea? I will if I can find the teapot," Amanda revised, looking at her husband and biting her lower lip. "Unk loved his coffee, but I couldn't find a teapot in this kitchen. Mine are still unpacked. How about some coffee?"

"Don't fret over that. Sit and let's chat a while before we take our leave," Maggie urged.

Amanda and Sam joined the Sisters at the kitchen table.

"We gave most of Uncle Will's clothes to the Salvation Army," Amanda said. "This house, like all old houses, has very limited closet space. We had no choice. And Uncle Will's *National Geographic*s! Oh my! Since Sam couldn't take off work, I asked a few of my former students to come over to help me pack them into the storage boxes I bought. We got them all organized by year, boxed, labeled and stored in the attic. I couldn't bear to part with them.

"Then," Amanda went on, "I got someone in to help me wash windows and put up new drapes and curtains, except for these in the kitchen, that we laundered. My Aunt Bonnie made these," she indicated, "and I want to keep them. They're still in good shape. Uncle Will was neat and clean, but he didn't keep house like a woman, so I've been concentrating on sprucing up and readying the house for our things. Now, we can start putting our touches to it, though I don't want to change much." She cast a tearful eye over the room. "I love this house, this farm. Always have. I've so many *wonderful* memories." She grappled with grief for control, swiping the back of her hand under an eye.

"Are you and Sam going to the Harvest Dance?" Raine asked, hoping to cheer her. "If so, I'll see you there. Beau and I are going."

"I don't feel like celebrating," Amanda voiced softly. "But I'm on the food committee. I promised three apple pies and a couple dozen apple tarts, so Sam and I will deliver my offerings to the Grange that evening for sure."

"I want to stay long enough to exchange a few words with friends and neighbors," he stated, sending his wife a warm regard. "I think it would be good for Mandy; and besides, we've been eating take-out for about three weeks now, so it'll be nice to stay long enough to enjoy some home-cooked food for a change. We can leave when the dance begins.

"Harvest Dance is late this year," Sam went on. "It's always in mid-October, but the renovation on the Grange wasn't complete. Still isn't. I *guess* Reggie Mason will have it all done for the rescheduled date. Originally, he promised the Grange board he'd have the work done by the second week of October, then he told them he ran into difficulties that held him up."

"Since we're guessing, what do *you* think happened?" Raine asked.

Sam didn't hesitate with his reply, and when he spoke, he did so scornfully. "In most people's opinions, including my own, he should have *foreseen* those difficulties. He gave his word, and he broke it. But that's not all. The renovation went about $25,000 over budget. He'd assured the board of directors that his original quote was set in stone, and it was in writing; so his father, Derrick Mason, stepped in to let the Grange know that DHM Construction would uphold their contract, and the difference would come out of Reggie's paychecks," Woods denounced with a slight pursing of his mouth.

"I have it on good authority," Sam continued, "that Derrick is really upset with his wayward offspring, more so than ever before, for making empty promises and not keeping them, for not getting a job done when that particular job could have been done on time, and for assuming too much and not looking deeper into the reality of the situation. The Grange, after all, is an *old* building, a former barn. He should have carefully checked everything, roof, plumbing, wiring– *everything*.

"So this newest chapter in Reggie's life gives him even *more* reason to want to get his greedy hands on *this* property. It just might be the prodigal son's last chance to prove himself to his father, who, I heard anyway, is about to boot him out of the business. As manager of Washingtonville Lumber, I've known Derrick a long time. Personally, I don't think he'll ever hand over the company he *labored* to build to someone who does not adhere to good business practices."

Out of nowhere, Amanda said, "I can understand wanting to prove one's worth to a parent. Reggie's probably no different from anyone else when it comes to wanting parental approval."

"I don't know why you're defending him," Sam questioned abruptly but not curtly, though his remark seemed to throw his wife off balance.

"I wasn't really defending him," Amanda returned in a somewhat uncertain tenor.

Raine tossed Maggie a poignant glance. "This discussion has jogged my memory," the raven-haired Sister began. "Have any of the people your uncle referred to as the 'pests' been plaguing either of you since the funeral?"

Sam tilted his head. "No one's been pestering me. Thus far, anyway." He looked to his wife. "Has anyone approached you, honey?"

For a moment, Amanda looked a bit sheepish before she answered, "N-no, nothing to be concerned about."

Maggie caught Raine's eye, and the Sisters exchanged a thought.

After the brief pause, Raine said, "Look, why don't we roll up our sleeves and help you today?"

"Oh, we couldn't ask you to work!" Sam exclaimed. "You're guests."

"We don't mind pitching in," Maggie replied. "You just direct us. If I might make a suggestion, the kitchen's the heart of any home. Why don't we go all-out on getting it in working order? Then we can rid some of these big boxes out of here, so you can move about better."

"We can cut up the boxes, and Sam can burn them out back," Raine added.

Now it was Sam and Amanda who swapped glances.

Sam reached for Raine's hand, turned it palm up to slap his palm to hers in the old way horse traders sealed a deal. "Offer accepted!" he laughed. "How about I go and get us a large pizza with the works and some beer to wash it down? Do you like pizza and beer?" he asked the Sisters. "If not, I could pick up something else. If we're going to put you to work, we can at least feed you!"

"Sounds like a plan," Raine rejoined, "and we can get started while you're gone."

Once Sam left the kitchen, and Amanda heard his car's engine roar to life out in the driveway, she rolled her eyes, and there was a notable change in her voice. "I get so much more done when he's out of the house."

The Sisters again traded significant looks– *and thoughts*.

"You and Sam seem to have such a close relationship," Maggie probed in her subtle manner.

Amanda looked stunned. "Oh, we do." The hangdog expression returned, and the color came up in her face. "I hope you didn't get the wrong impression. Understand, I'm just not over my uncle's death, and I-I'm … I'm a little uptight."

\*\*\*

When Amanda and Sam entered the Grange the night of the Harvest Dance, a cold, gusty wind was blowing. The sky was hard and leaden, and the cinnamon-brown hills that had gleamed in the sun the day before looked dark and bare. The east wind, like a razor, stripped the trees; and the leaves, crackling and dry, shivered and scattered in the gale's blast.

"Wouldn't you know?" Amanda said, her face, under the pixie hood of her coat, whipped with the cold to rosy. "That nice stretch of Indian summer days, and a storm has to blow in the night of the Harvest Dance!"

"Wind's drivin' in a front with hard rains. The weathermen have put out a warnin' for flash flooding," an elderly man passing by the couple commented. "*Black* winter my pa used to call this weather."

"I hope it doesn't deter people from coming out tonight," Amanda replied. "The committees always work so hard."

"Oh, I doubt that'll happen. No city slickers round here," the man laughed. "All country folk, farmers mostly, an' we're used to dealin' with weather."

"Looks like we're two of the first ones here," Sam said. He was holding a long open box filled with apple pies and tarts his wife had baked for the festival.

"The kitchen and food committees always come early to ready the food tables," Amanda replied, looking about. "Looks like they've set lots of food out already. Wow, the decorating team did a great job! Doesn't the Grange look nice?"

"Sure does," Sam replied.

Decorations in autumn colors of orange, brown, yellow, black, and red brightened the old barn and made it look and feel festive. On both sides of the stage, hay bales lent a harvest mood. Additional hay bales provided extra seating in all the old barn's nooks and crannies. A huge golden moon bearing the words, in red, black and brown lettering, *Welcome to the Annual Washingtonville Harvest Dance*, was pinned to the closed curtains on the small stage.

Encircling the large dance floor were round tables, each with six chairs. These tables were topped with colorful centerpieces, each featuring a copper-colored bowl of mums flanked by gourds, mini-pumpkins and dried corn. Wavy, long, orange, yellow, brown, and black streamers cascaded from the rafters. Pumpkins, gourds, and lanterns brightened the long food tables. And colorful autumn wreaths adorned the walls. The beams and doorway were festooned with garlands of colorful, faux autumn leaves and tiny twinkling orange lights.

"Sam," Amanda began, as he helped her off with her coat, "I must dash into the Ladies' to tidy my hair. The wind has turned me into a scarecrow; I'm sure. Would you mind arranging my apple treats on the dessert table for me?"

"I don't mind. Go ahead. When you come back in, I'll have a table for us and our salads to start. You can sit and relax. I know you're beat after all that baking."

Amanda glanced down at the plain, black sheath she was wearing. "Does this dress look all right? I guess I should've worn something nicer, but–"

"You look beautiful," he cut in, kissing his wife's pale cheek.

Sam carried the apple offerings to the long table holding the desserts. He carefully arranged Amanda's pies and tarts on the orange tablecloth and then moseyed over to the other food tables, delighting in all the tempting choices.

The first table held a bounty of salads, dressings, salad add-ons, and fresh fruit; the second table displayed the entrées, most of which were in warming dishes, including casseroles, covered dish items, pot pies, fried chicken, a variety of wings, ribs, chili, hearty soups, vegetables, breads, butter, and seasonings; the third table presented the desserts– cakes, pies, cookies, tarts, cupcakes, and handmade candies.

Once he had perused the row of tantalizing fare, Sam walked back to the salad table to choose something for Amanda and himself. There were Waldorf salads, tossed salads, potato and macaroni salads, and antipasti. He was hungry, so he decided on a particularly appetizing antipasto, one for him and another for Amanda. The bottled dressings presented yet another quandary, for there were several choices. He picked up three before he settled on one, adding the dressing to each of the salads.

"Ah–huh! You've chosen *my* antipasto," Washingtonville Town Council President Mildred Grimm bellowed, coming up behind him and giving Sam a start, as she peered over her spectacles at what he was holding.

"Antipasto is one of our favorite choices at the deli," he remarked bluntly, hoping the obnoxious woman would move off. He stepped away from her to pick up a couple of napkin-wrapped place settings.

"Humph!" Grimm muttered testily. "*My* antipasto is better than anything you'd get at the deli!"

"Then I'm certain we'll enjoy it." Sam looked about for the beverage table.

Realizing he had missed the drinks on a smaller table at the opposite end of the salad stand, he covered the short distance only to come face to face with Etta Story, the retired journalist and current president of the Washingtonville Historical Society.

"Good-evening, Sam," she said in a kind tone. "How's Amanda doing?"

"Better every day," he answered. "Thanks for asking." He glanced quickly around. "I don't see any trays. I'll have to make two trips."

"I'll take Amanda's to her. Which one is it?" Etta asked, eyeing the salads.

"Either one," Sam smiled. "That's nice of you. Our table is just over there," he indicated with a jerk of his head. "Can you grab her a water too? I know that's what she'll want with her meal."

"Sure. I'd like to say hello; perhaps chat for a sec," Etta remarked, setting Amanda's salad down. Several moments later, she snatched up a bottled water before taking the salad in her free hand to proceed toward the table where Sam was standing.

"Ah, here comes Mandy now." Having set the food things down on his chosen table, Sam raised a hand to signal his wife, who, seeing him, headed in his direction.

"Hello, Etta," Amanda said, upon arriving at the table. "Good choice, Sam. This salad looks scrumptious."

"I'm going to enjoy all the home cookin'," Sam stated with visible anticipation. "A month's worth of take-out has honed my appetite. I can't wait to sample as much of everything here tonight as I can."

"Mildred Grimm made the antipasto," Etta volunteered. "I brought the tossed salad, and she and I both supplied the dressings, as we do every year. I hope people don't get tired of my salad contribution. I've never been very domestic, but I do make, what I think anyway, is a tantalizing tossed salad." She looked to Amanda. "So how do you like living out at the farm?"

Etta reached down to move the bulky leather purse Amanda had set on the floor at her feet. She scooted it over a few inches, closer to Sam, so she could pull a chair, from the next table, into the space between the couple and sit and chat with them both.

"You know I love Witch-Tree Farm," Amanda responded genially. "Sam and I have spent so much time there, it's always been like home. We've Jasper with us, of course."

"You should come out for dinner some evening," Sam said, already diving into his salad.

"Yoo-hoo! Amanda! Glad to see you out and about!" called a plump, pleasant-looking lady from halfway across the room.

Amanda waved at the woman, a teacher at the elementary school where she had taught before being downsized. All around, there was a great bustle of activity in the hall now.

"I'd love to come over for dinner sometime," Etta replied to Sam's offer. "Witch-Tree Farm holds such *nostalgic* appeal," the ex-journalist stated with style.

"Any time," Sam answered. It was all he could manage with his mouth full. As he continued eating voraciously, his napkin slid from his lap, and he reached down to retrieve it.

Meanwhile, Amanda was speedily countering her husband's open invitation. "Of course we'd love to have you over, but right now we're in a mess, with boxes everywhere. That's what we're going to be doing when we leave here, unpacking boxes."

"You're not staying for the dance?" Etta's voice carried a shred of displeasure.

"No," Amanda shook her head. "I'm not up to that sort of thing. Not yet."

"Honey, eat your salad before it gets soggy," Sam said between mouthfuls, reaching for another napkin from the extras he had brought to the table.

"I will. Just unwinding first." Amanda turned toward Etta. "I'm all in. It's so much work, moving. One never realizes how much stuff even a small apartment can hold till moving time. Sam and I did it all ourselves, because we sold most of our furniture, so we could use Uncle Will's. Even so, packing boxes, moving them– it took us several trips in my SUV– doing windows and curtains, and ridding out. Then this baking … it's all been *so* tiring."

Etta's face darkened. "Oh no, Mildred Grimm is headed this way. I've had enough of her for one day. It was nice talking to you both. You take care of yourself, Amanda. You *look* tired. And if ever you … well, I don't have to express it in words. You know how our historical society feels about Witch-Tree Farm; or, at least, I hope you know. We'll talk again soon." With that, Etta rose and walked briskly away, just in time before Mildred Grimm arrived at the Woods' table.

"I've been watching you …"

What Amanda and Sam did not realize was, since their arrival, more than one pair of eyes were observing them.

"… and I see you haven't even touched my delicious antipasto," Mildred leveled at Amanda. "What did Sam do, tell you *I* made it? You won't get fare like that at any old deli." Grimm's eyes flicked over the younger woman before narrowing with a look that nearly wilted her. "I certainly hope you're not going to waste that! I put a lot of time and effort into that salad, not to mention all the costly ingredients. *My antipasto is to die for.*" The remark slid out in a semi-cooing voice over an undercurrent that came off as decidedly– *sinister*.

"And a cheery good-evening to you too," Amanda replied with a mirthless chortle.

The obnoxious woman bent to shove Amanda's cumbersome purse another couple of inches out of the way. Then, rising slowly, she eased herself into the chair Etta had vacated. "So," she smiled in a most deprecating fashion, "you got settled in at the farm, did you? I heard you'd–"

"You know very well we've taken possession of the farm," Sam cut in, coming to his wife's rescue, Grimm's thin, cruel smile provoking him to intervene with a sting of his own.

Mildred pulled herself up to her full height. "I trust you two know it's because of *you* Washingtonville will miss out on a fine new shopping center, with the unique shops and restaurants that would create jobs, generate more money for our town, and augment the tourism we've been working so hard to increase.

"There's our long-time rival, Haleigh's Hamlet, with several nice eateries, and then here's dear old Washingtonville with its one dinky little café and its fast-food dives. What tourists we do pull in drive over to the Hamlet to eat. The Hamlet benefits from the programs we stage! I hope you're able to live with that. Why do you two think you need that big place anyhow? Sam works long hours at the lumber company, and *you*," Grimm shot Amanda an especially caustic regard, "now that they downsized you from the school district, you're gonna be all by your lonesome most of the time out there in the boondocks. What in God's name are you planning to do with yourself on that farm?! It can get pretty scary out there at night. *Pret-ty* scary! Have you thought about that?"

The woman bulldozed on, not waiting for a response, as a stricken, wide-eyed Amanda sat still and stomached her acidic insults. "You could have all that money DHM Construction is offering, and you could live in style somewhere, *anywhere,* with that kind of ready cash, while giving our town what we n–"

"**Enough!**" A saturated Sam slammed his fork down to angle abruptly forward, so that his face was virtually nose-to-nose with their attacker. "That's quite enough harping from the town harpy. Take a walk," he uttered in a harsh undertone. "The fresh air would do you good, not to mention what it'll do for us."

Mildred hauled herself to her feet with a bluster, glancing nippily round at who might have caught Sam's remarks, her face flushing scarlet. Along with the color, a sudden malevolence rose in her expression. If looks *could* kill, Sam would have dropped from his chair, stone dead. Suspending them both in Time's shadowy grip, Grimm's mean eyes held his in wordless combat. Then with a bombastic "Humph!" she turned on her heel and stomped off, muttering darkly under her breath.

"Thank you," Amanda whispered to her husband, who reached over to pat her hand. She closed her eyes and allowed herself to settle, letting out a sigh.

"An incredibly rude and intolerable woman," he growled.

Amanda nodded, suppressing a yawn and thinking that she was more spent than she'd realized. Picking up her fork, she was about to take her first bite of salad when a loud wave of raucous laughter, from the doorway, carried to their table, pausing her. Several new arrivals entered the festive Grange, after which fragments of their conversation drifted over to the couple's ears:

"Rainin' cats 'n dogs out there!" a woman proclaimed, shucking out of her trench coat.

"Hope the ole bridge doesn't wash out!" a tall man rejoined. He doffed his tweed cap and shook it, as droplets of water sprayed the air.

"Well, if the bridge does go," an older fellow returned, "people will just have to take the long way in and out."

"Hey, our old Grange really does look nice! Guess it was worth the wait!" a woman toting a fiddle case declared.

"Let's just hope Reggie boy didn't take any short cuts that will translate Trouble with a capital T!" a heavyset fellow with apple-red cheeks spouted in a booming voice.

"Oh, I don't think his pa would put up with that!" the woman on his arm answered.

"I'm going up for something else." Sam stood, picking up his paper salad dish to discard in one of the waste baskets. "Can I bring you anything?"

"Not yet," Amanda answered, covering her mouth to give in to the persistent yawn. She glanced about to notice several familiar faces in the flux of people streaming in.

Someone must have popped a country-music CD into a player, for it blasted abruptly and momentarily from the loud speaker, before it was promptly reduced to a comfortable volume.

Dressed in a low-cut, rich purple dress that molded to her perfect figure and deepened her eyes to amethyst, Sirena Chambers approached the table where Amanda was sitting, poised fork in hand to dip into her salad.

Setting the fork down, Amanda thought, *What a beauty this woman is! She's captured the attention of every person in this room.* "Evening," she said aloud. "You're looking more like a gorgeous Liz Taylor every day."

"Thank you, Amanda," the young woman smiled. "I realize now's not the best time, but I just want to let you know that my father and I still haven't found a property we like better than Witch-Tree Farm on which to build the condos we spoke about. If you change your mind about selling, please call *us*." She glanced up to see Sam approaching. "It's not my intention to pressure you. That's not our way at Chambers Construction, so–"

Returning from the food tables with loaded plate, Sam nodded a brusque acknowledgment to Sirena, who quickly concluded, "I was just telling your wife that the offer made by Chambers still stands. I don't want to interfere with your dinner, so I'll wish you both a pleasant evening. Enjoy."

Again Sam gave an edgy nod. He took his seat next to his wife, leaning in, "I was hoping no one would stress you tonight."

"Actually, she was very nice."

Sam groaned, swiping crumbs from his mustache with his napkin. "Brace up. Here comes the Reggie."

The playboy looked spiffy in his tweeds this evening, and as roguish as ever. "Evening, folks," he greeted with his usual swagger, pausing at Amanda and Sam's table.

All around the dance floor now, couples and groups of people were coming in, finding seats, and queuing up at the food tables.

"Reggie, I think we've said everything there is to say," Sam stated tightly, attempting to head off a sales pitch.

"Sam, old boy! I can't let my competition outdo me, now can I? Gotta level the playing field, after all," he put across in an arch manner. "I'll tell you the same thing I know *she*," Reggie cast a swift regard after Sirena, "told you. DHM's offer still stands. Take a look around," he said, flinging out a hand. "Didn't I do a great job with the Grange? OK, so I didn't deliver on the October date, but as I told the board of directors here, 'Do you want it fast, or do you want it good?'" Humor played at his sensual mouth. "They didn't just want it fast, they wanted a freakin' miracle. But you have to admit, I delivered ***good***, huh? ***Huh?!***" he executed a reverse wave to rake in praise from his listeners.

"Yes," Amanda purred, seemingly fascinated, by him or the newly renovated Grange, it was difficult to tell, "you did."

His wife's comment, received by Reggie with a sexy grin, sparked flashes of annoyance in Sam's eyes.

Straightaway, Reggie adopted a different manner, sending the fay-like Amanda a subtle wink, his eyes searching. "You may not feel like selling today ..." he raked his fingers through his lustrous dark hair, and his grin broadened; but this time the gesture came off as almost menacing as his eyes shifted to Sam. "Maybe tomorrow you will. Things happen– we change our minds. Think about it, and when you do," his reassuring bonhomie bounced brightly back, "we hope you'll choose us. Because, remember, Chambers wants to put up condos, but my father and I want to build a shopping center. Think about all the good that will do the community, and how you'll be appreciably responsible *for* that good."

Noting that Sam transferred his glare to Mildred Grimm, who'd let loose a jarring cackle nearby, Reggie leaned toward Woods to say in a muted voice, his face lighting up with the spirit of pure mischief, "Ain't exactly an oil painting, is she? Wonder how much she charges to haunt a house?" A loud laugh burst from him, causing several people to turn and look. "An amusing thought," he crooned under his breath, laughing again.

"I was under the impression you and Grimm are buddies," Sam said tersely.

"Buddies," Reggie repeated in an abstract way. "Yeah, you could call us that."

Sam's handsome face wrinkled in a grimace, his focus on Reggie, whose eyes seemed to be combing the crowd in the hall. In a moment, the latter mumbled seemingly to himself, as if answering an afterthought that popped into his head. "That's it!" he snapped his fingers, a curious expression passing over his face. "That's what I'll do!"

"What?!" Sam flung back. "Tell your story walkin'?"

"Huh?" Reggie answered, coming out of his reverie and looking bemused. He dragged his gaze back to Amanda and, picking up her hand, lowered his voice– that took on an unexpected *dramatic* quality. "Again, I want to convey my sympathy for the loss of your uncle." Bending, he pressed his lips to the small, soft hand he was holding.

With obvious irritation, Sam stuck his chin out in a belligerent manner, a gesture not lost on either his wife or Reggie, who, not wanting to push his luck or the shopping-center issue further, for now anyway, moved hastily off to catch up with Sirena. Amanda– looking faintly reproachful– and Sam heard him call to her, "Hey, good-lookin', I hope you saved me a dance tonight!"

"What did he mean by '*Again*' he wanted to convey his sympathy?" Sam cocked his head to eye his wife dubiously, and his face took suddenly a forbidding line.

Seemingly befuddled, Amanda stuttered out, "I-I suppose … he meant after his words of condolence at the cemetery."

"Damn it! I was looking forward to a relaxing evening, hoping we wouldn't be bothered tonight. This whole business is *most* unprofessional," Sam muttered, returning with gusto to his food.

"Oh, it'll stop, Sam. You'll see. When they finally accept the fact that we won't sell–" She broke off, adding, "I never want to part with the farm." Amanda poked at her salad, but still did not take even a single bite.

His eyes on Reggie– where the Casanova stood, several feet off, chatting up Sirena– Sam gave a grunt of condemnation. "Look at 'im! He's off and runnin', doing what he does best. You should see him with the girls at the lumber office. What a jerk," he grumbled. "A blowhard. He's *so* full of it, he should run for public office."

Without comment, Amanda picked up her fork to finally dip into her salad. "Who's that, over there?" she indicated with a movement of her head in the direction of the entrance. "She looks familiar."

Sam turned partway round. "Oh, a local author, Ceane O'Hanlon-Lincoln, is doing a book signing here tonight. I saw the poster as we came in. She wrote that award-winning history series we read about in the paper the other day, County Something or Other."

"Chronicles," Amanda supplied. "*County Chronicles.* And her first name *isn't* pronounced *See-Ann*. It's *SHAWN-nee,* or *Shawn* for short. I thought she looked familiar. I've read from her works in my classroom."

Sam gaped at the author, who was busy arranging books on the table that would be her station. "Kind of a *wild* idea to have a book signing here, at the Harvest Dance, isn't it?"

Amanda surprised herself with a girlish giggle. "Oh, I think writers are prone to wild ideas." She reached over to place a hand on her husband's arm. "Bothersome pests or not, I'm glad you talked me into coming out tonight. You were right– I needed this."

He kissed her cheek. "I'm glad I talked you into it too, sugarplum."

Amanda smiled. "You haven't called me that for a long time."

"Guess it's because we haven't taken time out for relaxation in a long while. But things are going to change," Sam said, picking up her hand. "And you will always be my little sugarplum."

"Sam, you do amuse me."

Heading to the food tables, Moonglow and Starlight waited to stare a guarded moment at the couple, whilst the former visibly squared her shoulders before approaching the Woods.

"Blessed evening," they pealed, setting their purses down on the next table. "Amanda, would you mind keeping an eye on our purses, while we get something to eat?"

"Not at all," Amanda answered.

"Tell you what," Moonglow began, "let me set them here on the floor with yours," and she stooped to put the purses together, taking her time to carefully arrange them. "There, now they won't be in anyone's way. We'll leave our wraps on the chairs here to save our table. Robin will be joining us with her husband. So please try," she waved a hand over the table, "and save this place for us, if you can."

"Will do," Amanda replied.

"Here comes Raine and her date," Sam remarked, shoving a big forkful of chicken potpie into his mouth.

Amanda stood and motioned them over. "Sit with us," she invited, reaching out to take Raine's hand.

As was her habit, the Goth gal bewitched in black– a lace jacket-blouse that topped a Victorian riding skirt and high-heeled boots. Beau sported a navy corduroy jacket, similar to the beige one Sam was wearing, over a light blue shirt and dress jeans.

Settling into a chair at the table with Amanda and Sam, Raine asked Beau to get her some hot cider. She was watching Moonglow and Starlight, who were paused at the food tables to speak with Etta Story. The Sister was trying to determine if Etta had signaled them or if the furtive gesture she'd caught was merely a subtle greeting. The three had their heads together until the two Coven sisters felt Raine's eyes. Quickly then did they break to resume filling their plates.

"You better go up and get yourselves something to eat," Sam suggested, routing Raine's reverie. "The food is great, and it won't last."

"Shall we?" Raine said, as she and Beau stood and started off together to the first food table.

"I think I'll join them. I want another piece of fried chicken," Sam said, rising. "And I think I'll have another helping of that great antipasto," he lowered his voice to an intimate level, "even if the Grimm Reaper did make it. Can I get you anything, honey?"

"Not yet."

Noticing that she had not even begun to eat, Sam waited. "Don't you like your salad? If you don't, I can get you something else."

She shook her head. "You go on. I intend to eat this."

Shrugging, he moved off to join Beau and Raine, while Amanda finally got the chance to take her first bite.

Not long after Sam, Raine and Beau returned to the table with their food choices, they all noticed that Amanda's face was turning red, and there were hives on her neck. Her cheeks were puffing out, and her lips were swelling.

"Oooh," she huffed, clutching at her throat. "I'm having trouble breathing."

Beau and Raine looked to Sam, with Beau asking straightaway, "Does she have any food allergies?"

Already on his feet, Sam hurriedly swallowed the antipasto he had put in his mouth. "Yes," he began, "she–" His wife cut him off.

Struggling for breath, Amanda was desperately trying to articulate the word "Peanuts!" Her big brown eyes grew even larger with fright, as her words came out in jerky gasps. "I … I can't breathe! Sam … get … injector!"

Raine and Beau jumped up to try and calm the poor woman, who was, very rapidly, exhibiting panic, her convulsive movements alarming to watch.

"H-H-H-Help me!" She clutched at Raine, who put her arms around Amanda and began stroking her damp face and hair.

"Keep calm," Beau instructed the frightened woman with level voice. "Sam's getting your injector. It's important that you stay as calm as you can."

As soon as his wife had begun wheezing, Sam wrenched her large purse from the floor to the chair he vacated. Quickly then, he began a search for her epinephrine. He was so nerve-driven, his large hands fumbled with the purse's contents, and he appeared nearly as panicked as his wife.

"Her injectors have *got* to be in here!" he cried out. "She *never* leaves the house without them, and she always takes *two*, no matter where we go!" His hands were rummaging with frenzied need.

"Amanda," Raine asked, "did you put your injectors in your purse tonight?!"

Unable to speak, Amanda bobbed her head, her eyes wild with fear. "Ssssss-ide!"

"What's she trying to say?" Raine asked.

"Side," Sam replied, not pausing to look up. "She always carries them in the *pocket* of her purse, where she can get to them easily, if she needs them." He wedged his fingers into the purse's tight side pocket. "I checked there *first*, but–"

"I'm going to call 911," Beau cut in, reaching for his phone in the inner pocket of his jacket. "We don't want her to go into shock!"

"They've **got** to be in this purse!! I'll dump the damn thing out on the floor!" Sam shrieked. "Help me look!" Both he and Raine rooted feverishly through the spilled contents, as Beau called the emergency number.

"Could she have left the injectors in the car?" Raine asked, looking up from the jumble to Sam's frantic face.

"Never! The doctor told her never to do that. Neither heat n'r cold is good f'r th'm," he sputtered, yanking his car keys from his pocket. "Search our car anyway! I parked right by the door. It's the black–"

"I know it!" Raine snatched the keys he was shoving into her hand and made a dash for the parking lot.

"Ambulance's on its way!" Beau announced, slipping his cell back into his pocket. What all did she eat?" he asked, reaching to check Amanda's pulse.

"Nothing but that salad, *that antipasto*," Sam answered, not even glancing up as he delved through the purse's contents for the third time, opening every zipped compartment to pry inside with shaking fingers. "I ate the same thing, and trust me, there were *no* nuts in that antipasto. I'd *never* have given her anything with nuts in it!"

"What about the dressing?" Beau picked up the wheezing Amanda's arm to gently stroke it.

"I put Italian dressing on both our salads. What's that?!" he yelled, his demeanor wholly unnerved. "Olive oil, vinegar, herbs? I don't know, but surely not peanuts!"

"Is she allergic to any other foods, to *anything* else?" Beau pressed.

"Not that we know of!"

By now, Amanda was literally *gasping* for air. Her throat had tightened, and her chest felt heavy as she fought hard to breathe. Her face and lips were horribly swollen, and her face was bright red.

"Stand back! Give her air!" Beau roared at the people crowding around.

Sam's voice rose hysterically, "She had one of these attacks a couple of years ago here at the Grange. **Where're those damn injectors!**" he bellowed, so distraught was he. "I *know* she brought two with us tonight! **I know it!**" He grabbed Amanda's empty purse, and began jamming his fingers into every crevice, feeling for the pen-shaped items. **"I know she brought them! This is insane!"** he shouted, crazed with terror.

Stroking the poor woman's swollen face, Beau said softly, keeping his voice level, "Try to stay calm, Amanda. *Try.* Help is on the way." He poured a little of her bottled water onto his handkerchief and applied it gently to the young woman's forehead. Then he held the cool, damp cloth to her face and wrists.

In a few moments, Raine came rushing back inside. "No luck," she announced, breathless.

"I knew she wouldn't leave them in the car," Sam said, squeezing his wife's hand as he gaped at her puffy, distorted face. "Oh my God! God help me, I can't lose her!"

Amanda looked as though she weren't getting air at all, when Raine urged, "Beau, call 911 again and find out where the ambulance is!"

With a nod, he yanked out his phone and redialed the emergency number. In a moment, he said, "What's taking that ambulance so long to get to Washingtonville Grange! I told you this is a life-or-death emergency!" He held the phone so he and Raine could both catch the response.

"Let me check," the dispatcher said in swift reply.

Beau could hear her on the phone with the ambulance. In a moment, she said, "The flash flood took out the bridge."

"If we bring her to the bridge, could we figure a way to get her across to the ambulance?!" Raine questioned near to the phone, looking with troubled eyes to Beau.

"The water's too high and rapid for that, ma'am!" came the disembodied female voice from Beau's cell. "They've had to go around, the long way in, but they've turned on the siren, and they'll be there as fast as they can."

Beau shook his head, whispering to Raine, "That's a thirty-mile detour." He knelt down next to Amanda, whom Sam had placed on the floor, and it was at that precise moment when Raine gave a start, having caught the shockingly smug look on Mildred Grimm's face.

The Sister's sharp eyes quickly scanned the circle of staring faces. Etta Story, Moonglow and Starlight were all wearing the same anxious expression that could well have been anticipatory. While Reggie and Sirena were sharing a protracted look that, because their faces were turned, Raine could not interpret.

With his gasping wife's head cradled to his chest, Sam was rocking back and forth, repeating, "Hold on, Mandy! You gotta hold on! Help's coming!" He kissed her lips. "Please, baby, don't leave me!!" he rasped with a strangled cry.

The suffering woman swallowed convulsively.

Not quite five minutes later, Sam seized Beau's arm, clutching it, ***"What's happening to her?!"*** With terrified countenance, he lifted his wife toward him to kiss her again. "Mandy, Mandy, hold on; hold on, honey!" he begged, stroking her honey-blonde hair with trembling fingers. "Please don't leave me, Mandy! *Mandy!!"* Tears streamed down his face.

The frantic struggle for breath ceased, and Amanda went limp in her husband's arms.

Beau felt for a pulse, then raising his eyes to meet Sam's, he voiced softly, "I'm sorry, Sam. She's gone."

# Chapter Ten

The subsequent Monday evening, Aisling, Maggie and Raine found themselves at the McCutchen Funeral Home in Washingtonville. They purposely got there early, so they could have a few private minutes with Sam Woods.

When they entered the room where Amanda was being viewed, they were relieved to discover only a couple of other mourners there, in addition to Sam, who was standing at the coffin, somberly gazing down at his wife.

The Sisters went first to the casket to pay their respects and whisper their prayers, after which they moved close to Sam.

"Thank you for coming," he said, reaching out to take Raine's hand.

"Of course," she replied. "We won't be able to attend the funeral, because of work, but we'll be there in spirit. Beau won't be able to attend either, due to demands at the veterinary clinic, but he sends his sympathy."

"I understand," he responded. "And I am grateful to all of you for the kindnesses and compassion you've extended toward our family. Mandy appreciated your kindheartedness too. She said so several times." His eyes glistened from unshed tears, and he lowered his gaze, murmuring, "My wife was an extraordinary woman, you know. I was always proud of her."

The Sisters conveyed words of condolence, after which Raine lowered her voice to say—

"Sam, we realize this is not the time or the place; and, indeed, we don't wish to distress you; but with some things, time is of the essence. Would you mind terribly if we asked you a few questions? Perhaps we could move to that anteroom there," Raine gestured with a slight movement of her hand.

Sam studied the Sisters for a solemn moment, glancing over his shoulder quickly to make certain the other two people in the room were not within earshot of what he was about to say. "You don't think what happened to Amanda was an accident, do you?" he said in a barely audible voice.

"We don't know," Aisling answered quietly.

"Come with me." Sam indicated the adjacent, private alcove, guiding the Sisters inside.

When they had taken seats close together, Sam spoke again, his voice low. "I know your reputation, so I was hoping you'd think there might have been foul play, because *I* sure as hell do."

The Sisters exchanged looks.

"Do you think many people knew that Amanda had a peanut allergy?" Aisling opened.

Sam raised one blond brow, tilting his head. "This is a small town. You know as well as I that everybody knows everyone else's business in *any* small town."

"I recall you mentioning that Amanda had a couple reactions in the past, when the two of you were out together," Raine prompted, clearly wanting to be told more.

"She did, and one of those was at the Grange Harvest Dance two years ago." Sam closed his eyes, reaching, with visible pain, back in time, thenceforth clawing his way, almost breathless, in return to the present. "It was similar to the situation that occurred the other night, only her former reaction was from a dessert, brownies I distinctly recall. It didn't look like there were nuts in them; but the nuts, as it turned out, had been ground up in the batter, so elderly people who attend the Harvest function could enjoy them."

"Do you remember if the same people were at the dance, the previous time she had the reaction and this year?" Maggie inquired.

"Oh sure, the same people were at both dances, including Mildred and Etta." Sam paused again, adding, "What I remember most, though, is how frantic *I* was both times it happened. I admit I'm not very good in a crisis." He shook his head. "That's not exactly true. I am at work, but not when it involves—" his voice caught, and he broke off. "I was scared; Mandy was always so delicate. So, when I came runnin' toward my wife from the dessert table, I'd shouted, at the top of my voice, that her injectors were in the side pocket of her purse."

"When she had the reaction the *first* time at the Grange?" Aisling interposed, to be clear.

Sam nodded vigorously. "What I'm saying, and I've given this a lot of thought since the night of," he choked back tears, "Mandy's passing, is that everyone present at the Grange that night two years ago *had* to have heard me. I remember yelling, too, that she *always* carried the injectors *in the side pocket of her purse.* So, you see– I unwittingly provided a future murderer with the way to kill my wife!" The man looked devastated. "And don't think this doesn't torture me now!"

Maggie reached over to pat Sam's hand. "When you reacted in the manner you did back then, you most certainly weren't thinking of murder."

"All right, let's start at the beginning. Did anyone else handle Amanda's *salad* other than you?" Raine questioned.

Sam inclined his head in a pensive gesture. "Yes, in fact Etta Story came up to me and started talking when I was fixing Mandy's salad; after which I noted that, since there weren't any trays, I'd have to make two trips to carry the food, drinks, and flatware to the table I'd picked out for my wife and me. I must have mentioned the fact out loud ... you know, that I'd have to make two trips, because that's when Etta volunteered to take Amanda's salad to her. I thanked her and asked her to grab a water, because I knew that's what Mandy would want; and," Sam stopped to think, "she set the salad down on the salad stand and went off the few steps to get a bottle of water. I turned and walked to the table I'd selected; and after a bit, Etta showed up with Mandy's salad and water."

"So you turned your back on Etta after you handed her Amanda's salad?" Maggie murmured. "But you said you *fixed* Amanda's salad, so *you* put the dressing on it, right?"

"Yes," he answered, "but Etta could've done anything to that salad when my back was turned. She had it in her possession for several minutes."

"True," the trio of Sisters returned.

"Could there have been nuts in a salad dressing?" Sam questioned. "'Cause there sure weren't any damn nuts in the antipasto."

"We're thinking peanut oil in the salad dressing," Raine replied.

"But why would there have been *peanut oil* in *Italian* dressing? That's what I put on both our salads, mine and Mandy's. Wouldn't Italian dressing consist of olive oil and vinegar, garlic, herbs … I don't know," his voice trailed off, as he found himself shaking his head in bewilderment.

"Who brought the dressings to the function?" Aisling inquired. "Do you know for sure?"

"Mildred Grimm and Etta Story brought the salads **and** the bottled dressings. I know for certain because they each mentioned it to me." Sam's eyes narrowed. "Mildred harbors an especial *hatred* for Mandy and me both. She's made that crystal clear on more than one occasion, including the dance the other night."

Sam's eyes popped open with a start, and he clutched Maggie's arm in sudden recall. "Wait a minute! I just remembered something that could be significant. Mildred Grimm actually told Mandy and me, at our table, that her antipasto was, and I quote, '… to *die* for'!"

The Sisters glanced fleetingly at one another, before Maggie said, "That's a common phrase used frequently to mean–"

"I'm quite aware of what the phrase means!" Sam retorted. "But you would've had t' have *been* there to get *my* meaning. It was the *way* Grimm said it! I can still picture her face," his own face took on a faraway look, "and those hate-filled eyes when she directed those toxic words to my wife!" He looked to the Sisters, and his expression registered censure. "Do you suggest it was otherwise? Do you think I'm *imagining* all this? Is that what you think?!"

"Take a deep breath and calm yourself, Sam. We don't mean to upset you," Raine pled.

Sam's blond head dropped to his hands, and he shuddered, almost sick to his stomach. "Forgive me. I didn't mean to raise my voice to you. I told you I've been *tortured* over this. In addition to broadcasting the info about her injectors for all the world to hear, I talked Amanda into going to the dance in the first place. All she wanted to do was to drop off the desserts she made and then go straight home. But *I* talked her into staying! I thought it would be good for her to stay for a little while at least! Oh, God!"

The bereaved husband took a moment to collect himself, saying, "I'm thinking that Mildred, *that nasty piece of work*, could have wanted Amanda out of the way, thinking that I'd be more apt to sell the damn farm, that perhaps I wouldn't be inclined to live in a place that holds so many memories." Sam cocked his head for a considering moment, saying, "And then there's Etta."

His light blue eyes widened, as a thought broadsided him. "If something happens to me too, go after Etta Story, because with Mandy and me *both* gone, Witch-Tree Farm, according to her uncle's will, goes to the Washingtonville Historical Society." He blinked his now glistening eyes, and they appeared to spark, as his swirling emotions came to a boil and surfaced. "I'll tell you one thing for sure– I'd be wise not to turn my back on either of those women again!"

The Sisters swapped troubled looks as a flashback sprung upon them– the chilling portent Hester Duff's spirit had chanted at the *Samhain* fest: "Death doth come, the death of three."

"Perhaps I *am* imagining this," Sam was saying, his voice taking on a softer tone, "but I can't *help* this feeling I have. I just can't!" He shook his head, gazing intently at the Sisters. "And I think you three share my suspicion. I can tell by your faces that you don't think what happened to my wife was an accident either."

The Sisters traded thoughts but remained silent, not wanting to express their opinions right then.

"Sam, did you search for the two auto-injectors at home, the two that you thought went missing from Amanda's purse?" Aisling asked.

"Amanda was so distressed over her uncle's death, she could have neglected to put the injectors in her purse the night of the Harvest Dance," Maggie suggested.

Sam wagged his head again, this time with vehemence, brushing one eye with the back of his hand. "The two injectors she kept at home were *there*, right where she always kept them, in the bathroom cabinet, but no others; so yes, *the two in her purse went missing.* I told you– my wife *never* neglected to check her purse for two injectors anytime she went out. *Never.* She was *always* prepared. When she was teaching, she kept one at home and one at school, in addition to the two she always carried in her purse."

Aisling asked, "Did she perhaps change purses and forget to put the injectors into the side pocket of–"

"*No*," Sam answered before she finished the sentence. "Mandy always carried that big, black leather bag." He reflected for a moment, saying, "The thing dwarfed her. She was so dainty. I remember telling her once that she should carry a smaller purse." He thought for a moment. "That's another thing. The damn purse. It was … *distinctive*. Everyone would've noticed that it was the *same* one she always carried– the one I inadvertently let a murderer know held her life-saving medication in the side pocket!"

"You know, there is a chance the injector pens could've *fallen* out of her purse. After all, there was no zipper on that outer pouch where she regularly carried them," Raine commented. "I don't believe they fell out in the car though, as near as I could tell. I felt everywhere I could reach for them."

Again Sam shook his head. "No, I would bet my life they didn't fall out of her purse. And as for the car, I searched it yesterday myself. Mandy made a point to really stuff those pens all the way down inside that deep outer pocket, and the pocket was snug. I *can't* help believe that someone pinched the injectors from her purse. The whole damn Grange would've known they were there!"

His expression grew wistful. "Amanda was meticulous about everything. For instance, she never put anything else in that exterior compartment of her purse *but* the injectors, so that, if she needed one, she could grab it fast and not have to root through anything. And, like I said, she always carried *two* injectors no matter where she went. Before leaving the house, she made a practice of checking her purse for the pens. *Meticulous*, I tell you, about everything."

Raine sat forward in the folding chair on which she was sitting. "Did anyone handle Amanda's purse? Did you, by any chance, notice anyone coming into contact with her purse?"

Sam pressed the heels of both hands over his eyes and tried to think. "Well," he began, "Amanda went to the Ladies' Room when we first arrived at the Grange. It was windy, you remember, and she wanted to tidy her hair. She was in there a long time, which didn't alarm me, because as a husband, I know how long that sort of thing takes. Mandy's always–" he broke off, covering his face with his hands. "I'm ... God, I'm–" He wrestled with rising emotions. "I'm talking as if she's still alive."

Sam squeezed his eyes shut for several seconds, and when he opened them, they shone with fresh tears. "Forgive me," he rasped, pulling out his handkerchief.

The Sisters reached out to console him.

"I just can't believe she's gone. I can't–"

Finding no words, Maggie patted his arm reassuringly.

"When Mandy came back into the hall, from the restroom," Sam continued, "I waved her over to the table I'd chosen, and she set the purse on the floor at her feet, between us." He swallowed hard.

"That's when Etta carried Amanda's salad and water over to the table and set them in front of Mandy. Then she reached down and moved Amanda's purse over a few inches, which allowed her to pull a chair from the next table between us, so she could sit and talk. I saw her do it. I saw her *grab* the purse. I didn't see her take the injectors, of course, *but she could have.* I was hungry, so I'd started eating.

"Not long afterward," Sam sped on, as if suddenly fueled by a vengeance, "Mildred Grimm came up to our table, and *she* stooped down and moved the purse a bit more. I saw each of those women fiddle with the purse, but I didn't *watch* if they lifted anything from it. *I know now I should have!*"

"You had no earthly reason to watch for that." Aisling jotted a notation down on the pad she'd extracted from her bag.

"I don't know. I don't know anything anymore," he answered forlornly, slowly shaking his head in a distracted manner. Then, with the intensity of a man who just lost the wife he so loved, he blurted, "With the situation over that blasted farm, I *should* have been vigilant! But no, *no*, I was too busy stuffing my face. I hadn't had a good meal for–" He cut off, adding with passion, "I should have been **vigilant**!! I let her down, and now my wife is dead!"

"Don't blame yourself, Sam. And please excuse us, but if we're going to get to the bottom of this, we've got to ask these questions," Aisling said in a gentle but pressing manner. "Did you witness *anyone* else laying hands on that purse?"

"I appreciate your help, and I understand. Please bear with me; I'm in a fog, going *crazy* trying to process all of this myself." He gave a nod of approval, ducking his head then to mumble, "Let me think who else handled Mandy's purse."

In a moment, his gaze again met the Sisters'. "Two of the witches from that coven, or whatever it's called, in town. I think I heard Amanda call them Moonbeam and Starry Night or something like that," he said, erroneously reporting their names.

Sam looked down at his feet as his mind roved back to that fateful night, to when the two witches had come in contact with Amanda's purse. "I remember … they asked my wife if she would keep an eye on their purses and hold their table while they went to get their food. One of them set both their purses on top of Mandy's while they went to the food tables; and when they returned to their table, which was right next to ours, the other one reclaimed their purses, lifting them off Amanda's bag."

"What about the land developers? Did either of them come over to your table to talk when Amanda was sitting there?" Maggie queried. "When her purse was there, on the floor?"

Sam thought for a second. "Yes, they both came over to the table to speak with Mandy, individually."

"Did either of them handle her purse?" Raine and Maggie asked in near unison.

Sam took a longer moment this time to think. "I was at the food tables for part of the time when Sirena was talking with Amanda, and I was so busy eating when Reggie was there, that I just didn't notice. Come to think of it, I might've made a quick trip to the food tables when Reggie was talking to Mandy. I guess either of them could have gotten into her purse, though I doubt it was Sirena. I don't know how she would've been able to bend in the tight dress she was wearing. But let's not forget– someone could've lifted the injectors from the purse while Mandy was in the Ladies' Room. Both Mildred and Etta were already at the Grange when my wife and I got there. Either of them could have seen Amanda go to the Ladies', followed her and nabbed the injectors. And I happen to know, 'cause my wife mentioned this to me one time, that, depending on where she was, she sometimes didn't carry her big purse inside one of those restroom cubicles. If there was no hook inside the cubicle to hang a purse, she hated to set the thing on the floor, next to the toilet."

"Sooo, she could have left the purse on the sink, outside the cubicle?" Maggie mused.

"Right, and anyone in the restroom could have snatched the injectors," Sam replied. Again his head dropped to his hands. "My God! How could anyone, *anyone*, do something like this to Mandy? She was the sweetest girl who ever lived! You *must* find who did this! Promise me!"

"Be assured– *we will*," Raine answered.

A short silence fell upon them before Sam voiced his earlier thought. "I'm been thinking about this a lot, and I can't *help* thinking that Mildred Grimm might be figuring, with my wife out of the picture, I could be persuaded to sell to DHM Construction, so her pal Reggie can put up that friggin' shopping center the pair of 'em have been yappin' about. After all, Amanda was the one who really wanted to live on the farm, and with her gone–"

"And you didn't?" Raine cut in. It was not quite a question but displayed a desire for more information.

A sad expression settled over Sam's face, and his eyes went misty anew. "I would have lived anywhere Mandy wanted to live. I lived for her and through her. *She was my life*."

\*\*\*

The Sisters were keen to meet with their sleuthing set the following evening. They had arranged it upon their return from the funeral home, and the plan was that the coterie of sleuths would convene for a pick-up supper next door at Hugh's.

In happy surprise, it turned out to be an autumn picnic, as Betty christened it– cheeseburgers, hotdogs, baked beans, and potato salad.

After fixing their plates in the kitchen, everyone gathered before the living room's warming fireplace.

"Yes," Raine reiterated to their tight circle of sleuths, "when Sam said that if anything happened to him, we should go after Etta Story, the three of us immediately remembered what Hester Duff's spirit had forewarned at *Samhain*: "Death doth come, the death of three.""

"If Amanda and Sam were to *both* pass away, with no children, Witch-Tree Farm goes to the Washingtonville Historical Society, right?" Betty asked. "If that happens, Etta Story better have a damn good alibi!"

"That gives her glaring motive, all right," the Sisters responded, virtually verbatim and in unison.

"She would be the prime suspect, no question about it. We've learned it's been her aim to get hold of that farm for years." Raine took a bite of her cheeseburger. She'd put the works on it, and it was messy, so she leaned over her plate. As at every sleuthing session, she was sitting on the floor with Beau, the pair of them using a large, round leather hassock as their makeshift table.

Hugh and Betty were seated on the love seat, Maggie and Thaddeus on the longer couch, with Ian and Aisling sitting opposite one another in easy chairs.

"Great Goddess!" Aisling exclaimed. "Let's not program anything here!"

"*As it stands*, the one of the group that Will called the 'confounded pests,' who might have something to gain by Amanda's passing would be Mildred Grimm." Raine swiped her mouth with a paper napkin.

"Keep going." Hugh took a swallow of his iced tea, setting the glass down on the tray that rested before him on the coffee table.

"Sam pointed out that, in Mildred's way of thinking, DHM Construction would have an easier time convincing him to sell the farm, with Amanda out of the picture," Aisling repeated. "Memories and all."

"Bittersweet memories. Actually," Maggie interjected, "if Amanda's death was not a tragic accident, and by the bye, we don't think it was, that theory could be applied to the two land developers as well– they could each be thinking it will be easier now to convince Sam to sell Witch-Tree Farm."

"Sound logic," Hugh stated, turning to see that Betty was nodding her head in agreement.

"Has Sam gone to the police with his suspicions?" Ian wanted to know. As a former police detective, he could not help but pose this all-important question.

"He told us he's planning to talk to the police the day after the funeral … that would be tomorrow morning," Aisling answered. "Ian and I know the police chief over in Washingtonville well. Name's Michael Mann. Known in his district as 'The Man,' he's a bit of a hard case, but he's a good cop– tough but fair."

"By the way, did you notice anything suspicious at the Harvest Dance that verified what Eva Novak had shared with you at the Tearoom?" Hugh asked, looking to Raine and Beau. "Did it seem to you like any hanky-panky was or had been going on between–?"

"Indeed," Raine interrupted, so eager was she to reply to Hugh's query, "we caught a couple of things. You won't believe it, but …"

After discussing what first Eva at The Gypsy Tearoom, then Raine and Beau at the Harvest Dance had noticed about two of the central figures in their existing mystery, there was a lull, whilst everyone munched and mused over the comprehensive situation.

Finally, Ian's deep voice broke the silence, "Well now, what you just told us, in regard to the cupid component of our current challenge, throws a new light on matters."

"Or a brighter light," Beau quipped.

"We hope you'll keep your thinking caps on when we," Maggie stole a glance at her fellow sisters of the moon, "take a couple of short breaks from this probable whodunit."

"Right, the full moon's in three days. Thus we'll be time-trekking to find out more details as to what actually happened at the Witch Tree, and we'll be speaking with Hester Duff herself to learn as much as we can about her. We must execute our time-travel the night of the full moon." Raine put her cheeseburger down to sip her iced tea. "No way round that. We *have* to time-trek at that auspicious moon phase."

"And then, a couple of days hence," Maggie reminded, "the three of us will be heading out to Ohio to meet with Hester's descendant, Teresa Moore. No way to move that date either. We *have* to go when we have that break in our teaching duties at the college. Aisling, are you still willing to drive?"

"Yes, and let's be sure to get an early start that day. I telephoned Teresa, and everything is set for our interview with her, the day after Thanksgiving. In preparation, I've scheduled my SUV at the Auto Doctor's for a needed tune-up. It's been a while."

"Grantie Merry told us, via Athena, that Teresa has something in her possession that will help us clear Hester's name, and I can tell you that all three of us are burnin' to find out what it is," Raine said with her usual ardor for adventure. Due to Amanda's death, it's even more important that we connect the dots and prove Hester Duff's innocence, if we want to save that tree. In addition to which, we," she turned toward Maggie, "tend to think connecting all the dots about Hester will help us solve our current puzzle in connection to Amanda. Soooo, let us all keep calm and sleuth on until we come together again at Tara for Thanksgiving."

"What's going to be our portal this time-trek?" Maggie asked, glancing at Raine, then Aisling.

A moment of silent contemplation passed. Abruptly then, Raine and Maggie recited in-sync, as they were oft prone to do, from their thesis, "As always the entry should match the targeted destination."

"Well, we know from Athena's magickal movie that Hester's Colonial cabin was right close to the Witch Tree; so it would seem to me that the site of Hester's tree would be the very best portal this trip," Raine replied with aplomb. She popped a forkful of creamy potato salad into her mouth to fix her gaze on Maggie.

Next to her, Beau stirred, an intense expression crossing his face, as he murmured something incoherently. When Raine turned to regard him with searching eyes—

Maggie answered in response to the portal suggestion, "I agree. *Thaddeus*," she articulated teasingly, "are you up for going with us?"

With a glint in his vivid blue eyes, the professor replied, "Maggie, I'm *up* for anything you suggest. Need you ask? Count me in!" he practically shouted, tossing Beau a strange glance.

Out of the corner of her eye, Raine, still regarding Maggie, caught her Beau's subtle nod of thanks to Thaddeus. *There he goes again! I can't help thinking he's up to something. As Granny used to say, "The heart of another is a dark forest, always, no matter how close it has been to one's own."*

"How are we going to manage the Witch Tree portal without risking discovery?" the practical Aisling put to her sisters of the Craft.

"*Simple*," the more daring Raine answered, coming speedily back to earth. "We always embark on our time-treks at midnight; so, we just slip onto Sam's property— *and do it*. He'll most likely be in bed, asleep. Should he discover us, we just say we're doing a protection ritual for Witch-Tree Farm and the Witch Tree."

Aisling made an abrupt sound of accord. "We'll have to be stealthy."

"Sure thing," Raine laughed, quipping, "*Crafty* is our middle name."

"Can you see the tree from the farmhouse? Remember, the moon will be full that night, and it's only supposed to be partly cloudy." Aisling took the final bite of her burger, then picked up her napkin to dab at her mouth, depositing it on the folding snack table beside her chair.

"No," Maggie answered, "you can't see the tree from the house. Luckily, the Witch Tree's a good tramp from the farmhouse and situated in a valley." The redheaded Sister slid the last forkful of baked beans into her mouth. "Everything was delicious, darlings!"

"Thank you," Hugh and Betty answered.

"But I wish you'd have let us contribute to the meal this evening," Aisling chided.

"Baa!" Hugh huffed into his mustache. "It's only picnic foods!"

"*Comfort* foods," Raine said. "And they did the job. My appetite is satisfied and my passions positively piqued!" She slid Beau a sexy glance.

"Betty and I have another treat for you," Hugh stated. "And I'm not talkin' dessert, though that will be a treat too. We read both murder mysteries that Mildred Grimm checked out of the library in Washingtonville. In *Murder is Simple*, guess what? The victim, who is allergic to peanuts, is killed with peanut oil on a pasta salad."

**"What?!** Why didn't you tell us sooner?!" the Sisters exclaimed in unison.

"We wanted to save it for last," Betty interceded. "And after all we've discussed thus far, I'm glad we did." The former librarian leaned forward to set her paper plate down on the coffee table. "*There's more.* After we read both mysteries, we went a step further and drove over to Washingtonville's library to glean who else checked those same books out recently–"

"Whoa– time out!" Raine cut her short, signaling with her hands. "What was the *other* mystery about?"

"*Murder on the Road* is a newer mystery," Betty answered, used to Raine's impetuosity. "In that one, the murderer kills the victim by hacking into his car's computer." She took a quick sip of her tea. "But getting back to what I was saying: You were right. Mildred Grimm checked both those mysteries out, but Hugh and I figured it would be a *good* idea to see *who else* might have checked them out lately. And guess who did– right after Grimm brought them back to the library?"

**"Who?!"** rang out in chorus, prodding Hugh's sibling German shepherds, lying cozy before the hearth fire, to raise their heads and stare at the sleuthing set with questioning eyes.

Betty sat back in her chair and crossed her arms over her ample bosom. "*Etta Story*, that's who."

Beau gave a low whistle. "What Hugh and Betty ferreted out–"

"Thanks to Maggie's witchy notion to copy those titles down the day you interviewed Grimm and Story in Washingtonville's Abbott Library," Betty jumped in.

"Could prove to be *vital* information," Beau finished, pulling at his lower lip. "*Interesting.* Very, very interesting."

"Something's at work here besides coincidence," Raine muttered.

"Speaking of vital information," Aisling nodded her silvery blonde head, "Ian and I are going to be tied up with a case in Pittsburgh for the next day or so; nevertheless," she regarded her sisters of the moon, "you two should take a drive, after your classes wrap tomorrow, to Washingtonville to speak with Chief Mann. As I said, he knows Ian and me, so he's heard of the Sleuth Sisters. But to pave the way for you, I'll telephone him; and I'll put in a call to our own Chief Fitzpatrick, since we've worked with Fitz on several cases, to give Chief Mann an additional heads-up that you're coming in to talk to him. Like I said, 'The Man's' a tough old bird, but he's fair, and I'd bet my besom he'll welcome our help. Don't hold back. Tell him everything you've seen and heard thus far. I'm counting on you."

"Wiz–zard!" Raine exclaimed, with she and Maggie both bouncing back with –

"You got it, Aisling!"

"I always practice safe hex!"

~ A witch upon a time

# Chapter Eleven

The following day, after completing their teaching duties at Haleigh College, Raine and Maggie set out, in Maggie's Land Rover, for the Washingtonville Police Station to share with Chief Mann their suspicions, along with everything they had collected in connection with Amanda Woods' untimely death. Simultaneously, Aisling caught a break and was able to take her SUV into the Hamlet's Auto Doctor a day early for the scheduled tune-up.

"Aisling!" the receptionist Kathy Wise voiced with gentle surprise. "I haven't seen *you* for a while. Usually, Ian's the one who brings your vehicles in for servicing. How you doin', gal?"

Aisling smiled at the cute lady behind the counter. "Doing fine. Busy as ever. Ian and I had business in Pittsburgh this morning, that wrapped early, so I rang the Auto Doctor straightaway to see if you could tune my Jeep today rather than tomorrow as scheduled. There was a cancellation– *just as my witchy intuition had alerted me,* she thought– so here I am."

Undoing the clasp of her cape, at the throat, Aisling said, "Ian's going to pick up our daughter at school and take her to a ballet lesson this afternoon. If I'm finished here in time, I'll swing by the dance studio for Merry afterward, while he makes us dinner. At our house, my husband's the cook."

"You're lucky. When I get home from work, the first thing out of my husband's mouth is 'What's for dinner?'" Kathy, the supreme multi-tasker, had pulled up the file on Aisling's Grand Cherokee and located the work order for the tune-up.

Known throughout the Hamlet as "Savvy Kathy," Wise was exactly as her surname proclaimed. A middle-aged woman with a much larger personality than her petite frame belied, she possessed a head full of know-how and knowledge. The classic go-to gal, Kathy knew the answer to most questions, and she knew just about everyone in Haleigh's Hamlet and round about. Her super-short brown hair was heavily blonde-streaked and spiky, her clothing stylish. In summary, Kathy was streetwise, cute as a button, and someone the Sleuth Sisters always had an urge to hug.

"Where'd you park?" She was looking over the shoulder of Aisling's black wool cape to the entrance beyond. Before the Sister could answer, she asked, aiming a perfectly manicured finger at the black SUV she spied through the glass, "That's it, isn't it?"

"That's it. Here're the keys." Aisling handed them to Kathy, who gave a courtesy nod.

"OK, you're good to go." The receptionist picked up the phone and barked the order into the receiver, while replacing the file. "We just finished a tune-up on an SUV exactly like yours. Same make, model, and year. Only his was the brownstone color. Guy from over in Washingtonville. Sam Woods. He's the manager of the big lumber company over there."

"Has a vehicle just like mine, does he?" Aisling hummed, hoping Kathy would continue singing. Her information could be depended on for accuracy.

"It was his wife's car. He's going to sell it now she's passed away. Shame about that, wasn't it? So young and pretty, a dainty little bit of a girl. You know the type, sort of dreamy and not quite of this world. What a tragedy!"

"Sure was," Aisling agreed, not wanting to say more, so that Kathy might go on.

"I remember the first time Sam brought that Jeep in here, well over a year ago now. He bought it for Amanda because he wanted to make sure she had a heavy, four-wheel-drive vehicle, so she'd be safe. Said his wife was a nervous winter driver, so he'd gotten her something good in the snow." Kathy shook her head sadly. "Sam had even sought out a vehicle that sat a bit high, since Amanda was so small. You know, so she could see better, pulling out. He spoke so highly of his wife. It was always 'Mandy this' or 'Mandy that.' Sam was proud of the fact that she was such a good teacher. Told me several times how her students worshiped her. My God, you should've seen him. He looks *totally* different!"

"What do you mean?" Aisling pressed mildly, suddenly regarding Kathy with a curious expression.

"What I mean is Sam Woods was always a good-lookin' guy, and now he looks like hell, absolutely *dreadful*. He's taking his wife's death *hard*. Looks like he hasn't slept in a week. Looked too like the clothes he had on were straight from a jumble sale. He was always so," she reached for a word, "*upmarket,* or maybe *swanky* is the correct term; I don't know. All I know is I never saw him look like that, downright *sloppy*, and he's been coming in here for years."

Aisling raised her brows. "In here?"

Kathy nodded. "The Auto Doctor is known far and wide," she stated with observable satisfaction. "We offer the best service in the entire area; and as you know, we specialize in foreign and vintage cars. Sam drives a Mercedes. Anyway, the poor man said he was having nightmares."

Kathy leaned forward on the counter, toward Aisling, lowering her voice to a mere whisper. "He mumbled something about ..." she paused to recall the exact words Sam had used, "inadvertently blaring out something that might've brought about his wife's demise. Even muttered about ghosts, spirits, or some such boloney. Voices in the wind, I think he said, and strange noises in the house, nights. He wasn't really making much sense, but when he talked about it, he got real jittery, and his hands shook."

*Ghosts, voices in the wind, and strange noises out at Witch-Tree Farm.* Several thoughts were running through Aisling's head.

"Oh, he's been hit *hard*," Kathy repeated, oblivious of Aisling's wandering mind. "So much so, I'll tell ya the truth– I wouldn't be at all surprised if the poor fella doesn't end up having some sort of breakdown!" She shook her head. "You know what? I thought pigs would fly before I ever saw Sam Woods look shabby."

Aisling's face was pensive. "As Granny McDonough used to say, 'Pigs may fly, from time to time, but they're very unlikely birds.'"

\*\*\*

"As we always do before we time-trek, let's go over our reminder list," Raine said, snatching up the sheet of paper that dropped from the printer. "We don't want to forget anything." Her eyes scanned the items, as she mentally checked the roll of things they needed to take with them to the erstwhile Pennsylvania frontier. "Proper coins, in case we need them. Does Thaddeus have any we can use?"

"Yes," Maggie answered, "but, for this trip's targeted time and place, he has only three or four coins that would fit the bill, so let's hope we don't need more."

"I doubt we will. It's not like we'll be doing any souvenir shopping," Raine bantered.

Having returned from Washingtonville, the two Sisters were in Tara's tower room. It was early evening, and through the tall tower window, the Hamlet's lights twinkled charmingly.

The raven-haired Sister cast an eye down the list, reading aloud: "Appropriate Colonial attire that we'll rent from Enchantments costume shop downtown. I rang them a couple days ago with a list of what we need, based on our first trip back to the Pennsylvania frontier, and they have everything I mentioned. So tomorrow, after classes, we'll stop and pick up the order.

"To continue," Raine stated, reading from the paper she held: "A vial of Granny's powerful healing potion, just in case; a compass; Pennsylvania Long Rifle; all-purpose knife and a hatchet; a limited few grooming items and toiletries; of course our talismans, plus an additional piece, each, of our enchanted jewelry that will specifically aid us in this mission, but nothing ostentatious; and last but not least, our travel *BOS*," she pronounced, referring to their pocket-size, leather-bound *Book of Shadows* that contained the ancient chant that would transport them through the Tunnel of Time– and get them back home.

"Good thing Thaddeus purchased another long rifle," Maggie remarked, peering out the window to the snow-blanketed woods and fields below. It had snowed, off and on, all day, and now the landscape below glittered in the illuminations of eventide. "He replaced the rifle those Hurons snatched from us the last time we traveled back to the frontier. Like the stolen one, the new rifle's an excellent reproduction.

"As soon as we'd started talking about Hester Duff and the Witch Tree, Thaddeus began taking the rifle out, after classes, to the shooting range. Fires every time with the utmost accuracy, he was relieved to report, so he feels comfortable with it. 'Never take an untried weapon into battle or harm's way' is his motto. That man never ceases to amaze me. In more ways than one," the redheaded Sister murmured, the glossy ruby lips curving in the secret smile that was hers alone.

In a glimmer, however, Maggie snapped out of her romantic reverie. "Let's see now, Athena provided us with the date we needed; and we decided we're going to program our Time-Key for the day *before*, so that we might actually meet Hester Duff; in addition to which, we've decided on our portal, the Witch Tree. So all that's left for us to do in preparation for our time-trek is to pick up our frontier attire at Enchantments."

***

The next afternoon, Raine swung Maggie's vintage, green Land Rover into a parking space on the town square. After stepping out of the vehicle, she stood for a few thoughtful moments, regarding the Hamlet's pumpkin-and-cornstalk-bedecked gazebo.

Her emerald eyes swept the stately trees, devoid now of their autumn glory in expectation of winter's repose; the charming, genteel storefronts bordering the square, with their green-striped awnings and festive harvest and Thanksgiving decorations; the lacy wrought-iron park benches, bereft, in the November chill, of their familiar, warm-season occupants; the nostalgic Victorian lampposts with their outsized hanging baskets, the fall blooms, therein, bright and cheerful– and, as ofttimes happened, her heart flooded with love for Haleigh's Hamlet.

At moonrise the night before, staring out the tall windows of her woodsy-themed bedroom at Tara, Raine had gazed upon the waxing crescent and thought about the former occupants of their area– the Native Americans, so many years gone from where the Sisters now lived.

The Indians had christened the moons with such *illustrative* names. November's was the Hunter's Moon, the Frosty Moon, or Beaver Moon. If she peered deeply into the surrounding woods, she could almost see tall, dark figures moving, single-file and leaf-light, through the network of trees, returning perhaps from making council farther west or north, or from a hunt or a raid far from the relative safety of their villages.

Every time she walked in Haleigh's Wood, she felt the powerful presence of those Native Americans.

*I wonder if, this time-trek, we'll again encounter–* Her thought was interrupted as–

Coming round the Rover to stand next to her sister of the moon, Maggie said, "You're thinking about the Native Americans, aren't you?"

Raine gave an answering nod. "Thinking about how this land once belonged to them. As I tell my students, we're only lent our homes for a brief moment in time– as were they. We're all– and the Indians were right about this– *sojourners*, just passing through. We never really own the land, no more than we can own the sky, the rivers, or the ocean."

Maggie laughed her crystal laugh. "And as I told you before, darlin', I know this every time we pay our property tax!"

At Enchantments costume shop on the Hamlet's town square, Raine and Maggie walked briskly to the counter and rang the bell for assistance.

In a moment, the owner and manager, Lindsey Taylor, appeared from behind the curtain that separated the shop from the storage and alterations area.

"Good-afternoon, ladies," she smiled, securing a threaded sewing needle to her bodice. "I have everything packed and ready for you in shopping bags. Hold on, and let me get them. Be right back." The attractive brunette slipped behind the curtain.

In a moment, she reappeared, carrying three filled shopping bags that she set on the counter between herself and the Sisters.

"Here we go," she began, pulling the things from the bags to show Raine and Maggie. "Let's start with the ladies' things first. We'll save the gentleman's for last. For each of you, a plain linen, ankle-length, white petticoat called a 'chemise'; a wool over-gown, Raine's forest-green and Maggie's deep purple. For each of you, a short-gown. As you can see, it's like a blouse-jacket and should be hip-length, deep purple for Raine, rust for Maggie. It's held together … *closed* in front, by the apron you'll each be wearing. So, for each of you, a bibless apron that ties around the waist. For each, too, a large kerchief, both a lighter shade of green than Raine's frock; woolen black stockings that are gartered below the knee, with these." She held up the garters. "Black, leather shoes, the tops adorned with silver buckles; long, wool, hooded cloaks … capes that tie at the throat, both jet-black; and lastly, black, open-finger mitts. The open fingers afforded eighteenth-century ladies better use of their hands than the closed-finger gloves we wear today."

"Right. May we try the things on to make sure everything fits comfortably?" Maggie asked.

"I was going to suggest you do," Lindsey replied. "We can substitute what might not fit with comparable items. Then once you ladies are all set, we'll go over the gentleman's things."

Raine was already heading for the nearest dressing room, her items over her arm.

"Let's hope these frontier getups fit us," she said, ducking inside a dressing room.

About fifteen minutes later, the raven-haired Sister rapped on the separating wall between their changing cubicles. "How's it goin', Mags?"

"So far, good," the redhead answered.

"We'll be doing some walking, so let's make sure the shoes are comfortable," Raine advised. "For woodland walking, we really should take moccasins along with us. These leather shoes will be fine for indoors."

"True," Maggie agreed. "And the moccasins will render our forest footfalls quieter. Just thought of something else. Are we going to wear stays? Lindsey didn't mention them, but–"

"Hell no!" the Goth gal blurted. "We may have some long tramps through the woods, or we might have to run for our lives. *Nooo way* am I going to wear a corset! It's not like we've allowed our figures to run rampant!" She checked herself out in the dressing room's full-length mirror. "Need I remind you again, Mags, we're headed for the frontier wilderness, not a Philadelphia drawing room?!"

"Aw, pull in your Aries horns, you won't get an argument from me," Maggie retorted. "I'm all vested out in my frontier *getup*, to use your word, so if you are too, meet me at the long mirror out front."

When the Sisters emerged from their respective dressing areas, their eyes lit up at sight of one another.

"Surely, we'll pass!" Raine stated with vigor to Maggie. "I love these deep, rich colors; and we know, from our research, that they are authentic."

"Aye," Maggie answered, feeling the mood of the clothing. "Like me, Colonials loved bright colors; but dyes were expensive, so predominantly, their garments were of darker, even somber hues. However, red, purple, green, blue, and yellow dyes did exist."

The redheaded Sister looked to their poppet Cara, who accompanied them to the costume shop. When Maggie left the dressing cubicle, she set her purse, holding the doll, on a chair next to the mirror. Since Cara had lived on the Pennsylvania frontier, the Sisters valued her opinion. Glancing round to make certain no sales-staff or other patrons were within earshot, she asked in an anxious whisper, "*Will* we pass?"

Sticking halfway out of the designer purse's side pocket, the poppet bobbed her faded yarn head. "Ye look foine." The ragdoll trailed her words with a tiny giggle. "Like ye jes' stepped through th' Tunnel o' Time," she rhymed.

But the Sisters wanted that extra assurance, so engrained in all female essences. Before the full-length, wall mirror, each turned and twisted, this way and that, viewing themselves from all angles, as each smoothed, tugged, and adjusted their separate costumes.

Finally satisfied, Raine and Maggie stood for a protracted moment, staring at themselves in the tall glass. The women who gazed back at them– markedly with the hoods of their capes raised to cover their modern coiffures– were straight out of the eighteenth-century Pennsylvania frontier, and though their garments indicated that noblesse they were not, they looked fascinating, nonetheless.

Raine glided a finger along the black cloak's generous hood that becomingly framed her face. *"Witchy-Woman wicked,* don't you think, Mags?" she grinned, deepening the dimple in her left cheek.

*"Quite."* Maggie tossed her sister of the moon a playful *jeu de mots,* "We travel in style, darlin'.'"

When Raine lowered her hood, Maggie regarded that Sister's short, wispy, ebony locks. "Don't forget that new chignon you purchased! My hair's long enough to fashion my own bun, but make sure you remember to wear your faux one."

"Not to worry," Raine answered. "I set it out on my dresser, so in my excitement, I wouldn't forget." She glanced down at her Colonial-shod feet. "These shoes are quite comfortable. Very soft, and the square toes make them nice and roomy. I might not have difficulty walking in them; but having learned from experience, we'd better take a pair of moccasins for each of us, just to be safe," she concluded.

Maggie nodded, remembering well their other trip to the perilous Pennsylvania frontier, nearly a year earlier. She started to say something about that, to Cara, who stopped her with–

*"Whist!* She comes!"

"This is your lucky day," the approaching shop owner called to them, "I've just unpacked some ladies' pockets. Just got them in. They're exactly what the word implies– a large, deep pocket with a strong string cord that ties around the waist. It's worn over the apron to give the frontier goodwife accommodation for the tools she needs to go about her myriad of chores."

"Wizard idea, that!" Raine called after her, as Lindsey hurried off to fetch the string pockets. "We won't have to tote a pouch for what the Colonials called our 'possibles,' and our hands will be free for our pistols," she whispered.

"Lindsey never asks us what we need these costumes for," Maggie returned the whisper. "I'm relieved she doesn't, but I wonder–"

"Oh, she won't ask," Raine breathed, unabashedly admiring her reflection in the mirror. "I told her that, as history professors, we enjoy dressing in period outfits, the era depending on mood, with like-minded friends for a dinner party we host once in a while at Tara."

"When were you planning on telling me that?" Maggie hissed. "Suppose she would've asked me if we were doing something connected to our theatre group?"

Raine's kittenish face scowled. "She wouldn't have done that, goose, because *she's* a member of our theatre group!"

"Quit yer jawin'," Cara cautioned in her scratchy little voice, jerking her yarn-topped head in the direction of the advancing shop owner.

"Here you go," the woman said, handing each Sister a stringed pocket. "You said you always want to be authentic, so I think this is a nice touch."

"They'll do fine," Raine answered, reaching for hers and immediately slipping off her cape to tie it round her slim waist. She dipped a hand into the pocket to test the roominess. "Just right!" she declared more to herself than to Lindsey.

"You said you've assembled the frontiersman's outfit, suitable for actual travel through the woods," Maggie stated, turning from the wall mirror to face the saleswoman. "You know what I mean," she quickly amended, "one that would've been suitable for woodland travel." She rolled her emerald eyes at Raine when the clerk turned her head to direct an inquiring customer toward the shop's medieval section.

"All put together for you," the saleslady responded to Maggie. "We get a lot of requests for the frontiersman's costume during our Hamlet's Heritage Weekend, so we usually have several in house." She puckered her brow, her eyes making a cursory review of the Sisters. "I assume you plan on doing your hair to match the era; but other than that, you really look your parts. Come over to the counter when you've changed, so we can go through the man's outfit together."

Once the Sisters had exchanged their Colonial attire for their street clothing, they joined Lindsey at the counter.

The shop owner pulled the complete frontiersman attire from its shopping bag, saying, "One wool felt, low-crown hat, in brown; a leather haversack for the gentleman's 'possibles'; a loose linen shirt; a pair of linen breeches; wool stockings; high-moccasins; a warm frock coat; and a pair of leather leggings with leather garter ties. All in the sizes you asked for, but let's double-check everything," she suggested.

"Yes," Maggie affirmed once they'd finished, "this all looks perfect."

The next day was so demanding at the college that neither Raine nor Maggie found time to telephone Chief Mann. They wanted to follow up on what they'd shared with him two days before in connection to Amanda Woods' death. Finally, as they were having their tea at Tara's kitchen table, after gulping down the first food they'd eaten since breakfast, they decided to phone him.

When Raine rang off, she thought for a long moment, mulling over what the chief had said.

"Well, any news?" Maggie pressed, unable to stand the silence another moment.

"Sam was in to relate to the chief all his suspicions, but, other than that, there's nothing."

"Then why do you look as though there *is* something?" Maggie questioned.

***

Later that evening when Ailsing's SUV rolled to a stop before Thaddeus' imposing English-Tudor home, she pronounced the name, on the mailbox, of the neo-Gothic house, "*Joyous Garde*." Though a rather new home, the house possessed qualities of magick, enchantment, and most certainly, of beauty. "So, Sisters, did you ever find out? After *what* did the professor name his house– John Steinbeck's writing refuge or the idealistic refuge of Guinevere and Lancelot?"

"It's named for Guinevere and Lancelot's castle," Maggie replied without hesitation. "I put that question to my … *imaginative* professor right after you first asked me about it, months ago, but I kept forgetting to tell you."

Raine and Maggie were dressed for their Colonial time-trek, whilst Aisling was sporting her favorite black "uniform" of snug jeans and turtleneck sweater, leather jacket and high boots. Her ritual robe and everything the time-trekkers would need for takeoff was tucked into a large carryall that, for the moment, rested on Maggie's lap.

"Levitation!" Raine exclaimed. "I can't believe Thad's not waiting for us outside, rarin' to go, as he always is."

"Oh, I am getting forgetful! He rang me earlier to say he wants us to come in for a few minutes. We've time," Maggie said.

Kitted out in Colonial togs, Thaddeus fetched his Pennsylvania Rifle from its place above the fireplace in the den. Moving aside his karate trophies, he unlocked the gun cabinet to retrieve a filled replica powder horn, which he slung over his arm, and a couple of boxes of .45 caliber balls. To his costume, he made an addition of his own– a period backpack and blanket bedroll to which he had tied an ax. The eight-inch knife he carried in his right high-moccasin.

Now, as he held the rifle, almost lovingly, in his hands, he remarked, "I never named the long rifle the Hurons got from us–"

"No harm was ever done with it," Raine interrupted, adding smugly, "I *witched* that rifle."

"But, as I was saying," Dr. Weatherby continued, "I've named this one Ole Sure Fire. Couldn't really think of a better tag for her." He ran his hand over the beautiful curly-maple stock and the fancy inlay. "As we know, it was common practice for a frontiersman to have a name engraved on his long rifle," he tilted the flintlock toward the ladies, "which, as you can see, is what I have done, thus bestowing on this already individually crafted gun– a *personality*. In effect," he grinned, "I've *ordained* by bestowing the name Ole Sure Fire– *that it is so*." He sent the ladies a rakish wink. "Just a bit of added insurance."

"With most of Pennsylvania primitive woodland in the era we'll be visiting," Maggie commented, reaching for a fragment of classroom discussion, "settlers placed chief reliance upon their rifles for sustenance, security and survival. The Pennsylvania was the best investment a frontiersman could make."

"I've heard it said!" Thaddeus joshed. He gave the rifle an affectionate pat, "*dead accurate* the length of a football field."

Raine gave an abrupt nod. "Why, the Pennsylvania could bark a squirrel from the tallest tree, and fell man or beast at a hundred yards times three!"

When the ever-pragmatic Aisling cleared her throat, the professor got down to the real business at hand.

"Sit down there." He indicated a long, leather couch, surprising the Sisters with his intensity. "I want to talk to you. We've time before the moon is up."

He turned and reached inside the gun cabinet for a beautiful, ornate, ebony box the Sisters had seen on one other occasion. "Once again, I want both Maggie and Raine to carry one of these pistols *constantly*." He handed each of the fore-mentioned a pistol. "Pay attention. I don't know how much you remember about these. They're single-shot flintlocks, and since they are dueling pistols, each, like the long rifle, is dead accurate. However, unlike the Pennsylvania, these pistols are only lethal at close range, no more than twenty paces, but they're light weight and easier … *faster* to load and fire, which is why I've chosen them for you."

"I can't get over the workmanship and the real gold and silver inlay on these babies," Raine remarked in awe.

Maggie was closely examining the Goddess image on the carved pistol she held. *This is the main reason he's chosen these for us,* she zipped to Raine.

"Their real value is their precision," Dr. Weatherby reiterated. "They'll serve as strong protection. Since," he directed at Raine and Maggie, "we're all three history professors, I need not remind you, though I will anyway, of the dangers we'll be facing. Looking back in history, we know that the year we'll be visiting, 1787, translated extreme terror on the Pennsylvania frontier. Though the Revolutionary War had ended, the British, from their outposts beyond the borders of our infant nation, kept the Indians stirred to ever more treachery against the Americans, hoping to regain their lost colony."

He fixed Raine with his vivid blue gaze. "We don't know *what* we'll be facing, but I will tell you this, and *this* I promised Aisling, Ian, and Beau– when I say it's time to make a break for home, *we do it*. I've been abiding by your rules, ladies, and with this, you'll abide by mine. Clear?"

Raine cast Maggie a sideways look, the two of them shifting their eyes to Aisling, whose intense McDonough regard prompted their assenting reply, "Clear."

Dr. Weatherby tapped his bearded chin with a finger. "I *will* hold you to that covenant. Now, to return to our lesson: These pistols are English. If you recall, they take .52 caliber ball and, in addition to being plumb accurate, can inflict severe … *fatal* wounds. Here, take these too," the professor instructed, handing Raine a filled powder flask and balls. "Have a care now; each pistol is loaded."

Maggie and Raine rose, almost at once, to bestow on Thaddeus a grateful hug. Still in the three-way embrace, Maggie turned her head to kiss Thaddeus on the lips, after which he carefully reviewed with the Sisters how to load and fire the pistols, though both were comfortably familiar with flintlocks.

Since their first time-trek to the Pennsylvania frontier, Maggie, due to Thaddeus' prodding, had graduated from *capable* at their handling to Raine's *marksman* status. Whether or no the more emotional Maggie would be as steady under pressure– remained to be seen.

Aisling swung her long legs off the couch and stood. "The witching hour is nigh! In the midnight sky, the moon will soon be high! My question, then, to *you– **are you ready to fly?**"*

"More than ready!" Raine and Thaddeus enthused.

Maggie, however, was not as sure.

"As a result of the great Albert Einstein's Theory of Relativity, the time-traveler can say, "Let it happen!"
~ Author Ceane O'Hanlon-Lincoln

# Chapter Twelve

When they arrived at Witch-Tree Farm it was still about forty minutes till the stroke of midnight and the witching hour. The Sisters knew that turning points– "the betwixt 'n between"– such as midnight, the time between day and night; the meeting-point of shore and sea; or the turning of one season or year into the next were *magickal* transitional cusps. Even doorways were magickal portals to the Other Side.

Aisling had decided not to motor even partway up the long lane that led to the house for fear Sam would hear them approaching; hence they left the SUV, not far from the entrance of the drive, and walked through the woods onto the property. By chance, or the great Goddess' grace, with the aid of a flashlight, they struck a path that ultimately led them near to the Witch Tree.

It was, for the most part, a clear night, only partly cloudy but biting cold. The woods were extremely dark, and every once in a while, the little party stumbled against one another on the narrow trail. At one point, Maggie paused to take in a deep breath of air.

She loved the earthy forest smell, especially the scent of the tall pines. It was centering. Scent evokes memories, and the redheaded Sister was pleasantly reminded of a rainy forest encounter with lofty pines, years before, that had alleviated her stress and anxiety. Along with the redolence, a line from a favorite poem by Robert Frost drifted across her essence: *The woods are lovely, dark and deep, but I have promises to keep, and miles to go before I sleep– and miles to go before I sleep.*

Night noises permeated the otherwise quiet. An owl hooted and, in the distance, a fox barked a startling alarm. When the group exited the woods and set off toward the Witch Tree, its boughs reaching out as wide as it was tall, a small herd of white-tailed deer, foraging for food, raised their heads, snorted and bounded for safety.

Raine glanced skyward to check on the moon. It was something she did before every time-trek. Reassured to see no blood on the large golden orb this night, she drew a deep breath of relief, releasing the plea, *Oh hail, fair moon, leader of night! Protect me and mine until it is light!*

Of a sudden, a most frightening sound rose from the dark depths of the forest, an abrupt snarling growl followed by a loud hiss.

"What th' hell was that?!" Aisling muttered, stopping dead in her tracks and hunching deeper into her black leather jacket for warmth. She had switched off the flashlight as soon as they'd left the cover of the woods.

Somewhere, not very far away, a twig snapped with a sharp cracking noise, breaking the stillness of the night.

"Shhhhhhh," Thaddeus whispered, holding up a cautionary hand. "*Bobcat*. They can be more aggressive than a mountain lion. Out hunting, and *we* are interfering with that hunt. Let's give her a moment. Be still."

Everyone froze where they stood. It was quiet, except for the sudden rustle of something in the brush. Then, within the time it takes to cry "Gotcha!" they heard the squeal of the rabbit the hunt-cat caught, another quick snarl, and it was over.

Now it was Aisling's turn to release a sigh of relief. "Let's get down into the ravine, under the Witch Tree," she voiced quietly. "We'll be virtually invisible there."

"Good t'inkin', blondie!" Cara cracked wise. The poppet was sticking out of the blonde Sister's carryall so she wouldn't miss anything.

As they walked across the frosty meadow, Maggie grasped Dr. Weatherby's hard-muscled arm, "Did I ever tell you how handy you are to have around?" she breathed into his ear.

"Once or twice," Thaddeus replied with a low chuckle."

She turned her head to view the intrepid professor's profile in the moonlight and felt a rush of tenderness. *I love him more than I've ever loved anyone in my life.*

When they arrived at the foot of the Witch Tree, the redheaded Sister opened their last-minute checklist to full-sheet and began reading, "Pepper spray, just in case. With our magickal powers and Thaddeus' black-belt karate, we'll be safe enough, not to mention our weapons. However, we must keep in mind, at all times, that we can't do anything that will change the course of history."

"Pepper spray!" Raine answered, her hand slipping under her long cape to dip inside the deep pocket secured around her waist. "Check!"

"Our small, travel *Book of Shadows*." Maggie reached a hand into the pocket tied to her waist. "Got it!" Her eyes returned to the list, over which Aisling beamed the flashlight. "An ampoule of Granny's healing potion."

"Here!" The Goth gal held up the glowing purple vial. "I would never forget this!"

Maggie gave a short nod, continuing, "A few can't-do-without toiletries."

"Right!" she and Raine echoed in unison, with Maggie laughing, "Girls will be girls in any era!"

"Got my toothbrush," Dr. Weatherby remarked, thumping a hand to the leather haversack he was carrying over his shoulder. "And I brought my Colonial fire-starter, along with a few other items I think might serve us."

"Darlin,'" Maggie said, addressing Thaddeus, "are you wearing your contacts?"

"Yes," he replied. "And *yes* to the warning on your lips to keep my eyes tightly shut when we take off, so the wind in the blustery Time-Tunnel won't dry and irritate my eyes. Getting so I can read your mind, luv."

"Aye," Maggie rejoined, touching a finger to the side of her nose and endeavoring to get into Colonial mode.

"Aisling," Raine began, "I hope you remembered to bring a thermos of Eva's brew, Tea-Time-Will-Tell. Sorry we had to ask you to bring it again, but the one thing Maggie and I neglected to do was purchase a thermos."

"No worries," the blonde with the wand answered, "it's in my bag. I wouldn't have forgotten, not after you both reminded me at least half a dozen times today. Anyway, rest assured I get how much Eva Novak's special brew relaxes you enough to make your journey through the Tunnel of Time bearable."

As Aisling lifted a lantern from the satchel, she patted their poppet's yarn head, "Excuse me, Cara." This lamp burned fairly bright, and the senior Sister hadn't wanted Sam or anyone else to spy it. Now, in the relative safety of the ravine, she felt more comfortable lighting the thick candle inside. Hanging the lantern from a low branch of the Witch Tree, she said, "With the great Goddess' help and protection, let us, shall we say, *embark* on our evening's quest."

Aisling set the big canvas bag down on the bench under the majestic tree's far-reaching limbs. Opening wide the carryall, she extracted a thermos, then rummaged briefly through the contents to locate and draw out four collapsible plastic cups. After pouring the Tea-Time-Will-Tell special brew for the time-travelers and herself, she said, "Are we adding a drop of Granny's Easy Breezy Flying Potion to everyone's tea but mine?"

"Let's try *two* drops," Raine goaded.

"No!" Maggie argued. "Raine, darlin', you know you have a tendency to overdo. Let's start with one drop this trip. If we find that's not sufficient, we can add a second drop next trek."

"I agree," Aisling concurred, sending Raine a gentle nod. "Granny's flying potion is pretty powerful stuff!"

From the satchel she yet occupied, Cara handed Aisling a small, glowing vial of Granny's silvery flying potion.

"I believe a single drop per cup will do the trick." When Aisling went to return the vial to the satchel, Cara snatched it from her hand and deposited it safely inside the carryall.

"Aire ye no f'rrr-gettin' sumpin?" the haunted ragdoll asked in a querulous tone.

Aisling's tip-tilted McDonough eyes kindled. "Sorry about that, Cara." She reached in the bag to produce a flask and a child's cup. "This is good Irish whiskey, my little friend. I brought it especially for you." Having poured a drop into the tiny cup to which she first poured a small amount of tea, she handed it to the poppet.

"T'ank ye, lass." The doll lifted the cup to sniff the contents, the action stimulating a quiver. "*Uisce beatha.* Aye, 'tis good."

After handing Raine, Maggie, and Thaddeus each a filled vessel of tea laced with flying potion, the blonde with the wand smiled. "As last time, I think this calls for a special cheering cup. Thaddeus, would you again do the honors?"

Dr. Weatherby cocked his head and raised a finger in a wordless plea for "One moment," then he gave the dry little cough with which he sometimes prefaced significant remarks. "May the great Goddess keep us safe, and may we achieve a smooth homecoming, armed with the information we need." With that, he raised his cup. "To the full success of our mission!"

**"So mote it be!"** the Sisters and Cara chorused.

The poppet– that is, the ancient spirit who occupied her little rag body– drew in the sensation of her drink.

Everyone drank, presently draining their cups, as thoughts turned to their work at hand.

In the glow from the lantern, three pairs of McDonough green eyes sparkled, as Aisling, the senior Sister, regarded the time-trekkers, sending them a special blessing of safe travel.

"Before takeoff, let's go over some important data," Maggie said, breaking the transitory silence. "Thaddeus and I are a married couple, *Maggie and Thaddeus Weatherby*. Best to use our real names, like we've done on previous trips. And as on prior treks, Raine is my sister. Raine will be using her real name, and we all hail from out East, but came west for the same reason all the settlers did, for the freedom that life on the frontier could provide.

"We know the history of Braddock County well," the redheaded Sister went on, "so we'll have no difficulty answering any questions about it, should any be put to us. Raine, Thaddeus and I have concocted a likely story as to why we are in the vicinity of what is now Washingtonville, which, by the bye, used to be called Catfish Camp, after an old Indian chief whose encampment once occupied that site."

"The fewer people you actually engage in conversation, the better," Aisling advised. "Just get what you need and get back as quickly as you can."

"That's our usual MO," Raine murmured, hurriedly checking her face in the compact-mirror she pulled from her pocket. The lion-faced compact, having belonged to the lion-hearted Granny McDonough, had become a good-luck charm to the Sisters, providing an extra measure of the magickal mix of protection, assurance and conviction.

Except for a light dusting of powder and a natural-tint lip gloss, Raine and Maggie were not wearing makeup. Both, of course, had nixed their signature nail polish, Raine her ebony, and Maggie her scarlet-red.

"As we have with each time-trek," Aisling reminded, "we'll cast the same magickal spell to deal with the era's speech."

After momentarily conferring with Raine and Maggie on the ritual they would be performing, the senior Sister continued, "Within our secret chant, we'll weave a spell that will *witch* your speech– *hear and tell.* In other words, your speech will be heard by everyone you encounter as dialect familiar to them. The enchantment will work in the reverse as well, so that *everything* spoken to you and around you will sound … that is, will *translate* to your modern ears like our modern dialogue, slang, and patterns of speech.

"As I told you before each takeoff, the enchantment is not perfect," Aisling recapped. "Some words and phrases may flee the charm, but the spell *will* work." She gave a long sigh. "I think that just about covers it."

"Except for Cara," Maggie said, indicating their poppet, who, unusually quiet, was taking everything in. Cara rarely missed anything.

"Leave her here with me," Aisling instructed.

"Of course," Maggie replied. "She's here because, as always, she wants to see us off and wish us well."

"*Och!*" the doll squawked, lifting her little arms, as she raised her gaze to the stars. "Sure 'n haven't I tole ya over an' yet again not t' talk 'bout me as if I ain't here!" She ducked her yarn-covered head, and her reedy little voice softened. "You bet yer knickers I want t' be here f'r yer leave-takin'! Godspeed, me darlin's, and Goddess bless! This here's th' blessin' from yer granny. Muuuuuuuuu-waaaaaaaaaaaa!" She brought her wee mitt-hands to her mouth to blow a dramatic kiss, flinging her arms out as far as she could from her rag-stuffed body.

From the bewitched poppet's smeared, crooked mouth came a rush of crystalline faerie dust, silver and gold and shimmering, that wafted to the time-trekkers to settle over them, brightening and polishing their auras to a Divine brilliance with the Light of Protection. The farewell kiss had become a pre-takeoff tradition that the Sisters set great store by, for they could *feel* Granny McDonough's presence infusing them with power.

Now, with Thaddeus, they thanked the little doll.

*It was time.*

Reaching into her satchel, Aisling extracted her black ritual robe, slipping it on over her street clothes, and because it was so cold, even over her leather jacket.

Raine's emerald gaze swept the others, "Are we ready?"

"More than ready!" Dr. Weatherby almost shouted, so eager was he to begin their passage. He reached behind him to make certain his backpack and bedroll with the tied-on hatchet were all secure. He checked to make sure his haversack was closed and his low-crowned felt hat firm on his head. Then he picked up his Pennsylvania long rifle and, unbeknownst to the others, whispered a prayer of protection of his own making. "Maggie, Raine, have you the pistols?"

"Yes," they responded, each feeling for her weapon, tucked, as they were, in each Sister's belt under their capes. At the last minute, Thaddeus had fetched Maggie and Raine belts before they departed from his home.

"Sisters," Aisling commanded, "Thaddeus, let us spiritually and mentally prepare ourselves for your journey. If all goes as well as your preceding time-travels, you'll be back in a literal flash, with no actual lapse in time, for we are scientifically mindful, as well as spiritually aware, that the past, present, and future are simultaneous." She glanced skyward at the moon– directly overhead. "Let us proceed."

As Aisling delved into her carryall for her magickal tools, Raine caught her breath. A feeling of imminent danger skittered along her spine, chilling her like a dip in an ice-crusted river. It was a feeling she had experienced before other time-treks, and she knew well what it meant. "Maggie," she whispered, "do you feel it?"

Rooted to the spot where she stood, Maggie was listening intently, scarcely breathing. "Yes," she returned in a whisper, "I do." *We'll have to be especially vigilant,* she added telepathically.

Raine tilted her head, covered with the hood of her long, black cape. For a fleeting moment, she thought she heard a frightful scream of terror coming from somewhere distant. *Perhaps it was the fox, or the bobcat. Either can sound like a person screaming.*

Oblivious of the exchange between Raine and Maggie, or the terrified shriek carried on the wind, Dr. Weatherby's vivid blue eyes reflected the excitement he was striving to contain within his own bubbling essence.

Watching him, Aisling thought, *He always reminds me of an astronaut ready for launch, or the way the pilgrims must have looked when first someone shouted, "Land Ho!"*

"Sisters!" she said, waving her hand before both Raine and Maggie in an effort to bring them out of their reveries, "Our chant will incorporate all the particulars. The date you've chosen to visit is Tuesday, 30 October 1787, the day before the mysterious incident at the Witch Tree.

"Though it is midnight now, we'll program for the three of you to reach the woods near the Witch Tree and Hester Duff's cabin at 7:00 in the evening, so you'll have more time to accomplish what you need to do. Since where you're going, it will be late October, it'll already be nightfall, and the woods where you'll land will be plenty dark for cover. Your visit should provide you with sufficient time to meet Hester and learn whatever you can about her, and then, the following day, to observe exactly what happened at the Witch Tree."

Aisling cleared her throat. "I strongly advise you to stage your return in the dark of night from the woods. If everything goes smoothly, when you do reenter your own time, as I said and we all know from experience, not one minute will have passed from your departure. I'll be right here, waiting for you."

"Aye, an' I'll be here, a-waitin' too! B'tweenwhiles, I'll keep Aisling company." Cara emitted a mischievous giggle. "As witches we know– ye're niver too old t' play wit dolls! Safe journey, me darlin's!!"

Turning toward Dr. Weatherby, Maggie addressed him with the old-fashioned schoolmarm ring of authority she used when instructing her college students. "I know we've gone over this at the onset of each of our time-treks, and at this point in our relationship, I feel I hardly need to; but, nonetheless, I'm going to say this. When we arrive, you must not interfere with our plan. Simply put, we three will be witnesses to history. And that is all. We must not, any of us, *in any way,* alter history."

"I quite understand," Dr. Weatherby assured his beloved. "And I hope you both," he especially directed his intense blue gaze to Raine, "keep the covenant you struck with me. We come home when I deem it right. We *must* put safety first this trek due to the precarious situation into which we'll be dropping."

"Agreed," the Sisters echoed, though Raine's voice carried reluctance.

As was her practice, the raven-haired Sister was bracing herself for the Time Tunnel's bluster. Lowering the hood of her cape, she checked to make certain her faux ebony chignon was tightly pinned in place. Then she raised the hood and double-knotted the cape's tie at her throat. Next, she felt under the cloak, in the deep pocket for her "possibles," lastly running her fingers over the cool grip of the pistol secure in her belt.

Taking her cue from Raine, Maggie did likewise, preparing herself for takeoff.

"Talismans at the ready!" Aisling commanded. Reaching under the bodice of the ritual robe, the leggy blonde pulled her gem-encrusted amulet free from its resting place beneath the black jacket and sweater she was wearing. She lifted the heavy silver chain over her long, silky hair. The talisman's center-stone sapphire and scatter of tiny jewels glittered and sparked energy in a beam of moonlight that streamed through the network of tree cover.

Thus impelled, Raine and Maggie removed their amulets from around their necks. In addition, each wore a medieval ring of great significance and strong arcane energies. Hundreds of years old, worn and dulled by Time, the rings' brass shafts bore faded secret symbols etched into the sides of the mounts that held, in each, a large blue moonstone. Already, the ancient rings were beginning to emit a shared bluish luster, a glow that looked particularly eerie in the Witch Tree's shadowy gloom.

Under Dr. Weatherby's watchful eyes, the Sleuth Sisters held out and fit together the three necklaces bequeathed to them years before by Granny McDonough, whose influential presence her magickal granddaughters now sensed even more keenly. In each pair of Sisterly hands, the powerful talismans actually felt warm against the skin– as they verily hummed with energy.

"Thaddeus and fellow sisters of the moon," Maggie enunciated in her mellifluous voice, "for the original definition of the word *talisman*, we must hark back to ancient times. Before it was known as a magickal symbol, *talisman* carried a far older meaning. From the Greek word *telesma,* meaning 'complete,' a talisman, in olden times, was any object that completed another– *and made it whole.* I say this to remind and assure us, here present this night, under this arboreal cathedral of the great Goddess– of the majestic Power of Three." Taking her beloved by the arm, she said, "Move in close, darlin', betwixt Raine and me."

The full moon, sliding from beneath a cloud, whence it had briefly cached itself, flashed a timely and quite dazzling blaze of light off the fitted talismanic pieces, as the Sleuth Sisters united their voices to invoke in perfect harmony, "With the Power of Three, we shall craft and be granted our plea! With the Power of Three, so mote it be! With the Power of Three, so blessed be!"

Holding her antique heirloom out to her cousins, Aisling said, "I don't need to remind you that Merry Fay is my reason for not accompanying you; however, take this with you again. You *must* maintain, as much as possible, the sacred and supreme Power of Three," she asserted.

Raine and Maggie hugged Aisling for a long, loving moment, as memories of all they had accomplished together came flooding back to the three of them.

*In the moon-drenched dell of the Witch Tree, it was a moment of supreme empowerment.*

Then Maggie, the middle Sister, slipped the senior Sister's amulet around her neck, together with her own. Raine put her talisman on again, as Aisling reached into the canvas bag she carried over her arm for the container of sea salt, a fire-starter, and a bundle of white sage handed to her by Cara.

With the salt, the senior Sister drew a circle of protection around the soon-to-be-traveling three people, whom, after her daughter Merry Fay and her husband Ian, she loved most in all the world. Flicking on the fire-starter, she lit the sage-bundle that she secured inside a small Pyrex bowl drawn from the satchel. In an instant, the air around them filled with the sweet, pungent aroma of the good, smoking essence.

Walking a circle with the smudge deosil– clockwise– the blonde Sister cleansed the area of negativity.

Finally, Aisling nodded to her sisters of the moon, as the powerful threesome chanted a strong incantation of protection, ending with the petition, "God-Goddess between us and all harm!"

As one, the Sisters again began to chant, "Wind spirit! Fire in all its brightness! The sea in all its deepness! Earth, rocks, in all their firmness! All these elements we now place, by God-Goddess' almighty strength and grace, between ourselves and the powers of darkness! So mote it be! Blessed be!"

In the glow of the tree-hung lantern, and with careful expression, the Sisters and Thaddeus intoned aloud the ancient Gaelic words, the arcane phrases Raine and Maggie had, over the years, so diligently ferreted out, the secret text neatly handwritten across their small *Book of Shadow*'s final pages– the ordaining language that programmed and powered their sacred travel through time.

*The Time-Key.*

Since the ancient chant was in Old Irish, in order to get it *letter-perfect* each time, it was best for the Sisters to *read* the words from their *Book of Shadows,* though the chant had almost burned itself, by this point, into their collective memories. After his first spell-trek with Maggie and Raine, Thaddeus's eidetic mind had snagged and stored the Time-Key, a fact that saved their lives on one, especially problematic, occasion in the past.

Their unified voices rising with each line in crescendo, the Sisters closed the current segment of their ritual with the words, "To honor the Olde Ones in deed and name, let Love and Light be our guides again. These eight words the Witches' Rede fulfill– 'And harm ye none; do what ye will.' Now we say this spell is cast, bestow again the Secret we ask! **Energize the Time-Key!** So mote it be! Blessed be!"

In perfect stillness did they wait.

Not a sound broached the silence. The night, at some point, had become totally hushed. The moon cast murky shadows through the Witch Tree's lacy canopy of boughs to the cold ground, as the surrounding woods seemed to breathe a message that was just beyond hearing.

The Sisters and Dr. Weatherby knew from past experiences not to panic, and so they used the interval to further center themselves, drawing in their breaths and breathing out slowly, sustaining the calm bestowed on them by Eva's tea.

And as it had been with their previous time-treks, it was as though Time waited– as though something momentous were about to unfurl within their established circle.

"Let us restate the passage," Aisling wisely proposed. "You have made your choice, and now you must focus! You've woven your intent within the ancient chant. You *will* arrive at your programmed destination. Put aside– each of you– any and all doubts, fears, and," fixing Thaddeus with her piercing McDonough gaze, "*impatience*. The magick cannot be rushed. Free yourselves from all negativity– and simply allow the Great Secret to happen. For happen it will! Give yourselves up to it!"

Again, the Sisters and Thaddeus chanted the ancient evocation, hands raised in calling forth. Prompted by Aisling, they added at the last: **"Now is the time! This is the hour! Ours is the magick! Ours is the power!"**

Having repeated the afterword *thrice*, the Sisters' ancient talismans, resting against their skins, radiated with heat– and the super Power of Three– as the conjured energies sparked, swished and swirled around them. They could feel those energies rising in a steadily growing cone of power– *a huge witch's hat, ghostly and omnipotent–* above their heads. It was the way of strong magick, and thus it did not frighten the trio of witches or their colleague the least bit.

For a fleeting moment, both Raine and Maggie thought they caught sight of something filmy white and vapory within the shadowy tangle of Witch-Tree limbs silhouetted against the moonlit sky.

*Could it be the spirit of Hester Duff?* they asked themselves, zipping the thought to each other.

They listened intently. *Were those her elusive words– suppressed and carried eerily away upon the whispering wind?*

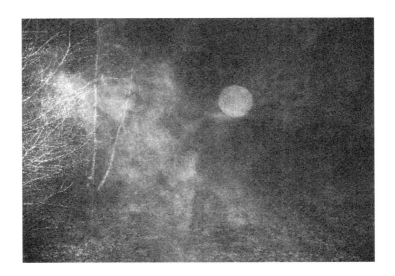

Though they strained to hear, they could not make out what the lost words were attempting to convey to them; and then, in the tradition of ghosts, the vaporous form vanished.

Raine and Maggie waited in sharp anticipation, but there was nothing, only the tree, the wind, and, beyond, the surrounding woods and textured darkness.

"Ah!" Thaddeus suddenly exclaimed, a glimmer of a smile flitting across his features.

There came, softly at first, then louder, an electrical crackling sound, as gleaming sparks and orbs of white light zigged and zagged above and around the human circle, turning the tree-shrouded scene increasingly eerie.

*Magick crackled in the very air they breathed.*

Slipping in and out of cloud cover all evening, the elusive moon slid free of its veil, choosing to show itself brilliantly at the express moment when Aisling took a step back, outside the circle of time-travelers. Her long blonde hair, silvered even more by moonlight, blew out behind her, as a terrific gust of cold, bone-chilling wind rushed across the area.

Otherworldly in its timbre, the wind carried on its breath the enchanted flutes of the mysterious race of people from Ireland's ancient past, the mystical *Tuatha De Danann*, from whom the Sisters had gained the coveted Time-Key.

From its supporting branch, the lantern began to swing precariously from side to side, causing the thick candle therein to flicker wildly. The wind moaned, and carried on its breath, too, the Sisters and Dr. Weatherby distinctly heard the melancholy hooting of an owl.

Seconds later, when the mystic wind blew the sputtering flame out, Maggie grasped her professor's arm, gripping hard. "Steady on now, darlin'! We know what's coming!" she called over the din, as the ghostly gale tore at her long, black cape and her layered skirts beneath.

As always, the Sisters were impressed by Dr. Weatherby's show of courage. His upturned face looked calm, serene, and his eyes were closed. Pushing his hat tighter on his head, he shouted, "Let it happen!"

Those words had no sooner left Thaddeus' mouth when, in a burst of light, a bevy of ethereal faces, skeletal figures, and vaporish human forms appeared in the rising, swirling mists, their gaunt arms widening beseechingly, their mouths opening in what looked to be silent screams. As the strange beings zeroed in on the time-travelers, the threesome caught snatches of the Time-Key chant.

In a blink of an eye, another burst of bright light, and the figures' claw-like hands snaked tightly round the time-trekker's ankles, heaving Raine, Maggie, and Thaddeus, with supernatural strength, toward the vortex of a pitch-black tunnel– a twister of helical wind that threatened to pull them into its infinite void with the force of a gigantic vacuum.

So strong was this gale, howling and whirling with accelerated ferocity, that the Witch Tree and the entire encircling woods seemed to strain and shriek. Not wanting to be separated, Raine, Maggie and Thaddeus held fast to one another, strengthening their power and protection with the intense love they shared.

Simultaneously, just outside the circle and their established Doorway of Time, the senior Sleuth Sister stood her ground. With her long, blonde locks blowing violently about her upturned face, and her black robe billowing out from her tall, slender body, her arms shot skyward, as her chant carried on the wind to spin faster and faster around the time-travelers.

Aisling's confidence never failed to infuse pluck and purpose into Maggie and Raine. Each locked hands with Dr. Weatherby, and for a magickal moment, the time-trekkers seemed limned in silver– each a nimbus of light! Raising their joined arms, the three of them– keeping cadence with the chant of the wraithlike figures– repeated the last line of the arcane passage yet again.

A thick, vaporous cloud was rising from the depths of the cold November ground– that started quivering and rumbling beneath their feet– even as the air around them continued to swish and swirl like the mightiest of whirlpools. Lightning cracked, and a tremendous roll of thunder assaulted their ears with a mighty **RO————AR!**

Maggie squeezed Thaddeus' hand. "It's happening!" she called out, determined to stay calm.

"Brace up!" Raine shouted. "It won't be long now!"

Suddenly, the churning atmosphere opened with a violent suction– making them feel as if they were being swept down a giant drain! Rapidly then did the Tunnel wholly swallow Raine, Maggie, and Dr. Weatherby, as Aisling disappeared from their view in a brilliant burst of blue-white light, her voice rebounding after them, **"Bles————————sed Beeeeeeeeeeeeeeeeeeeeeeeeeeeeee!!"**

Quicker than any one of them could answer "Blessed be," the time-travelers were forcibly hauled deeper and deeper– into the long, black Tunnel of Time.

Above the blustering din, Maggie's voice echoed through the dark corridor, **"Hold tight to one another! We can't chance being separated!"**

**"Wherever we go,"** Raine's words rumbled down the mysterious passageway– **"we go together!!"**

*** 

With a thud, Raine landed on her tush, the touchdown cushioned by a mound of leaves banked against a soaring pine that acted like a backstop. In expectation, the raven-haired Sister glanced quickly around, but it was too dark to see Maggie and Thaddeus.

In an anxious, strained whisper, she called, "Maggie? Thaddeus? Are you here ... with me?"

Silence answered, and Raine's heart skipped a beat. *Perhaps they didn't hear me.* "Mags! Thad!" she called again, holding her voice, as best she could, to an undertone.

Still there was no response. The Sister listened, but the only sound was the wind hissing and groaning through the tall pines. Other than that, the forest was hushed. Not even the sounds of the wily creatures of the night did she hear– and *that* alarmed her even more.

Without warning, something– *or someone*– gave rise to a rustling sound. Hardly breathing, Raine strained to hear. Were those nearing footfalls she heard? *Likely a critter scurrying for its burrow*, she told herself after several daunting moments.

Keeping her fears in check, she started crawling on hands and knees on the leaf-blanketed forest floor, calling out, in raspy whispers, as she went, "Mags! Thaddeus!" *We've never gotten separated before*, she sent Maggie the brainwave. *Where are you?!*

"Over here!" came a familiar voice.

Her heart swelled with gratitude and relief that Thaddeus had answered. He and Maggie were sprawled beneath another towering pine several feet from where Raine had landed.

"Thank you, God-Goddess," she breathed. Then the Goth gal filled her lungs with the crisp, cool air, fragrant with the woodsy autumn aroma of decaying leaves, her gaze sweeping their milieu as her eyes attempted to adjust to the murk. "It's too dark to see anything clearly, but it sure smells like October," she said.

After taking a deep breath, Maggie's eyes shifted to the surrounding forest to perceive where capricious Time had dropped them. "If all went as planned, we should be in the woods near the Witch Tree and Hester Duff's cabin." She sucked in another deep breath. "Aye, it's definitely October. Let us hope 30 October 1787." She took yet another breath and released it slowly. "One thing I do know: This landing was *far* easier than our previous passages, even our last one, which was darn good!" Her hands came up to lift the hood of her cape to her head, after which she twisted toward Thaddeus. "Darlin', what say you?"

"I say we hold our tongues. No tellin' who, of our fine feathered friends, might be lurking about in these woods." Satisfied that his long rifle was beside him, he began feeling over his person, checking that everything was intact. "Stay put and *quiet*," he commanded in an emphatic whisper. Getting to his feet, he dusted leaves and bits of tree bark from the seat of his breeches, then picked up his rifle. "I want to orient my compass. I'll be back directly."

"No more of that horrid nausea we used to experience!" Raine exclaimed, moving close to her sister of the moon and holding her voice to a murmur; as, with her hands, she began taking stock of her own costume. Everything seemed "to rights." After a moment, she said, keeping her voice low, "I still think we need just a *tad* more of Granny's Easy Breezy Flying Potion." *Ah! Trekking back in time does provide such nice, clean air!* she thought, filling her lungs again. "This fresh atmosphere tells me we've definitely time-traveled."

"Raine, I still hold that two drops would be over the top. If we'd overdose with Granny's powerful flying potion, we might just revert back to the horrid nausea. And who knows? We really could end up disconnected from one anoth–"

Thaddeus loomed over them, and though they could not see his features in the forest gloom, they most definitely *felt* his discontent in his harsh whisper. "Hush!!" His bright blue eyes had adapted to the lack of light, and now they probed deeply into the shadowy foliage and thick underbrush, searching as absorbedly as his sharp ears were listening. "Shhh," he hissed, sensing approaching danger and holding up a hand for silence– a hand that the Sisters perceived, though faintly.

A crow cawed from the uppermost branches of a tall, dead tree that, moaning on the wind, gave forth a lonely, forlorn sound. When a night creature sent out a call of alarm, the crow took suddenly to the sky, complaining raucously. Then, as though an unseen hand had flicked a switch, the forest went quiet– *too quiet.*

Dr. Weatherby hurriedly pushed the women down to the damp forest floor, behind some accommodating boulders. "Shhh," was all he breathed, but in such a manner, they instantly obeyed. Instinctively, they knew not to move a muscle.

Then they heard it, the soft sound of moccasin-shod feet on the leafy path– just inches from where they were hiding.

Within a few moments, nine warriors trailed past. They were moving along at a good clip, single-file and silent. In a beam of bright moonlight from an opening in the canopy of trees, the crouching "chrononauts" saw that the Indians were grotesquely decorated for war. As the Sisters' tip-tilted eyes slid sideways and upward, they got a chilling glimpse of a scarlet-red, vermilion-covered body and visage, a black hand painted over the face, the stiff roached hair adorned with feathers.

As the last warrior tread lightly by, a rabbit dashed across the narrow, leaf-strewn trail, causing the Indian to abruptly stop and turn about. He ventured back a couple of feet, coming precariously close to where the time-trekkers were secreted behind the boulders.

Gingerly, Dr. Weatherby felt on the ground for a pebble. Picking it up, he lobbed it across the trail into the tangled forest vegetation. Of a sudden, either that rabbit, or another, stirred in the underbrush, darting out and fleeing to safety.

Hardly daring to breathe, Raine, Maggie and Thaddeus waited for what seemed like a time without end, Maggie with her hands over her mouth, her eyes closed in silent prayer.

A few seconds later, with guttural expression, the Indian hurried to catch up with the war party, satisfied that it was a four-legged varmint he'd heard.

The redheaded Sister slipped a hand under the layered bodices of cape and dress to run her fingers over the treasured amulets around her neck– and finally let out a long breath of thanks.

Releasing his hold on the knife at the top of his high moccasin, Thaddeus stood, clutching the long rifle and glancing cautiously about. "I know which way we need to go, and be grateful it's in the opposite direction from those Shawnee," he murmured, pulling Maggie to her feet.

Raine removed her hand from her pistol, then making certain of her own talisman, rose and, speedily brushing leaves from her long, black cape, adjusted the cloak's hood over her head.

"I'll feel better," Dr. Weatherby pressed in a keen whisper, "when we're out of these woods and in the shelter of Hester's cabin. I'll lead. Raine, you bring up the rear, for you're the next best shot. *No talking*. Stay close, and keep your weapons at the ready, but have a care you don't trip on an exposed root 'n shoot yourself, me, or each other. Let's move."

## Chapter Thirteen

From the dark tree line where they were paused, the time-travelers could see, in the misty moonlight, Hester Duff's lone cabin in its clearing. It was a one-room log dwelling with a stone chimney, from which smoke curled invitingly. Through a chink in the shuttered window, either a candle or the hearth-fire glowed.

"We'll wait till the moon slides behind those clouds," the professor whispered. "Then we'll move fast and low across the clearing to her door. Keep your mouths closed and your ears 'n eyes open. This time, Raine goes first, and I'll bring up the rear." Thaddeus gazed upward, uttering after a few moments, "Now!"

The threesome dashed across the open area, keeping as low as they could. When they reached the cabin, Thaddeus, who had walked the last several feet backward, rapped lightly on the thick wooden door.

"Yer name an' yer business!" a strong female voice from within called.

"Travelers seeking vittles and a warm place by your fire for the night. We can pay," Dr. Weatherby answered, yet guarding their backs.

The plug in the thick door's rifle loop was unsealed, and an eye peered out at them before the barrier creaked opened a couple of inches. Hester must have been satisfied, for she moved the creaky door wide enough to allow the time-trekkers entrance. Her visitors immediately noted that she was clutching her rifle, and her bearing warned she would not hesitate to use it.

"You'd best come in out of the cold and harm's way," she asserted in a voice that bespoke self-assurance. "Ordinarily, I would not accept coin f'r common kindness, but iffen yer offerin', I'm acceptin', f'r me gut's tellin' me I might be needin' the coin in near future."

"Obliged," the professor answered. "Name's Weatherby, Thaddeus Weatherby. This is my wife, Maggie, and her sister, Raine McDonough. And whom do we have the pleasure of addressing?"

The woman was sizing them up, making certain that her decision to allow them access into her cabin had been a sound one. She was, as legend chronicled, strikingly beautiful with glossy raven locks that flowed down her back and over her shoulders. Her ankle-length, linsey-woolsey dress was dyed a deep midnight blue to match her eyes, and her long, bibless apron was snowy white. Milky fair was her flawless skin, and there was a rosiness to the cheeks that suggested her Highland ancestry.

"Hester Duff," she replied. Her tone hinted that she was glad she'd opened her door to them, for a flicker of a smile curved her lips to accompany the name and sweeten it, though she still held ready with the rifle. "F'rgive me lack iv manners. H'ain't used to company. G'on; git yerselves warm by the fire. I'll rustle ye up sumpin t' eat. I got some stew in the pot there I kin dish up fer ya, and I'll put the kettle on f'r tea. Got some leftover cornbread from yest'rdy, iffen y' ain't bothered that it hain't zacly fresh; but yer welcome t' crumble it inta yer stew, if ye've a mind ta."

"To echo my husband, mistress," Maggie repeated in a soft tone, "we're obliged." *Well now*, the redheaded Sister thought, scanning the woman before them and her cabin, *If cleanliness is indeed next to godliness, then our Hester is truly a goddess.*

The cabin was small and cozy with a wide-plank floor that was graced, here and there, with a bright rag rug. There was a tiny sleeping loft with crude but sturdy ladder. A yawning fieldstone hearth dominated the sole room. Over the fire, which was kept burning at all times, was a big, black cook pot suspended from an iron swing-arm known today as a "fireplace crane," known then by the more fascinating moniker "witch's arm." Resting next to the fire was a large, cast-iron, three-legged skillet the era's goodwives called a "spider." The three history professors recognized it instantly as the main cooking utensil on the frontier. Fireplace and kitchen tools, as well as a hodgepodge of odds and ends, hung on both sides of the hearth opening.

The fire in the hearth provided the cabin's only light. It was wasteful, even reckless, on the frontier to burn candles needlessly, though the small, single window was shuttered now, day and night, against the late-October chill and the threat of Indian attack.

In one corner was a spinning wheel, and occupying the place before the hearth was a long wooden bench, or "settle," that doubled as a storage chest. Its high, solid back served to protect against the bitter cold of winter nights.

The room's low ceiling, beamed by the stout logs from which the cabin was constructed, lent an air of security and protection. Dried herbs, most of which the Sisters recognized as curative, hung from a section of the beams. The log walls were studded by pegs that held Hester's long, hooded cloak, as well as various household items necessary to the harsh and demanding life on the Pennsylvania frontier.

"Indeed," Raine was saying, "'tis good to be inside, safe and warm. We thank you."

Hester, meanwhile, was staring intently at Raine. "F'rgive me gawkin', but sure 'tis as if I ken you, lass."

*You do **know** me, Mistress Duff, from our wind talking*, the Goth gal thought, though she merely smiled to say aloud, "Mayhap we chanced upon one another at the trading post at Catfish."

Hester shook her head, seemingly recalling something the Sisters couldn't quite pick up. "That ain't it." She shrugged, redirecting her thoughts. "Forest ain't zacly the safest place t' be nowadays."

Whilst Mistress Duff continued to stare at her visitors, Thaddeus stood his rifle against the wall and slid the pack off his back, lowering it to the floor by the hearth. On a peg there, the time-trekkers hung their wraps as well as Thaddeus' haversack, the Sisters setting their pistols down next to the professor's things. They kept everything together, so not to forget anything at their departure on the morrow.

All the while, Hester was guardedly watching them. Finally, she placed her own rifle– that Dr. Weatherby noted was an Indian trade gun– in a corner next to her powder horn suspended from a hook. Without further delay, she set about brewing the promised tea and dishing up the rabbit stew, into wooden trenchers, from the big black pot over the fire.

"Sit ye down, folks, 'n make yerselves t' home," she gestured, indicating a rough-hewn table and two chairs. "Mister, do me a boon and fetch us down those two extra chairs from the wall pegs yonder."

Thaddeus did as she bid, arranging the chairs at table. "Sure smells good," he commented, for lack of something else to say. He reached into his shirt pocket and produced two coins, placing them on the table. "For your hospitality."

"Allow me to divine, sir, yer callin'," she said, her eyes probing. "Might y' be a schoolmaster?"

"Aye," he grinned. "That I am … *was*," he looked to the Sisters, continuing, "some years back, in Philadelphia, whence we've come."

"I been to Philadelphy," Hester stated, setting the trenchers of stew, along with crude, hand-fashioned wooden spoons, on the plank table before her visitors. Forks were rare on the frontier, but since so many of the meals were soupy, it mattered little.

"Don't rightly remember it though," she adjoined in reference to Philadelphia, putting a hand to her thrust-out hip. "Was only a *bairn* then, whin me folks carried me here to America from th' Old Country." She glanced at her guests. "G'on, eat, eat! We don't hold on ceremony here in the back country," she hooted, turning to see about the leftover cornbread and their tea.

As she did, she continued talking. "Me folks been gone f'r many winters now. Injuns killed 'em whaire we lived up near Loyalhanna. Wud'iv kilt me too, or carried me off, iffen I hadn't been at me mither's friend's cabin. Sarah Campbell was a wise woman. That's who raised me thenceforth. I learnt many a useful thing from Sarah; bless her. Lived with her till Sarah's husband died an' she took a new man. A real sonivabitch that-un, and whin he thought he'd have his way wit me, I up 'n left. Lit out an' headed west. Ended up here in the Catfish area. Always felt bad 'bout leavin' without s' much as a by-yer-leave from Sarah f'r all she done f'r me, but cudn't be helped, that." Hester tilted her head, remembering. "Suspect she *knew* though. Sarah weren't nobody's fool." With that, Mistress Duff let out a howl of laughter. "An' I reckon she taught that horny ole billy goat a lesson he ain't niver f'rgot!"

The Sisters and Thaddeus, who had been hanging on Hester's every word, suddenly remembered their food and dipped their spoons into the wooden trenchers to warily taste it. After a spot of the steaming pottage, Mistress Duff's visitors decided that her stew was surprisingly palatable, thick and savory.

"Ambrosia," the professor pronounced, as he crumbled cornbread into his fare and began in earnest to eat.

"H'aint nothin' fancy, but it sticks to th' ribs," Hester said, looking pleased as she poured the black tea into three wooden noggins she lifted from the fireplace mantel.

"Right tasty," the Sisters commented, certain now they would eat Hester's offering.

She set a noggin of tea before each of her guests, and sat at table with her own tea, which she had poured into a small, hard gourd, revealing that she owned but three cups.

"We nearly shook hands with a Shawnee war party," Thaddeus stated, taking a breath from his stew. "Headed east down that old bison trail yonder," he indicated with a wave of hand in the direction of the forest. "Nine of them."

"Shawnee don't shake hands, mister. You were lucky." Hester took a long sip of the strong tea. "It ain't none of me niver-mind, but wud y' object ver-ry much t' tellin' me whaire yer headed?"

"I don't mind," the professor answered. He was doing most of the talking, since that was the custom of the era into which they had dropped. Women were subservient in Colonial times, most women anyway, barring the one he was addressing at the moment. "West. We're headed northwest, to a point beyond Buffalo Creek."

Hester didn't press for more, but her eyes told her guests she ached to hear their story, so Thaddeus indulged her. As history professors, he and the Sisters were acquainted with the fact that it was lonely on the frontier for women. A neighbor's chimney smoke was a *rare* sight. Women yearned, as did many men, for news, especially good tidings, and for what the Irish and Scotch-Irish call *craic*. The time-travelers knew, too, that Hester Duff, shunned by most of the other settlers in her area, was *especially* lonely and eager for chatter.

"We were burned out. Lost everything– our harvest, our cabin and everything in it," Thaddeus announced, glancing cursorily at the Sisters, then taking a draught of his tea.

When he did, Maggie slipped into the role, with an expression that backed up the professor's sad words. She was so convincing, Hester reached a hand toward the redheaded Sister to pat her arm.

"Raiding party swooped down on the lot of us," Raine gladly took up the story. "The big bell at the blockhouse rang– *McCabe's Blockhouse* 'twas– with fair warnin', thanks t' our good rangers; and most of us got inside, though in the nick o' time. But 'tweren't long afore we could all see our cabins goin' up, one after another, the columns of black smoke tellin' the tale, for each of us, of loss 'n woe."

Raine peered inquisitively at Hester, hoping what she was about to add would spur Mistress Duff's story in return. "Don't know if you ever had to make do, crowded inside the walls of a blockhouse, where the air loses all purity and sweetness! An' I tell you true: I don't know which is worse– the terror on the outside of the walls, or the filth, dirt 'n reek on the inside! From my recall, each time the blockhouse bell rung, we all rushed inside friends and neighbors, glad f'r the company and strength in numbers; but each time, too, at the end of a few days cooped up with one another, not everyone parted friendly like."

The Sisters noted that Hester's face had darkened at the mention of the word *blockhouse*. Or was it at mention of the word *neighbors*?

"Aye, I understand yer feelin's; but I hope ya know, the Buffalo Creek area ain't gonna be much safer f'r ya," Hester stated mildly.

Thaddeus set his mug down on the log table. "Likely not, f'r a while anyroad, but we're hopin' things smooth down now that the war is over. Cornwallis surrendered six years ago. The peace was signed three years ago. Things will settle down."

Hester raised her ebony brows, and her eyes widened. "Yer aff yer heid, man!" she spouted in her Scottish brogue. "You don't know the British!"

"And you do?" The professor's tone was mild, though slightly teasing. *Off my head, am I?* Dr. Weatherby thought. *The lass is bold for her era!*

"*Och*, ivery Scot 'r Irish knows the British! They ain't gonna give up their prize colony so quick, mister. They've been proddin' the Injuns to iver more treachery agin us, and they'll keep at it till they git wha' they want."

"I agree. They will keep at it– *till they're stopped.* And they will be. Mark me, *they will be.*" Thaddeus' eyes flashed blue fire.

Hester shrugged. "Mayhap yer right, mister; but till that day comes, we're all in f'r it!" She rose and, going to a shelf, lifted down a jug. "Payment f'r a healin' I done," her eyes skimmed the cabin's single room, "as purt' near everything I hold, includin' th' raisin' of this here cabin. I prefer the barter way o' payment mos' times. Kaint toss a coin in the fryin' pan 'n eat it. Kaint pour a jigger iv coin on a cold winter night neither." She set the jug on the table. "He'p yerselves. Got no sugar f'r the tea; an' I dinna fancy blackstrap. Too heavy, but that there whiskey'll sweeten th' tea f'r us. 'Tis good rye, but have a care, ladies; it packs a wallop," she laughed.

With an approving nod, Thaddeus picked up the small jug to "sweeten" the Sisters' tea, then his own. "Obliged, Mistress Duff. You've a kind heart."

"F'r some folks I do," she replied in a dry voice. "H'ain't like me to mollycoddle, but I like you three. Tell me, if ya care to, have y' *kin* up on Buffalo Creek?"

Dr. Weatherby shook his head, initiating the story he and the Sisters had contrived before embarking on their time-trek. "Going to stay with a friend, a widow-lady, whose ranger husband was killed. We," he spared the Sisters a glance, "knew them well in Philadelphia and traveled here to the frontier in their company several years back. They've lived in the vicinity of Buffalo Creek the past twelve years. Tom was a fine man, a brave man." He stroked his beard. "Built his wife Rebecca a good, strong stone house when he returned home from war ... thought they'd grow old there together, but 'twasn't to be. Anyroad, when we were burned out, and I heard that one of our rangers was to make a tramp to the Buffalo Creek neck of the woods, I asked him to carry the letter I'd penned to Tom and Rebecca. McLaughlin's their surname. At the time, I didn't know Tom had been killed, of course," he clarified. "In the letter, I inquired could we winter with them, workin' for our keep till we built ourselves another cabin." He sipped his tea to wet his whistle.

"The *express*," the professor continued, using the more common word on the frontier for *ranger*, "delivered us the widow's answer to 'Come ahead.' Said she lost Tom to the Indians and doesn't fancy spending the long winter alone. She wrote that we were welcome at her place for as long as we wished, and she hoped we'd decide to stay. Said their original log cabin was still there, on their eight hectares of land. She thought Maggie and I could stay in it, and Raine in the house with her. 'Course during signs of trouble, we'd fort up together in the house." The professor cocked his head. "So there you have it."

Hester looked keenly at the Sisters, and they feared she might guess that what Thaddeus had related was fiction. By the look on her face, she sensed something was amiss. "Wudn't ye rather rebuild yer cabin on yer own land?"

The Sisters exchanged looks, with Thaddeus stalling by clearing his throat and taking a swallow of tea. However, Raine, the accomplished storyteller, came to their rescue.

"No!" Feigned fear flashed in her emerald eyes. "After thrice runnin' f'r the blockhouse and each time makin' it by th' skin of our teeth, Maggie and I both said 'No more!'"

"No more!!" Maggie iterated with evident resolve. "Oh, we know the dangers still exist where we're headed; but, at least, as my sister said, they'll be strength in the many gathered there. More blockhouses the countryside round, more settlers too than there be further south whence we've come. And, lest we f'rgit that Rebecca's big house is stone– 'like a fortress' she wrote!

"We had a terrible fright end-a last winter," Maggie went on, "'twas a good thing we had a sleigh, one Thaddeus crafted for us." She looked to Raine, sending her a telepathic message to pick up the tale from a true frontier happening, one they both recounted in their classrooms during discussion of escalated terror on the frontier in the aftermath of the Revolutionary War.

The raven-haired Sister gave a subtle nod of understanding. "'Twas last March. Spring had come, but since snow still covered the ground, we thought we'd git a bit more reprieve from the eternal vigilance of watchin' day after day f'r Injun sign. 'Twas jus' turnin' dusk, whin the express come to thump on our cabin door, hardly standin' still long enough t' shout th'r was thereabouts *twenty* of th' painted devils close on his heels. 'Run f'r McCabe's!' he hollered, and that's sure what we done.

"Thaddeus and I hitched up the sleigh," Raine sustained the tale, "but we'd no sooner jumped in it, whin we seen 'em– painted in that hideous way that meant they was meanin' t' take scalps or die tryin'. Anyways, there they was, of a sudden like, bold as brass, 'cross the cabin clearin' at the treeline, the leader on horseback. Well, faster 'n you kin spit out th' words 'Take aim!' Thaddeus shot the horse, and me and him acted as rear guard on foot b'hind the sleigh, whilst Maggie slapped the reins down, hard as she could, on our horse. Poor Thunder was so tetchy from the shootin', his big eyes showin' white, he reared straight up in the air, close on t' upsettin' the sled!"

Thaddeus was bobbing his head as if in vivid recollection. "I yelled **'Git goin'! And don't look back!'** Maggie got control, and off they dashed! Then, kneelin' in the snow, Raine and I got off another round, and the attack quickly turned into a runnin' fight."

"You bet it did!" Raine interjected with fire, thoroughly enjoying herself. "Him and me kept stoppin' t' kneel, load 'n fire, so's t' hold th' devils off, then we'd run like hell– fast as we could in the deep snow– to catch up with Maggie and the sleigh."

"I was fearful the blasted war party would get ahead of my wife, so we **had** to stay within shot of the sled!" Dr. Weatherby rejoined with vigor.

"'Tis a hair-raisin' remembrance; I kin tell you that!" Maggie put in. "Racin' f'r our lives along that narrow, rough trail through the thick, black trees in a fast-descendin' twilight!"

Raine sent Maggie a congratulatory look. *Good one, Mags! I'm impressed!*

*Must be this 100-proof rye!* Feeling bolstered, Maggie carried on. "At one point, in the fadin' light, the poor horse shied again from the loud shootin'; and leap he done, fast 'n sudden-like, t' one side, *slammin'* the sled inta a rock. I all but fainted, f'r the sleigh just about went over that time f'r sure! I had to git out and, with my hands quakin' s' bad from the cold and m' nerves, secure the shaft in the gloom and shadow of near nightfall. Musta took me nigh onta fifteen minutes, but it felt like an eternity! It *sure* felt like an eternity!"

Raine jumped in again. "All the while Maggie was tightenin' the shaft," she threw a glance at Thaddeus, "we knelt in the cold snow t' reload 'n fire as fast as our freezin' fingers wud let us. And not t' brag, but we picked off a goodly number of 'em! Didn't we, Thad?"

His cup to his lips, Dr. Weatherby gave a vigorous nod.

"When," Maggie continued, "we was finally within sight of McCabe's Blockhouse, my husband's boomin' voice reached my ears over the shootin': **'Go, Maggie Mae! Go like th' devil!!'**

"My heart was in m' throat," the redheaded Sister pressed on, a hand to her chest, "but I slapped the reins with all my might, and with a sideways look at husband an' sister, who I did *not* know if I would *ever* see again alive, I yelled f'r all I was worth, **'Y-yaaaah!!'**

"Ears laid back, our good Thunder leaped into full gallop, right as the alarm was shouted from the parapet to open the blockhouse gate jus' wide enough t' let us in. We raced through to safety, whilst several men rushed toward our lathered horse t' gain control of the excited beast.

"A few minutes later, by the grace of the Divine, Thaddeus and Raine tore through the narrowly opened gate, breathless, but miraculously uninjured.

"That was the first time I tole m' husband I was not going back to the farm. My mind was set, but he *talked* me inta goin' back, and then we lost everything. *No more.* Th' place holds *bad* memories. I will never go back to that farm!" Maggie picked up her wooden cup and took a long pull of the whiskey-laced tea. "Whew! You weren't joshin', Mistress Duff," she remarked to Hester, raising the noggin. "'Tis not my wont to babble overmuch, but this mash doth pack a wallop!"

"Injuns took our mare, Fidelity, and her foal," Raine said, looking truly downcast. "I jus' hope they treat them well. Took the cow too, they did."

"Injuns respect Nature 'n animals. I seen that f'r meself. I 'spect they're takin' mighty good care of the horses. The cow, you kin bet, they et." Hester gazed speculatively into the crackling flames of the hearth fire before saying, "Been hard on us settlers. First the French, then the British all along roustin' the Injuns agin us, payin' well for scalps 'n f'river teachin' 'em new tricks."

"Aye," Dr. Weatherby concurred, "three generations of Indian troubles here on the frontier, soon near to half a century of what I call 'eternal vigilance.'"

"But lest we f'rgit there be rights 'n wrongs on *both* sides, good an' evil on each," Hester said with pluck. She rose to poke at the fire. With a fiery spray and crackle, the flames in the hearth shot higher.

Thaddeus coughed gently. "Well now, we've done a heap of jawin' about ourselves," he stated after a brief hush had settled over the comfy cabin, aglow from the fire in the stone hearth. The professor was satisfied they'd gained Hester's trust. "What about you, Mistress Duff? What is *your* story?"

The Sisters cast him a grateful look. After all, they were here to learn all they could about *her*.

Their hostess sat back down to take a deep draught of her tea, and for a long while, Hester was silent, so that the time-trekkers wondered if she would reveal *anything* of herself to them.

"Neighborin' Injuns don't bother me none. Not no more, they don't," she said when she was ready, her sudden response causing Maggie to jump. "I don't know if they put a mark somewhere on my place, carved into a tree mayhap– that's sumpin' they do– or if they flat out tole one another t' leave me be. I see 'em sometimes, autumn 'n winter mostly when the leaves 'r down, movin' along the trail, yonder," she flung a hand toward the shuttered window, "but they don't make no trouble fer me. 'Course th' British set Injuns on us from Canada an' who knows whaire! So iffin I hear the blockhouse bell, I run like all the rest. But leastways th' Injuns *round about* leave me be, 'n I do likewise. I reckon it's b'cause of what I done for an important shaman-a theirs, old Delaware fella name-a Windwalker.

"One of his sons come to me cabin." She thought for a moment. "Oh, 'bout four winters ago now. In broken English and sign, he asked me to help his father. The poor ole man was devilishly sick with fever and the shakes; couldn't breathe either. Injuns die from white folks' ailments, even the ord'nary complaints. Well, sir, I made a poultice, and I put it on his chest. Kept watch over him all through the night, I did. By sunup, his fever broke, and he cud breathe again.

"Ole Windwalker and me become fast friends. Once in a while, I look up, and *there he is* at me cabin door. Niver hear 'im; he jus' appears, like a ghost. I give him food, and we trade herbal remedies an' secrets." Hester looked pensive, saying after a moment, "I've come t' see there's a kinship … a *likeness* betwixt Celts 'n Injuns. I suspect the wily British seen it too. Anyhoo, Windwalker is a great shaman among his people. I learnt many useful things from 'im, and mayhap he learnt sumpin' from me. I reckon that's why the Shawnee, a goodly number of 'em annyway, don't bother me none, though ya niver know which-a way a Shawnee's gonna jump!"

Hester settled back into her chair. "The Shawnee call the Delaware 'Grandfathers.' 'Grandfathers to the North,' to be more faithful to th' name. Anytime y' might stumble upon a Shawnee village, ye'll find a Delaware camp due north. Least that's wha' they tole me in their stories, 'n them Injuns 'r *sure* good f'r spinnin' yarns," she chortled, sending the Sisters an unexpected grin, "almost as good as we Celts!"

Hester's tone turned suddenly thoughtful. "My folks brought lots o' stories with 'em from the Old Country. And I'll tell ya agin: There's many-a likenesses between Celts an' the Injuns. The war paint, war drums, the love an' respect for Nature and our animal brothers. Love-a jewelry and ornaments. Mayhap even love-a spirits– the liquid kind I'm talkin'." Her dark brows lifted, "Though the Injuns aire keen on t'other kind-a spirits too, jus' like us Celts."

"Shoot," she slapped a hand down on her knees, "I dinna help that ole fella t' win friendship 'r annythin' else, but I'm mighty glad f'r how it turned out." Hester's voice dropped. "Windwalker's damn near the only *true* friend I got round here of late."

"Has something happened?" Maggie feigned ignorance, her voice benign.

"You cud say that. Storm blew in couple days ago that took the harvest. Most iv th' farmers round here lost everythin', and the lot of 'em aire blamin' me f'r it."

"Why would they do that?" Raine questioned with innocent expression.

Hester managed to keep her emotions out of her voice. "Because they say I'm a witch."

"Are you?" Thaddeus asked, not unkindly, his tone matching hers.

Hester laughed low in her throat, darting her houseguests a penetrating gaze. "I might put th' same quizzin' t' you three."

The Sisters' eyes flicked to Thaddeus with an unspoken question of their own.

"No need f'r anny of us t' answer," Hester said abruptly. "We each know who we aire and what is in each iv 'r hearts."

Hester's words threw Maggie a wistful vibe. Lost for a moment in thought, she rested her chin in her hands, elbows on the table. "To be a witch is to soar among the stars, whilst still on earth. The voice of the Goddess calls to us through the mists of another time." She heaved a sigh, reaching out to cover one of Hester's hands with her own. "To be a witch is to know the ways of the Olde. People fear what they do not understand– they taunt 'n trouble you b'cause they fear what they cannot twig."

"And wha' they kanna twig is a whole heap! Th' varmints! They pitch aside th'r fears quick enough t' seek me out whin they need me!" Hester snapped.

"Aye, throughout the ages, we're ofttimes needed but rarely welcomed," Maggie replied.

"Mind, no matter wha' they done t' me, I niver refused to help anny one of 'em, though I've been tempted. *Oooh, I've been tempted!"* Her blue eyes flashed in the glow from the hearth fire. "But I tell you I won't suffer the'r black hearts much longer!"

*Be ye witch by birth or witch by choice, we must all listen to our inner voice.* "There be jealousy 'n revenge in th' mix with the fear. Is that not so?" the always bold Raine questioned aloud.

"Aye." Hester's generous mouth twisted in a sardonic half-smile. "I won't trouble t' spill all inta yer ears; but more 'n one iv the good Christian husbands 'ave come t' me door seekin' o'er 'n above a potion, balm, or herbal remedy. One thing I've leant 'bout men in me twenty-four–" she tilted her dark head for a reflective moment, "'r is it twenty-five years?" She shrugged. "Lost count. Men don't fancy bein' put off. They git notions 'bout someone like me, an' well," she shrugged again, "y' git wha' I'm tryin' t' say.

"Then thars the good Christian wives, who think because a lass is comely, she's a tart after layin' with the'r husbands. If they wud practice wha' they preach–" she shook her mane of ebony hair. "Bloody hell! A witch h'ain't evil! We *battle* evil!" Hester took a long swallow of her tea, polishing off what was in the gourd. "I'm partial to the company of me four-legged friends of th' forest. And I *sure* as hell understand 'em better."

Maggie's crystal laugh lightened the moment. "We know what you mean … *sister*." Their eyes met and held with renewed empathy.

"Religion should be personal and private– like a fella's *wand*. It's a fine thing for a-one to have and take pride in, *but* should some scoundrel whip it out t' wave in my face– *we got a problem!"* Raine quipped, her words prompting a peal of laugher from the others round the table.

"Ahhh," Hester said, her tone softening, "I'm grateful f'r me struggle; f'r without it, I wud niver have stumbled upon me strength!" Her eyes fluttered closed. "Looking behind, I am filled with gratitude. Lookin' forward, I am filled with vision. Lookin' upward, I am filled with strength. And looking *inward,*" Hester put a hand to her heart, regarding her guests, "I am filled with peace. Windwalker taught me that prayer– and it is filled with truth.

"I *say*," she exclaimed a moment later, "I'm *endurin'* glad I opened me door to ya! Ye've done me hear-rt a boon. Bless you, the three of ya!" She stood and, fetching the kettle from the hearth fire, poured each of them more of the strong tea. Then she picked up the jug and sweetened each measure of tea with the strong whiskey. "Yer welcome t' stay f'r as long as ye wish."

"Thank you, mistress; appreciate it; but we'll be taking our leave on the morrow. We want to stop by the blockhouse to see if there be any further news of or from our friend, and then we'll be headin' out." Thaddeus picked up his noggin to take a long swallow before saying, "I'd be happy to fetch you some water from the nearby creek before we put down for the night. And come first light, I'll chop some wood for you. I notice you seem to be a mite low for this time o' year."

"Brother," Hester pronounced softly, looking almost dazed that someone was offering her kindness, "I'd be obliged." She glanced across the room, stood, and, moving to the stone hearth, put a couple of logs on the fire, tossing in a few pine cones as well, after which she fanned the flames with her generous apron. "Whativer ya do, don't let the fire go out t'night. I'd hate like hell t' have to tramp the ten miles to ole, grumpy Curry's place in the mornin' for a chunk-a fire. He is a neighbor, but what he *ain't* is neighborly."

Thaddeus nodded his understanding. "I'll be heedful." He inclined his head, listening. "Wind seems to have kicked up."

Hester, too, listened to the moan and shrieks of the wind, her brow furrowing. "'Tis a banshee wind that howls round the cabin this night. It portends something … *dark*. Dark indeed."

Suddenly, a death-chilling sound from the encircling wilderness reached the four people snug inside, the great logs crackling and flaming in the open hearth, the air fragrant with the pine cones Heather had chucked into the fire. A deathly stillness descended on the shadowy room, and by the look on the Sisters' faces, the frontier woman could readily see they held a question.

Hester's eyes narrowed. *"Catamount.* Sounds like a *woman* screamin', don't it? Not to worry, it won't bother us. Painters got better sense th'n to come sashayin' round humans. Out huntin' is all. But ye'd best take yer rifle whin ya go f'r the water. Cud be a mama with cubs. Cubs'd be six months old b' now, but they'd still be with their mama, and no beast is more protective of her *bairns* than that th'r big cat."

She closed her eyes and tilted her head. "I sure miss my da on nights like this. He cud drown the howlin' wind and the eldritch forest voices with th' magick of his fiddle. Mayhap, in the Summerland, he's a-playin' that fiddle yet." She swallowed hard and opened her eyes, smiling softly to herself. "I mean wha' wud the place be without fiddle music, good whiskey, an' dancin', huh?!"

"I'll drink t' that!" Thaddeus rejoined, tossing back the last of his whiskey-tea.

When Maggie and Raine polished off their tea, the professor rose from the table to fetch his long rifle. "I'll be goin' for the water now, and if you ladies wish to take a stroll down by the creek or the trees, now's the time."

Hester handed him a wooden bucket. "Tarry not, 'n haste ye back."

The Sisters rose and, pulling on their capes, followed Dr. Weatherby out the cabin door.

When the threesome arrived at the creek, Thaddeus bent to fill the bucket, saying to the ladies, "I suggest you take a short fast walk into those trees. Don't talk or dawdle. I'll keep watch."

Raine took a step and paused. "What's your impression of Hester," she whispered to her companions.

"She's a gifted healer, an effective sister of the Craft, and she's terribly lonely," Maggie answered.

"I'll second that," Thaddeus voiced *sotto voce*, "though I'll add my take to your assessment. She'd be the *wrong* person to push to real anger. Like you, she's the kind of woman who gets what she wants. As my students would say, 'She walks her talk.'"

When the Sisters entered the tree cover, they quickly began to tend to Nature's call. Raine had no sooner gotten to her feet, when she heard the hunt-cat's snarl. Lifting her gaze, she glimpsed its great yellow eyes glowing out of the darkness. In the next instant, the moon, sliding from cloud cover, revealed the full-grown male cougar– eight feet long if it was an inch– crouched on a sturdy limb directly above them, and it was ready to pounce on Maggie!

Its open mouth bared its formidable teeth; and for a timeless time– though truth be known *it was but a flash of time*– the angry catamount, with flattened ears, fixed its gleaming eyes on Raine, letting out a protracted, low menacing growl followed by a drawn-out hiss. The mesmerized Sister could not help thinking how like war paint the dark markings on its face were when it snarled again, raising a paw to unsheathe its lethal claws. Swift as lightning then, and with a bloodcurdling scream– it leaped! It all happened so fast!

Frozen in place, Maggie, whose eyes were riveted on her attacker, screamed too as a shot rang out, echoing loudly in the still of night. With a thud, the big cat dropped on the leaf-strewn forest floor– just inches from where the redheaded Sister crouched. She let out a second cry, her wide, frightened eyes shifting to Raine, who, somewhat stunned, was regarding the smoking pistol she held in her hand.

"Oh, Raine, Raine darlin'!" Maggie gasped, a hand to her pounding heart. "You saved my life!"

When they returned to the cabin, Hester was standing on the porch. "Wha' happened?! I heard the catamount and–" The sentence went unfinished when–

"Thaddeus appeared from the shadows, the cougar slung across his back. Maggie followed, with Raine carrying the long rifle and bringing up the rear, her own weapon tucked safely back into her belt.

The professor dropped the big cat on the ground before their hostess. "I'll skin it for you first light. It will make a nice hearth rug."

"Oooh, I wish you dinna have t' shoot him. He's a beauty," Hester said, bending down to stroke the tawny fur, "but I'd wager there was no he'p f'r it. I heard the screams."

"I shot the cat, sister," Raine interjected without bluster, sadness tinging her voice as realization set in. "And no, there was nothin' else I cudda done." *Not in that split second anyway*, she told herself. *As **determined** as that cat was, I would've needed a bit of time, and that was the one thing I didn't have.* "No," she whispered to the Goddess, "there was no help for it."

Afterward, when Hester reentered her cabin, she found her visitors stretched out on Thaddeus' blanket on the floor before the fire. They had moved the settle to make room for their blanket. Maggie and Raine were sharing the professor's pack for a pillow, their capes over the pair of them. Next to Maggie, who was in the middle, the professor was snug under his frock coat.

Noticing that he had no pillow, Hester climbed the ladder to her sleeping loft. A few moments later, she stood over Dr. Weatherby to proffer one of hers. It was stuffed with lavender. "F'r yer head."

The professor smiled his thanks, sniffing the stuffed linen. "The lavender will bring me restful sleep and sweet dreams. Thank you."

"See y' don't let that fire go out," she reminded. "And to the three of ya– *peaceful night*."

The morning dawned bright but frightfully cold for the end of October, so the time-trekkers thought anyway.

Thaddeus rose early to go outside, with his rifle for company, to chop a small pile of wood for Hester, stacking it to dry on the cabin's rustic porch. He spent the bulk of the time skinning the cougar, after which he tacked the salted hide to the sunny side of the cabin to cure. *Though Hester won't get use out of this wood and panther skin, someone will*, he thought with a self-conscious contentment that neither would go to waste.

The Sisters spent the morning talking with Hester, trading spells, a select few secrets, and girl talk, some of which reached across the centuries to prove the veracity of the old saying that "Some things never change."

After a light meal of mush and molasses washed down with Hester's strong black tea, the time-trekkers made ready to go.

Having adjusted his backpack to his satisfaction, Dr. Weatherby picked up his haversack. Reaching inside, he drew out two small items– an LED flashlight, about four inches long, and its 3x3 solar panel. To the Sisters' surprise, and with brisk motion, he set the objects down on the split-log table before Hester. "A gift," he announced, "from the three of us."

Both Maggie and Raine started to demur, but inexplicably thinking better of it, held their tongues.

Hester studied the items for a mystified moment. "Wha' is it?"

Thaddeus thought carefully, answering, "A sun stick. 'Tis a sacred item, hence you must never share it with anyone, and never let anyone else handle it." He figured correctly that as a sister of the Craft, she knew not to let others handle her enchanted items, thus he clutched at that by way of his explanation. In reality, he did not want the item, incongruous with Hester's era, to be discovered by anyone else.

Hester looked closely at the professor's offering, picking up the flashlight to examine it. "Wha' might it be fer?"

"This part," Dr. Weatherby replied, "captures light from the sun. Come outside, and I'll show you."

The group filed out of the cabin to gather beyond the porch in the sunlight.

"You must set this," he indicated the panel, "in sunlight for a whole day. It must set in *direct, bright* sunlight," he reiterated. "Thenceforward, when you plug the sun-gatherer into the sun stick," he pushed the small button at the base of the lighter, "it loans the sun's light to the stick. And, as you can see– *light!*"

Hester drew in her breath, her dark blue eyes growing large with awe.

Thaddeus went over the steps again to make certain that she knew how to charge and operate the sun stick.

"Use it wisely, for it only *borrows* light from the sun. It has not the sun's endurin' power, hence it will not last forever," the professor instructed.

As if freed from a trance, the Sisters suddenly rallied. "Use it in good health." Stepping forward, they embraced Hester, who, in turn, gave voice to a traditional blessing of her own–

"Good fortune attend you; Godspeed and Goddess bless!"

With that, the Sisters and Thaddeus, satisfied with their Hester encounter, took leave of their friend, each with the pang of wistfulness to the heart.

Standing on the cabin porch, Mistress Duff called after them, dabbing at her eyes with her apron, their magickal gift secure in the deep pocket. "Watch yer backs! Best be safe th'n sorry!"

The caution registered well with Raine, for the voice she heard was not Hester's but Granny's!

When the time-trekkers arrived at the blockhouse, several people were milling around both inside and outside of the stockade– sharpened logs standing upright, side by side, that surrounded the log structure itself.

"Everyone's staring at us," Raine whispered to Maggie. "Have our faces gone green or something?"

"Since they've never before set eyes on us, they're curious," the redheaded Sister answered.

"Remember," Thaddeus whispered to them both, "Stick to our plan. We are just passing through. We listen and learn what we can in connection to Hester, then steal back to Mistress Duff's, ahead of the settler mob, to hide near the Witch Tree and witness, first-hand, what happened."

"Right," the pair answered in sync.

Noticing that an artesian spring flowed through the blockhouse property, Thaddeus pretended to be in need of water and set forth asking if anyone minded their filling their leather water pouch.

"He'p yerselves, strangers," a robust man in buckskins answered. "Jus' passin' through, are ya?"

"That's right," Dr. Weatherby replied. He said no more, not wishing to trade dialogue with the fellow.

"You'd best watch your topknots then," another man, sparer and younger, remarked, giving all three time-travelers a brash, cursory look.

"We intend to," Thaddeus answered. He leaned on his rifle. "What news? Any Injun sign reported of late?"

"Two of our rangers just come in," the second man said, pointing to the two express, around whom a small group was assembling.

"Obliged," the professor responded with a short nod, heading, with the Sisters, toward the gathering.

"We picked up an Injun trail headed toward the cabin of Joshua Gray," the taller ranger was saying. Close to six feet, the man, sporting breechclout and leggings in the Native style, appeared lean and fit as a racehorse, his face golden brown with sun, his somewhat aquiline features cast in that brooding yet watchful repose characteristic of the backwoodsman and the Indian. "Josh had been out huntin', and whin he spotted us, he fell in with us. When we got to his place, all that was left was smolderin' logs 'n ashes. There was no trace of his missus or his two young'uns, a son an' daughter, th' girl a babe still clingin' to her mother's breast.

"Straightaway, we followed the war party for a day 'n a half, right to the banks of the Ohio. The devils had made camp, and we seen the Grays with 'em. Trouble was, there was nine iv them an' only two of us, so we hunkered down and waited till they was asleep. Then we crept forward, into th'r camp. Took down two of 'em with our rifles, then with tomahawks and knives, four more. Three took off runnin', but I think I might-a wounded one iv them. In the dark, they didn't make out there was only two iv us. Mrs. Gray 'n th' young'uns 'r reunited with Josh, and that's what we set out t' do."

"I see the Grays did not accompany you here," a heavyset woman who had moseyed up to the gathering remarked. "Where are they stayin'?"

"We escorted 'em over t' Wolf Creek, to Josh's brother's place," the second ranger said. "They'll winter there."

"Seen any Injun sign over that-a way?" the robust fellow who had first spoken to Thaddeus asked. "These here folks are headed in that gin'ral direction."

The shorter ranger looked to Dr. Weatherby, pointed out by the burly man in buckskins. "The English are payin' a right smart price f'r scalps, mister. Keep yer nose to the wind, and yer eyes and ears open, hear?"

"I will do that," Thaddeus answered firmly, giving a nod of thanks.

"We didn't see any fresh sign goin' or comin' back, but that don't mean things can't change, and change they ofttimes do in these parts," the taller ranger warned. "We'll be goin' back out in the mornin'."

"What about our other problem?" a tall, scrawny man in a wool hunting shirt and breeches asked. He clutched a dirty, grey blanket round his shoulders.

"I say we pay a visit to Hester Duff's cabin before dark!" another man shouted from the group of listening settlers.

"Drive her out and away f'r all time!" yet another hollered. "'Tis enough we have the flamin' Injuns to vie with. We won't suffer a witch too!"

Somewhere in their midst, a frontiersman stammered, "Aye, drive her away, lest we consort further with witches!"

From the horde rose murmurs and grumbles, most of which the Sisters could not quite catch.

"I say we hang her, like they done in other places t' rid themselves iv her kind!" a male voice, whom the Sisters could not see to put face to, boomed in a markedly vicious tone. "Th' witch has brung her lot on herself!"

Maggie took hold of Raine's arm, leaning over to whisper into her ear. "Stay calm, Sister. We know they did no such thing. We'll be leaving this place soon."

"Ignorant varlets," the Goth gal hissed.

"I will be no part of a hangin'!" a deep male voice rang out.

"Nor I!" another avowed loudly.

"We agreed to scare her off, and we'll abide by that, or we don't do this thing," decreed the man who spoke up to have no part in a hanging.

"Nathan's right!" a new voice ventured upon an assertion. "We stick to our plan. We all agreed!"

"Good lads! At sundown!" one of the rangers shouted, with the others tossing in their unified agreement.

As the group broke up, Thaddeus and the Sisters garnered several remarks about their new friend. As a result, they discovered what they'd suspected all along was true. The Sisters were able to clearly read that many of the women were jealous of Hester; and several of the men, who had been rejected by her, sought revenge. Nonetheless, the main emotion that spurred Hester's neighbors to rally against her was their fear. They feared, as Maggie had said earlier, what they did not understand; and over the centuries, this was one thing that had not changed.

After having casually milled about to catch snatches of settler conversation, the time-travelers settled down, sometime later, on a log inside the stockade, to share the left-over cornbread Hester had given them, washing it down with the cool, sweet water from the spring.

"These little forts, the salvation of the frontier settlers, weren't much to look at," Thaddeus remarked quietly. "And many of them were poorly sited from a military point of view, but they served the purpose. Just a few men and women, inside a blockhouse, armed with the deadly Pennsylvania," he patted his long rifle, "could and did hold off war parties of fifty warriors or more– as long as they didn't run out of lead, powder, or water. That's why many blockhouses, like this one, were built over an artesian spring, and that's why some, like this one, weren't in the best spots militarily speaking."

"In addition to location, it was the *design* of the blockhouse that mattered," Raine added, content to pass the next few minutes discussing history, before they could slip back, in the fading light of day, to Hester's cabin. "To make it easy for my students to visualize, I tell them a blockhouse was, virtually, one log cabin atop another. The one above," she indicated with a jerk of her dark head toward the log structure, "overlapped the bottom cabin, enabling the settlers inside to fire downward, preventing any warrior from rushing the door. The loopholes all around the lower and upper levels gave riflemen the opportunity to pick off attackers in all directions."

"And," Maggie interjected, "with the two-hundred-foot clearing surrounding the blockhouse, none of the painted foe could sneak up on the little fort. The Indian was no fool. His forté was woodland fighting, ambush and stealth. Siege warfare was not in his nature."

"Right," Thaddeus affirmed. "Native Americans quickly tired of sieges to melt back into the forest to fight again another day– when the element of surprise was on their side, or when they were on their own woodland turf. Arguably, there was no greater guerrilla fighter than the Native American."

"Not that I agree with, or in any way condone, what these people are going to do to Hester; but, in a way, I can understand what has them fired up. Living in constant fear must've been nearly unbearable. Fear of the Indians, disease, and starvation– since that storm took their harvest. And talk about 'cabin fever'!" Raine exclaimed, still managing to keep her voice low, "imagine being shut up in here for days, weeks, or months!" She looked to her companions. "Nothing short of dreadful. We've talked about settler blockhouses to our students, and even to Hester." Her own words streamed back to her, *Blockhouses ... where the air loses all purity and sweetness!* "But *physically* being *in* this situation really drives home what we've taught in our classrooms, doesn't it?"

"Overwhelmingly," Thaddeus snorted.

"Utterly dreadful," Maggie reiterated. "I can hardly breathe for the stench. Imagine being cooped up in here in the heat of summer!"

"What gets me," Dr. Weatherby remarked, holding his voice down, "we have seldom read first-hand reports that included, not much anyway, the quarrels, the sickness, or the terrible hardships of living crowded in restricted conditions. Perhaps they were *so* ordinary for the times, so probable, that they were, by a cat's whisker, hardly worth mentioning."

"It was a tough way to get any farming done," Maggie commented. "No small wonder these folks are enflamed over the loss of their harvest. They would've had to leave their families packed into these wretched blockhouses round about, petri dishes for diseases, whilst the men took turns planting at each farm last spring, with an armed guard around each field. They're angry, and they're scared, and they want to blame someone, so they're blaming Hester– because she's different."

"They dare not blame the storm that took their harvest on a natural disaster. To them, that would be like blaming God. These folks carry a rifle in one hand and a Bible in the other," Raine quipped. "Or imaginably I should say, a jug of 100-proof rye in one hand and a Bible in the other, with their Pennsylvania rifles always near at hand."

Thus, the time-travelers whiled away the afternoon, observing, listening, and talking to one another **and** the penned-up settlers, a few of whom did concede that Hester Duff had, at one time or other, healed them, a member of their family, or even their livestock. In essence, the time-trekkers did not hear one solitary negative thing about Hester– *except that she was a witch.*

"They say the word as if it's a bad thing." Raine gibed disdain for the ignorance of those she always referred to, *après* Harry Potter, as "muggles."

Due to the rangers' report that they'd spotted no further Indian sign, several settlers left the compound during the course of the afternoon. Others chose to stay until "The matter of the witch was settled." Those who remained within the confines of the blockhouse drove their livestock inside the stockade with them, so the situation was yet crowded, smelly, and way beyond anything any modern mind could fathom as salubrious.

The Sisters, especially, were relieved and happy to walk out of the tall, sharpened-log enclosure just before sundown. They wanted to arrive at the Witch Tree ahead of the irate settlers, so they could locate a good hiding place and cache themselves in the underbrush.

When Raine, Maggie and Thaddeus arrived at the tree, the late-October sun was just setting, and twilight was fast approaching. In the forest gloaming, near to the Witch Tree, they found the perfect cover. Hunkering down, they waited– quiet and anticipating.

Before long, the threesome spied the glimmerings of the lit torches and heard the rabble tramping through the woods on the same old bison-turned-Indian path they had followed earlier from the blockhouse. With sadness, they beheld the same scene that their crystal ball Athena had faithfully shown them days before.

With bated breath, they watched as, tied to the tree, Hester looked skyward, uttering her curse, in tandem with her Indian friends' diversion of a staged attack. This time, however, the Sisters heard Mistress Duff call upon her ancestors to aid her. It did not surprise them; for, here, where they time-trekked, it was *Samhain*, when the veil between the worlds lifted. *Samhain* was *the* time to call upon the ancestors.

Thenceforth came the literal flash– an ear-shattering crack of lightning louder than any shot fired in the trick Indian attack. The Sisters each gave a start as the bolt crashed against the Witch Tree, felling a huge limb only a couple of feet from their hiding place.

Smoke covered the area.

When they had viewed the scene in their crystal ball, the Sisters had *not* been able to see the two Native Americans creeping up behind Hester. Swiftly, under veil of smoke and night, the Indians untied her, retied the rope, and silently melted, *with Mistress Duff,* into the dark forest. Now, too, the Sisters and Thaddeus, cached close by in the underbrush, were able to catch the trilogy of words Hester softly uttered: "Windwalker! Bless you!"

Crouched down in their leafy hiding place, the time-travelers listened as the Indians, staging the distraction, got off a few more scattered shots, accompanied by their bloodcurdling yells and shrieks. Then, as it had been in Athena's crystal depths, the scene grew unexpectedly quiet, when, realizing the Indians had ceased firing, the settlers' gunfire, from the cabin, also ended.

Some minutes later, the time-trekkers watched one of the rangers cry out, after having ventured beyond the clearing, "The witch is gone! The rope is yet tied, but she has–!"

His words were piercingly interrupted by another great bolt of lightning that forked the sky, lighting up the area with the great force of its energy. As Athena had revealed, concurrent with the lightning flash, a faction of the frontiersmen rushed forth from Mistress Duff's cabin, where they'd taken refuge from the attack, to see, in the bright burst of light, the name H-E-S-T-E-R burned deeply into the greyish-white bark of the tree's rough trunk.

"On this day, 31 October 1787," one of the frontiersmen proclaimed in a somewhat quaking voice, "we have witnessed something not of this earth! *God protect us!!*"

It was at that point when Athena had become cloudy with the grey swirling mists that told the Sisters their crystal ball's magickal movie had ended. Now, they saw and heard what happened next.

"Mayhap the Injuns carried her off," one of the men proposed.

"And **re**tied the rope to the tree?!" another shouted. "Don't be daft, man! She's *vanished*, and there be the proof– that Hester Duff be a witch!"

"Let's git outta here!" yet another bellowed, glancing furtively around. "Afore the Injuns or the witch returns to do us harm!"

A bloodcurdling scream from the surrounding woods reached their ears, whether human or beast, of this world or the next, the Sisters knew not. There was a realm of possibilities– for it was *Samhain* after all!

"C'mon! Let's git!!" the same voice repeated though louder this time, his words met with a roll of thunder. "We'll race th' storm," he cast an eye fretfully about, "and *whatever else* back to the fort!"

With that, the throng hurriedly dispersed, heading back down the well-worn trail toward the relative safety of the blockhouse.

After a few minutes, the time-travelers stood. Their legs were cramped from crouching in the cold and damp of their forest lair.

"Did you hear Hester call upon her ancestors? We should have guessed *long* ago that such powerful magick had been cast on *Samhain*," Maggie stated quietly.

"Let's try and pick up Hester's trail to follow, for at least a short distance. Perhaps we can figure out where she's headed," Raine urged in an excited whisper, her pulse quickening.

"*No!*" was Thaddeus' swift response, taking firm hold of her arm and glancing cautiously about. You gave me your word we would whisk ourselves home when I deemed it necessary, and that time is *now*. We saw that Hester was rescued by her friend, the shaman Windwalker. Hester has a Delaware escort to transport her through dangerous Shawnee territory. We do not. I trust you will keep your word."

Granny's, as well as High Priestess Robin's, wise caveats bolted back to the raven-haired Sister as blaringly as the lightning that hit the Witch Tree. "You're right, of course," she acquiesced. "We'll rely again on Athena to view Hester's escape from here."

"Yes," Maggie concurred, "and the rest of what we need to know, I've a witch's intuition, we'll learn from Hester's descendant, Teresa Moore."

"I can hardly wait!" Raine whispered.

The woods were fully dark now when Thaddeus came suddenly alert at the not-too-distant howl of a wolf. Virtually in response came the gobbling of a turkey from the opposite direction. A newcomer to the frontier might have taken those wilderness sounds for granted, but these seasoned history professors and time-travelers were *no* greenhorns to the precarious Pennsylvania frontier.

Holding his voice to the quietest whisper, Dr. Weatherby said, "We're not alone. Do *not* make any visible reaction whatsoever. Had a feeling we were being watched. I think they're waiting till we make camp to jump us, so let's oblige 'em. My guess is they've come from the river and are not part of the faction that left with Hester."

All the while he was whispering, the professor, his rifle slung over his shoulder, was unpacking his bedroll as if he were about to make camp. Handing Raine the hachet, he said as loudly as he could, "You ladies chop us some firewood for tonight, and I'll make us a fine supper. **Stay close.**" Lowering his voice again to a whisper, he said, "Get to the river and find their canoes. Keep the best one for us 'n scuttle any others. If I don't join you within fifteen minutes or so, go down river 'n Time-Key home without me."

When Maggie started to object, he breathed his response, almost inaudibly, into her ear, kissing her. "Don't fret; I'll do m' best t' join you at the water's edge. It's our only chance."

As casually as she could, Raine, still holding on to the hachet, made a show of pulling her loaded pistol from her belt with a silent nod to Maggie, who, freeing her pistol, followed.

"Go on now! I'll start a fire!" he said cheerfully out loud, indicating with subtle gesture of his head which direction they should go.

As the Sisters started away, Dr. Weatherby, drawing the attention of their watchers to himself, stretched and yawned loudly. His rifle at hand, he began singing as he pulled out his fire-starter and quickly got a campfire going. Then he slung his rifle back over his shoulder and sauntered off a few feet from the firelight, fumbling with the front of his pants, as though he were preparing to relieve himself. He took several more steps away from the glow of the fire; then ducking into the trees, he broke into a run to head for the river.

At the water's edge he immediately saw Raine and Maggie looking anxious in a canoe that was afloat. He dashed past a second canoe with its bottom hacked out. Shoving the *bateau* with the Sisters aboard as far as he could out into the water, he leaped into the stern, whilst he and Raine, at opposite ends, began paddling for all they were worth down river, Maggie in the middle.

"Glad you copped two sets of paddles!" he said. "Faster! **Faster!!"**

They were far out on the Ohio before the two waiting Indians realized they had been duped. Rushing down to the water's edge, they began firing, but by then, the fleeing time-trekkers were out of range.

"Figured there were only a couple of 'em, or they would've rushed us straightaway," the professor declared.

"Thaddeus, you're a wizard!" the Sisters replied.

"I don't know about you two," Raine affirmed, "but I'm more than ready to click my heels together thrice 'n repeat that time-honored phrase, 'There's no place like home!'"

Some time later, the time-travelers put ashore on the Pennsylvania side of the river. Venturing into the woods, they paused to momentarily center themselves.

Maggie reached under her cape to draw, from the deep pocket of her apron, their small, travel *Book of Shadows*. Opening the grimoire to the ribboned final pages, Raine, Maggie and Thaddeus clasped hands tightly to begin the ancient Gaelic invocation, *the magickal Key that would unlock the door of Time–*

And take them home once again.

# Chapter Fourteen

The day after their time-trek, Raine and Maggie were grateful their Thanksgiving break at Haleigh College had begun so they could sleep in. After a light breakfast, they prepared Athena for scrying. They were glad, too, that Aisling would be joining them for the session. Magick was always better with the Power of Three!

An hour later, when the trio of Sisters, accompanied by Cara and the Merlin cats, reached their sacred attic space, they slipped into their ritual robes, cast their circle and smudged. Then they sat before Athena in the soft illumination of the lamp Raine lit behind the large amethyst crystal ball.

"Maggie," Aisling said firmly, "you lead us."

With a nod, Maggie dabbed a little of the Lemuria oil she extracted from the pocket of her robe on the third-eye area of her forehead, passing the ampoule round, so that Aisling and Raine could do likewise. Then, with their enchanted poppet sitting on her lap, the redheaded Sister began a deep breathing pattern, allowing stress and negative energies to flow completely out of her body as she exhaled. Her two sisters of the moon followed suit, breathing deeply, as each meditated: *Healing energies in ... negative energies out ...*

After repeating the exercise thrice, Maggie opened her eyes and began focusing on an area of the ball to which she felt drawn. "Focus," she pronounced in her silky voice, "focus on a portion of Athena's crystal depths that calls to you."

"Athena," the redheaded Sister began to chant, "as we go into a trance/ Bestow on us the magick glance/ Take us back in time today/ Reveal what happened come what may/ The *Samhain* clash at the Witch Tree: We ask what followed; ***this*** our plea/ Show us Hester Duff's flight, through the woods in dark of night/ Take us back for the sight/ Of Hester's escape, from hence her plight/ This is what we wish to learn/ For ***that***, Athena, we now return!"

As the Sisters' vibratory levels rose to harmonize with the antique crystal ball, they began to feel Athena's powerful energy coursing through and around them in the shadowy attic. *It was electric!*

The magick was working faster than ever it had!

*All three witches immediately thought how well everything was going for them of late, how everything seemed to be falling into place. The "magickal childe," that bundle of powerful energies they had passionately created with their soul mates, was serving them ever so well.*

"Yes … that's it," Maggie's soft voice crooned. "Let go. Allow the mind to become as clear as the crystal. *Relax.* As we gaze fixedly into the ball's deep crystal cavern, we *know* we can do this. We've done it successfully before. We can do it again … and evermore."

Keeping their regards focused, not blinking an eye or moving an inch, all three Sisters smiled inwardly as, in the time it takes to utter the words "Show me," within the huge crystal ball's amethyst depths, a ghostly mist was forming.

"Our connection with Athena has been made," Maggie drawled softly. "The door is opening. Keep your focus. Let Athena's mists draw us inside," she whispered.

"Off we go," Cara crooned, "into the wild purple yonder."

The ethereal mist swirled inside the mystical sphere, slowly at first, then faster, then slowly again, before the quartz crystal began to clear.

"Let us drift," Maggie hummed along serenely. "Light as feathers … inside Athena's crystal cave, for like Merlin's, it will show only Truth. Soon, the light and sound images, everlasting and eternal, will reveal what we seek, or what Athena feels we should know. We shall see …"

"What we shall see," the poppet droned.

"Remain calm," Maggie murmured, "so not to break the trance with emotions."

As the mists cleared, Maggie lightly mentioned Grantie Merry's caution, "We might see and hear what we do not expect. But that is fine."

"Pur-r-r-fectly foine," parroted Cara.

Maggie released her breath. "Simply allow Athena to take us where she will, in order to show us–"

"*What she will,*" the poppet completed in rhyme.

"That's it ... *calm and centered.*" Maggie's full lips were parted, as she sighed softly, endeavoring to keep her own serenity. "Do not try and make sense of anything till everything has faded away. Simply *allow* the scenes to flow, one into the next. We will know when Athena's magickal movie has ended, for everything will fade and dissolve." Maggie drew in another breath, slowly releasing it, as she kept her focus and her gaze.

Within the Sisters' circle of protection, the Merlin cats appeared wholly relaxed, sitting, as was their habit within a sacred space, with half-closed eyes, purring like little motor boats, sailing along on waves of contentment.

Of a sudden, out of Athena's evaporating mists, rose an image of Hester Duff and two Native Americans, walking single file, through the dark woods. The Sisters noted that Hester was wearing moccasins, and history professors Raine and Maggie instantly figured this was so she and her companions could tread silently through the wilderness. Too, they reckoned the Indians gave Hester the moccasins so that any rangers tracking them might not realize a white person accompanied them.

Striving to hold their focus, the Sisters hardly dared to breathe, as the scene within the purple sphere rivetingly played out.

At one point, it looked as though the threesome within the crystal ball lost the wooded trail that cloudy night, for the two Indians were attempting to find it by crawling along the dark forest floor. It was then Hester pulled from her apron pocket the sun stick Thaddeus had given her. The Sisters watched as the Indians uttered, in their guttural tongue, exclamations of surprise and wonder.

With the beam of light to guide them, they soon struck the trail once again.

Thanks to Hester's sun stick, she and her companions moved swiftly along despite the black sky devoid of moon and stars. Moreover, the Sisters could clearly see that no rangers followed. Heeding Thaddeus' warning not to waste the sun stick, Hester *intermittently* flashed the light to make certain that she and the two Indians were keeping to the narrow path.

As the Sisters continued to gaze at their crystal ball, Mistress Duff and her escorts arrived at the river. The witches knew it was the Ohio, the river the French explorers had named "*La Belle Rivière*," across which lay what was then, outside the original thirteen colonies and fledgling new United States of America– "Indian Country."

Immediately, Hester's rescuers began searching for the three birch bark canoes they had cached, under brush and tree branches, near the water's edge. It was then the war party that had staged the diversion attack on the settler mob appeared from the tree line. Watching attentively, the Sisters saw Hester use the sun stick for her rescuers to quickly locate the hidden bateaux.

Without delay, Mistress Duff and her Indian friends slipped into the canoes and headed across the Ohio.

*Their canoes were stashed at a different locale from where we cast off*, Raine and Maggie both reasoned.

It was easier, with each scrying session, for the savvy Sisters to keep their focus. As they continued to watch the canoes glide away, they saw that one of the Indians aboard the light, narrow boat in which Hester was riding lost his oar when it struck a log floating in the dark water.

Jamming a hand into her apron pocket for the sun stick, it looked as though Hester was about to use the light again, to locate the oar, when she spied the thing floating near enough to grab. Leaning precariously over, from her seat in the center of the canoe, she nearly capsized the boat, grasping for the paddle. Though she succeeded in capturing the oar, the risky action caused her to panic, resulting in the loss of both the sun stick and the charger.

Athena clearly revealed what happened, causing Raine to lose her concentration. "Oh no, she lost the sun stick!" she blurted with unexpected disappointment.

All three Sisters lost focus then, for the images blurred, faded, and vanished in Athena's now-familiar, swirling grey mists. Beyond a shadow of a doubt, their current session with Athena was over.

"Bloody hell!" Raine exclaimed. "I'm so sorry I lost focus and ruined it for us, Sisters!"

"No matter," a familiar voice from Athena's crystal depths rebounded. "You know now that Hester Duff headed for Indian Country– *Ohio*. And that's where *you* will soon be headed, my dear girls!"

The Sisters blinked to see Grantie Merry smiling at them from inside the great crystal orb.

"Athena's magickal movie was about to end anyhow," their great-aunt disclosed. "But never you mind; you will discover the rest of what you need to know about Hester Duff from her descendant, Teresa Moore, day after tomorrow. Make certain you *keep* that appointment, my angels! And do get an early start. It *is* a holiday weekend, you know!"

With that, Grantie's image, too, vanished, and Athena became– crystal clear.

"Leave it to Grantie Merry to make us feel better. You gotta love her, don't you? I'm sorry, Sisters," Raine groaned, "but I *so* hated to see Hester lose her sun stick and charger!"

"Thaddeus' gift served its purpose," Maggie assured, leaning back in her chair to stretch in her feline manner.

"Historically speaking," Aisling cut in, "it's a good thing she did lose it. They'll be no record of the incongruous thing in history." The blonde Sister's face clouded. "I was, to put it frankly, *astonished* that you allowed Thaddeus to give it to her, though I have to concede that, really, it did *not* alter history."

"Not one jot," Cara put in firmly from Maggie's cozy lap.

Raine struck a pensive attitude, saying after a weighty moment, "Nooo, it didn't interfere with history. It was as though Thaddeus *knew* Hester and her companions would need the sun stick to make their journey easier-going; and then," she raised an ebony brow, "it was almost as though he *witched* it. You know what I mean– caused it to be lost to the river."

"Hmmm," Maggie mused, "and I'm certain you've noted that he always knows exactly what we'll need on each of our time-treks."

The Sisters exchanged looks with the thought–

*Makes you wonder yet again if our multi-talented Dr. Weatherby is the Keystone Coven's mysterious wizard.*

"Time will tell," the ornery poppet giggled to herself.

After Aisling departed, Raine and Maggie got down to the business of preparing for the following day's Thanksgiving dinner. They needed to food shop and then prepare a few side dishes for their sleuthing set whom they would be hosting at Tara on the morrow. The only additional guest would be Aisling's pre-teen daughter Merry Fay.

"Done!" Maggie exclaimed, as she ran her eyes down their grocery list. "I added some good French cheese, Brie, Camembert, perhaps some Gruyère. Aisling and Ian are in charge of the turkey and stuffing. And Merry Fay's making our favorite garlic mashed– or as she calls them, *smashed*– potatoes."

"Betty and Hugh are baking the pies– sweet potato, pumpkin, and apple," Raine stated, sitting down at Tara's kitchen table, across from Maggie, to sip a cup of restorative tea.

Magick, after all, can be draining.

"Beau and Thaddeus are bringing the wine, Beau red, Thaddeus white," Maggie said, sliding her pen behind her ear. "I reminded Thad to include a good pinot grigio."

"And *we're* in charge of the side dishes," Raine declared. "Granny's fluffy turnips; cranberry and nut salad; tossed salad; just plain, baked sweet potatoes in their skins. None of us like them candied, and everyone can dress them as they like. Oh, of course, Granny's creamed pearl onions. That's what we're making with our own little hands, but the broccoli casserole and Sophie's delicious cranberry and orange sauce we're picking up today at Sal-San-Tries."

"Lest we forget to stop at The Gypsy Tearoom! We need more of Eva's special brew, Tea-Time-Will-Tell, and we can wish our good friend a Happy Thanksgiving as well," Maggie rhymed.

"Hark y' don't f'rgit to set a place f'r me at Thanksgivin' gobble-up!" Cara cautioned with the unbridled passion she applied to just about everything.

Raine reached toward the poppet– who was sitting on Maggie's lap, this time at table with a cup of whiskey-tea before her– to pat the faded mop-top head. "Do we ever forget you?"

"Reckon ya don't. I don't let ya!" the doll jibed. "Have t' protect me own interests, I do."

"Did you order anything special from the Tearoom for tomorrow's dinner?" Raine asked Maggie.

"I did. Festive cranberry cake and pumpkin cornbread," the redheaded Sister said, making double sure she had all the ingredients they needed on their grocery list. "We'll stop at the deli and the Tearoom after we shop, Tearoom last."

"Don't forget," Raine commented, "Hannah's coming over today to give the house what she calls a 'lick and a promise.'"

"Right," Maggie repeated. "Let's get going!"

When Raine and Maggie returned from their errands, their housekeeper Hannah Gilbert was just finishing up.

Humming a holiday tune, *Over the River and Through the Woods*, the Sleuth Sisters' devoted housekeeper bopped across the clean kitchen floor on signature purple sneakers that matched her flamboyant personality.

"Howdy, chickadees!" she greeted, and though her voice and manner were brass– her heart, as the Sisters were wont to say, was pure gold. Heart of gold aside, Hannah was not one to demur. "The ole place is as tidy as a candy shop, so see you keep it that way through the holiday. I'll be back in two weeks to do a more thorough job for the Christmas cleanin'."

*Twenty-four karat.* Raine tossed the thought with a wink to Maggie.

Despite her penchant for gossip, along with a tendency to be a mite bossy, Hannah was a nurturing soul. She took splendid care of the Sleuth Sisters and Tara, scrubbing and polishing the old house with almost religious fervor, and she regularly looked after Aisling's daughter, Merry Fay.

"Thank you, Hannah," chorused the Sisters, each giving the loyal maid a warm hug.

Raine reached out to snatch a large cobweb that floated from the housekeeper's ear, then she handed her an envelope with her pay, including a holiday tip. Picking up a bag from the food items they'd just brought home, she extended it toward the older woman. "Sal-San-Tries' chunky, white chocolate and cranberry cookies, two dozen, fresh out of the oven this afternoon. Happy Thanksgiving, Hannah!"

Hannah lit up, wiping her hands on her garish Hawaiian muumuu, her standard cleaning "uniform." "Gotta have one right now with a cup of that tea I just brewed for you. C'mon join me."

"Sit down, Hannah; I'll serve," Raine said, pulling out a kitchen chair from the round oak table.

Hannah plopped her ample bottom into the chair with a slack movement and a blown-out huff.

Maggie finished putting away the last few grocery items, whilst Raine poured the tea.

"Hey, I got a newsflash for ya," Hannah said, beginning to chew the big bite of cookie she had chomped off.

"I hope it's not bad news," Maggie replied, snapping shut a cabinet door.

"Hubby–" It was all Hannah could manage due to cookie interference. She raised her pointer finger in a gesture that asked for a moment. "Went over to Washingtonville yesterday to pick up a load of lumber he ordered. That's where he always buys that kind-a stuff. He's deep inta another one of his projects. Been fixin' up a part of the garage for a workroom for hisself. You know how the man loves to tinker! Anyway, he told me the manager there, at the Washingtonville Lumber Company, was like a *whole different person.*"

"What do you mean?" Raine sat down with her cup of tea.

Maggie cozied up at table too.

"Well, Jim said he looked like, and these were his exact words, '*Death warmed over.*' He–" Hannah wrinkled her brow, tilting her grey head, with its neat bun, in thought, "What's the fella's name? Can't remember."

"Sam Woods," Raine supplied, glancing at Maggie.

"Yeah, that's it," Hannah replied. "He looked plumb awful Jim said. Lost weight, so that he smacks of a straggly scarecrow; and he had dark circles under his eyes like he ain't slept in days. Pale as a ghost, he was," she lowered her voice to a sinister tone, "*or like he seen a ghost.*"

"What makes you say that?" Maggie wondered, knowing their housekeeper's habit of keeping them in suspense when she had news to share.

Hannah took a swallow of tea before answering. "I'll tell ya what makes me say it. Jim said that when he asked Sam if he was feelin' all right– m' husband told him he looked white as a ghost– what do you think his answer was?"

"What?!" the Sisters responded at the same time, leaning swiftly forward in their chairs in eager anticipation.

"He said, and I quote– 'That's b'cause I *seen* a ghost.'"

"Seen a ghost?!" the Sisters echoed.

"That's what he said. And when Jim asked him to explain, he mumbled somethin' m' hubby couldn't make out; so Jim repeated the question, but Sam just shook his head and dummied up. Now whatd'ya think of that?" Hannah took another big bite of cookie, washing it down with a gulp of tea. "See, I remembered when Jim and I saw Sam Woods' wife's picture in the paper. Poor thing. She was such a pretty girl, and so young! And then," she looked to Raine, "you mentioned that you and Beau were there the night she died, at that Harvest Dance. I figured you'd want to know what Jim told me."

"Yes," Raine said in an absent way, anxious to get back on the case as soon as they returned from Ohio, "Beau and I were there that night."

"Sam and his wife– Amanda, wasn't that her name?– must-a been really close." Hannah clicked her tongue thrice. "I seen this happen b'fore," she declared. "A husband or wife takin' the other's death s' hard they go off the deep end." The housekeeper glanced at the antique railroad clock on Tara's kitchen wall. "Would ya look at the time?!"

Hannah downed the rest of her tea and stood, setting her cup in the sink. "Gotta run. Have-ta warm a casserole in the oven for supper." From a hook near the back door, she grabbed her purple coat, the exact color of her sneakers, along with her grey wool hat, yanking them on hurriedly. "Jim and I are goin' to his nephew's for dinner tomorrow, so I don't have to cook. Made a couple-a things to take is all. OK, baby girls," she said, blowing the Sisters a kiss, then snatching up her purse and bag of cookies, "you have a great holiday. I'll see you in a couple-a weeks! And thanks for the goodies! Love ya!"

"Love you too, Hannah!" the Sisters called.

When their housekeeper had gone, Maggie breathed, "Our darlin' Hannah, always peeping through the shutters into other people's lives. But she's the most *lovable* busybody we know, isn't she? And, great Goddess, I don't know what we'd do without her!"

Lost in contemplation, Raine said in a vague sort of way, "Savvy Kathy told Aisling rather the same thing about Sam." The Goth gal's eyes kindled with another thought as she took direct cognizance of Maggie. "Remember that scream we heard right before we took off on our time-trek? That might not have been a wild animal. It could've been Sam! I can't wait to get back to Amanda's case. I still say it was a *murder* and not a tragic misfortune."

"We haven't been wasting time; that's for sure," Maggie stated. "And I have a witch's hunch that everything we're gathering will turn out to be connected."

"Hmmmm," Raine answered, clicking her ebony nails against the table top in a musing gesture. "That's our forté, connecting the dots." She rested her little chin in her palms, elbows on the kitchen table. "We have our suspicions, Mags, but–" she cut off, switching tones, "Oh, if only someone at that Harvest Dance saw something. Someone like Hannah, you know what I'm saying, who doesn't miss a trick."

"Y' mean like a gawper?" Cara, who materialized on the kitchen counter, asked in her tinny little voice.

"A gawper?" Maggie questioned. "Care to illuminate us, darlin'?"

"*Och*, whatd'you Yanks call it? A pryer? Nooooo ... a meddler– a **busybody!**" the poppet squealed in satisfaction.

Raine jerked to attention, raising her head, her fertile mind working frantically. "*Shutters!* **That's it!**" she exclaimed, her slanted eyes sparking with green intensity. "It's so simple! I don't know why I didn't think of it before!" She jumped up and ran from the room.

"What's simple? Where're you going?" Maggie called after her in frustration.

"To get my phone. We've got to call Robin!"

\*\*\*

The carpet of red, gold, and purple leaves Jack Frost had deposited on the Hamlet's grounds slowly faded to somber hues by Thanksgiving. The open fields, round about, took on a cinnamon tone, and only a few stubborn leaves clung resolutely to the trees, reminding Raine and Maggie of the Celts and Germans who first settled Braddock County. "Those stalwart pioneers held on, through thick and thin, to weather every hardship that came their way," the Dr. McDonoughs were inclined to recount to their history classes.

By Thanksgiving, Indian summer was a sweet memory, for now there was a wintry chill in the air. The Hamlet often got snow for Thanksgiving, and Hannah's off-key rendition of *Over the River and Through the Woods* harked the Sisters back to the magickal Thanksgivings they had experienced with Granny.

Raine and Maggie both rose early Thanksgiving Day. When each peered out a bedroom window, neither was surprised to see snow blanketing Earth Mother, pristine clean, white, and sparkly as faerie dust.

"Yeeeaaaa!" Raine yelled, as she danced down the stairs that morning. It wasn't their first snow of the season, but she was always as excited as a child to see snow over the holidays.

The Sisters had decorated the front door with Indian corn tied with raffia and hung as a simple but pleasing swag. Cornstalks festooned the brick front-porch pillars, and pumpkins lined the front and back steps. A bright scarecrow stood sentinel at the massive front entrance. He was holding the sign Maggie crafted the day before that read: *Merry Meet and Welcome!*

Inside, the fireplace mantels were bedecked, too, with tasteful harvest decorations– faux autumn leaves, colorful gourds, and antique wooden alphabet blocks that spelled out– GIVE THANKS.

Hannah had especially polished the dining room to perfection. This was one of Tara's most colorful rooms, the furnishings and hangings showing strong evidence of the Sisters' discriminating good taste. A trilogy of stained-glass windows took up one entire wall, the varicolored glass depicting a scene of faerie-tale castle with knights and ladies fair. A second wall displayed a transom window also of stained-glass, this one of a simple grape and grapevine motif, since that window faced the backyard grape arbor. Hand-painted grapes and vines swirled over the wall under and along one side of the transom.

A third wall sustained a built-in china cabinet with diamond-shaped leaded glass doors, behind which sparkled jewel-toned wineglasses, Waterford crystal, and the set of fine china, hand-painted with wee shamrocks, that had belonged to Granny McDonough.

The Victorian dumbwaiter had cleverly been converted to a wine cabinet, its door inset with stained-glass grapes and vines in keeping with the theme of the transom and wall art. Ornate pocket doors of enduring English oak, that matched the rich, dark woodwork throughout the house, took up the final wall and opened into the adjoining parlor.

The dining room's high tray ceiling was graced with a mega, milk-glass chandelier, the light fixture encircled by a ceiling medallion that restated the red-and-purple-grape-and-green-vine theme. The dark oak furniture, imported from England, was massive and lavishly carved. The walls were tinted the hue of candle glow, and over the gleaming hardwood floors, the area carpet was a shade darker than the walls. All in all, it was a lovely room, warm and friendly like its owners.

The Sisters had decorated the buffet with tiny orange pumpkins and a colorful spray of faux leaves. Knowing they would be pressed for time, they set the table the evening before, after delivering their food donations to the local soup kitchen. Anonymously, they left food baskets on several Hamlet porches as well. This was something their granny had always done, and the Sisters Three carried on the tradition at each and every holiday.

Glancing round the dining room with appraising eyes, Raine and Maggie thought everything looked festive: the orange and brown linen tablecloth set with the Thanksgiving-theme dishes bearing acorns and leaves, Granny's holiday wineglasses, and the centerpiece– a trilogy of orange candles, graduating in height and festooned with a spray of bittersweet and leaves.

The bittersweet had been sent to them from a sister of the moon in New England. Raine thoughtfully captured a picture of their readied Thanksgiving table to email the cherished friend, along with their wishes for a "witchin'-good Yuletide." A gift of their own making would follow before Yule.

When the antique doorbell sounded, Maggie let out her usual complaint– "One day I really will rip that annoyance out! Bloody thing puts me in mind of the change-of-class bell at the college!"– whilst Raine rushed to answer it.

Everyone seemed to arrive at once, each bearing tempting offerings, and one and all entered with the traditional Tara blessing on their lips– "God and Goddess bless this house and everyone in it!"

After taking the food to the kitchen, where Maggie, with Aisling's help, began the pre-dinner preparations, the arrivals relinquished their coats to Raine. Then everyone streamed into the parlor, where a lively fire in the hearth welcomed them, and the savory smells from the various holiday foods drifted throughout the big, old house to whet everyone's appetite. Tara seemed to be bursting at the seams with comfort and joy!

"I daresay you all strike a jolly good note!" the raven-haired Sister remarked.

Beau, Hugh, and Thaddeus looked quite the "country gentlemen" in their tweeds. Ian sported dress jeans with a black turtleneck sweater and tan corduroy blazer. Betty, as might be expected, was Southwestern chic in a long jeans skirt and fringed suede top. Aisling exuded witchy-woman wow in a black knit dress that fit her like the proverbial glove. Merry Fay's denim dress was embroidered with fall leaves and a cute scarecrow. As might be anticipated, too, Maggie's attire screamed *color*– a peacock-design, Fifties-era pencil-skirt topped with a black cashmere sweater that showed off the antique emerald necklace with which Thaddeus had gifted her the year before. Raine's signature diamond magick-wand brooch glittered against the soft black fabric of her Gothic dress. All in all, as Raine exclaimed– they were a *festive* group.

The first thing Merry Fay did was run upstairs to entertain herself with the telly, Cara, and the cats. Maggie and Raine poured wine for their guests, then settled down in the parlor to fill their sleuthing set in on what transpired during their time-trek. As Raine talked, everyone sipped wine and partook of the hors d'oeuvres– smoked salmon-stuffed puffs, deviled eggs, stuffed celery, hummus and pita chips– from the tray on the rose-marble coffee table.

"That's everything that happened during our time-trek. Now, let me refill your wine glasses, and I'll fill you in on what we gleaned from our last session with Athena," the raven-haired Sister said, getting spryly to her feet.

In a few moments, she plunged excitedly into what their crystal ball had revealed, ending with, "So we know Hester escaped into Indian Country, Ohio, and that's where we're headed tomorrow to meet with her descendant, Teresa Moore, whose name and contact info we got from Grantie Merry. Bless the dear woman!"

Betty gave a whoop, catching the spirit of the Sisters' excitement. "Wow, then you should reap enough information to save that historic tree!"

"We've a feeling we'll discover from Teresa the remaining pieces of the Hester puzzle, yes," Raine replied.

Maggie rose. "I'd better see to our dinner. Everything will be ready in about fifteen minutes, and I hope the wine and hors d'oeuvres have revved up your appetites!"

"We've enough food to feed an army," Raine remarked. "Enough for everyone to take home leftovers, which we all so enjoy late-night and next-day."

Aisling stood too, to follow Raine and Maggie into the kitchen, instructing Betty to remain where she was, so she could "Keep the men in line."

"Pass me more of Merry Fay's delicious garlic potatoes!" Beau said with genuine enthusiasm. "And I wouldn't mind another of her rolls either."

"I'm glad you like them," the blonde pixie smiled charmingly.

A beautiful child, Meredith "Merry" Fay, named for Grantie Merry, possessed the best of both her parents, though she mirrored her magickal mother in looks, including her long, silvery blonde locks. Merry had also inherited the witchy talents of a long line of McDonough women.

"You did a great job, sweetheart," Hugh stated, reaching for the bowl of creamy potatoes.

"We're very proud of Merry Fay," Aisling said. "She got all A's on her report card again."

"And that includes math," Merry rejoined with a blush. She brushed a finger over the magick-wand pendant Raine had given her for Christmas the previous year. "I envisioned myself getting all A's, and it helped me to actually do it. Thoughts are magick wands, powerful enough to make anything happen– anything we choose. Right, Auntie Raine?"

"You bet!" Raine answered.

"*Is maith sin!*" Cara cried in Irish. "Brilliant!"

The poppet was sitting at the head of the table in a doll's high-chair, supplied by Merry Fay from the Gwynn's attic, the tray of which held a small dish of holiday foods, as well as a wee cup of whiskey-tea.

"Fourth grade this year!" Betty exclaimed. "Merry, you're growing up so fast. Have you thought about what you want to be?"

"Yes, Mrs. Donovan, I have. I want to be an archeologist and travel to all the *mysterious* and *magickal* places in the world."

"Well, it certainly runs in the family," Raine and Maggie stated with pride.

"We're just glad she doesn't want to go into law enforcement," Ian commented under his breath.

Merry Fay made a slight grimace. "Well, actually, I have considered becoming a detective, but archeologists," she looked to Raine and Maggie, "*and* historians *are* detectives."

"Yes they are, darlin'!" Maggie replied, zipping the thought to Raine, *Archeologists and historians are detectives accustomed to bones and death.*

*Not to mention– magick! Archeologists* **know** *real magick exists.* "Oh, our conversation has struck a chord," Raine said aloud. "Aisling, have you spoken with Chief Mann of late? What news?"

"No news at all," the blonde with the wand replied, helping herself to more of the savory stuffing. "But trust me, after what I shared with him of our observations and suspicions, he's *on* the case."

"Well, after our meeting with Teresa Moore, we plan on delving into this mystery with gusto," Raine informed. "One thing at a time. As Granny used to say, 'If you chase two rabbits, both will escape.'"

"Tell them what we heard from Hannah," Maggie encouraged. She reached for a second helping of the cranberry and nut salad. It was a favorite holiday treat of the redheaded Sister.

Raine shared the Hannah account, comparing it with what Aisling had learned from Savvy Kathy at the Hamlet's Auto Doctor. She closed with the comments from both sources, that the balance of Sam Woods' mind had been disturbed, and it appeared, anyway, that he was on the verge of a breakdown.

"Then, yesterday," the Goth gal went on, "I happened to think that every small town has its busybodies. Our Hamlet sure does, so, I am certain, has Washingtonville. I called our friend High Priestess Robin to ask her if she thought any of their town snoops would've been in attendance at the Harvest Dance, the night Amanda died. She told me she'd have to think on it, do a bit of research and call me back, which, of course, she did. And guess what? She said their village's biggest busybody was working in the Grange kitchen the night of the dance."

Raine paused for a sip of wine. "Picture this." She drew, with her fingers, a large imaginary rectangle. "There's an opening in the wall, at the Grange, between the kitchen and the main hall. The opening has louvered shutters, which I noted were open– the louvers, not the shutters. Anyone peering through those louvers would've had a ringside view of the food tables. I'm hoping the town gossip saw something that will help us. We have our suspicions, but we need proof."

"You got the town gossip's name, I presume?" Beau asked.

"We did. Gracie Seymour," Maggie answered. "Raine and I intend to set up a meeting with her as soon as we return from Ohio."

Hugh helped himself to a sweet potato and began dressing it with butter and pepper. "Betty and I reread the mysteries Maggie recommended, the titles that Mildred Grimm and Etta Story both checked out of the library. We like to *savor* a mystery, reading aloud to one another, with discussion at the end of each chapter. It helps us fine-tune our sleuthing skills."

Maggie put her fork down. "Best turkey you ever did, Ian! To go back to what Hugh said: In the first mystery, *Murder is Simple*, you told us the murderer killed her victim, who was allergic to peanuts, by dressing a pasta salad with peanut oil, right?"

"Right," Hugh answered. "Pass the turkey, please. Maggie's right, Ian; your best ever."

Ian grinned his appreciation for the compliments that rang out. "My pleasure."

Maggie picked up the turkey platter and started it down the long table to Hugh. "And in the second mystery, the killer tinkers with the victim's car computer?"

"You got it." Hugh forked a slice of turkey onto his plate.

"May I be excused?" Merry Fay asked. "May I take Cara with me, and may I use your computer, Auntie Raine?"

"You may be excused," Aisling answered. "We'll call you for dessert."

"Go ahead, sweetie," Raine told Merry in regard to her request about the computer and Cara. "And you *both* know the *rules!*" she called after them.

"*Och*," the poppet exclaimed, as Merry lifted her from the highchair, "imagination *rules* the world!"

For the next several minutes, the sleuthing set continued discussing the various aspects of their latest challenge, thrashing it all out and repeating themselves, whilst the hands of the chiming mantel clock moved slowly round.

"You're reasonably sure, then, who killed Amanda Woods?!" Betty goaded some time later.

"At the present, we can't be a hundred percent certain, but we have *a very strong suspicion*," Aisling hurriedly put in.

In a blaze of questions, the brainstorming resumed with lively exchange. At one point, after rehashing what happened on their time-trek, the Sisters looked to Thaddeus, asking how he knew to gift Hester with the sun stick.

Dr. Weatherby finished chewing the buttered pumpkin cornbread he had popped into his mouth. "Heavens, you both know it's a *given* that a light of any kind would come in handy to anyone living on the eighteenth-century Pennsylvania frontier!" He flashed Beau a spectral of a smile asking that he pass the broccoli casserole.

The professor's nonchalant attitude and response made the Sisters wonder why they had posed the question in the first place.

It was only later that a second question surged through their minds.

# Chapter Fifteen

The following day, bright and early, the trio of Sleuth Sisters were on the road for Ohio in Aisling's black SUV, Raine and Maggie leaving their poppet at Tara to house and cat sit. A dusting of snow covered the ground, and light, tranquil flakes floated down, sprinkling the crisp, cold air with enchantment.

"Once we get to Washingtonville, we want to merge onto I-70, heading west," the blonde with the wand stated. She looked to Maggie, who was sitting next to her in the passenger seat. "You man the map, Mags."

"Right, darlin'," the redheaded Sister answered, looking up to glance out the window. "I hope we don't have bad roads this trip."

"I don't think we will," Aisling replied, keeping her eyes to her front. "Most of the snow we were supposed to get, we got, so the weather report says only flurries today and tonight. Same goes for Central Ohio."

"It's magickal, isn't it?" Raine asked from the backseat. "The snow flakes, I mean."

"Lovely," voiced Maggie and Aisling, with the former adding, "There is a quietness in snow that covers the slumbering Earth Mother with a blanket of peace."

"Well said, Mags. Snow always puts us in a holiday mood." The raven-haired Sister giggled. "I'm remembering snowy days when we were kids, and Granny would laugh and say, 'The angels are having a pillow fight.'

"I'm dying to know what Teresa Moore will share with us. Grantie Merry made it seem *momentous*, and I've never known the woman to be wrong, or to lie." Raine redirected her gaze out the window at the passing rural scenery cloaked in glittering winter white. "Over the river and through the woods to 'Mother Teresa's' we go!" she caroled. Bursting with eagerness, the Goth gal knew, with her keen witch's intuition, that Grantie hadn't dramatized the situation one iota– Teresa Moore had something categorically significant to reveal to them!

Nigh on to three hours later, the Sisters were in the small, picturesque village of Brinkhaven, Ohio.

"Turn left," Maggie said, as they rolled down Main Street. "Here!"

Aisling navigated the turn, drove on for a quarter of a mile, then pulled off the road to consult the handwritten instructions she had gained, over the phone, from Moore herself. "OK, Maggie, from this point, we'll follow Teresa's directions. We're close." She handed her notebook to the redheaded Sister, saying, "We continue on this road for a short distance until we see the turnoff for Shawnee Lane. Keep your eyes peeled for it, both of you."

Aisling waited till a closed Amish horse-drawn buggy went trotting past, then she pulled out, back onto the road. The horse's sleek brown body gleamed, and so did the highly varnished black vehicle the handsome bay was pulling. The carriage was plain, with no dashboard or other trim. Aisling gave a little shiver. "Betcha it's cold in those Amish buggies, winters."

"Oh, the Amish use buggy heaters," Raine remarked. "They run on propane gas, I think."

"And, of course, they have buggy blankets," Maggie interjected.

"I figured they used cozy lap covers," Aisling replied. "Listen, Teresa alerted me when we talked that if we come to the famous Bridge of Dreams, we've gone too far."

"Oh, but we *have* to visit the bridge before we leave here," Raine begged. "I looked it up. It's the longest covered bridge in Ohio and the second longest in the nation. The 370-foot bridge spans the Mohican River, on the Mohican Valley Trail, connecting the villages of Brinkhaven and Danville. And here's the best part– it's a great place to make a wish!"

"Not to worry, we'll be sure to see it," Aisling smiled. "Oh," she exclaimed a few seconds later, "there's the bridge. Look!"

"And that means we've gone too far," Maggie stated, peering down at the notebook she held in her hands.

"We might as well pull over and take a quick look. We're *here!*" Raine pressed.

Aisling noted the time on her watch. "We're early for our meeting with Teresa. Why not?" And she could sense rather than see Raine's dimpled grin in the rearview mirror.

The Sisters enjoyed the subsequent few minutes walking through the Bridge of Dreams.

Gazing down on the shining ribbon of serenity and bliss that was the Mohican River, Raine suggested they all make a wish *together*. "For good luck via the Power of Three," the raven-haired Sister whispered.

When they were ready, they each cast a penny, with their unified wish, into the sparkling water.

"With the Power of Three, so mote it be!" the magickal threesome ordained by their chant.

"Now, watch for Shawnee Lane," Aisling charged, as they climbed back into the SUV.

They had only driven a short distance when Maggie and Raine both cried out, "There it is!"

Since no one was behind her, Aisling slammed on the brakes in time to navigate the sharp turn. "No wonder we didn't see it before. The sign is twisted, likely by wind and tree branches, making it difficult to see from the opposite direction."

Snaking through the woods, Shawnee Lane was narrow, only wide enough for one car at a time.

"Great Goddess!" Maggie exclaimed, "what if we meet another vehicle coming in the opposite direction?"

"One of us finds a place to pull over and let the other pass," Aisling answered evenly. "When Teresa said she lived back in the sticks, she wasn't kidding!"

A few minutes later, the Sisters saw, through the trees, the "tiny house," or at least that's what Teresa had called it. They couldn't *help* but see it, for they had never seen a more *colorful* abode.

"Wiz—zard!" Raine nearly shouted. "It's a Gypsy caravan like the ones we saw in Ireland!"

"Wow!!" Maggie concurred, amazed.

Whilst the blonde Sister declared, "What a beauty!"

As they passed through the driveway that gave admission to Teresa's fascinating residence, they noted that the open wooden gates, on both sides, were carved with what the Sisters recognized as Irish lion faces– symbolic of protection, courage, and strength.

Teresa's home looked to be a genuine Gypsy caravan. It was bright lipstick red, with embellishment of purple gingerbread and a variety of vivid, hand-painted, varicolored symbols and figures. The small, round window frames were painted Kelly green. On one side of the caravan, the picture window was gorgeous, and the Sisters could image the woods viewed through that big, round window the turning wheel of the seasons.

Smoke curled invitingly from the wee chimney. A wooden sidewalk led to the door– an entrance that was nothing short of breathtaking, replete with protective symbols painted in a royal blue shade and accented with a paler, sky blue. There was a bit of an overhang, highly decorated with gingerbread in happy hues, that protected from rain. To the right of the door, an ingenious recess with a hook held an umbrella splashed, like an Impressionist painting, with dabs and daubs of bright colors!

Off to the side, under the trees, was an old-fashioned picnic table painted the same green that decorated the caravan. A stone footpath meandered round to the rear where a small, circular metal building could be seen in the distance amid the trees. *Barely* seen, for it was painted to blend with its woodsy surroundings. A vintage 1949 Overland Jeepster convertible, in a shade Raine would call "forest green," was parked behind the Gypsy caravan.

*Everything other than the caravan blends into the natural surroundings*, Maggie thought, *so nothing competes with the faerie tale dwelling for attention.*

The Sisters noted the herb and vegetable garden, "put to bed" now for the season. Raine and Maggie both had a simultaneous flash of the bright, multi-colored flowers that, during the warm period, lined the path leading to Teresa's unique home.

By this time, Aisling was rapping lightly on the ornate door.

In a moment, the mistress of the caravan appeared. "Come in! I just put the kettle on when I heard you drive up. Did you have any problems finding me?"

"Not really," the Sisters intoned.

Greetings and introductions were made, as the Sisters and Teresa warmed to one another.

Noting that their hostess was not wearing shoes, only warm socks, Aisling, Maggie and Raine removed their boots, leaving them on the dry wooden step at the door, under the overhang.

The Sisters speedily discovered that Teresa Moore was as colorful and one-of-a-kind as her home. Her snow-white hair was shoulder length. It wasn't curly, nor was it straight, but, rather, soft and wavy. She wore a long flannel dress of a deep rust hue and, over it, a long, green tunic, the generous, pixie-style hood of which hung partway down her back. The tunic, as the dress, flowed to her ankles and clasped in front, under the bust, the generous sleeves dripping from her wrists in a medieval flair. Teresa's eyes, once a vivid green, had dimmed slightly with age, but they still glittered with the joy of life. Despite her age, her face was comely, and the Sisters could tell she was once a great beauty.

Meeting Teresa, Maggie, the consummate history professor, was swiftly reminded of a quote by Eleanor Roosevelt: "Beautiful young people are accidents of nature, but beautiful old people are works of art."

Picking up the thought, Raine sent the redheaded Sister a subtle nod.

As soon as they'd stepped inside, the Sisters could tell that every inch of her home echoed *Teresa*. Everything held a story; everything had a special meaning and significance in and to her life. Entering the caravan was truly a magickal experience– like walking into a beautiful *objet d'art*. And the interior resonated with even more color and charm than the outside!

"My goodness, there's more space in here than we thought there would be," Aisling remarked, glancing about.

"Oh, there's a place for everything, as long as everything's in its place," Teresa laughed. "Lots of hidden storage. Not an inch of space is wasted. Do sit down and make yourselves comfortable. I hope you like tea."

"We do!" the Sisters chorused.

"I'm off the grid here, but not without a few essentials. I have a well and a generator, and my bathhouse is out back, the round, green building that blends into the woods– toilet, shower, and hot tub. There's a second outbuilding yonder," Teresa pointed. "Another round, painted metal building that also disappears in the trees. That one is for extra storage. I've a little stone springhouse too.

"You see," she talked on, "I had the land. This was my ancestor Hester Duff's and her husband Captain Colin Moore's land. Their house was close to where my caravan is, not far. I can take you later to see their graves. They're buried here. I always intended *to build* on this land; but this is nicer, I think. It reflects who I really am– *a free spirit*. Actually, if I get the wanderlust, my caravan is movable. All I'd have to do is hitch a truck up to it and pull it anywhere; but this spot is my true home, so here I'll stay."

Teresa cast a glance about and smiled, and the Sisters could see that she was really comfortable in her own skin, as well as in her unique surroundings. "I don't have a computer, or television, or a land phone, and I don't miss them. If I want to watch a particular TV program or search the Internet, I visit one of my tolerant friends who have those things. If I want to listen to music, I can, on my CD player, thanks to my generator. I do have a cell phone, as you know. That reminds me, how did you get my number?"

Obviously, the magickal trio could not reveal that information, so they told a little white lie that was partially true, almost completely true, and hurt no one.

"I'm a former police detective," Aisling said. "So I'm used to connecting the dots, as we like to say. Raine and Maggie are history and archeology professors at our local college; consequently, they are, in essence, detectives as well."

"While we were doing our homework, one clue or piece of information led to another," Maggie shrugged, "one person to another."

"It might take a year. It might take a day," Raine chanted, "but what's meant to be, will always find its way."

Teresa tilted her head to further scrutinize her visitors. "I understand. You don't wish to divulge your sources." She grinned. "The important thing is– *you're here*."


As the Sisters and Teresa exchanged pleasantries and small talk, getting more and more comfortable with one another, the Sisters took in the caravan.

The kitchen consisted of a tiny sink, under which was storage; a hotplate; a small microwave; a tiny fridge; and shelves, one of which held a variety of teas in quaint and unusual tins. The small table dropped down from the wall, around which everyone was now seated, the padded seating adorned with a spectrum of pillows, each a different color and design. Hanging in the big, round picture window, above the kitchen sink, was an attention-grabbing mobile. A wooden spoon served as the rod, sky-blue, over which goddess symbols had been painted. From this decorated utensil, suspended by virtually invisible fish line, hung fancy, wire-wrapped crystals of all different sorts, sizes and colors, as well as a variety of charms, and tiny, vivid Guatemalan worry dolls crafted and cast to lift fears and uncertainties from their owner.

The caravan's curved interior walls were painted the same lipstick red as the exterior, the inside, as the outside, covered with hand-painted symbols and figures. The Sisters recognized Wiccan, Celtic, Viking, Native American, Jewish, and Chinese symbols for protection, health, longevity, creativity, success, happiness and joy.

Raine sipped her tea, asking Sister Teresa after a reflective moment, "Did you say you were a schoolteacher?"

"I didn't say, but yes, I was a teacher for many years." She gave a dour chortle. "Felt like many. Let me think. For eighteen years, I taught history at the local high school."

"You sound as though you didn't like teaching," Maggie said, her voice level.

"Oh, it wasn't that I didn't like it. I did, at first anyway; but as time went on, I felt confined, restricted. What I'm endeavoring to say is that I couldn't really be who I am. So after eighteen years, I retired from the teaching profession and opened a small shop in town, where I lived, upstairs. It was a metaphysical shop. You know the sort of stuff– herbs, all perfectly legal, of course," she laughed, "balms, candles, sage, tarots, runes, jewelry, crystals, gemstones, books on the Craft, et cetera. And *that* I thoroughly enjoyed."

Teresa took a quick sip of her tea. "I closed the shop last year to live here. I already owned the land, as I said. Inherited it from my parents, along with Dad's old Jeepster." She rolled her eyes. "That thing's got over a hundred-fifty thousand miles on it, but it's still dependable. Gets me in and out of here in the winter. But getting back to what I'd started to say– I had a sister who died at birth, and my brother passed over about three years ago. Sooo, as I always wanted to do, I retired here when my caravan was ready."

"Custom built, I assume," Maggie probed, "your caravan?"

"Yes, I designed it and even helped construct it," Teresa stated with pride.

"Creativity is intelligence having fun!" Raine and Maggie recited, quoting Thaddeus.

"Your home is so *cozy*, and you are *sooo* creative! I love the little fireplace," Aisling commented. "Darling!"

"Thank you. That's my favorite thing about the place," Teresa commented. "Keeps me snug and warm winters.

"I designed the windows to open in the warm season, and I even have custom screens for them. I get a refreshing breeze through the caravan when the windows are open. It's lovely to smell the wild flowers in spring and summer and the woodsy, nutty smell of the fallen leaves in the autumn."

There was a tiny toilet that Teresa called a "convenience," since her bathroom was in a separate building to the rear of the caravan, cached within the privacy of forest. "When it's too cold to go out back during the night," she said with a titter.

At that, a black cat, that had been sleeping on the bed, under one of the caravan's small, round windows, rose, arched her back and stretched. Across from where the four witches were seated, the queen-size bed was high off the floor, with a huge storage area of drawers beneath. A sliding ladder, painted the caravan's lipstick red, provided access. Since the bed was a built-in, there was no need for headboard and footboard. Rather, the walls at the head and foot were covered in vibrant swatches of velvet, in a patchwork design that matched the velvet quilt. Atop the bed, too, a multitude of pillows in rich, jewel-tone colors and a variety of shapes and designs added to the cozy ambiance.

"Ah, the queen is up from her nap!" Teresa's eyes held amusement. "Puss-puss, come here."

The cat mewed and came forth to jump into her mistress' lap. "She's my baby. Her real name is Magick, but she is so regal, I'm given to calling her Queenie." Teresa stroked her furry companion, bringing forth a steady purr. "I always wanted a cat, but couldn't have one in the apartment where I lived above my shop in town. I rented that building, you see. Here, I am free. Free to live my life and be me!" Her handsome face shone with joy when she pronounced those words. "I never married, so I have no children. It's just Queenie and I, and we're an in-step pair. Kindred spirits, aren't we, Queenie?"

The cat opened her half-closed, golden eyes, looking up at Teresa to meow, as Raine perceived, a *positive* response. *A mutual admiration society.*

The Sleuth Sisters suspected strongly that Teresa hadn't always been without a human companion. There had been, they speedily divined, several lovers over the years; and yet today, there was a special someone in her life; though they picked up, too, that, like Raine and Maggie especially, she wanted to retain her own space, identity, and freedom.

Teresa's age was difficult to determine, so unlined was her face, and so youthful her laugh and vitality. But the Sisters reckoned she was likely in her late sixties or early seventies.

"Now," their hostess said, after she poured them all a second cup of tea and passed round a tray of organic oatmeal and raisin cookies, "suppose you tell me why you've come to speak with me."

Raine revealed their quest— how they wanted to clear Hester Duff's name and find out everything they could about her in order to obtain a Pennsylvania marker, which would designate the Witch Tree a historic site. The Goth gal told their hostess everything about the land developers, everything surrounding the tree, save the murder they suspected. "The more we learn about Hester, the better," she finished. "As we said, and we're certain you understand as a former history teacher yourself, if we can gather enough information to gain that Pennsylvania historical marker for the Witch Tree, that would go a long way in saving the tree. We're hoping you can help us. That's why we're here."

"We don't want to waste your time unduly, but *can* you help us?" Maggie asked with pleading look and tone.

"I can ... *and I will*," Teresa answered, getting to her feet. She bent to raise the lid of the padded seat upon which she'd been sitting. Reaching inside, she lifted out a metal box along with a pair of white, cotton gloves, setting them on the fold-down table around which she and her guests were assembled. Opening the casket, she extracted a timeworn, leather-bound notebook, wrapped in an oilcloth.

Teresa fixed her green eyes on the Sisters. "I keep this in the safety deposit box at my bank in town, but I *knew* I would need to get it out for your visit."

The Sisters hardly dared to breathe, so excited were they. *Was it, perhaps, a journal written in Hester's own hand?*

"Before you go, as I promised, I will take you to Hester's grave here on this property. Hester and her husband, Captain Moore, two of their five children, and Hester's Native American mentor– I suppose you could say *savior*– are buried here on this land where they lived."

The Sisters exchanged looks, with Raine blurting, "The shaman who rescued Teresa is buried here?!"

"So you know about Windwalker?" Teresa asked in a tone that did not convey disbelief.

Raine eased up. "We heard rumors. He's part of the *mysterious* legend surrounding Hester."

"Before I explain this," she patted the wrapped, antique book, "allow me to tell you the story of Windwalker."

The Sisters sipped the fragrant, delicate green tea and settled back against the soft pillows of their cushioned seat for what they knew would be a compelling account.

In her rich, mellow voice, their hostess related the exact episode with which the Sisters were now familiar, thanks to their crystal ball and their Time-Key. When Teresa got to the part of the story where Windwalker and his faction of Delawares rescued Hester, she informed her listeners that Mistress Duff's Native friend had caught the gist of the irate settlers' intentions at the Catfish trading post. By the time Teresa mentioned that the Indians and Hester headed across the Ohio in canoes, the Sisters could hardly contain themselves for want of what happened next.

"Windwalker took Hester to a trading post, east of here, where she stayed with the French family who ran it. She lived with Monsieur and Madame Bonheur and their two children for the next year until she met Colin Moore, an army captain, and they were subsequently wed.

"But lest I get ahead of myself in the tale," Teresa continued. "In parting from Windwalker, after he'd escorted her to the Bonheur Trading Post, a grateful Hester presented her rescuer with a white handkerchief– it was the only thing, except for a couple of coins, from her belongings she had on her, because she'd fled her Pennsylvania cabin in such haste. On the handkerchief, neatly embroidered in black, silk thread, was a five-pointed star and her name, 'Hester Duff.'" Teresa stopped to sip her tea.

The Sisters did likewise, though they were full to bursting with the excitement of discovery.

"Seven years later, in late August of 1794, Hester's husband, Captain Moore, commanded a force under General Anthony Wayne at what was to be the final defeat of the Indians on the Eastern frontier. The fight, as I am certain you know, was the Battle of Fallen Timbers, here in Ohio, near Maumee. After the bloody fray, Moore discovered an elderly Indian sitting forlornly on a log deep in the forest. As the soldiers approached, the old man pulled from a leather pouch a white handkerchief.

"He had been a warrior for many moons he told Captain Moore. He had fought in what the Whites called the French and Indian War, Pontiac's War, Dunmore's War, and the Revolutionary War. He had fought at Fort Ligonier, at Bushy Run, against St. Clair, and now against General Wayne, whom the Indians called the 'Black Snake' due to his uncanny ability to wage war in the same manner as they.

"'I am old now,' the elderly Indian declared, 'tired and sick of war. I wish to live my final days in peace. The Old Ways are long on the path of yesterday– gone now forever. The fight is over,' he rasped. Tears glistened in his old eyes. *It was done.*

"With that, he proffered the white handkerchief, as worn and ragged as himself, toward the uniformed soldiers before him.

"Officer Moore glanced down at the symbol of surrender and drew in his breath. Often, over their years together, had his wife Hester related the story of Windwalker. He extended his hand and smiled, closing the Indian's leathery fingers over the tattered keepsake."

Teresa paused again to sip her tea, as the Sisters hung in anticipation and suspense.

"Captain Moore took the old man home with him, where Hester and Windwalker had a heartwarming reunion. Windwalker lived five additional years– with the Moores. He became a beloved mentor, a grandparent to their children, teaching them many useful and wondrous things about the forest, our animal brothers; and as I said, he is buried here, on their homestead land, with the Moores in the family plot."

"What a delightful story!" Raine and Maggie remarked. "It deeply touches us."

Teresa looked pleased. "Whenever you hear or read something of a spiritual nature that moves you ... touches your soul, you are *not learning* something. You are *remembering* what you have always known."

The Sisters turned to one another and nodded. *Granny told us the same thing once.*

"Did you discover the Windwalker account in that journal?" Aisling asked.

"Not a journal, a hand-written manuscript," Teresa corrected. "Captain Moore's biography of his remarkable wife Hester Duff Moore." She waved a hand toward the oil-cloth-wrapped book. "It's all here, her entire life story, including all the good she did in this world, her countless healings; and lest I neglect to mention here today, the woman was a peacemaker and a healer between the Native Americans in her area and the Whites."

Raine was about to pose a question but stopped herself, not to interrupt Teresa, who, after a brief silence, began anew to speak–

"Captain Moore, as he states in the prologue of his book, wanted to surprise his wife with the publication of the manuscript on which he secretly worked for over three years; but he passed away just before he finished it, so this biography," Teresa gave the treasure a pat, "was never published. He hid the book from his wife after each writing session, so that it *would* be a surprise. Hester never learned of the manuscript's existence– *not in this world anyway.*

"Moore was making the final comments, a concluding segment to round out his literary work in an epilogue, when he passed away. Little did he realize when he penned the last word to paper, and he hid the manuscript that last time, that he would have only a day or so left on this earth.

"My great-great-great grandparents discovered the manuscript in this metal box under the floorboards of the log cabin that Moore had built for his wife here on this property. Stories passed down in our family claim it was a very large, roomy log cabin, quite cozy and nice. But nothing, including wood, lasts forever. Logs weren't treated in those long-ago days. The cabin was going to ruin, though the tall, stone chimney stood sentinel here for years until Time claimed it too. My people eventually abandoned it and moved closer to town, where they were merchants, though they held on to this land– *and* the historic manuscript which we've always treasured as a family heirloom.

"When our parents passed away, my brother and I sold the big house just outside of town, and I used my half of the money to open my metaphysical shop, where I lived until I retired last year and moved into my Gypsy caravan; but I told you all that." Teresa glanced around, as if looking for something.

"Let me read a bit of the prologue to you." The affable woman lifted her eyeglasses from a small shelf next to her, carefully removed the protective oil-cloth wrap from the leather cover, slipped on the pair of white, cotton gloves, and even more carefully opened the manuscript.

"'Every word of this manuscript about my beloved wife, Hester Duff Moore, is absolutely true. I swear this on my honor as a retired officer in the United States Army and as a God-fearing man, who faithfully obeyed both God's and man's laws my entire life.'"

Teresa looked up at the Sisters, who were moved to find their hostess' eyes brimming with sadness. "As if he knew that posterity would not hold honor as sacred as his generation, Captain Moore went to a notary, and with his hand on the Bible– Moore was a Christian– avowed that what he wrote was true. It's signed by the notary and two witnesses."

The Sisters traded looks, with Raine shooting the thought to her cousins, *This would prove everything we've always suspected **and** what we discovered without jeopardizing our Time-Key. **And** it would provide enough historic data to get the Pennsylvania marker and save the Witch Tree!*

Teresa seemed to be eagerly studying the Sisters for a long, private moment.

"We always believed Hester Duff was a good person," Raine said quietly, almost to herself.

"She was; but, as my great-granny always maintained, she was no one to goad into a fight," the fascinating woman commented, reminding Raine and Maggie that Thaddeus had said practically the same thing. The dark legend about my ancestor holds some truth, you know. By the way, Hester's nickname was 'Dark Star.'" She peered curiously at the Sisters. "As I suspect you're aware, *Duff*, in Gaelic, means Black or *Dark*; and *Hester*, anglicized from the Gaelic *Ó hOistir*, translates *Star*.

"Oh, Hester battled evil," Teresa cried out, "yes, as many witches do; but she was no one to fool with if she felt someone needed to be taught a lesson. My granny used to say that Hester's credo was 'I'm a witch. I don't have to wait for Karma!'"

"We're most of us grey, I suppose," Maggie said, with a measure of understanding, "differing shades of grey. One hardly ever encounters out-and-out saints or devils."

"Teresa," Aisling began, "would you consider letting us use this piece of history to bring your ancestor's story to light, preserve it, and save what has become known over the centuries as the Hester Tree or Witch Tree? Irrespective of what we always believed about the farm and the tree especially, we have no documentation of any kind. Hester Duff has always been shrouded in mystery. With *this* material, we could secure that Pennsylvania marker. Getting Witch-Tree Farm, with its Witch Tree, declared a historic site will go a *long* way in saving both from destruction at the hands of land developers, or anyone else for that matter."

"Like you, I've done my homework." The former teacher sat back against the pillows and held her visitors' eyes. "Done some detective work of my own," she stated with a quick bob of her head. "After you telephoned me, I looked you up on the Internet, at a friend's home, an ex-police officer; then, together, we made further inquiries. The police call on me, from time to time, to aid them in locating a missing person and so on. But I digress," she smiled.

"To return to what I was saying, I learned *all about* the famous Sleuth Sisters from Haleigh's Hamlet, Pennsylvania. I'm satisfied that you are good people, good witches, and that you do good works.

"It pleases me to no end, that, with your sterling reputations, you're making it your *personal* quest to bring my ancestor's true story to light and to save Witch-Tree Farm and the Witch Tree. It's especially gratifying that you are historians, with doctorates no less," she gestured toward Raine and Maggie, "as well as archeologists. What I'm saying is, you *realize* the historical significance of this manuscript, and you know what to do and not do to handle it properly in order to preserve it. Into the bargain *you*," she indicated Aisling, "were in law enforcement, so that gives me added comfort."

Teresa picked up her cup to down the remaining tea. "I've decided to allow you to borrow this manuscript that has been in my family for over two-hundred years. I want it back, however, as soon as possible, and in the same near-pristine condition in which I am loaning it to you. Now," she said, rewrapping the leather-bound book, "how about another cup of tea?"

## Chapter Sixteen

With the historic manuscript in tow, the Sleuth Sisters had no sooner set out, on their way home to Haleigh's Hamlet, when Aisling's smart phone sounded with the programmed music of Rowena of the Glen.

"Answer my call," the blonde with the wand said to Maggie, who was sitting next to her in the SUV's front passenger seat. "I don't like to talk on the phone when I'm driving, especially at night *and* on a road I'm not that familiar with."

"Hello," the redheaded Sister voiced into the phone. Maggie listened for a bit, her expression registering alarm. "Great Goddess!" she exclaimed. "Hold on!" She turned toward Aisling, behind the wheel, and Raine, who, by now, was leaning forward from her position in the rear, her hands gripping the backrest of Aisling's seat in anxious anticipation.

"It's Robin." Talking into the phone again, the redheaded Sister said, "Robin, please slow down, darlin', and tell us what happened from the beginning. I've put you on speaker."

"Sure." The High Priestess drew in a long breath. "My husband was listening to his scanner; when all of a sudden, I overheard the police say something like, "'Car fifty-two, we have a victim of a possible sabotage. Vic's lost control of vehicle and called 911, hysterical, to alert that his car's computer was compromised. Reported having no steering, no brakes, no way to control fast-moving vehicle, no way even to bail out. Victim is now on the runaway-truck ramp toward the bottom of Three Mile Hill. Take a report, call EMTs, if needed, and a tow to impound vehicle in question for investigation.'"

Robin sucked in another big gulp of air. "I can't recall *verbatim* what was said over the police scanner, but that was the gist of it. Sisters, guess who the victim of this car sabotage is?!" Robin all but shouted.

"Who?!" the Sleuth Sisters chorused.

"Sam Woods!" the High Priestess shrieked in her wound-up state.

\*\*\*

Several minutes earlier, en route home to Witch-Tree Farm, Sam Woods was just starting his descent down the treacherous Three Mile Hill.  In the owl light of the early November evening, he was thinking about his deceased wife Amanda, when suddenly, he realized he had no rule over his vehicle.

*Someone's tampered with my car to take control!* he told himself with sudden terror.

Wrestling with his fear, he tried pumping the brakes; however, pushing the pedal to the floor did absolutely nothing!  In fact, his car was picking up speed every second, as it *raced* down the steep, winding incline!

Gripping the steering wheel with white-knuckle fear, Sam strained but could *not* turn off the road onto the first runaway-truck ramp.  In panic, he lunged for the door handle in a frantic attempt to bail out but fast discovered, to his increased terror, that all the doors were securely locked.

He was trapped in a speeding runaway vehicle on a downhill chase of imminent death!

Laying on the horn, he tried the only way he could to clear his path and elude collision.  As he sped on, cars and other vehicles on the road, with screeching tires and blaring answering horns, were veering sharply out of his way.

Grasping for his cell, he yanked it out of his pocket, his shaking fingers frantically dialing 911.  When the dispatcher answered, Sam screamed into the phone, for as High Priestess Robin reported to the Sleuth Sisters– he was indeed *hysterical*.

"Help!  **Help me!!**  I'm speeding down Three Mile Hill with no control of my vehicle!  Someone's messed with my car's computer!  **Get outta the way!  MOVE!  MOVE!!**" he screeched at an SUV in his path, slamming his hand down on the horn and catching a fleeting glimpse of the female driver's terrified face.

The loud, stretched-out horn of his car, along with the extreme reacting horns of the impeding SUV and other vehicles, blasted into the dispatcher's ears.

"They're trying to *kill* me!" He yelled into his cell. "They killed my wife, and now they're trying to kill *me!*" Sam's words were dashed together and shouted frantically with the panic the man was experiencing. Again he tried his door, throwing his shoulder against the panel with no better luck.

"Are you *sure* you have *no* control of the car?" the operator asked.

"Sweet Jesus! **Are you deaf?!** No brakes; can't steer! Nothin' but lights!"

"What about the emergency brake?"

"Burned it out!! Can't even turn th' damn car off! **Noooooooooo! Move! Move, you idiots!! Get outta th' way!!"**

The dispatcher again heard the long-drawn-out blare of a car horn followed by another spun-out horn in response.

"Can you bail out; do you think?"

"Tried, doors locked!" In the next instant, Sam shrieked, **"Aaaaaaaaaaaaaaaaaah!** There's a woman standing in the road!" He fought to turn the wheel, but it refused to obey. **"Get off the road, y' stupid hippie! My God, I'm going to hit her!!"**

The now-frantic dispatcher heard yet another prolonged scream of horror, then the line went quiet. "Hello! Are you still there? Hello! **Hello!!** Sir, are you OK? **Hello?!"**

Letting out his breath, Sam picked up the dropped phone, gasping, "Y-yes, I'm ... I'm OK ... I think." He waited a moment till he began breathing normally. "All of a sudden, I-I *regained* control of my car! I'm ... toward the bottom of Three Mile Hill on the runaway-truck ramp, stuck in the gravel. Send help! Send a police car! **Someone's tried to murder me!!"**


Stunned by this turn of events, the first thing the Sisters did, when they arrived back home in Pennsylvania at Tara, was telephone Sam Woods at Witch-Tree Farm.

"I don't know if he'll be home or in hospital," Raine said, looking up from the little black book she kept by the kitchen phone.

After several rings, she was just about to disconnect when Sam answered. "Sam, are you OK?!"

"Who's this?" His voice sounded raspy.

"Dr. McDonough … Raine. We heard from a friend who has a scanner that you–"

"What an ordeal!" he cut in. "It was traumatic … **traumatic**; I tell you! I'm lucky, damn lucky, to be alive! The same person who killed my wife is trying to kill me!! I **told** you this would happen, didn't I?! And I was right! You gotta **help** me!"

Raine was holding the land phone so her two sisters of the moon could also hear what Sam was spouting. "I know it's difficult, but please tell us everything. Aisling and Maggie are here with me. We'll try to help you."

The words of Hugh and Betty– after they read the two mystery titles Maggie had copied down at Washingtonville's Abbott Library– sped through the essences of all three Sisters: *In Murder on the Road, the murderer kills the victim by hacking into his car's computer.*

The flash was staggering – *both* Mildred Grimm and Etta Story had checked that title out of the library, as well as *Murder is Simple*, in which the victim, allergic to peanuts, was given a salad dressed with peanut oil!

Concurrently, Sam was rattling out everything that happened to him on Three Mile Hill, after which Raine asked with bated breath, "Great balls of fire! Did you *hit* the woman who was standing in the road?"

"Crazy hippie! What th' hell was she doin' standin' on Three Mile Hill Road, in the black of night?! Must-a been high on dope!" Sam shouted, not waiting for or even wanting an answer. "The stupid b–" he skidded to a stop, saying instead, "*blockhead* was just *standing* there, in the middle of a steep, winding mountain road in the dark– and dressed in dark clothing to boot!"

"Did you *hit* her?" Raine pressed.

"No, thank God! That's when I suddenly got control of my car, and I jerked the wheel just in time to go up the runaway-truck ramp. It was a *miracle* I got control of that vehicle at the express moment when I did!"

"Thank goodness," Raine echoed, exchanging thoughts with Maggie and Aisling. "Look, I know this is upsetting for you, but could you *try* to tell us what the woman in the road looked like?"

***

Raine and Maggie drove to Washingtonville the following day with two stops on their agenda. They needed to make their meeting with the woman who, Robin told them, was the town gossip, a woman who had been one of the kitchen workers the night of the Harvest Dance. Then they planned on speaking with Police Chief Mann in the privacy of his office at the Washingtonville Police Station. Aisling could not accompany them. She and Ian were tied up all day with clients at their Black Cat Detective Agency.

Behind the wheel of Maggie's Land Rover, Raine said, "Keep your eyes peeled for Darling Road. That's where we turn right."

"There it is!" Maggie pointed from the Rover's front passenger seat.

Raine navigated the turn and rolled slowly down the quiet street, looking for the correct house number. "We want 602," she stated, her eyes searching the houses along the picturesque, tree-lined lane. "This street is aptly named. The homes *are* darling." And she began romanticizing about the people who resided in those houses.

"The street's named for John Darling, a Washingtonville industrialist who—"

"I *know* that, Mags, I was simply making a little *jeu de mots!*" Raine retorted.

"We're going the right direction," Maggie said, untouched by Raine's snippy tone. One or the other of the Sisters took what Granny used to call a "hissy fit" on occasion, but neither meant any harm. In a moment, Raine said—

"Sorry, Mags. I was just being peevish."

"No need to apologize. We've each allowed ourselves to become stressed. Oh, here's 600. And *there's* 602!" the redheaded Sister indicated with a wave of hand.

Raine pulled to the curve and turned off the ignition. "Grace Seymour's expecting us." She glanced at her watch. "We're only a couple of minutes early. *Darling* house," she remarked, sending Maggie an impish grin.

The charming grey-stone house beckoned, as Raine and Maggie strode up the brick walk to the gabled front door.  Maggie rang the bell, which sounded as antique as the one at Tara, causing the redheaded Sister to roll her eyes.  Then, looking to Raine, she whispered, "I know how you like to talk; and according to Robin, Grace does too, so make sure to stick to our plan."

Before the Goth gal could reply, the door opened with startling suddenness, and there loomed Washingtonville's neb-nose and gossip *par excellence*– Grace "Gracie" Seymour.

"You're right on time.  I like that!" the imposing woman enthused, indicating that her visitors should enter.

Inside, the breath of lemon oil and old wood hung on the air.

"You have a lovely home!" the Sisters remarked, as they repaired to the living room with its gleaming expanse of parquet floor, upon which were dotted expensive Persian rugs.  For all the costly items in the room, they couldn't help notice that the old-fashioned, Victorian-style parlor was far "too busy," crowded, as it was, with antiques, knickknacks, and gingerbread of all sorts.  Even the wallpaper, behind the wealth of paintings, bore a busy *toile de Jouy*, the pattern printed in a garnet red.

"Thank you," Gracie said in response to the compliment on her home.

Both Raine and Maggie could tell immediately that here was a woman of very sharp and definite personality.

"My late-husband was an attorney in town, but when he had time, he loved to restore antiques.  Like me, he was a *stickler* for perfection," she stated, standing there and looking like the acme of decorum.  A second later, she signaled with extended arm, "Do sit down."

*A busy house for **the** busybody*.  Raine flashed the notion to Maggie, who ducked her head to hide the smile tugging at her glossy-red lips, as the pair seated themselves on the plush, velvet sofa.

The Sisters took in the lady of the manor at that juncture. Big-boned, rather than heavy-set, she was a large woman, who appeared to be on the back side of sixty – "Big enough to hunt bear with a stick," Granny would have said. Gracie wore her greyish-brown hair feather-cut in a short pixie, a style that did not suit her and made her head appear too small for her body. Her tortoiseshell spectacles were outsized and *round*, lending her an owlish appearance, which induced the Sisters to think how like an owl Gracie was, not for the totem's sagacity, but for Owl's swivel head and wide range of binocular vision.

Completely devoid of makeup, Gracie's chiseled face displayed a somewhat pinched expression, as though she were thinking hard about something. She had unusual ears, pointed at the top, like the ears of an elf. Her dark-brown skirt reached far below her knees, to the shins, and her pale-blue, long-sleeve sweater looked to be the finest cashmere. Sturdy, sensible shoes completed her attire, and it occurred to the Sisters that these were the sort of shoes she always wore. Small gold hoop earrings and her wedding rings were her only adornments, but the Sisters could not help noticing the diamond– it was big enough to choke a horse. Gracie Seymour looked prosperous if not completely dignified.

"I don't drink coffee. Never keep it in the house, but I can offer you tea?" Gracie said, filling the parlor doorway.

"No, thank you," the Sisters replied, so anxious were they to begin the interview. They could feel the woman's myopic eyes taking in every detail of their appearance.

"I learned to love tea when I was in England. After my husband died, I traveled for a while, with a cousin. God rest them; they're both gone now. Travel packages mostly, where you rush from London to Paris, dash on to Madrid, Rome, Athens, Geneva, Cologne, and back again. Wouldn't have the energy for that sort of madness nowadays."

*Oooh, I hope we can keep her on track!* Maggie shot to Raine, who was searching her bag for her pen and notepad.

Gracie took a seat in a beige wingback chair opposite the Sisters, who were seated, side by side, on the long, brown couch. "Sooo," she stared, "you're the famous Sleuth Sisters from Haleigh's Hamlet."

"In the flesh," Raine answered, turning her head to exchange a quick look with Maggie.

Gracie cocked her head, looking up over the tops of her glasses. "Aren't there *three* of you?"

"Yes," Maggie replied. "Aisling couldn't make it today."

"I've read about you in the papers, even seen you on TV a few times when you were interviewed by the news media, but never did I think I'd be sitting in my own living room– *chatting* with you!" Gracie smiled wryly, leaning slightly forward in her chair, and the eyes behind the sizable spectacles kindled. "You're on another case, aren't you? What do you need from me? Daresay I'm a very *observant* person, as anyone who knows me can tell you."

"So we've heard," Raine replied. "It's come to our attention," she skipped on, "that you were working in the kitchen at the local Grange the night of the Harvest Dance. I recall that there's a large opening in the wall that separates the Grange's main hall from the kitchen. Shutters veil the opening, and the night of the dance, though the shutters were closed, the louvres were open. Anyone looking through those louvres would've had a grand view of the food tables. We were hoping that perhaps you might have seen something–"

Gracie broke in with intensity. "I saw *everything* that went on at the food tables. I told you I'm very observant. I have volunteered to work in the kitchen at the Harvest Dance well over twenty years now, and I've been in charge of the kitchen crew for nearly that long. *Nothing* gets by me; I'll tell you that!"

*I, I, I, me, me, me* Raine whizzed to Maggie. *Let's hope she wasn't so self-absorbed the night of the dance!* Aloud to Gracie, the Goth gal said, "That's exactly what we're counting on. We've heard how meticulous you are in everything you do," Raine gushed, endeavoring to stroke their egocentric hostess. "Now, tell us, Mrs. Seymour, were the kitchen crew the first people to arrive the night of the dance?"

Gracie answered in a split second, "*No!* Mr. Porter– the handyman and janitor– was the *first* to arrive. He opened up for us and let us in, then he went around, turning on all the lights."

"By *us,* when you said 'He let *us* in,' you mean the kitchen crew?" Maggie queried, pulling a small notepad and pen from her purse.

"That's right," Gracie replied. "There were five of us working in the kitchen that night. Usually we have six, but Norma Smythe had a dreadful cold, so–" she cut off, tilting her head, as a shrewd mien manifested on her sharp features. "You think Amanda Woods was *murdered,* don't you? *I've* been saying it all along! That's what this is about, isn't it? Well now, first off, let me state for the record that, my thought notwithstanding, our Washingtonville is a very *unsuitable* place for a murder! *Ours* is a nice little town, not like …"

As Gracie rattled on, the Sisters swapped glances with the thought, *Stick to the plan; keep her focused on subject!*

Maggie abruptly cleared her throat. "We don't know if there was foul play or not. We're merely gathering as many facts as we can," the Sister remarked, making a notation on her pad.

Gracie's crafty expression deepened, and her eyes, behind the owl glasses, sparked. "Uhhh-*huh.* Well, we … *the kitchen crew* always get to the Grange ahead of the others, so we can ready the kitchen. Actually, I was the first one there after Mr. Porter, because, as I told you, *I'm* in charge of the kitchen. We *have* to arrive early because we've all the setting up to do– make sure the coffee and tea urns are clean; then we brew the coffee; get the iced tea made and the hot-water urn ready for hot tea; and we set all that up on the beverage table. We always see that the food-warmers are ready for use; cover all the food tables with cloths; put out paper plates, paper bowls, napkins and silverware … I should say *eating utensils.* The flatware we use looks like silverware, but it's really plastic. We set out stacks of napkins and napkin-wrapped utensils." She gave a shrug. "As I said, we get all the tables ready for and with the food. I always say–"

"Who arrived next, after you kitchen ladies?" Raine deftly interposed.

"The first two food people to arrive were Mildred Grimm and Etta Story." Gracie paused a beat, interjecting, "They each brought salads."

"And they each brought salad dressings too, right?" Maggie questioned, looking up from her notepad.

"That's right. Mildred Grimm's husband helped her carry her salads and dressings in, then he went outside and lent a hand to Etta Story with her food items, before he darted out back. I saw him sneak out." Her voice lowered to a conspiratorial level. "He's a smoker, you see, and I don't think Mildred can do anything with him, in spite of the fact that she's as dictatorial as they come. Why, I remember when he …"

*Great Goddess, Robin was right! We'll have a job keeping her on track*, Maggie whisked to Raine.

*Yes, but her words and manner are telling us she never misses a trick!* Raine shot back.

"… so I don't think he'll ever quit smoking!" Gracie concluded after her rambling response. Noting the two pairs of McDonough eyes fixed on her, she immediately jumped back on target. "The next thing I noticed was how Mildred and Etta were eye-balling each other's contributions, as they arranged their things on the salad table. Those two are always in competition with one another, you know … or maybe you don't know. There's bad blood there. Every year, they try to outdo one another with their salad creations."

The witchy McDonough stare kept Gracie moving along. "After Mildred and Etta finished arranging their salads the way they wanted them, they headed for the Ladies' Room to freshen up before the others started arriving, and the place began filling up."

"How do you know that?" Raine interjected. "That Mildred and Etta went then to the Ladies'?"

"Because that's when *I* took a quick break to visit the Ladies' myself," Gracie replied in a tone that suggested she didn't like being doubted.

"Who all was in the Ladies' when you went in?" Maggie asked. "Think back carefully. This is *very* important."

Gracie gave a huff. "I don't need to think hard, because the question is an *easy* one. Only Mildred and Etta were in the restroom when I went in. Mine was a flying visit because I don't dare leave the kitchen unsupervised. You wouldn't believe–" Again she was stopped short by the Sisters' witchy gaze. "Anyway, as I was leaving the restroom, Amanda Woods was just popping in."

"You're certain it was Amanda?" Raine questioned. "You said you were in a hurry."

Grace stiffened and drew herself up in her chair with an even greater bluster. "Oh, hurry-scurry! Of course it was Amanda! I've known her since she was knee-high to a grasshopper, as the saying goes! I held the door for her as she went in!"

"So Mildred and Etta were in the Ladies' Room the same time Amanda was there," Maggie repeated to herself, bringing the pen to her lips in rapt thought.

"That's what I just said," Gracie snorted in a most indelicate manner. "I seized a fragment of something they were saying to one another in the Ladies'. Mildred said something about *strange bedfellows*, and Etta muttered that the operative word was *strange* all right."

Raine's eyes grew large with excitement. "Were they referring to *themselves* as the strange bedfellows?"

Gracie nodded. "I believe they were. They were each in a cubicle, when they were talking to one another; and when I came in, they heard me and shut up."

The Sisters exchanged a thought, as Gracie continued talking.

"When I got back to the kitchen, I directed the crew to start filling the big tubs with ice for the bottled water and soda pop."

"Where was Sam Woods at that time?" Raine queried, jotting something on her notepad.

"Well, when he first came in, he was alone in the main hall at the food tables, arranging his wife's baked goods on the dessert stand. I saw him do that, then walk over to the salad table to look over the choices there. He looked the salads over carefully before making his selection. He then started helping himself to *two* salads, I figured for him and his wife. He did the same with the salad dressing."

Maggie glanced up from her pad. "By that you mean that he looked the salad dressings over carefully before he put them on the two salads he took?"

"That's what I said," Gracie retorted with a roll of her eyes.

"Was anyone milling around Sam, talking to him?" Maggie probed.

Gracie thought for a moment. "Hmm, the rest of the food people were all coming in by then, the *entrée* people … the folks bringing hot foods. They began trooping back to the kitchen to transfer their contributions to warming dishes, which my crew started carrying out to the proper table. I gave the order for that to be done right away. A few of the entrée people had brought their offerings that morning, you see; and my crew had taken those things out of the fridge and set them out in chafing dishes already. We *have* to be prepared. People come hungry as bears!

"Anyway, by that point in the evening, more of the dessert people were coming in too. Even some attendees were starting to arrive by then. Mind, I couldn't see the new arrivals at the entrance, from my position behind the shutters, but I was catching bits and pieces of conversation and laughter. I noted several young women hanging about in groups, giggling and flirting with the men. It's *disgraceful* the way young people conduct themselves today, don't you think?" When the Sisters neglected to respond, Grace carried on. "I did see Mildred Grimm and Etta Story talking to Sam."

Raine furrowed her brow. "Together? Were they both talking to him at the same time?"

"Lord, no!" Gracie said firmly. "Weren't you listening to me? I told you those two despise one another. First Mildred started bragging about her antipasto salad to him." She gave a particularly loud "Humph! Looked to me as though she practically *forced* him to make her antipasto his selection because she started yammering to him about it when he was at the salad table. Anyway, when Sam got away from her– and I could *clearly* see that he was trying his best to break away from Mildred– he then came face-to-face with Etta Story at the beverage table. I heard him mention that he'd have to make two trips, carrying his food to the table he picked out for himself and his wife. It was then I heard Etta volunteer to carry Amanda's salad."

"Think really hard about what happened next," Maggie urged. "It could be *very* significant." The redheaded Sister studied their hostess with almost bated breath, as the latter's mind reached back to the moments in question.

"All right," Gracie began, reflecting, "I remember … that Sam asked Etta to grab a bottled water for Amanda. Then I saw her, *Etta,* set Amanda's antipasto down on the salad table while she got the water." The older woman stopped, as though suddenly remembering something else.

"Then what?" Raine pushed, growing impatient.

Gracie's thin lips tightened, and two spots of color rose to her cheeks. "That's when one of my kitchen workers bothered me for an extension cord, and I turned around and pulled the kind they needed from one of the drawers back there. When I returned to my station at the shutters, I saw that Etta was talking with Amanda at the Woods' table."

*Great balls of fire!* Raine sent telepathically to Maggie. *She can't tell us if she saw Etta, or anyone, alter Amanda's salad! Wouldn't you know it?!*

"Do you recall noticing if anyone handled Amanda's *purse?*" Raine asked suddenly. "Hers was a large, black leather bag that she plunked on the floor between herself and Sam, at the table where they were sitting."

Gracie tilted her mousey-brown head in a musing gesture. "Y-y-yes, I *do* remember several people shoving that bulky purse of hers out of their way."

"Again, this is extremely important, so we need for you to give this careful thought," Maggie petitioned. "Who were the people you recall, *in any way*, coming into contact with Amanda's purse?"

"Etta was the first one I saw moving it … sliding it over to make room for a chair she pulled from the next table, so she could sit *between* Sam and Amanda and chat for a spell." Gracie gave a short, quick sigh. "Let me think. OK, after that, Mildred moseyed over to the Woods' table. She started right in on the couple about selling Witch-Tree Farm to make way for that shopping center she has her sights on. I don't know how well you know Mildred Grimm, but she's like a bulldog with a hunk-a red meat once she's sunk her fangs into something."

The Sisters exchanged looks.

*Pretty much what Robin told us about Etta Story!* Raine shot to Maggie, who replied telepathically that *perhaps the strange bedfellows, the unlikely allies, were more alike than meets the eye. But why would ...*

Noting that her Grimm comment had made an impression, Gracie saw fit to add, interrupting the Sisters' thought transfer, "You keep your eyes on that one! Mildred's mean as a rattlesnake and twice as dangerous. I know what I'm talkin' about!"

"Hmmmm, let me ask you this." Maggie fixed the older woman with her McDonough stare. "Did *both* Mildred Grimm *and* Etta Story bend down to move Amanda's purse, or did they simply shove it out of the way with a foot?"

Gracie thought for only a second before responding. "I can tell you for certain *both* women bent to move that big, ugly purse Amanda always lugged around."

"Each moving it with hands?" Raine wanted to make absolutely certain. "You're sure they didn't just slide it with a foot?"

Shaking her head and surveying the Sisters critically, Gracie reiterated, "Etta and Mildred each bent down and moved the purse, *each with hands*," she said, fluttering her hands before her face in an exasperated manner. "I really don't see why you–" the busybody stopped herself in sudden realization. "Ahhh, so that's how your mind is working! You think–"

Raine cut her off. "Before we move on, did you see anyone else come into contact with that purse?" the raven-haired Sister pressed, holding the older woman with her emerald eyes.

After a few quiet moments, Gracie said, "On reflection, I did. Those two weirdos from the local coven, or whatever that ring of heathens calls themselves. "Looney or something Moony, and Starry Night, or maybe it's–" She threw her hands in the air. "I don't recall their silly names, but I'm certain you know who I mean," and her voice was accusing, "since I saw *you* hobnobbing with them soon after you arrived at the dance." She leaned back and crossed her arms in disapproval.

The Sisters looked to one another, as Raine strove to hold her tongue.

"Moonglow and Starlight?" Maggie offered in a quiet tenor.

"*Whatever*," Gracie bristled, and her tone and manner were condemning. "I heard them ask Amanda to keep an eye on their purses and save their seats while they visited the food tables. They'd taken a table right next to the Woods, you know. Then I saw them set their purses on the floor *with* Amanda's bag. It was right after that," Grace gave a curt nod of surety, "yes, *right after that* Amanda had her attack."

"And those were the *only* people who stopped by the Woods' table to chat?" Raine asked, wanting to make sure they were reaping as much information as they could.

"I didn't say that," Gracie snapped tersely with a gesture of annoyance, after which she let loose a snappy pair of connected tsks. "Honestly, one would think you'd be better listeners! Sirena Chambers then Reggie Mason talked briefly with the Woods at their table, in that order, and right before the two weirdos."

*Soft of eye and light of touch, speak we little, listen 'n learn we much*, Maggie meditated. Aloud, she said, "Did you see either Sirena or Reggie come in contact with Amanda's purse?"

"Hmmm, noooo," Grace answered as if she were thinking it over.

A sensation of doubt flooded both Sisters, with Raine questioning, "You're sure about that?"

The McDonough stare overpowered Gracie's ego. "I best not answer that," she determined, lowering her eyes and pursing her thin lips, "because when those two were talking to the Woods, I wasn't at the shutters the *whole* time. A couple of kitchen issues arose that *I* had to handle. Let's say *duty called*. I like to post myself at the shutters in between, so I can watch the food tables and see if there is anything we need to replace or refill, spot if someone spills something … you know, things like that. I always try to be on top of matters."

*And to spy on everyone you can without being seen; but in this case, it's a good thing you **are** such a thumpin' yenta*, Raine thought to herself.

"Frankly, I did *not* see Sirena or Reggie handle Amanda's purse; but, as I said, I was not at the shutters the whole time they were chatting with the Woods," Gracie admitted, prompting Maggie to zip Raine the thought–

*She's an **honest** snoop.*

"Did you notice anyone paying especial attention to Amanda Woods?" Maggie happened to think, voicing it aloud to their hostess.

"Well," Gracie began, wagging a finger at the Sisters, "now that you mention it, there were *two* people, especially, who seemed to be," she groped for a word, "*studying* both Amanda *and* Sam. At least that's the impression I got."

In the twinkling of an eye, the Sisters turned to one another, excitedly shifting their focus back to Grace.

"Who were they?" Raine blurted a tad too loudly.

Approximately a half-hour later, the Sisters posed one final question to Grace Seymour.

"Tell me," Raine lowered her voice, "and this is likely *the* most important question we will put to you today– do you recall witnessing anything that you thought was odd or unusual the night of the Harvest Dance? Anything, aside from Amanda's passing, that was out of the ordinary?"

Gracie knitted her brow and considered the Sister's query for a long, weighty moment. Then, with sudden eagerness, the eyes behind the owl glasses lit up with recollection. "Yes! As a matter of fact, I *did* notice something, a couple of things, that, at the time, I thought odd but insignificant. I distinctly saw …"

\*\*\*

Chief Michael Mann was a tall, robust police officer, middle aged, who beheld his job and the law with the utmost reverence. He had a high color, as a lot of Irish do, and his iron-grey hair matched his grit– determination the Sisters could easily detect in his eyes. It was difficult to discern the color of those eyes, a mélange of grey, green and brown.

*Hmmm, people with eyes of that sort are said to be risk-takers, courageous, and quick tempered*, Raine chucked to Maggie. The Sisters were seated across the chief's desk in the privacy of his office.

"I've known fellow brother and sister in blue, Aisling and Ian, many years," Mann stated, "and I am aware of the crime-solving skills of the famous Sleuth Sisters." He smiled just a little when he spoke those words, revealing even, white teeth. "Your reputation, as the saying goes, heralds you," he gave a gracious nod, "and I am duly impressed."

"The Man" pulled himself up in his desk chair. "In addition, I have spoken at length about you with your Hamlet's Chief Fitzpatrick. Fitz and I go *way* back, so I am going to welcome any assistance you might be able to give me on this case. Needless to say– but I'm going to say it anyway– anything we discuss in the confines of this office, stays within these walls. What I'm about to share with you is *not* to be disclosed."

"We fully understand," the Sisters replied.

"And we wouldn't have it any other way," Maggie pledged.

"Now," he said a bit louder and getting down to the business at hand, "we've, thus far, four persons of interest. Etta Story, Mildred Grimm, Reggie Mason, and Sirena Chambers. And thus far, it seems our Washingtonville Historical Society President is the *top* suspect, for Story has the most to gain. If something happens to both of the Woods, Witch-Tree Farm goes to the Washingtonville Historical Society. That, I discovered, has been Etta Story's vehement quest all along, to have the society in possession of the farm and the tree."

The Sisters traded looks.

"We may have a murder *and* an attempted murder to solve. As I'm sure you know, cars nowadays have a black box similar to those on planes. The one from Sam Woods' vehicle is being processed as we speak. The crime lab will be able to tell us by tomorrow if someone interfered with that car's computer.

"Clearly, Town Council President Mildred Grimm has been on an all-fired quest of *her* own as well. With Amanda Woods gone and out of the picture, perhaps Grimm's scheme is to *frighten* Sam Woods enough, so he'll turn around and sell Witch-Tree Farm to her buddy Reggie Mason; and then she'll see the realization of *her* dream, that of a glitzy shopping center here in Washingtonville. The 'jewel in the crown' I've heard her mention after council meetings to newspaper reporters."

Chief Mann cocked his grey head. "I've uncovered that Grimm has an even bigger dream– she plans to run for state rep and then state senator, stepping stones to the governor's mansion. Personally, I don't think she has a snowball's chance in Hell, but it's obvious *she* thinks she has. As for someone trying to scare the owner of Witch-Tree Farm off his land– I'd say that hair-raising ride down Three Mile Hill gave Sam Woods a fright, wouldn't you agree?"

Before the Sisters could respond, the chief continued. "I've been getting reports that Woods has been hearing *strange* noises, even voices in the wind, out at Witch-Tree, and some say he's been babbling about ghosts. Could be that his nerves, after losing his wife, are just getting the best of him. That farmhouse is old, and old houses emit lots of strange noises. *Or* it could be, as I was hypothesizing, that someone's *staging* all the crazy, odd-ball things Woods is experiencing– to *scare* him enough to sell his farm."

The Sisters remained quiet to give the chief time to talk.

"Look," he brought hands together, locking the fingers in a tepee shape, "we've learned that Reggie Mason is a whiz kid on the computer. Used to design web sites for spending money when he was in college, and his dad cut him off for being such a royal pain in the butt. My question is this– is Mildred Grimm in cahoots with Reggie Mason? Do we have a collusion at work here? Reggie's a spoiled brat who got older but none the wiser. Nothing like his father, that lad. Derrick's a hard worker, an honest businessman, and withal a damn likable fellow. As for the other land developers, Sirena is the rich daughter of a loudmouth multi-millionaire, self-made– or so he likes to brag– but the whole town knows he inherited a ton o' money from his father." The chief furrowed his brow. "Could even be more than one collusion at work here." He fixed his eyes on the magickal pair before him. "Remember, ladies, everything we discuss stays between us.

"Etta Story's a computer whiz in her own right," the chief went on. "Does all the computer stuff for the historical society. You know, she was a journalist for many years, so she's definitely computer wise. Then there are the two witches from the local coven. I almost forgot to mention them as persons of interest– Moonglow and Starlight, or whatever handles they've hung on themselves." He laid his hands flat on the desk in front of him. "They've been on, to say the least, an *intense* quest to save the Witch Tree, 'At all costs,' is the word about town."

Noticing the look on the Sisters' faces, he promptly added, "Oh yeah, they've been passing out flyers and getting people to sign their petition, all the while shootin' off their mouths, from one end of Washingtonville to the other, how they will do anything, *anything*, to save that tree; and I quote, 'No matter what it takes!' And guess what *they* do for a living?" Without waiting for an answer, the chief hastened on, "They're computer tutors and web designers. *Successful* computer gurus, I might add. Used to be computer programmers for public broadcast television in Pittsburgh. That's where they met."

Mann tilted his head in a sudden pensive gesture. "I wonder … . Those two cyber sibyls might be adept at what is called in the entertainment industry 'special effects.' Who knows what hocus-pocus, what black magick, those two could brew up? *They* could be staging the ghostly shows out at Witch-Tree Farm to scare Sam Woods off his land. Not to mention scaring away prospective buyers."

"Hmmm, *noises off*," Raine murmured to herself, her green eyes widening.

"What's that?" the Chief asked, meaning that he didn't quite hear what she'd uttered.

Raine came out of her musings. "A theatrical term, sir. Just sorting out a notion of mine."

"The Man" shook his head as if to clear it from all the data and suspicions whirling round in his brain. "Aw, everyone's a computer expert today, even kids. But you gotta admit, it's feasible, very, very feasible, that our top suspects might *all* know how to meddle with a car's computer, among other devilment for personal gain!" Once more, he wagged his head, slower than before, as if revisiting his own thoughts. "Mum's the word, ladies," he repeated of a sudden.

"Of course," Raine and Maggie replied.

"Sooo," the chief leaned back in his chair, "to review: Our top suspects are Story, Grimm, the land developers, and the two witches, and I've told each of them not to leave town."

Again the Sisters looked from one to the other.

"We've uncovered a couple clues we think might be significant information, *and* we've some hunches of our own we'd like to share with you, if we may," Maggie said, pulling her notepad from her purse.

"*Please*," Chief Mann responded, extending a hand, palm up, "say what you like. I'm of the belief that women have an intuition that is denied men."

Raine gave a nod. "You might be surprised by our findings, perhaps not, but nonetheless, here goes …"

Sometime later, Raine asked, "Chief, perhaps your top suspects would be more inclined to level with *us*. I mean, not being uniformed officers of the law, we might be more apt to pull information out of them. You know what I'm trying to say. There's, for some folks, blue-coat syndrome when talking with police, just like there's white-coat syndrome for some people in the doctor's office. What say you? Would you give your OK for us to interview each of the suspects, to learn, among other things, where each was the evening the computer in Sam Woods' vehicle went haywire?"

"By all means, talk with them," Chief Mann answered. "Find out anything and everything you can, then report back to me. We want to get to the bottom of all this!"

# Chapter Seventeen

That night was anything but restful for Sam Woods. After finally drifting off to a fitful sleep, he began tossing and turning in his bed, racked as he was, with gruesome nightmares. The chill, November wind whipping round the old farmhouse was filled with strange noises and ghostly voices.

Each night, since Amanda's death, was worse than the last; and lately, Sam shrank from the challenge of retiring to his bed for the evening. He never knew what awaited him during the course of the night; and, most of all, he feared what might be looming in his dreams. He had taken to staying up as late as he could, rising in the morning for work, tired and jittery. He told those who mentioned to him how exhausted he looked that he blamed himself for what happened to his wife, muttering that he should have been more vigilant.

Shaking their heads, friends and co-workers discussed among themselves how *tortured* Sam was. Nothing anyone said or did seemed to lighten his self-reproach for his loss.

Mumbling and thrashing about on his bed, Sam was reliving his ride of terror down Three Mile Hill. Yet again, he had no control of his car, as speeding down the treacherous, steep and winding slope, he raced on, narrowly missing one vehicle after another, whilst he laid on the blaring horn, screaming and sweating and gnashing his teeth for the violent impact that would signal his death.

Suddenly, with a cry, he sprang upright in bed. "Oh, God, I thought for sure I was going to hit that woman this time!"

Drenched in sweat, though the house was cold, the heat turned down for the night as he preferred, he was breathing hard, as though he had run a long, long way. With a groan, he raised quivering hands to his matted hair. "Oh, God!" he cried again. "I can't go on like this! I can't go on like this!" He rubbed the space between his eyes, wishing he could make his head stop pounding.

The night wind howled, shrieking and moaning like the dreaded Banshee. Mustering what strength he had left, he was about to step out of bed, when his eyes were drawn across the room, to the large antique mirror, atop the tall dresser, that had belonged to Amanda's uncle Will.

Within the glass, in the misty moonlight streaming through an opening in the drapes, he saw a silhouette that appeared to be a human shape.  Emerging from the mirror, the shadow remained motionless next to the dresser, and Sam got the distinct feeling that it was– *waiting*.

*Waiting for what?!* he asked himself.

Upright in bed, the tormented man sat frozen in place.  Never before had *this* happened!  With a mix of ghoulish curiosity and paralyzing fear, he remained still, unable to move, as a flow of wraithlike orbs began appearing from the mirror– one, two, three, four … five.  He watched as they started drifting– closer and closer to his bed. *And then it happened.*

An ethereal substance floated from the antique looking glass.  This was not the first time he was seeing this particular vapor, and with each appearance, it struck new fear in his heart– for, instinctively, he knew this was a *powerful* entity.  Before, when it had glided from the dark depths of the mirror, it hovered above the bed, over him, his screams vanquishing it with the sudden disappearing act for which ghosts are known. *Tonight, however, was different.*

For the first time, the mist began to take on a recognizable shape– the unmistakable form of a woman.

As the ghost drifted closer, the orbs flanking it, the room turned icy cold.  With held-in breath, Sam's eyes were glued to the advancing entities.

Beyond, he could see that the shadow-figure, like a sinister sentinel, held back, remaining at its post, next to the glass.  While he stared, two red, glowing eyes kindled and sparked in the shadow-man's face.  The evil glow was there a mere instant, but that's all it took to send an even greater frisson of fright surging down Sam's spine.

As the relentless talons of fear seized him, he tried to move, to leap from his bed and run; but, try as he would, his legs would not obey.  It was like those dreadful nightmares, in which he was trapped, prisoner and victim to the tortures of the night!

When the filmy white specter was directly over him, Sam's heart was pounding so rapidly, he thought his chest would burst.  He couldn't move; he couldn't speak; he could not even scream.

With a sudden, quick movement, the thing reached for him, the hands claw-like and threatening, the face taking on a familiar guise!

**"You!"** Sam raised *his* hands to ward off what he thought would be an attack, letting out a horrified cry that brought the dog Jasper to his closed door, barking for all he was worth on the opposite side of the wooden barrier.

Since the ghostly activity began at Witch-Tree Farm, Jasper was terribly afraid. For a time, Raine quelled the Airedale's fears, but, of late, the dog refused to enter the master bedroom. Jasper's whining and barking kept Sam from falling asleep, and so he had taken to closing his door nights.

At once, Sam's sudden scream brought forth yet another transformation– the specter's face and hands changed to those of a skeleton, the thing's open mouth emitting an unearthly shriek that, reaching Jasper in the hallway, raised the fur on the poor beast to send him racing from the farmhouse's top floor to the basement, where he cowered under the steps with the cobwebs.

Letting out an even louder yell, Sam freed himself from his temporary paralysis. Springing from his bed, he threw open the bedroom door, letting it crash against the wall, the impact causing an oil painting of an old mill to thud and thump to the floor.

With a wail, Sam dashed down the stairs in the dark, where he tripped over a living-room chair to fall, face-forward, into the kitchen. Slowly, he dragged himself to his feet, feeling, with shaking fingers, for the light switch.

"I must be losing my mind!" he uttered, leaning against the wall for support, his breath coming in gasps. "I can't ... can't take much more of this. My nerves are shot. God help me– *something's got to give!"*

Little did Sam Woods realize how foretelling his frenzied utterance was!


The subsequent day would have seen Raine and Maggie back at Haleigh College for a special Sunday seminar that had been scheduled for months; but a stroke of fate afforded them a couple of more days off when burst pipes in Old Main resulted in the cancelled session, not to be rescheduled until after the Christmas break.

The Sisters had risen early, but having received word that their history seminar was cancelled, they were sitting at their breakfast table, preparing to galvanize into action, Sleuth-Sisters style.

"This means we can get our interviews with Chief Mann's top suspects realized straightaway," Raine said, rubbing her little hands together in anticipation, her emerald eyes sparkling. "What say you, Mags?" She could sense Maggie's mind ranging over the names on their list.

"Sounds like a plan," the redhead replied. "Look, we don't know how much time we'll have before we have to return to our classrooms, so why don't we split the chief's suspects up between the three of us. We can each interview two, and when all done, compare notes."

"That's exactly what I was thinking!" Raine exclaimed. "Great minds think alike! Listen, I rang Aisling right after the college phoned us with the news of the cancellation, and she's more than willing to do this. How do you want to divide the suspects between us? Aisling said she'll go along with however we do it." The raven-haired Sister bit off a piece of buttered English muffin, swiping crumbs from her mouth with a paper napkin.

"Why don't I interview Moonglow and Starlight? You take Sirena and Reggie, and Aisling the chief's topmost two– Mildred and Etta?" Maggie took a long swallow of tea, draining her cup. With a shrug, she added, "I can't say why precisely, but to me, that distribution seems like a good fit for each of us."

Raine nodded contentedly, "I think so too. And since we have a pretty clear vision where each of the persons of interest will be, we won't give them a heads-up that we want to speak with them. That way, they won't have time to cook up any false stories. One more thing: Let's you and I begin this evening on the intense paperwork required to gain the Pennsylvania historical marker we're after for the Witch Tree. We want to make that a *fait accompli* ASAP, and the sooner the better, for the safety of the tree!" she spun her charm.

Maggie refilled their teacups from the pot ensconced in Granny's shamrock-sprinkled cozy. "Right, and that way, we can return Teresa's manuscript to her before long, to put her mind at ease about it. I'm nearly finished reading it, then I'll pass it to you." She drew in her breath. "Tomorrow, we must drive out to Witch-Tree Farm and talk to Sam."

Raine came back with, "Right! We'll ask Aisling if she can accompany us to Witch-Tree, but *we* go anyway, with or without her, agreed?"

"Agreed." Maggie worried her full lower lip, deep in thought.

"Who knows? We may just wrap this whole case before we have to resume regular classes on Tuesday!" Noting the anxious look on Maggie's face, Raine said, "Don't worry, Mags. Everything will work out the way it's supposed to, for all concerned. *We'll* see to that," she concluded with passion, downing the rest of her tea and rising.

She glanced at the railroad clock on the kitchen wall. "Let's hustle. Aisling will be stopping by momentarily to pick up Mildred's and Etta's addresses. I figure we'll all drive separate cars, conduct our interviews independently and simultaneously– that way, our persons of interest won't be able to compare notes– and we'll meet back here at Tara by what ... four o'clock or there about?"

"Sounds good," Maggie answered. "I hate driving, but at least the roads are clear today, and there's no snow or ice in the forecast."

Tara's antique doorbell pealed loudly, causing Maggie to groan. "One of these days!"

"That's Aisling!" Raine announced needlessly, rushing to answer the door.

On the way to Washingtonville, Raine wanted to make a quick stop at Belle's Notions, a Hamlet beauty salon. Though it was Sunday, and Belle's was closed, Raine knew the owner often did her paperwork in the shop on Sundays. Raine was out of the organic shampoo and conditioner she purchased from the proprietor, so she'd telephoned for the beautician to have the items ready to go. All she had to do was pop in, grab the bag, hand Belle the money, and be on her way.

At the Hamlet's Victorian town square, Raine whipped her MG into a space in front of the beauty shop, stepped out of the car, and was about to enter, when who should exit Belle's Notions but Sirena Chambers, one of the persons of interest with whom the Goth gal was hoping that morning to question!

"Hello!" Raine greeted with a happy smile (that the happenstance spell she'd cast earlier had turned out so well). "What a blessing running into you! Could we go somewhere for a cup of tea or coffee? I really need to speak with you." *Looks like she picked up some hair products too*, the Sister told herself, noting the bag Sirena held that bore the name of Belle's shop.

Sirena checked her watch. "I can do that. Where do you want to go?" She creased her brow, "Now? Or did you want to see Belle first?"

"No," Raine answered, checking her own watch for the time. I was just going to pick up some hair products, but I can do that after we talk. Let's go to The Gypsy Tearoom. It's right around the corner."

"I know it," Sirena answered. "Shall we walk? I'll leave my car here."

"Let's," Raine replied, falling briskly into step beside the land developer.

The Gypsy Tearoom was nearly empty when the women entered and slid into a private booth in the rear, opposite one another. Within a few moments, Eva, menus in hand, received them warmly, asking if they would be eating or just having tea.

"Just tea," they both answered.

"Darjeeling for me," Sirena stated, removing her leather driving gloves.

"I'll have the same," Raine said, getting a vibe from the quick-moving Eva that the proprietress knew she was there on Sleuth-Sisters business.

"You've been here before?" the raven-haired Sister asked.

"Oh yes, several times," Sirena answered. "I'm very fond of this place. I have to drive over to the Hamlet to have my hair done. Belle's the only beautician I know of in the whole area who uses only organic products, and I like to pop in here, afterwards, for lunch. Today, however, I wasn't planning on lunching here, due to the pile of papers waiting for me at the office. Sunday is often the only time I can work quietly, to wade through the paperwork I have without interruption. So I guess I'll just order take-out back in Washingtonville, though I do so hate eating at my desk."

"Sirena, I have to ask you a few personal questions, and I hope you'll be straightforward with me. Where were you this past Friday, between five and five-thirty in the afternoon?"

Visibly taken aback, the woman was silent for a long moment before answering, and when she did, her response was to ask a question of her own. "Why do you want to know?"

"There may have been an attempted murder committed at that time. My cousins and I are assisting Chief Mann in the investigation, and—"

"An attempted murder!" Sirena cut in. "Surely, you don't think *I* had anything to do with an attempted murder!" Her violet eyes deepened, and her cheeks took on a rosy hue.

"Are you going to tell me where you were?" Raine asked quietly. "It would be better to tell *me* than to have the police question you at the station." She extracted a small notebook and pen from her purse.

"Am I a suspect?!"

Declining to answer, Raine merely tilted her head, her gaze never leaving the other woman's face.

"The very idea! This is preposterous!"

Raine raised an ebony brow. "You knew, before this weekend, that you became a person of interest in a related matter, and you were told *not* to leave town. Tell me where you were Friday. I won't mince words; you're a suspect in what might be a murder and an attempted murder." Her strong voice released the words harsher than she had intended.

Eva, who caught a snatch of Sirena's exclamatory remarks, set the tea on their table and quickly departed, without a word, to the kitchen, to allow Raine to continue with her interrogation.

*Bless you, Eva!* Raine thought, sending the wish to the proprietress and fixing Sirena with the green fire of her McDonough gaze. "Are you going to tell me where you were?"

Sirena lowered her eyes. For all her boldness in business, modesty forbade her reply. "That's a rather delicate question. Will my statements be kept confidential?"

"Yes." Raine did not lower her affecting scrutiny. She kept looking steadily at her subject, trying to decipher what was in her mind.

"I was with a man at a hotel," the young woman said quietly.

"What hotel, where?" The Sister forced her own stunned suspicions aside and willed herself to listen impassively.

Sirena raised her eyes to meet Raine's. "It was out of town. The Green Gables up the mountain past Jennerstown."

Raine intensified her look.

"It's the truth. I know you'll check on it. I didn't use my real name, of course; but you'll take a picture of me, I'm sure, to show the desk clerk up there; and you will find that I'm telling you the truth. The name I used was Elizabeth. We registered as Mr. and Mrs. Smith."

*Most original*, the Goth gal thought, as she jotted data down in her notebook. "What time did you check in?"

"At noon, Friday, and we checked out last night, around ten. We were going to stay till today, Sunday, but … I wanted to get back home."

Straight-up, Raine asked, "Who were you with?"

Sirena drew in a deep breath, releasing it along with the man's name.

It was not the name Raine was expecting to hear; but coolly, she exhibited no reaction, as she scribbled the name on the pad, then poured their tea, picking up her cup and sitting back against the tufted leather seat. With a studying regard for the woman opposite her, she slipped her pen behind her ear. "I've a few more questions."

Surmising that the Sister already knew a portion of what she was about to reveal, Sirena answered, "OK, but my father is *never* to learn of this. **Do you understand?**"

"I hope *you* understand that you either come clean with me, telling me everything, or you'll be hauled down to the station to be interrogated by the police, and then I can promise you the shite, as we Irish say, will hit the proverbial fan. I'll *reiterate*– this case has spun into a probable murder and attempted murder." Raine's emerald gaze held Sirena's violet one.

It was on the tip of her tongue to snap at the Sister; but, instead, Sirena took a sip of her tea, swallowing hard to send Raine an agreeing nod.

"Did you use a computer or your smart phone at all on Friday?" The Sister guessed what the response would be, but she wanted to hear it anyway.

The young woman did not have to think too long before answering. "No. There was no Internet access in our room. The place is dead-zone remote. I couldn't get a signal with my cell, so I used the hotel's land phone at the desk to let my father know I arrived OK. I'd told him I was meeting a couple of friends to share some girlie time. You know … a day of shopping, spa, mani-pedi, good food, drinks, and catching up."

"I think you know what my next question will be," the raven-haired Sister stated, regarding the other woman steadily, "and I hope you'll be as honest with me as I think you've been thus far."

Her poise shaken, and perceiving the inference, Sirena's beautiful face flushed a deep pink with embarrassment. "I know what you're going to ask," she hung her head a moment before continuing. "I know, too, you won't believe me; but I am ashamed, so ashamed …"

Several minutes later, in a mirror on the wall, Raine caught Sirena's reflection, staring after her as she exited The Gypsy Tearoom. And the face the Sister saw was very, *very* frightened.

With her interrogation of Sirena under her belt, Raine dashed back to the town square, where she had parked, to finally pick up her package at Belle's Notions. Opening the door, she entered the charming establishment where the décor was art deco, the color scheme black and white with touches of silver.

Belle was behind the counter. Having just finished her accounts, she was about to pull on her coat and leave the shop. "Hello! I thought you forgot. I have your shampoo and conditioner all ready to go." She reached under the partition to produce a silver bag with the name of the shop on the outside. "Here you go."

Raine opened her purse, pulled out a couple of bills and handed them to the beautician.

The Hamlet's Whispering Shades' makeup and hair artist, for their "Little Theatre in the Woods," and the area's most popular beautician was a petite lady with platinum-blonde hair cut in a bob that framed a pleasant face.

"You never told me that Sirena Chambers is a patron here," Raine let drop casually.

"You never asked," Belle replied, slipping the bills Raine had given her into the cash register and handing the raven-haired Sister her change. "Like you, she stopped in to pick up organic shampoo and conditioner."

Knowing how Belle was always careful not to gossip about her customers, Raine glanced quickly around to see that there was no one else in the shop. "Belle, I need to ask you something, and I really want you to level with me. This is a literal matter of life and death to do with a case my cousins and I are working on."

"Come into the back," the blonde replied. "I don't want anyone to see us in here and drop in for something. I'm done for today. I want to lock up and get home."

When the two of them entered Belle's private room in the back, Raine said, "Look, I know how patrons spill their guts to beauticians. Beauticians and barbers are like bartenders; they hear all the scuttlebutt. Their clients like to vent and tell them their personal business in exchange for advice. You know, too, that what you tell me and my cousins we never repeat. I need you to answer this question as honestly as you can. Has Sirena ever mentioned a lover she's had in the past several months?"

Belle winced. "Oh, I do so hate to divulge anything a client tells me in confidence; but I'm fully aware of your reputation and the good work you do, so I'll help you. Yes. In fact, she just told me today she'd finally broken it off."

Raine reached out to take hold of Belle's hand. "Did she say why? This is *very* important."

"I know you wouldn't be asking me if it weren't," Belle whispered. "She said she broke it off when she realized the man might be dangerous. '*Extremely* dangerous' are the words she used."

When Raine arrived at DHM Construction, she caught a glimpse of Reggie at his desk through the long, buff-brick building's front window. She could hear him whistling a tune as he sorted through a stack of papers. *Wave my wand!* she thought. *I was hoping I wouldn't have to go to his father's house to speak with him. This morning I got a clear vision of the prodigal in his office– and here he is! Thank you, Goddess!*

As soon as Raine opened the door to enter the building, Reggie stopped whistling and stood. "Sorry, we're closed today. It's Sunday! A holiday weekend! I just had to stop in here to pick up something. Whatever it is, it will have to wait till tomorrow when we re-open."

With a faint smile on her lips, Raine pulled the blind on the door, that held the Closed Till Monday notice on it, all the way down, making the sign even more obvious on the outside; then reaching behind her, she turned the lock. "That's not very welcoming, and I haven't stopped in on business, Reggie. I want to talk with you alone. I've a few questions about a private matter."

One ebony brow lifted. "Alone … a private matter? Now this sounds *interesting*," he drawled in a sexy tone. "I thought little girls were taught quite young not to ask indelicate questions, and especially not to a man," he winked.

*What man? I don't see a man*, Raine mused.

"What's this about … *little girl?*"

With a glamour, the petite Raine pulled herself up to her full height, the gesture beginning its magick on her subject. "Murder and attempted murder," the Sister's deep voice rumbled succinctly and in a no-nonsense timbre. "If I were you, I'd sit back down. This might take a while. I want to know where you were all day Friday and with whom. I need specifics."

In a trice, Reggie's breezy tone darkened, and the fierceness of his blue eyes flamed with irritation. "You can't come in here and dictate to me. I don't care *who* you think you are!"

Raine smiled inwardly. *Underestimate me– this'll be fun!* Aloud, she said with icy calm, "Sit down, Reggie. You can talk to me or to Police Chief Mann at the station. Your choice."

He dropped slowly but surely down in his leather desk chair. Meeting the Sister's stare with one of his own, the brash player lowered his *gaze*, too, but still was not talking.

"Choose wisely. It'll be a lot rougher downtown, especially since you were told not to *leave* town."

"OK, you win. I don't have anything to hide; I just don't like being browbeaten. Yeah, I did leave town, but I'll be damned if I was going to give up what I look forward to every Thanksgiving!"

Raine's gaze was unremitting, as she leaned close to Reggie's face to lock eyes with him, her hands resting on the desk between them. "Enlighten me."

He shifted uneasily in his chair. "I hook up with two of my college buddies to watch football, drink, eat, and hang out."

"Partying with the boys, were you?" Raine's eyes flashed emerald. "Where?"

"My one friend's family owns a mountain cabin. That's where we were, and I assure you we didn't murder anyone. Who th' hell was murdered anyway?!"

"*Don't push me! I've got a wand, and I'm not afraid to get all bippitty-boppitty-boo on your ass.* Audibly, she replied, "**I'll** ask the questions. Now, I told you I need details. So start talkin'!" The Sister whipped out her notebook and pen, taking a seat in the chair across the desk from the red-faced Reggie. "And start at the beginning!"

His face tensed, and a muscle in his jawline twitched. "You know what you are? You're a—" Her eyes halted him, and he began his recitation with a huff. "I had an early Thanksgiving meal with my dad, like I do every year, 'cause he knows I meet my buddies at the cabin. I drove up the mountain; the cabin's not too far from Ligonier— that's where the guy's from who owns the place— then we hung out. As I said, we watch football, drink, eat— the cabin's always stocked with plenty of good food and liquor— and we talk about old times. Is there any law against that?"

"Depends," Raine replied calmly. "Let's talk about Friday, the day after Thanksgiving. Did you use a computer or your smart phone at all on Friday?"

Again Reggie shifted uneasily. "Funny thing about that."

Raine raised a brow. "*Amuse* me."

"I have a strong signal all the way up the mountain, and then, at the top, I don't."

"That wasn't my question. I asked if you used your computer or smart phone on Friday."

He shook his head. "I didn't."

Rained fixed him with a look. "No?"

"No, that's what I tried to tell you. The cabin has no Internet access. I didn't even bring my cell inside. Left it in my car's glove compartment. When I take a break, I wanna be completely unplugged. No way do I want to get messages from clients, pain-in-the-ass clients, who think they own my soul."

Noting the look on Raine's face, which Reggie took to be disbelief, he blathered on, "Hey, I deserved a break with my buddies. I've been working hard, long hours too, and my dad's been noticing. I think he's pleased with what I've been accomplishing. He'll be even more pleased in the weeks to come!"

"Oh? Why do you say that?" Raine leaned forward anew to study her subject, resting her chin in her hands and looking directly into his eyes.

"Hey, I don't have to reveal business deals to you. I'm answering your questions now, because I've nothing to hide, but I'm sure as hell not going to let you in on business secrets!"

"Uh-huh. Were you at the cabin the whole time you were up there?"

"Yep, the whole time."

"When did you leave?"

"This morning after breakfast. We had to shop last night to replace some of the food and drink we consumed, then tidy up to make sure we left the place as we found it. The owner, my one buddy's dad, always takes the cabin over for the rest of the Thanksgiving weekend, with a couple of his own friends. They're hunters. The Monday after Thanksgiving's the first day of deer season, so we always have to be out by Sunday to make way for them. We left this morning, like I told you."

"You know I'll be checking your story out, so I need the names and contact info of your two pals." Raine picked up her notepad, then slipped her pen from behind her ear, poised to write.

"You do that," Reggie gibed, having recovered some of his bluster. "I answered your questions because, as I said, I have nothing to hide," he stated for the third time, prompting the Sister to think otherwise, "but don't think *I* won't be checking out *your* story with Chief Mann."

Several minutes later, as Raine was getting into her MG, Reggie was picking up his phone.


While Raine was conducting her interrogations, Maggie was speaking with Moonglow and Starlight at their colorful Washingtonville home.

The two Coven sisters resided in a small Craftsman-style bungalow just outside the city limits, on a quiet, tree-lined street suitably named Shady Lane. A pentagram crafted from grapevine and a beribboned besom, both decorated with bright autumn leaves, hung on the front door. Inside, the home was brimming with witchy items, including protective symbols, gemstones and crystals, books on the Craft, and just about everything you could shake a wand at connected to the Sacred Feminine.

Maggie sat at the Coven sisters' kitchen table, across from the pair, who appeared to be a trifle edgy, a wary look in their eyes.

"I'm not going to beat around the bush," Maggie opened firmly. "The situation is far too serious for game-playing. We, the Sleuth Sisters, are working with Chief Mann, so we know you were told, as persons of interest, *not* to leave town. This case we're working on just might include a murder and a related attempted murder. *I* volunteered to question you. I'll help you, if you cooperate with me; and I *hope* you choose to do that, because it will go a lot easier for you if so. Needless to say, your rash ... *impetuous* conduct has poor Robin beside herself."

"Yeah, she was absolutely *livid* the last time she lectured us." Moonglow turned to look directly at Starlight, seeming to send her an unspoken communication. "I know we shouldn't have left town Wednesday evening, but we didn't want to forfeit the money we paid for our room. We go away every Thanksgiving. It's become a tradition with us. We stay at Whispering Pines Inn."

"Where is that?"

"It's in Potter County, about a hundred fifty miles north of here," Moonglow replied. "That's where we were; check it out." She reached up to flip a mess of curly, red-gold hair from her eye.

"Are we going to be in trouble with the law for leaving town?" the more petite Starlight asked, wringing her hands, the large, doe-like eyes in her olive face anxious. In fact, through the course of the entire interview, Starlight would continue to sit there uneasy, like a guilty child, toying with the long sleeve of the Renaissance top she was wearing.

Their reactions caused Maggie to look upon the twosome sharply, and with more than a little suspicion.

Under the McDonough gaze, the ultra susceptible Starlight flushed and murmured something inaudible. "Are we in trouble for leaving town?" she repeated in a small voice.

"I can't speak for the chief," Maggie answered bluntly, "but it will go a long way if you cooperate now, by telling me everything, and by telling me the whole truth." The redheaded Sister pulled her notebook and a pen from her bag. "What time did you leave town Wednesday evening?"

To stall for time to think, or due to nerves, Maggie knew not which, the stronger Moonglow adjusted the belt around the waist of the witchy green dress she was wearing. She had a very small waist for one so buxom. "We left right after we finished working. Mostly, we work from home; but Wednesday, we had to set up and program three computers at the high school, for the administration, and we couldn't do that remotely. By the time we finished, drove home, and threw our suitcase in the car, it was about six when we finally rolled out of town."

Maggie put starch in her normally soft voice. "Then what? And don't leave anything out– *I'll know*."

"We drove straight through to the inn, checked in, freshened up, and went to dinner." Moonglow looked to her partner, who gave a concurring nod.

"Where?" Maggie asked, glancing up from her notepad. "Where did you dine?"

"We ate a light supper at the Lone Pine Diner. It's about a mile down the road from the inn where we stay. Lone Pine's a favorite eatery of ours when we break at Potter County, very rustic, as is everything up that way. We love it there." This time Moonglow sent Starlight a tender look.

Maggie fastened her emerald gaze on the duo. "Keep going."

"Well," Moonglow said with a sensual hint to her voice and an ultra-naughty expression, "then we went back to our room, where we spent a cozy evening together." Her words took suddenly a protesting tone, "You sound like a trial lawyer the way you're cross-examining us!"

"Let's hope it doesn't come to that," Maggie replied in her best schoolmarm manner. "What did you do Thanksgiving Day?"

"We slept in late," Moonglow answered, noticeably sobered by Maggie's bearing, "and enjoyed a continental breakfast sent up to our room. For what was left of the morning, we lounged around, then dressed and went for a nice, leisurely walk in the woods."

"The inn property has gorgeous walking and horseback riding trails," Starlight appended. "That took about two hours, then we went back to the room, showered and dressed for dinner."

Maggie picked up the pen she had set on the table in front of her. "You ate at the inn?"

The lithe, dusky Starlight looked to Moonglow for the OK. "No, we drove the five miles to Indian Creek Lodge for Thanksgiving dinner, after which we returned to the inn, had a drink on the back patio, wrapped in a warm blanket, star-gazing and thanking for blessings. Then we spent the night in our room."

"*Friday*," Maggie articulated louder. "Tell me every detail about Friday, the day after Thanksgiving. I need a blow-by-blow account."

"Well," Moonglow began, "again we slept in to about nine-thirty. That's late for us. We're always so rushed off our feet for one reason or another, so when we go to our favorite place, it's nice to kick back. Anyway, we showered and dressed, then walked the mile on one of the trails through the woods to brunch at Lone Pine. Following the meal, we rushed back to our room to freshen up, before we took off for the annual Thanksgiving psychic fair and witch auction. It's one of the reasons we go up there every year."

"Where did the fair take place?" Maggie asked.

"It's always at the Indian Creek Lodge, where we had our Thanksgiving meal the evening before, spread out over their three largest conference rooms. Everyone knows us at the lodge, you could easily check out what I'm telling you." Moonglow locked eyes with her other half who, by now, was clearly in a flutter.

"We were at the fair and auction all afternoon into evening," Moonglow continued. "It's a spectacular event. Everything is staged to purrr-fection, complete with special effects to make it a truly magickal experience. We've," she cast an eye to Starlight, "given them a lot of tips on that sort of thing over the years. You should look into Indian Creek's psychic fair and auction for next year. You'd love it!"

Maggie sensed correctly that Moonglow was endeavoring to whisk them away from what they were about, and she fixed her with a keen look. "Funny you should say that."

"Say what?" Moonglow asked, matching Maggie's mien.

"What you said about *staging* and *special effects*. That's the express focus of my next line of questions."

Starlight's fidgeting caused her to tip over a glass, spilling water onto the tablecloth. With nervous movements, she grabbed a handful of paper napkins to mop up the spill.

"Leave it," Maggie ordered after a few moments. "Both of you listen closely to what I am about to ask you. And to reiterate– *I want the whole truth and nothing but the truth.*

Several minutes later, Maggie, having made a few notes, retraced her attention. "What time did you leave the witchy doings at the lodge?"

Moonflow replied without reflection, "When the fair and auction ended, about six-thirty–"

"It was a little later than that, honey," Starlight interposed quietly. "I remember glancing at my watch when we got into the car. It was almost ten to seven."

"You didn't eat at the lodge Friday night?" Maggie was unconsciously tapping her full lips with the pen as she continued to study the pair.

"No," the winsome Starlight answered, "because they were passing round hors d'oeuvres all afternoon, and we didn't feel like having a regular meal, so we decided to drive back to our inn and enjoy a light snack before bed in our room. They've snacks in the lobby, with beverages, for the guests. Nice healthy stuff– fruit, yogurt and the like."

"Were you on a computer, laptop, tablet, or a smart phone at any time on Friday?" Maggie asked in an abrupt fashion.

The couple exchanged looks, and it was but a split-second before they answered.

**"No!!"** the pair vehemently declared, *together*, which struck Maggie as a tad unusual.

"There was no need to be on any of 'em!" Moonglow stressed, and the timbre of her voice came across– a bit too strong.

While Raine and Maggie were conducting their investigations, Aisling was making every effort with *her* two persons of interest.

Peering over, and not through, her eyeglasses, which were perched precariously on the end of her long nose, it was infinitely apparent Mildred Grimm wasn't in any mood to spend her holiday Sunday being questioned by one of the Sleuth Sisters.

"Why didn't you call first?!" she hurled at Aisling, who was still standing at the door in the cold.

Not giving any outward sign of aggravation, the blonde with the wand answered calmly, "I work during the week, and my days are crammed full of commitments. This won't take long."

"Well, *I* work too, and *my* days are just as hectic as yours. More, I'd wager!" The obnoxious woman rolled her haughty, indignant gaze over the Sister. "Come on in, and let's get this over with!"

Mildred unceremoniously ushered Aisling to the parlor of her Colonial home, where Mr. Grimm was reading the Sunday paper. When Aisling entered the room, he started to rise.

"No need to stand or leave the room, Mr. Grimm. I don't want to interrupt your reading."

Mildred emitted a sharp expletive of vexation. "But you don't mind interrupting *my* day! Sit down," she ordered, taking a seat, uneasily, in an overstuffed chair across from Aisling, who sat on the couch. "All right, what is so rip-snortin' urgent that you have to barge in here on a holiday weekend to annoy me?"

Remaining calm, Aisling grasped her purse and took out her notebook and pen. Looking up, she asked, "Let's begin with where you were on Friday. I need details of your day, please."

Confronted by the unexpected, Mildred's mouth opened in wordless tremor, whilst her face went a literal chalk white. "How is that any of *your* business?" she asked after a silence and in her usual arrogant manner.

"I am working, along with my two cousins—"

"The Sleuth Sisters at it again, huh?! Snooping into other people's affairs!" And there was more than a hint of malice in her voice.

"Hardly. We're working with Chief Mann and his department on a case that could involve both a murder and an attempted murder." Aisling caught a glimpse of Mr. Grimm in her peripheral vision, taking cover behind his newspaper, though she sensed he was listening to every word.

Meanwhile, Mildred had drawn herself up in her chair with a loud huff, her face unattractively creased by distress and anger. "What's this muddle to do with me?!" she snapped, her shrewd eyes narrowing, as she crossed her arms over her chest in what the blonde Sister recognized as a defensive gesture.

"You, ma'am, are what we term a 'person of interest.'"

"A **suspect**! Are you *insane?*! **Me!** The very idea! I've never broken a law in my life! Never got so much as a parking ticket! I always had my doubts about Chief Mann– I've told our idiot mayor that several times– and now I **know** Michael Mann is not fit to hold the office he occupies! I'll sue; that's what I'll do, and don't think I won't!"

Aisling looked thoughtfully at the woman sitting across from her, at the taut mouth, the deep lines from the nose down, the hands now tightly pressed together. Tilting her head, the blonde with the wand replied calmly, "You knew before this that you were a suspect, when the chief told you *not to leave town*. I strongly suggest you talk to *me*, Mrs. Grimm, and answer my questions truthfully. I assure you it will be a great deal better for you than being hauled downtown for questioning."

Grimm's face went purple, and she wheeled upon Aisling, who remained cool. **"How dare you!!"** the obnoxious woman bellowed in a clear, priggish voice. "I *refuse* to answer! I'm going to telephone my attorney; and I promise you; your two cousins, sisters," she ran her scorching gaze again over Aisling, "or whatever you three are; the chief, and his whole questionable department that you will regret ever having included *me* in your *irresponsible* investigation! **I'll make you rue the day you met me!!"**

Not the least bit flustered, Aisling queried evenly, "Are you going to tell me where you were on Friday and what you were doing?"

"I most certainly am *not!* It's none of your goddamn business where I was!" Mildred slid, in a secretive motion, a sidelong glance at her husband, after which she leaped from her chair and started for the hall, where the land phone rested on a small desk. "I've learned a thing or two in my day," she directed at the Sister through the open doorway. "Silence can never be misquoted!"

*Oh, yes it can*, Aisling retorted in her head.

It was then Mr. Grimm lowered the newspaper from his face to say in his quiet manner, "Milly, you best tell her where you were. She's going to find out anyway."

Nearly an hour later, Aisling, fresh from the impact of Mildred Grimm, was sitting in Etta Story's Victorian living room, wondering what Chief Mann's leading suspect would say in answer to her questions: "Where were you on Friday last, and what were you doing? I need you to be specific, please."

Looking unmistakably uncomfortable, Etta chewed her lip in visible disquiet, and her eyes filled with sadness. She swallowed, determined not to cry. "You know I left town, don't you?"

Aisling didn't know for sure, but she had guessed. She could tell by Etta's expression, body language, and hesitation to respond that she was hiding something. Now, she merely gave a studying nod. "You defied the chief's warning, didn't you?"

Etta folded her hands, which were shaking slightly, in her lap. Sitting at one end of the claret-colored, velvet couch, angled to face Aisling, seated on the opposite end, Miss Story was the picture of decorum– except for her hands. It was those that fully betrayed her. "I did leave town. Chief Mann told me not to, but I had to. I felt compelled, you see," she dropped her gaze, "*obliged. I had to do it.*"

The anxious woman swallowed again, visibly struggling to collect her wits, as well as the shreds of her dignity about her. But the hands told the tale– and the jaw, which she clenched and unclenched in an attempt to gain control of her nerves.

When she continued, Etta's voice carried a strong measure of nostalgia. "Perhaps," she closed her eyes an agonizing moment, "perhaps if I tell you my story, you will understand better and not be so quick to judge me ..."

"Stupidity is the friend of evil."
~ Anon

## Chapter Eighteen

By four that afternoon, the Sisters had completed their interrogation sessions. Meeting back at Tara, they quickly compared notes, then put in a call to Chief Mann. Unable to reach him, Aisling left a message, asking him to return her call as soon as he could.

"Tomorrow, we must drive back to Washingtonville and speak with Sam," Raine said with fervor, as the threesome entered Tara's kitchen. Aisling, can you go with us? Our classes resume on Tuesday— I just know they'll have the pipes fixed by then— so tomorrow's our last free day till the weekend."

"I think Raine's right; and our evenings will be crammed with all the paperwork it's going to take to secure that Pennsylvania historical marker for the Witch Tree," Maggie added.

Aisling deliberated a moment before replying. "Sisters, why don't we split the tasks up again? Ian and I will check out the suspects' alibis. It's what we do, so we've developed a nose for that sort of thing ... should only take us four or five days tops. I just need you to share your notes with me before I head home. You two get that paperwork done for the tree, in addition to driving over to Washingtonville to talk with Sam. When you've done that, and *while* you're there, go over everything with the chief too. Get him up to date. Don't tarry; time is of the essence!"

Raine looked to Maggie, who gave a nod. "Copy that! Aisling, can you ring us after you speak by phone with Chief Mann, *if* he calls you before Mags and I meet with him in person tomorrow?" Raine started taking down the tea things to brew the three of them a nice pot of green tea.

"Of course," the blonde with the wand answered. "I'll ring you the instant I hear from him."

The following morning, Raine and Maggie were on the road to Witch-Tree Farm, with the raven-haired Sister behind the wheel of the Land Rover. A half-hour earlier, when Raine telephoned the Washingtonville Lumber Company to ask Sam if he might take a few moments out of his work day to speak with them, she was told he'd called in sick. Thus, the Sisters decided to drive straight out to the farm.

They were nearly there, when Maggie's cell sounded. "Hello," she said. "Aisling, we're almost at Witch-Tree. Sam called in sick today, so—"

"Chief Mann just returned my call," Aisling cut in. "Get this, Sisters! There's *no* evidence *whatsoever* that the computer in Sam's car was compromised."

"Are they certain?" the redheaded Sister asked, putting the phone on speaker so that Raine, too, could hear what Aisling was saying.

"Absolutely certain," Aisling replied loud and clear. "No one fooled with that car's computer. When the chief called Sam to report this, he said Woods went berserk, ranting on and on about someone trying to kill him. As we speak, the car's being towed to the Auto Doctor in the Hamlet, so they can go over everything. Could be that the computer short circuited or something."

"Where are you now?" Raine voiced from behind the wheel.

"Ian and I are on our way up the mountain … just coming into Ligonier now. We're going to be checking out alibis all day. Listen, you two watch your backs."

"Ditto that to both of you," Raine answered. "There's a killer on the loose, and whoever it is, he or she is *mercilessly* dangerous."

*** 

Pulling up to the old farmhouse at Witch-Tree held nostalgic memories for the Sister pair, as they got out of the Land Rover. The first thing they noticed was the gargoyle they'd gifted to Amanda. It had been removed from the house to the back porch. Raine and Maggie quickly sent each other the telepathic communiqué not to mention the guardian to the already-distraught Sam.

When a gaunt, hollow-eyed Sam Woods opened the door, Jasper leaped out to pounce on Raine. Placing his front paws on the shoulders of her black wool cape, he began licking her face.

"Jasper!" Sam hollered. "Get down!"

"It's all right," Raine laughed. "He's fine. How are you, Jasper old boy?" she asked quietly, stroking the Airedale's wiry fur. The dog whined and looked at the Sister with sad eyes, sending her the brief messages that he missed Will and Amanda terribly and how frightened he was of the torturous spirits at Witch-Tree.

*We'll look into that today, old boy. I give you my word*, Raine answered. As the raven-haired Sister stroked the dog, he unburdened himself to her.

"Well, don't stand out here in the cold, ladies," Sam said, attempting with only a trace of success, to stir a dash of joviality into his voice. "Come in. Come in. Trust me, I am happy to see you! We both are. Aren't we, Jasper?"

"Sam," Raine said, as soon as they were inside his kitchen, "we just found out that your car's computer was not hacked."

"So you're working with the police?" he queried. "Please, sit down. I remember you prefer tea to coffee. I'll put the kettle on."

"Thank you," the Sisters spoke at once, with Raine adding, "Tea will hit the spot on a dark, gloomy day such as this!"

"To answer your question," Maggie began, "we *are* assisting the police."

"Good!" Sam answered with ardor. "I don't think they know what th' hell they're doing! As you've heard, they're insisting my car's computer was not messed with, but it *had* to have been. I had *no* control over that vehicle. **None!**"

"Perhaps the computer system in the car is malfunctioning in some way. Things happen," Raine stated.

"I had the car towed to the Auto Doctor in Haleigh's Hamlet. They'll find out what's what. I've been going there for years. They know what they're doing." Sam set the water boiling for the tea.

"Sam," Maggie said delicately, "don't take this the wrong way, but is there a possibility that since you've been so distraught, you could have imagined–" *Imagination can be a dangerous thing!* "… imagined," she repeated, "that you had no control of your car?"

**"No way!"** the wearied man answered without hesitation. He closed his tired eyes for a long moment. "There *have* been moments lately when I've questioned my sanity. I concede to that, but in this, I *know* I did *not* imagine anything. Someone is trying to kill me, the same someone who found it necessary to murder my wife!"

"Murderers almost always find murder *necessary*," Raine muttered, glancing at Maggie.

Sam's face flushed hotly as he grappled with his emotions.  With sudden despairing vehemence, he drove one clenched hand into the palm of the other.  "Someone's trying to *kill* me; I tell you!  Why doesn't anyone believe me?!"

"Don't work yourself up."  Spying a bottle of cognac on the counter, Maggie filled a small glass, handing it to Sam.  "Drink this.  It will do you good."  She sat back down, as the old adage raced through her mind.  *Speak the truth and shame the Devil.*

With shaking hand, Sam tossed back the liquor.  It burned a fiery path to his empty stomach, hitting bottom like a lead sinker.

Maggie held up the bottle, proffering another glass.  Sam shook his head.

"It's not that no one believes you, Sam; but the police, the courts, need *proof*," Raine offered.  Her voice was indulgent, almost maternal.  "Why don't you sit and tell us– as calmly as you can– exactly what happened Friday, when your car was out of control?"

With weary acquiescence, Sam sank down in a chair at his kitchen table with the Sisters, giving them a detailed account of what transpired.  He paused only to pour their tea, as well as his own.

"And that's not the only thing that's happened to me," he pushed on.  "There's," he glanced anxiously over his shoulder, pronouncing in a near-whisper, "*spirits* in this place."  Leaning forward, he said, "Do you want to know what I think?  I think someone's put a curse … some kind-a *hex* on me.  They've put the ***Evil Eye*** on me with black magick!  You should know about this stuff.  Wax figures and pins; voodoo, hoodoo!  I read about it in one of Will's magazines.  Strange things made to happen in Africa and the West Indies, but people practice the Black Arts here too.  These people can cause pain and even *death*!  Isn't that possible?  It *is* possible, isn't it?!"  His expression was one of terror, and the Sisters couldn't help but note, with the hollows in his cheeks and shadows under his eyes, how much the man resembled a ghoul.

They looked to one another, answering, "Yes, it's possible, but–"

"I knew it!"  Sam broke in with a shout.  He began gushing his ghostly accounts, revealing to the Sisters his nightly torments.

"If anyone would know about this kind-a stuff, it's *you*," he concluded at the end of his lengthy narrative, running nervous fingers through his unkempt blond hair. He was badly in need of a haircut, and even his mustache looked straggly. "I'm thankful you came by today. I can't take any more of this. The whole thing is a nightmare! Please help me! *Can* you help me?!"

"We can but try," the magickal pair replied.

With a groan, he reached for his teacup. It rattled against the saucer.

Raine sent a look to Maggie. "Shall we do the *Malocchio*, Mags?"

The redhead assented with a nod. "Sam, we're eclectic witches, mostly Celtic, but eclectic; thus, we draw from a variety of sources for our magick. We've found the Italian *Malocchio,* often pronounced *maloik,* to be the most effective for telling us if someone has put the Evil Eye on someone else."

"I don't give a rat's ass where it comes from, or anything about it. **Just do it!** I'm *sorry*," he said almost immediately. "I didn't mean to raise my voice. I wish I could be more entertaining today," he put forth wryly, "but a haunted house hardly lends itself to gaity. The other night one of those," again he glanced fleetingly over his shoulder, "*spirits,*" he whispered, "tried to *strangle* me! I felt its cold, bony hands closing around my neck! Woke me up with a start; I can tell you that!"

"People do tend to wake when they're being strangled," Raine jested in an attempt to lighten the situation. The look she received from Maggie, however, curtailed her effort.

"We'll try to help you," Maggie said, sending Raine another unspoken communication.

"There's more than one way to do the *maloik*, but we'll do it the way *we* know. We need a bowl, water, olive oil," Raine directed, "salt … sea salt if you have it, if not, *we* do, in the witch kit we carry in the car." She thought for a moment. "Two sewing needles and scissors."

Sam rose and filled a fairly large bowl with water. He set a bottle of olive oil on the table next to the bowl. Yanking on a kitchen drawer, he rummaged through the contents, finally ferreting out a couple of needles and utility scissors, to set them next to the water-filled bowl. "Will this positively tell us if someone's put the Evil Eye on me?"

"It will," the Sisters answered.

"I'll get the witch kit out of the car," Raine said, springing to her feet and exiting the kitchen.

When she returned, the Sisters drew a strong circle of protection. They took from the canvas bag, Raine had carried in, two smudge sticks of white sage. Lighting them, they began in earnest to cleanse the space, all the while chanting a cleansing mantra, as they fanned the good-smelling smoke, each using a feather, into the kitchen's every nook and cranny.

"Just sit there calmly and quietly," Maggie instructed Sam, who was at table, looking anxious, "and let *us* handle this."

"It'll be all right," Raine assured, pulling a container of sea salt from the witch-kit canvas bag.

Once their circle was cleansed to the Sisters' satisfaction, they sat with Sam at the kitchen table.

Without preamble, Raine picked up the two sewing needles, passing them several times through the smoking sage, which rested in twin Pyrex bowls before them. She inserted the tip of one needle into the eye of the other, as her deep voice rumbled, "Eye into eye … the hatred cracks and the eye bursts!"

Across the room, outside the circle of protection, where the kitchen opened to the parlor, a pair of red glowing eyes appeared in the shadows. They were there a mere instance, but the Sisters and Sam each saw them; for at that express moment, Jasper, his eyes on the frightful red orbs, let out a hair-raising howl. The dog had been stretched out on the kitchen floor, head on front paws, at Raine's feet; but now, he stood, fur on end and eyes wide, as he whined and whimpered in fright.

"It's OK, Jasper. Be still now, boy." Undaunted, the raven-haired Sister handed Sam the olive oil, clicking the side of the bottle with an ebony fingernail. "Shake three drops of oil into this bowl of water. Three exactly."

With visible fear in his eyes, Sam reached a trembling hand for the bottle. As carefully as he could, he shook three drops of the oil onto the water's surface. Then he set the bottle down and waited, whilst the Sisters intoned something he could not comprehend– thrice.

The only sound in the old house, other than the Sisters' chanting, was the clock on the kitchen wall. Almost gruelingly, the minutes ticked by.

Then, to Sam's amazement, the oil, floating atop the water, formed the unmistakable shape of an eye! Instantly, his face went as white and still as a waxen mask.

The Sisters exchanged a thought as yet another look passed between them. Immediately, they began anew to chant; after which Raine let fall the needles onto the oil, and Maggie tossed exactly three pinches of sea salt onto the oil-drop eye staring at them from atop the water.

Sam stammered out a word, but Raine cut him off with a curt wave of hand, as she picked up the scissors, passing it several times through the smoking sage, before she used them to cut the air above the bowl, working the scissors three times, the action bringing an unearthly howl.

This was not Jasper. Rather it sounded like the howling of an unearthly voice straight from the bowels of Hell!

"It is done," the Sisters voiced in sync, murmuring their closing chant.

"Well?" Sam questioned at their sullen nod when they had quieted. "There was an Evil Eye on me, wasn't there?!"

The Sisters traded glances, with the Goth gal waggling one hand in a yea-nay gesture–

"Let's just say you appear to be the target of some–"

**"I told you! Didn't I tell you?!"** Sam yelled with wan face and wild eyes. **"I knew it!!"**

"Now," Raine finished, rising from her chair. "If you permit, we'll move on to your bedroom!"

Grasping her sister of the moon's arm, Maggie whispered, "Let's proceed cautiously."

As soon as the Sisters entered Sam's bedroom, they immediately sensed the paranormal activity there. Having refused to follow, even Raine, into the room, Jasper waited outside the door, in the upstairs hall, with a pacing Sam.

Without delay, the Sisters, shaking off any shred of fear or apprehension, drew their circle of protection and smudged the room for nigh onto twenty minutes, chanting the strong cleansing mantra they had used downstairs earlier.

Raine caught Maggie's eye, and a deciding brainwave passed between them.

"We will make use of an ancient ritual of our granny's," Raine announced, casting a glance at Sam, who was peering into the bedroom from the hallway.

No sooner had those words left the Sister's lips, when misty white images began forming in the antique mirror atop Sam's dresser.

No one moved. Jasper's fur stood on end, as he gave forth an eerie whine, spinning abruptly round to race down two flights of stairs for his hiding spot under the cellar steps. That was it for Sam too. Bolting down the stairs, he snatched his coat from a hook near the door and tore out of the house onto the frosty back porch.

While that was unfolding, the Sisters were staring into the mirror, where the ghostly images had manifested– quite clearly by this point. Without difficulty, they recognized Amanda, who was flanked by an older man and woman. They also recognized Will, standing with a woman whom they guessed to be his wife.

For the next half-hour, Raine and Maggie spent their time with the Witch-Tree spirits, then they opened the circle, thanked and released the energies they had conjured.

When they returned downstairs, they found Sam shivering outside on the porch, his hands thrust deep into the pockets of his jacket, the collar up. The wind was blowing strongly, tossing his blond hair wildly. As he stood there uncertainly, the wind seemed to cut him to the bone.

"It's all right, Sam," Raine called. "You can come in now."

Without moving from the spot where he stood, he stamped his feet and blew upon his hands. "Have you rid the house of them? Are they gone?" he asked. "Gone for good?" Presently, he moved to the door, gingerly stepping inside.

"Come in here, Sam, to the parlor," Maggie requested.

When the three of them were in the old-fashioned living room, Raine pointed to the wall of framed photographs that depicted family members. Indicating a portrait of a preteen girl between a man and woman, she inquired, "This is Amanda with her parents, is it not?"

Seeing the image, to which the Sister was pointing, Sam answered. "Yes."

"And this picture here," Maggie indicated, "I assume is Will with his wife on their wedding day?"

"Yes, the woman is Amanda's Aunt Bonnie. Why?"

"Because those are the people we saw in the antique mirror," Raine revealed.

"And those are the five orbs you saw." Maggie straightened Will's wedding picture on the wall. "Deep peace to you," she whispered.

"Who's the other woman, the one who appears as the white filmy ghost?" he questioned, afraid but impatient to hear their response.

"That is Hester Duff, the spirit who has always haunted this farm and the Witch Tree," Raine stated firmly. "She is here to protect her tree, but she has unfinished business here too. It's quite common for spirits to hang about when there is unfinished business."

"Unfinished business? What are you talking about?" Sam questioned, shaking his head, mystified.

"Well, for starters, she wants her name cleared," Raine replied.

"Did you see the shadow-man?" he asked warily. "The entity with the glowing red eyes?"

"No, not upstairs we didn't, only family and Hester," Maggie answered quietly.

**"They're trying to warn me!"** Sam cried out suddenly, his watery blue eyes widening. "I'm *sure* of it now! They're trying to tell me I've fallen into a **trap**! I gotta get rid of this place and clear outta here," the frightened man argued in a panicky voice, "and the *sooner*, the better!"

Noting the look on the Sisters' faces, he shrieked, "Don't you see?! I *know* you see! Something *evil*'s come to Witch-Tree Farm! I'm in danger, *real* danger here if I stay!"

\*\*\*

When the Sisters arrived at the Washingtonville Police Station, Chief Mann welcomed them into his private office.

"We want to share with you in detail everything we garnered from our interrogations, Chief," Raine said, as they sat opposite his desk, facing him.

"In addition, we've done some research of our own," Maggie added.

The chief sat back in his leather chair. "I'm all ears."

Over forty minutes later, Raine was closing with a discussion of the spirits they experienced at Witch-Tree Farm.

"Wait a minute! Wait a minute! You're sayin' the ghosts out there are *real*?" the chief asked, with more than a little skepticism.

"Yes," answered the Sisters, "very much so."

With a chortle, Raine interjected, "'When one door closes and another opens– *the house is haunted*,' our granny used to quip."

Maggie threw the Goth gal a warning look, causing the latter's face to instantly sober.

"Well," Mann mused after a moment, "if you're sure about this– and I suppose if anyone *could* be sure of such things, it's you– then no one is *staging* the goings-on at Witch-Tree."

"We didn't say *that*," Raine and Maggie answered mysteriously.

The chief was the picture of confusion.

"Again," he pressed, raising his grey brows, "*I'm listening.*" However, he immediately turned pensive, fitting various scraps together in his fertile mind.

Maggie and Raine both started to speak, not getting far when, suddenly, Mann's Irish flared, and his face went blood-red, as he cut in with a roar, "I'll tell you one thing– the fact that my suspects *all* left town, after I warned them not to, makes me want to issue a warrant for their arrests, the *lot* of them! Their conduct this weekend, after comparing notes with you and with Aisling, makes every one of them even *more* suspect! We can't close our eyes to the theory that there may be a collusion at work here, or as I said before, even more than one!" In a moment, he got control of himself, saying, "Sorry to interrupt. Please," he insisted with a wave of hand, "go on."

"Let me back up a bit. As we said when we arrived," Maggie reported, "Aisling and Ian are checking out your suspects' alibis as we speak; *thus far*, however, this is what we think …"

"Sooo," Raine concluded with confidence some minutes later, "by this point, we're fairly certain who the killer is."

Chief Mann had listened carefully, bobbing his head occasionally whilst the Sisters were speaking.

*"The Man" doesn't seem at all surprised by what we had to say*, Maggie shot to Raine.

With a subtle nod, the raven-haired Sister answered Maggie's thought, affirming evenly to the chief, "In a few days, we'll know for sure."

"The energy that you put out in the world comes back to meet you.
That's a law– and its name is Karma."
~ Author Ceane O'Hanlon-Lincoln

## Chapter Nineteen

Raine and Maggie were always swamped after returning to their classroom and college duties from a break; but, nonetheless, they were determined to labor every evening to plow through the paperwork required to secure a Pennsylvania historical marker for the Witch Tree. At the same time, Aisling and Ian were meticulously checking out the alibis supplied to them during the Sisters' recent interrogations.

Mid-week, whilst Raine and Maggie were having a light breakfast at their kitchen table, they were more worried than ever that Sam would sell Witch-Tree Farm to one of the two land developers.

"Mags," Raine said, putting her teacup down in its saucer, "it's almost as if we're starting back at square one! On the other hand, I'm glad we thought to contact Robin to call a special meeting of the Coven. The girls met last night and will meet every evening to ask the Great Goddess to do whatever she deems appropriate to make this all turn out right! I refuse to lose hope!"

"We're all doing as much as we can. Remember what Granny used to tell us in situations like this? 'Never lose hope. It's usually the last key on the ring that opens the door.'" Maggie cast a glance at the antique railroad clock on their kitchen wall. "Hannah will be here any moment. It's her day to clean the downstairs. Let's have another cup of tea; we've time."

Raine gave a nod, picking up the cozy to refill both their cups.

In a twinkling, there came a trilogy of light raps on the back door, after which it opened, and their housekeeper tramped in. "Morning, chickadees!" she sang. "Funny weather we're having, isn't it?" She shucked off her coat and hat, hanging both on wall pegs by the door.

"Morning, Hannah!" the Sisters chorused.

The colorful maid padded, via her bright purple sneakers, to the kitchen counter, where she switched on the radio, an oaken replica of an arched, Gothic-style radio from the Forties. "I want to hear the weather report. Ahhh, you put the coffee on for me. Appreciate it!" She poured herself what she called a "cup of ambition" and, mug in hand, flopped down in a chair at table with the Sisters. "Got an interestin' piece-a news for you," she announced, pausing to take a long sip of the coffee, which she drank strong and black.

The Sisters leaned eagerly forward, as Raine, chin in hands, voiced, "What's the scoop?!"

"I told you that my hubby is fixing up a portion of the garage for a workroom for hisself."

"Right," the Sisters interjected.

Hannah stopped again to sip her coffee.

Raine fidgeted anxiously, twisting an enchanted jade ring on her left hand.

"Well," Hannah set her mug down on the table, "Jim was at the lumber company over in Washingtonville yesterd'y, and what do you think?" Without waiting for a reply, she ran on, "He heard some news I thought you should know. The scuttlebutt is that Sam Woods is going to sell Witch-Tree Farm to Chambers Construction. The talk up there is that the Chambers daughter– can't remember her name. Starts with an 'S.' Anyhow, rumor has it she never nagged like the other builder did, and Chambers upped their offer for the place, topping the rival company. Blast if I kin think of that name either. What *is* that other builder's name?"

"Mason," the Sisters supplied.

"Yeah, that's it. Lordy," Hannah shook her grey head, "Jim told me again that Sam Woods looks like death warmed over. Said, too, he heard at the local pub there in Washingtonville that the poor man's comin' apart at the seams." The housekeeper copped a quick sip of coffee, then chattered on for another five minutes, relating the gossip her husband had soaked up in the Washingtonville pub.

"What's the name of that pub; do you know?" Raine queried. *We should pop in there soon for a pint.* She sent the thought to Maggie, who gave a nod in response.

Hannah's eyes laughed. "That's an easy one! The Owl 'n the Pussycat. I remember 'cause it's the name of a faerie story I used to read to Merry Fay. Oh, I knew that hubby of mine would stop at a saloon after he left the lumber yard. I don't like him to drink and drive; but, at least, he limits hisself to one beer, or so he tells me.

"Anyhoo, Jim said the whispers at both the lumber company *and* the pub were that Woods won't be stayin' in these parts after he sells the farm. Too many, whadyacall, bitter-sweet memories f'r him. Once he gets all that dough– and the buzz is that it's over three million– he'll give up his job as manager at the lumber company and," she lifted her shoulders, "move to some fancy-spancy place." Hannah picked up her coffee mug. "I don't know … California mebbe."

"Oh!" the Sisters exclaimed, their identical McDonough eyes big with sudden disquiet.

While Hannah was talking, the song drifting from the radio was Bill Monroe's plaintive rendition of *Wayfaring Stranger*, the lyrics, "I'm just a-going over home," poignantly reminding Raine of Will and their solemn promise to him.

The brunette Sister was about to say something, when Hannah waved her to silence, as the radio began spitting out the weather report on the local country music channel to which the housekeeper listened whilst she cleaned: "Well, folks, rain and sleet late this afternoon and into tonight when we're in for what the weather people call a 'thundersleet.' With the warm frontal thunderstorms they're predicting, we're gonna get freezing rain and even winter lightning, so if you don't have to go out later– *don't!* Hey, that's what happens when warm air clashes with cold, but here's somethin' that'll cheer you. Bill Monroe and his Bluegrass Boys will carry you away from this imminent foul weather on the– *Wabash Cannonball!*"

"If heavy weather's brewin', I'd better drive today, Mags, and we'll take your Land Rover," Raine said resolutely. Standing, she set her dishes in the sink and glanced out the window at the gathering grey clouds scudding across the sky. "Looks kind of peculiar out there. Sure as taxes and death, it's a *threatening* sky, but it's not doing anything yet. Later on, though, like the radio said, we'll be in for it."

"Great Goddess!" Maggie cried, fueling Raine to augment the plea–

"Please don't let Sam sell that farm!"

Fifteen minutes along, when the Sisters drove off for their day at Haleigh College, Raine asserted, "We're just about done with the paperwork for the Pennsylvania marker. Let's make certain we *do* finish tonight. I want to post those forms with our carefully worded cover letter in the morning, overnight delivery."

"I agree, darlin'," Maggie answered. "And I suggest we consult Athena tonight after we finish with our Witch Tree project."

"Wiz-zard, Mags! Grantie advised us when she gifted us with Athena that our crystal oracle won't reveal much of anything if we don't do *our* part, our own investigations first– and to her approval. The Goddess helps those who help themselves, after all. Surely, we have furrowed out enough info now to ask Athena for more. If our session tonight shows us that we're right about who the murderer is, then we've got to think of a way to trip the killer up, so we can nail h–"

"Take heart, Sister!" Maggie blurted unexpectedly, a hand flying to her forehead. "I just had a vision that our killer is going to trip up without any prodding from us whatsoever!"

\*\*\*

That night, as planned, the Sisters finished the paperwork required to petition for a Pennsylvania historical marker. After sealing and addressing the large brown envelope to the Pennsylvania Historical and Museum Commission in Harrisburg, they gave a joint sigh of satisfaction.

"Now we can telephone Teresa Moore that we'll be returning her manuscript to her in person over our Christmas break. What time is it?" Raine asked, stretching to relieve the tension in her muscles.

"Going on nine-fifteen. Are you sure Aisling said she was coming over?" Maggie stood, scooping up the thick packet to carry downstairs to the kitchen counter, where they would be sure to see it in the morning and remember to take it to the Hamlet post office on the way to their late-morning classes.

*Thank the Goddess we're free the early part of the morning tomorrow*, the redheaded Sister thought.

"Aisling said she'd be here before nine," Raine answered. Of a sudden, she tilted her head, listening.

Tara's antique doorbell sounded loudly in response.

Snatching the large brown envelope from her sister of the moon, Raine said, "I'll put this on the counter and let Aisling in. You start preparing Athena for our session, Mags!"

"Right!" Maggie seized their poppet from the desk and dashed from the tower room, where they had been working at their computer, to the attic. There, accompanied by the Merlin cats, she drew their crystal ball from the locked cabinet and began its preparation.

Downstairs in the foyer, Raine was unlocking the front door to let Aisling in. "Galloping gargoyles, Sister! We were beginning to worry what happened to you." She stepped forward to give the blonde with the wand a hug.

"Sorry I'm late, but I was delayed with a client, then Ian wanted to talk with me about Merry Fay."

"Merry Fay? Has something happened? Is she OK?" Raine closed and relocked the front door.

"Oh yes," Aisling replied, shucking off her hooded, black cape, "more than OK. There was a girl at her school being bullied, and Merry solved the problem like a true McDonough woman. She advised the girl to stand up for herself, that bullies are usually cowards, and she told her she'd be right there with her. Long story short, when the first of the two bullies went to grab Merry's friend, and the frightened girl raised a hand to ward off an anticipated blow, her defensive move magickally waxed to a Karate chop that dropped the first bully to the ground. Then the second of the tormenters sprang forward to experience the same knockback. Off they ran, leaving Merry's friend unharmed and glowing with a new confidence.

"But that's not all," Aisling stated with pride. "Merry advised her friend not to get too much of a rush from what happened, that she should *ignore* bullies whenever possible and, to use her words, '… not make them her world.' Later, I heard her telling her friend over the phone, 'Haters don't really hate you, Nina. They hate themselves because you're a reflection of what they wish to be.'"

"Wiz–zard!" Raine exclaimed. "Our crafty little witchypoo is growing up– and before we know it, she'll be a *wise woman!*"

En route to the attic, Aisling was in the process of telling Raine how she and Ian were checking out the alibis of the chief's top suspects. "We should be finished tomorrow or the day after; and thus far, everything is pointing to the person *the three of us* believe is the killer. We should take satisfaction in that we've all done some first-rate sleuthing, and I think Athena will be more than willing to reveal to us what we're after tonight." She laughed. "As Ian says, 'Sleuthing is ninety percent leg work and ten percent brain work.'

"I would've suggested we wait to consult Athena till Ian and I checked out *all* the alibis; but as I said, we'll soon be done, and we have to move fast now– time is of the essence– since Sam is panicking," Aisling concluded. She slipped into the black ritual robe she'd lifted from a wall peg at the attic stairs leading to their sacred space.

Raine pulled on her robe, rhyming, "Of one thing we have *no* doubt– Sam's ghosts have really freaked him out. Sis, are you finding anything … *interesting* as you're workin' those alibis?"

"With Reggie's we did," Aisling answered, "but that doesn't really surprise us, does it?"

"On the subject of playboys, our top suspect, we've been discovering, has a history of using his power over women. In fact …" Raine talked on for several more minutes, until–

Maggie stated, "Ready when you are," as her sisters of the moon emerged from the top step into the attic's spacious room.

"Then let's give it a go!" Aisling and Raine answered with the combined fire of their Leo and Aries sway.

As the Sisters sat in a half-circle facing their huge amethyst crystal ball, Maggie dabbed Lemuria oil on the third-eye area of her forehead, passing the ampoule round, so that Aisling and Raine could do likewise. With the poppet Cara perched on her lap, the redheaded Sister began the familiar deep breathing pattern, allowing all the stress and negative energies to stream out of her body as she exhaled. The others followed suit, breathing deeply, each at her own pace, as each meditated: *Healing energies in ... negative energies out ...*

Silence prevailed during the centering preliminaries. After several moments, Maggie opened her eyes and began focusing on the area of the ball to which she felt a strong pull. "Focus," she said in her silky voice, "focus on an area of Athena's crystal depths that draws each of you in."

A particularly peaceful stretch of time passed, after which Maggie began to chant softly: "Athena, as we go into a trance/ Bestow on us the magick glance/ Take us back in time today/ Reveal what happened come what may/ Back to Washingtonville's last Harvest Dance/ To Amanda Woods' murder or happenstance/ Show us what we need to see/ To know *for sure*; this is our plea/ Take us to the Grange hall for the image above all/ Of who dipped a hand into Amanda's bag/ For her injectors the killer did snag/ If there be proof for us to learn/ For *that*, Athena, we now return!"

As the crystal ball's powerful energy commenced to surge around the seated, black-robed Sisters, their vibratory levels rose to harmonize with the antique crystal sphere– to make the needed psychic connection.

Within a few minutes, each Sister began to experience the tingling sensations that signaled their mystical union.

"We know from experience now, we must clear away any and all expectations. We will see what Athena wants us to see– nothing more, nothing less," said Maggie quietly, keeping within the trance.

"Our minds are clearing ... becoming as clear as the crystal," Maggie said soothingly, her soft voice carrying them to their desired destination.

"*Relax*," the poppet swayed. "Ree–laaaa–ax."

"Look into the ball's deep crystal cavern. Hold your gazes, Sisters. We *know* we can do this. We've done it before … and with great success. Ooooooh yes, we shall see …"

"What we shall see," Maggie and Cara crooned in concert.

Aisling was more tranquil than she had been during previous sessions, and stealing a peek at Raine, she noted that Sister, too, appeared more relaxed.

Within mere moments, and within the big crystal ball's purple depths, the familiar ghostly mist was manifesting.

"Our mystical connection with Athena has been made," Maggie drawled softly. "Our oracle is ushering us inside. Let us enter now all the way," she droned. "In we go … *purrrrrrr-fect.*"

The Sisters watched as the ethereal mist swirled inside the amethyst globe, slowly at first, then faster, then slowly again, before the crystal began to clear.

"Um-hmmmmm, let us drift," Maggie hummed serenely. "Light as feathers, let us drift inside Athena's crystal cave. Whatever we see and hear will be right. Athena knows best. She will take us where she will; and so, for this, I must instill– chill, dear Sisters, *ch–ill.*"

"Aye," the poppet swung rhythmically to and fro, "with the flow, off we go."

Maggie sighed softly. "That's right. Let go. One into the next, *allow* the scenes to flow."

The only sounds the old attic held were the Sisters' soft breathing and the loud purring of the Merlin cats. As always, their presence within a blessed circle was reassuring and comforting.

"Ahhhhh," Maggie sighed again. Out of the evaporating mists, from the quartz depths of their oracle, an image of the harvest-decorated Washingtonville Grange came swimmingly into view until everything was crisp and clear. Ever more, the magickal trio and their poppet were drawn deeper inside the ball's crystal cavern, there to witness exactly what had unfolded that dreadful night when Amanda Woods lost her life.

The hall looked empty, but the Sisters could clearly see that the salad table held its offerings as Sam Woods began arranging his wife's baked goods on the dessert table. Aisling, Maggie and Raine could all make out, behind him, the open louvered shutters between the Grange hall and kitchen.

Watching intently, the Sisters strove to remain calm, as they saw the person they believed to be the killer stealthily approach the salad table and, pulling a bottle of dressing from inside a jacket pocket, position it in a prominent spot with the other dressings. They had no trouble discerning the bottle's taped-on printed label that read "Homemade Italian Dressing."

Scarcely drawing breath, they dared not move, as they endeavored to remain centered.

Athena's mists returned to obliterate the scene and swiftly replace it with another. The Sisters were now witness to Etta Story making her offer to Sam to carry Amanda's antipasto to her. They watched as she set the salad down, their eyes never leaving the historical society's president as she picked up a bottle, afterward following Sam to his table.

For a few unsteady seconds, the whole scene wavered, threatening to slip away. Making use of every witch's trick they knew for calming, the Sisters regained focus. With bated breath, they watched Etta reach down and move Amanda's large purse, so that she could position a chair from the next table between the Woods couple and chat with them.

People were milling around in the Grange hall now, as several came close and into view. Now and then, one of them greeted Amanda and Sam. Then, at long last, the Sisters observed the hand of the killer, the person they suspected all along, slither into the side pocket of Amanda's purse and snatch the two injectors.

The final scene Athena presented to them was one at the end of the Harvest Dance, when everyone was packing up and making ready to leave. The crystal ball clearly showed Etta Story clasping the homemade Italian dressing to put it in her box of things to take home.

With that, Athena's swirling, effacing mists reappeared, and the Sisters knew her magickal movie had ended.

"Now we know *with absolute certainty* we're right about who the killer is!" Raine declared intently, after they'd taken the proper steps to end their scrying session. "But how do we *prove* this?!"

"Part of what Athena revealed to us we can prove by what Grace Seymour told us she saw. As for the rest, I told you I had a vision of the killer tripping up," Maggie said, stretching to relieve the stiffness in her neck. "At least I *think* that's what the vision meant."

"We're going over to Etta Story's house to get that dressing," Aisling stated firmly, springing to her feet.

Maggie glanced at her watch, though she needn't have, for the Westminster mantel clock downstairs in the parlor was just chiming ten. "Do you mean **now?!**"

"**NOW!**" the blonde with the wand answered, already pulling off her black robe and heading for the attic door. "I just hope we can make it to Washingtonville in this foul weather." She paused to peer through a clear segment of the attic's Irish-harp stained-glass window. It's getting treacherous out there!"

***

Etta Story's Victorian home was completely dark when the Sisters pulled up to the curb in Aisling's SUV.

"OK, so how do you want to do this?" Raine asked leaning forward from the backseat.

"Let me do the talking," Aisling said. "You *know* what to do and not do. C'mon, let's go."

***

When the large grandfather clock at the farm was striking the witching hour of midnight, Sam Woods was dozing downstairs on the parlor couch. He could not bring himself to sleep in the bedroom anymore. He felt he'd be safer downstairs away from the antique mirror whence the entities always seemed to emerge.

About an hour earlier, he finally drifted off into a fitful sleep, but the old nightmare was merciless, as he tossed and turned, mumbling to himself on the uncomfortable, lumpy couch. As before, he was speeding like a demon down the dangerous steep curves of Three Mile Hill. Laying on the horn, he screamed whilst he narrowly missed one vehicle after another, until again he saw the woman he called a "hippie."

She was standing in the middle of the road, staring at him, not moving, her long, black cape billowing in the wind.

**"Get out of the way!!"** he burst into speech, moaning loudly and bounding to a sitting position on the couch, as the sweat poured from his face and body. Clapping his hands to his head, he rubbed his throbbing temples. "This can't be happening! It can't be! Can't be!"

Simultaneously, the dog Jasper leaped up, with a whimper, and dashed from the room, fur standing on end, paws scrambling as fast as he could make them go to carry him to his hiding place in the cellar.

"Noooooooo!" Sam wailed when he saw the misty image of the caped woman, floating closer and closer, reaching her hands yet again for his throat. **"NOOOOOOOOOOO!"**

"It's time, Sam," the fearsome specter summoned in its ghostly voice, like the dismal tolling of a requiem bell.

Never before had the thing spoken to him, and in his gut he knew this was *not* a good omen.

"*It's time*," the apparition restated.

Behind the woman, the orbs began appearing, all five, morphing gradually into the spectral figures he identified as his deceased wife Amanda, her parents, her Uncle Will and Aunt Bonnie Granger. This was the first time *he* was seeing the orbs for the true entities that they were.

"*It's time, Sam*," they echoed eerily, taking up positions on either side of the caped woman.

In the very next instance, the shadow-man appeared in his accompanying black mist. He was standing aside, *waiting* as before, his eyes, like hot coals, glowing red and boding evil.

It was glacial cold in the room; and outside the forecasted winter storm was raging in all its fury, wild wind howling with ominous banshee voices, sleet beating against the doors and windows of the old farmhouse, rapping and rattling loudly, as though something malicious were trying to get inside.

Still sitting up on the couch, sweating and shivering simultaneously, Sam yelled hoarsely, "What do you want?!  Get out, and leave me alone!  Leave me alone!!"  Beads of perspiration trickled down his face and neck.

*"It's ti——me,"* the spirits announced, their combined voices blaring hollow, as if coming from an echo chamber.

They had reached Sam now, all of them, except the shadow-man, who still held back, waiting for whatever it was he knew was coming.

"*Ple—ase,* leave me alone!" Sam whined, lowering his pounding head to shaking hands.

The caped woman's eyes narrowed to midnight-blue slits.  Then, with swift force, her hands shot toward Sam, grasping, claw-like, for his throat, her pleasant face morphing into the demonic features of the shadow-man, the glowing red eyes horrifying, the howling mouth open to reveal– beast-like fangs.

With a shriek of terror, Sam jumped up and darted for the kitchen door.  Fumbling with the locks, he *burst* from the house into the stormy, black night, screaming like a man who had completely lost his senses.

Dashing across the back porch and away from the house, he ran aimlessly through the sleet and rain, nearly falling face forward several times on the slippery, muddy ground.  The starless sky discharged bolt after bolt of lightning; and thunder rumbled and rolled, as the wind continued to howl.

At one point, the crazed man halted briefly, standing motionless and listening, his hands rushing to cover his ears.  **"No!** Stop!  Stop, I tell you!  **Stop!!"**  But it was his own voice that ceased its bawling, dying away in a long, choking gasp.  He cocked his head to one side, to listen, with open-mouth, his breath coming in jerky, laborious pants.

It seemed like the voices in that glacial wind were relentlessly pursuing him, trailing him– baying after him like frenzied hounds for a kill. He couldn't believe what he was hearing, and he slowly turned his head to look back over his shoulder.

"It's time, Sam. **It's … ti———me!**"

"*Noooooooooooo!*" he wailed again, wrenching round. "*No! No! No! Nooooooooooooooooooooo!!*"

Wherever he darted, the caped woman, in a literal flash of light, appeared. Hence, he'd turn and dart another direction, glancing around wildly. But no matter which way he spun, she was *there*– omnipresent, everywhere he turned– *everywhere he ran!*

There was no escape; and always she met his white, frightened face with the fateful words, "*It's time, Sam.*"

He waited, his head turned to the wind, when of a sudden, he realized he was standing beneath the winter boughs of the Witch Tree! With paralyzing punch, a gut feeling froze him in horror where he stood, dizzy and devoid of all determination, as he stared at the fearful tree's snarled limbs, big enough to form trunks of ordinary trees, twisting, as they were, down almost to the earth and rising into the charged air like the arms of a menacing monster.

"The bitch has led me to the tree!" he blurted aloud, rubbing his dripping face and matted blond hair with hands that felt like they belonged to someone else.

"Not bitch, Sam— **witch!**" the caped woman corrected, and the word *sizzled*, over the raging tempest, like the wrathful hiss of a wild cat.

A powerful bolt of lightning forked the sky and lit the night bright as noon. In turn, thunder trolled, rolling the name branded in the tree's trunk decisively over Sam's quaking essence–

*Hester*

It was the last thing he saw before a second bolt of lightning, closer and ever so much louder, struck an overhead branch, sending the heavy limb crashing down upon him.

Meanwhile, back at Tara, Maggie had no sooner gotten comfy in her bed when she bolted upright. "It's *over!*" she told herself. "It's all over now."

Amidst the smoke and wind, rain and sleet, the shadow-man made his concluding appearance at Witch-Tree Farm. Emerging from his black vapor– that began to surround and contain Sam's body– the dark spirit spewed the only words he would speak as the latter let out his final breath.

"I've been waiting for you– *it's time, Sam.*"

# Chapter Twenty

[Three days hence …]

Aisling, Raine, and Maggie were seated across the desk from Chief Mann in his private office at the Washingtonville Police Station.

"We learned, early on, that Sam Woods was having an affair with Sirena Chambers," Raine was saying. "That was our *first* clue that Sam murdered his wife. There would be other signs."

"Murder in the family is common; and we see, nation-wide, many spouse-as-killer cases," the chief replied. "Usually, it's the first thing we think of, though this case did not quite fit the pattern."

"As we related to you several days past," Raine talked on, "our friend who owns The Gypsy Tearoom in our Hamlet was witness to the lovers cozying up to one another in her most private booth, in addition to which, Eva caught fragments of Sam's dialogue to Sirena." The Goth gal tipped her head in thought. "To broadly paraphrase, he said he'd do anything– whatever he *had* to– in order to sell Witch-Tree Farm to her father. We pieced that together over time.

"Likely his goal was to get rid of his wife, sell the farm to Chambers Construction for the three million-plus they offered, and talk Sirena into marrying him. He had 'married up' with Amanda, and his plan was to gain an even better social position 'marrying up' with Sirena. That would've made him a very wealthy man, with a gorgeous wife on his arm, who stood to inherit yet another windfall," Raine recounted. "And, as Eva overheard Sam tell Sirena in the booth at the Tearoom, he was watching *us,*" she indicated her cousins and sisters of the moon, "to keep tabs on what we were doing. Apparently, he feared we might get wise to his game."

"For a while," Maggie interjected, "I wondered if Sam, or someone, had hired a pair of thugs to stalk Thaddeus and me. You know, to frighten us, the Sleuth Sisters, off the case. But as it turned out, the attempted break-in I told you about, Chief, at our remote mountain cabin, was an isolated incident with no connection to the events surrounding the Witch Tree."

"Even though you're not pressing charges, I intend to hold on to the pictures you gave me of those punks and their ID," Mann returned.

"That was the plan," Maggie concurred. "Thaddeus and I sent the pics to Chief Fitzpatrick too."

"We're certain the reason Sam chose to kill his wife at the Harvest Dance was because she'd had a similar incident at the dance a couple of years ago," Raine cut in. "Sam knew that many of the same people would be in attendance, and he planned on using *that* to place suspicion on some of those people. He told us the earlier incident had happened when Amanda ate a brownie with nuts in it. Said he remembered running across the dance floor, yelling at the top of his voice that she always kept her injectors in the side pocket of her purse. But what I'd started to say was this: At the dance, he kept stalling when Beau and I wanted to call 911," Raine continued. "And that kiss on his dying wife's lips … oh, that was the Kiss of Death, the evil SOB's *assurance* that Amanda would perish. Due to a fresh helping of the antipasto salad with selected dressing– the peanut oil was on his lips." The raven-haired Sister let out a breath, readjusting herself in the folding chair upon which she was sitting.

"Nasty business!" Chief Mann's steely eyes mirrored the force of his words.

"I wish we could have *warned* Amanda; but that early on, we didn't have an inkling her husband was planning to *murder* her," Maggie declared.

"I wish we could have warned her too," Raine said, "though I don't think she would have believed us. It was *during the murder* when our serious suspicions about Sam arose," the Goth gal interjected.

"It appeared, for a while anyway, that everything was falling into place for the duplicitous Mr. Woods," Aisling remarked. "The first thing was when, at the dance, Etta Story inadvertently moved Amanda's purse, closer to *him*, so she could pull a chair from the next table *between* the couple, sit and chat with them."

"Sam purposely let fall his napkin," Raine broke in, "so that he could bend down, and while retrieving the napkin, dip his hand into the side pocket of Amanda's purse and swipe the two injectors. Holding them with and under his napkin, he deposited them into a pocket of his sports jacket.

"When we questioned Grace Seymour, who was in charge of the kitchen at the Harvest Dance, she told us she saw Sam, through the louvered shutters, drop and pick up his napkin, then stuff the napkin into his jacket pocket. Gracie never misses a trick. She thought that an odd thing to do. You know what I'm saying– stuff the napkin into his jacket pocket rather than put the napkin back on his lap or even on the table; but she didn't connect it with murder because she didn't realize Sam had lifted the injectors.

"It wasn't the only oddity Grace witnessed that fateful night," Raine went on. "Peering through the louvres earlier, she'd caught sight of Sam taking a bottle of something out of the inner pocket of his jacket, to position that bottle with the dressings on the salad table. At the time, she thought nothing of it, only that he probably brought his own dressing, a favorite dressing, and simply set it on the table with the others. She'd plumb forgotten about it until Maggie and I questioned her."

"I followed up your questioning with my own quiz session with Mrs. Seymour," the chief responded. "If it hadn't been for that eyewitness, it would have been much more difficult proving that Sam Woods murdered his wife."

"Seymour was the 'Saving Grace,'" Raine quipped.

"Nonetheless, that was damn good sleuthing on your parts, ladies," Mann remarked. "Our crime lab matched the printed label reading 'Homemade Italian Dressing' to Sam Woods' work computer– the paper matched up perfectly. It was a lucky thing for us that Etta Story took the killing dressing home along with her other bottles, and that you were quick to get it from her, Aisling."

"Part of the job," the blonde Sister shrugged. "I guess police work's in my blood."

"You are your father's daughter," said Mann in cheery response. "The lab report proved, beyond a doubt, that the dressing contained *peanut oil*, just as you three suspected."

Aisling nodded. "Etta Story didn't realize, of course, that *was* the killing dressing. She simply took home the dressings left behind on the salad table after Mildred Grimm had packed her dressings off.

"As I'd begun to enumerate," Aisling went on, "for a while, it seemed as though everything was falling into place for Sam Woods. The bridge washing out the night of the dance and delaying the ambulance. His out-of-control car racing down Three Mile Hill was something he used from, excuse the puns, the *get-go*– and he *ran* with it! Never did he miss an opportunity to rant that someone was trying to kill him– the same person who killed his wife he told everyone whose attention he captured."

*Everything fell into place for us too*, Raine flashed the brainwave to Maggie, *due to the powerful bundle of energies, the "magickal childe," we created with our "other halves"!*

"Another clue that Sam was the murderer was the statement he made to us." Maggie caught Raine's eye, inclining her red head. "How did he phrase it? 'Someone is trying to kill me, the same someone who found it **necessary** to murder my wife!' When Raine responded that murderers almost always find murder necessary, he lost his cool."

"We know for sure that the ghost of Hester Duff, the spirit who haunts the Witch Tree, is the entity who took control of Sam's vehicle," Maggie enlightened. "We're relieved, however, there's no need to try and prove *that* in a court of law!" she said, a twinkle in her eye.

"When," the redheaded Sister continued, "Sam described to us what the woman looked like– the woman he called a 'hippie' who was standing in the middle of the road toward the bottom of Three Mile Hill– he described, to a 'T,' Hester Duff."

"The way legend tells us she looked," Raine was quick to add, directing a wink at Maggie.

"Hester's legendary beauty is backed up by her husband's manuscript loaned to us by a direct descendant of Mistress Duff; and, lest we forget to mention, we saw Hester's ghost for ourselves at Witch-Tree Farm," Maggie reminded.

"Another thing Sam attempted to use to his advantage– the hauntings at Witch-Tree!" Raine remarked with her usual vim. "He droned and moaned about his otherworldly experiences to make himself look so devastated over his wife's passing that he was having a breakdown. He did his mumbling at his work place, at his favorite pub in Washingtonville, at the Auto Doctor's in our Hamlet– as we said, to anyone who would lend him an ear." The raven-haired Sister considered a moment, saying, "It's just occurred to me that evil is often more attention-getting than good. Sam had to make a show– to startle."

"Of course, as with any case, we had to be certain," Maggie remarked. "We three figured we could start checking the other suspects off your persons-of-interest list, Chief, once Aisling and Ian began checking out the alibis." She turned to send the senior Sleuth Sister a look of pride. "And Aisling and Ian did a first-rate job."

"You bet they did!" Chief Mann exclaimed, gazing respectfully at the magickal trio before him. "You *all* did, and our department is most grateful for your assistance." A rarely seen grin lifted the corners of "The Man's" stern mouth. "With all the paranormal activity connected to this case, I welcomed *specialized* assistance."

"We did our best to justify your confidence in us," Aisling stated, sending the thought to her cousins– *There's quite a satisfaction in solving yet another mystery, isn't there?*

*Quite!* Raine and Maggie replied telepathically.

"Though we were pretty sure Sam was the killer, we *had* to interrogate the other suspects and investigate their alibis. You gotta admit," Raine chortled, "when we discovered that two of our persons of interest, Mildred Grimm and Etta Story, checked murder mysteries out of the library, in which the victim of one is killed with peanut oil, and the victim of the other is killed by the murderer hacking into a car's computer," she shook her dark head, "well, that was a bit disconcerting, to say the least."

"I must admit, for a while there, I was postulating, with regards to Grimm and Story, what seemed to me a logical assumption," the chief conceded.

"Understandably, and you weren't alone ... *for a while there.* And what complicated matters further was the fact that nearly every one of our persons of interest was savvy enough on computers to have sabotaged Sam's car. But, as it turned out, no one– *of this earth anyway*– tampered with that vehicle," Maggie put in with passion.

"I'll tell you now," the chief divulged, "that during one of my interrogations, Etta Story let slip to me that she checked those two murder mysteries out of the library. She said she *knew* Mildred Grimm was a mystery buff, and she was more than curious to find out what sort of murders Grimm was reading about. Probably the reason Etta neglected to share this with you is that she had a very real fear of Mildred Grimm."

"Normally, I'm not a believer in coincidence; but," Aisling conceded, "I suppose there's always room for happenstance."

"Every one of the suspects told us the truth in regards to their whereabouts when Sam Woods' vehicle was supposedly hacked ... all except Reggie, that is," Aisling said after a brief silence. "He lied to protect Sirena."

"After he left his buddies at the mountain cabin, he was with her the Friday after Thanksgiving at the Green Gables Hotel," Chief Mann stated, glancing toward Aisling.

"Yes, as I said, he lied to protect her reputation," Aisling concurred.

"One of the clues I gleaned that Reggie wasn't telling me the whole truth occurred at the end of my interview with him," Raine interposed. "Through the window, I saw him using his cell phone. His desk phone was right there, but he grabbed his cell as soon as I left his office, so I figured he wasn't telephoning the police, as he told me he was going to do, to check out my story that I was working with Chief Mann. Rather, he was ringing his buddies to make certain they would back up *his* story."

"Reggie told Ian and me he intends to marry Sirena, that he's always been in love with her, but could never even convince her to step out with him for a cup of coffee before. Seems Reggie caught her at a vulnerable moment, and she succumbed to his advances on the rebound from her affair with Sam Woods." The blonde with the wand gave a slight shrug. "With Reggie's playboy rep, it was no wonder Sirena shied away from him as long as she did. Sirena admitted to us she's always had a crush on Reggie, an attraction that reached back to grade school, but she was afraid of getting hurt. We believe they will be a good match, one her father will have to accept; but one, we think, will delight Reggie's father."

Maggie was envisioning the pair. "They'll make a striking couple; that's for sure."

"When my beautician tipped me off that Sirena told her she'd broken off with a former lover because she thought he might be dangerous, the man she dumped, of course, was Sam," Raine disclosed. "At the end of my interrogation of Sirena, she confessed that she was deeply ashamed of her affair with Sam Woods. She said he pursued her relentlessly and quite effectively until she gave in to him. It didn't take her long, however, to see him in a true light."

Raine paused to clear her throat. "Gracie Seymour told Maggie and me that, the night of the Harvest Dance, she noticed Sirena studying Sam with his wife. After Amanda's death, the astute Miss Chambers, no longer blinded by infatuation, started becoming more and more aware that Sam was not the *mensch* he pretended to be."

"Right!" the chief uttered in his strong voice. "When we questioned Sirena Chambers, after you shared that information with me, we learned she'd begun to suspect that Sam had murdered his wife. People so often do look and act embarrassed when questioned by the police, but my years of experience tell me she harbors genuine remorse over her affair with Woods."

"Sirena," Raine pronounced, "is a charming young woman, and a clever one in business; but when it comes to matters of the heart, she seems, to me, too credulous. Hopefully, her affair with Sam Woods has taught her a valuable lesson."

Chief Mann raised his brows and, tilting his head, gave a brisk nod. "Miss Chambers conceded to us that Woods continued to *pressure* her into making a commitment to him– not exactly a man distressed over a beloved wife's death. Becoming more and more suspicious of Sam Woods, she fobbed him off as best she could, while he kept promising that, when the time was right– *and he promised it would be soon*– he would sell Witch-Tree Farm to her father."

"Oh, he was planning to make it look like he couldn't take any more of the paranormal activity out there. Very convenient, that. And the more exhausted he looked, the more frazzled, the more it fit his design that everyone believe he was having a breakdown over losing his wife," said Maggie, crossing her shapely legs in their black stockings. "He was hoping, too, that folks would think the farm held too many bitter-sweet memories for him. He mentioned that to his 'audiences' on more than one occasion."

Raine gave an abrupt nod. "Sam Woods was a *helluva* good actor when he set his mind to it, not to mention *cunning*. I'd wager he deceived a *stream* of people in his life."

"A sure bet!" Maggie agreed. "We know from our psychic abilities and via our tools of magick, Chief, that Sam Woods had discovered Amanda's Uncle Will was dying of pancreatic cancer. When Sam learned of this, he *urged* his wife to release her uncle from his promise to leave them Witch-Tree Farm. He didn't tell her that her uncle was dying; but, instead, pretended to want Will to have the money and freedom to travel and enjoy his golden years. He advised Amanda to talk Will into selling the property; for, in truth, he preferred to inherit the three million he knew Will wouldn't have time to spend on travel or anything else, rather than inherit a property that required constant attention. Sam had absolutely *no* sentimental attachment to that farm."

"Though he was formulating a plan to use the ghostly encounters out at Witch-Tree as an excuse to sell the place, they had begun to frighten him, more and more; and combined with the guilt that was riding him, it eventually broke him and did him in. We picked up some guilt, not much, but some," Raine concluded.

After a lull in the conversation, Maggie turned her gaze on the chief, "Moonglow and Starlight were exactly where they said they were, Chief."

"Yes," he replied, "they were. And no matter their blustery talk, there was never any harmful intent from either of them, or the Coven. I know that now."

"When I questioned them, I perceived *no* wickedness in their home," Maggie stated.

Aisling inclined her blonde head. "Mildred Grimm ... now, *there* was a person of interest, if ever there was one! Raine and Maggie learned from Gracie Seymour that she was the other person who had been staring at Sam Woods and his wife the night of the dance. Staring fixedly, like a cat watching a mouse with sharp-clawed paw ready to pounce." Aisling shook her head. "A maddening woman! Maggie had the 'old tabby' pegged from the start.

"At her husband's prompting, during my interrogation of her, Grimm finally confessed to me that she had been at her regular AA meeting in the next county. A very small and private circle of people who do not want the fact that they are alcoholics to get out. Due to her political ambitions, Mildred's always careful to keep under wraps that she'd been a secret drinker for years. And Etta Story ..." again the blonde with the wand shook her head. "Her alibi *is* a *story*, one that could be translated into a novel."

"Nothing we say will ever leave this office," the chief restated firmly. "Seems Etta was having an affair with a married man for years, a prominent one, US Senator James Byrne. They met years ago when she interviewed him for an article she was doing for a major news magazine. Byrne's wife has been institutionalized for years, since the early 1980s. He did everything he could for her to his recent death. Always made certain she got the best of everything. He just could not bring himself to divorce her, primarily because of their daughter, though his wife didn't even know him most of the time when he visited, which was, to his credit, often. As you know, the senator passed away this past summer of a heart attack. The daughter now sees to her mother."

"But getting back to Etta Story," Aisling reentered the discussion, "she and Byrne met two or three times a year, always at Thanksgiving, at the Summit Hotel atop Chestnut Ridge. This year was the first, in many, they weren't together.

"Etta shared her story with me, and I admit, I was touched," Aisling confessed. "She never married, or even dated anyone else, because she truly loved Byrne. Thus, she never had a complete life, a family, only those few stolen days each year with the man she loved but could never really call her own.

"When he passed away," Aisling went on, "Etta felt she *had* to go to the Summit, if only for that one last Thanksgiving, for closure; since, of course, she was not with the senator when he died, nor did she attend the funeral. The lonely woman never purchased a home, only rented the one she's lived in for years. She said she always wanted to be free to join him when and if *he* would be free." Aisling wrinkled her brow. "Sad really."

"Well," Maggie began, "now that the Washingtonville Historical Society owns Witch-Tree Farm, Etta has accepted their board's proposal of taking up residence there. As president and docent, she will live at Witch-Tree full time, beginning–"

"She's there now," Raine interpolated. "I just spoke with Robin on the phone this morning, and she informed me that Etta has moved into the farmhouse. The house she rented was fully furnished, so she had no furniture to move, only her personal things, clothes and such. She had to take possession right away, and then there's Jasper, so–"

Now it was Maggie's turn to interrupt. "Will she keep Jasper?"

"Oh yes!" Raine exclaimed with enthusiasm. "Robin said they took to one another like old friends!"

"That's wonderful!" pealed Maggie and Aisling.

"Witch-Tree Farm will soon become the *official* home of the Washingtonville Historical Society, with Etta's private quarters upstairs. The society has so many things to put on display there; and, of course, their annual picnics and holiday gatherings will be staged at Witch-Tree from now on." Raine paused to take a breath. "We should be getting that authorized Pennsylvania historical marker before too long, declaring the farm with its Witch Tree a historical site. So, our days of worrying about the fate of that venerable old oak are over!"

"It was thoughtful and kind of Hester Duff's descendant, Teresa Moore, to allow us to make a copy of Captain Moore's manuscript for the Washingtonville Historical Society, as well as a copy for us," Maggie said. "We plan on using it in our classrooms. We teach *some* local history."

"Everything has worked out quite well," Aisling beamed. "As Granny and Grantie would both say, "It all turned out like it was supposed to.""

From the police station, the Sleuth Sisters got into Aisling's SUV to head home to Haleigh's Hamlet.

They were just about to set forth, when Maggie turned round in the front passenger seat to glance back at Raine. "Who rang you when we were finishing up with the chief?"

"Ben," the raven-haired Sister answered. "I went outside to take the call; couldn't get a signal inside." Raine was referring to the Braddock County Coroner, Dr. Benjamin Wight. "Sorry. I was so elated over Jasper and Etta ... I was just about to tell you about Ben. He wants to see us in his office today, if we can swing it."

"What's he doing at the morgue on a Saturday?" Aisling asked, bemused.

"I don't know, but somehow, I feel *I ought to know*– oh dear!" she cut off, groping for the elusive witchy clairvoyance that was, like dandelion fluff on the wind, just beyond reach. "Whatever it is, Ben says he'd appreciate seeing us today when we get back from Washingtonville," Raine answered. "And I daresay– he sounded *strange*."

"Strange?! Whatever do you mean?" Maggie queried, imaging the always professional and most capable coroner.

Raine frowned. "His voice sounded peculiar. I think we'd better get on over there."

"On our way!" Aisling replied, turning on the ignition and checking her mirrors before exiting the parking lot at the police station.

When the Sisters pulled up to the Braddock County Morgue, they immediately saw the coroner's dark blue Mercedes parked in front.

Entering the long, low building, they were met by Dr. Wight as though he had been waiting impatiently for them, his hands jammed into the deep pockets of his spotless white lab coat. The Sisters sensed he'd been pacing, for he gave a fairly good impression of a caged panther near feeding time. Moreover, every bit of color was drained from his face. And, just as Raine had suggested, his voice and manner seemed quite out-of-the-ordinary.

"Come into my office," he said without preamble, turning on his heel and briskly leading the way.

Dr. Benjamin Wight was a tall, fastidious man in his mid-fifties with slightly wavy, black hair frosted heavily with grey. His eyes, too, were the color of steel, and though he looked like he strode straight out of the silky pages of *Gentlemen's Quarterly*, it was steel he was made of. In brief, Dr. Wight did everything as meticulously and as accurately as humanly possible– *perfection* was his life's credo.

The Sisters always took notice that Ben's office was as pristine as he was. It made them wonder if working with dead bodies had increased his natural tendency toward impeccability.

"Ben," Raine couldn't help but blurt, "is something wrong?"

He indicated the chairs against the wall, across from his desk. "Please, sit down. I'm glad you could make it here today." The coroner took his seat at his highly polished desk, cleared his throat, and pursed his mouth, which had been set in a grim line.

The Sisters exchanged quick looks but remained quiet, waiting for the coroner to begin.

Dr. Wight's throat clearing gave way to precise and measured speech. "I called you in here to tell you something and ask for your … *enlightenment*, I suppose one might say. When Sam Woods' body was brought in, I examined it for cause of death. Of course, blunt force trauma, the result of lightning felling the heavy branch that knocked him to the ground, was the obvious cause of death. However, the expression on the face looked to me as if he'd been *frightened to death*; thus, I wanted to find out if he had *literally* been scared to death. The autopsy revealed cause of death due to *both* cardiac arrest and blunt force trauma."

The Sisters had never seen Ben Wight so disoriented. They wondered what in the world it was that had him so rattled. As it turned out– it was nothing of this world.

"Before I began the autopsy, when I rolled the slab out of the cooler, I ..." the coroner hesitated, grappled a moment privately with his Higher Self, and went on, "Forgive me." Regaining his composure, he tried again. "I looked down at the body of Sam Woods to see a word burned into his chest. It was only there for a second, but it was *there– I saw it*." This last was uttered as though the coroner were struggling to convince *himself*.

"You three know me, have known me a long time," Wight hurried on, as if fearful he would change his mind about speaking to the Sisters at all about this. "You know I don't exaggerate or fabricate in any way. I am nothing if not *exacting* about everything I do, and if you ever mention this to anyone, I will categorically deny it. However, I trust you'll honor my request to keep this between us."

The shaken man fixed the Sisters with an intense look. "On the other hand, I know *you* and the work you do; thus, after careful consideration, I felt I should tell you this," he rambled, abruptly stopping to catch his breath, his eyes searching their faces for answers.

The Sisters again traded thoughts.

"Ben," Aisling said softly, verbalizing what was on all three Sleuth Sisters' minds, "what was the word you saw burned into Sam Woods' chest?"

The coroner's response came appositely. "*Karma*," he answered. And that was all he had to say.

\*\*\*

The following day, Sunday, the Sisters again took to the road in Aisling's SUV to drive to Washingtonville, to High Priestess Robin's home, for a celebratory gathering of the Keystone Coven.

"I think Ben was relieved to speak with us. He seemed to be doubting his sanity until we filled him in on Hester's story and some of the particulars of this case," Raine said from her usual position in the backseat. "If this doesn't cure him of what skepticism he had left, working with us over the years, nothing will."

"Well, it was good … and *gutsy* of Ben to share his paranormal experience with us. Hester was trying to tell us that *she* didn't kill Sam. He brought it on himself with the Karma he earned," Maggie replied, looking over at Aisling behind the wheel.

"The fate he fully deserved!" the blonde with the wand stated with vehemence.

They turned into the driveway at Robin's charming, faerie-tale house, Moonstone Manor. This visit, it was festively bedecked with Yuletide decorations. Rounding the arched, scarlet-red front door was a garland of fragrant pine that bore shiny red Yuletide bulbs and pine cones. Tall, glassed, antique-style lanterns stood on either side of the door; and on the steps, cauldron-style pots held, in harmony with the garland, fresh pine, red bulbs, and pine cones. In the leaded-diamond windows– and the Yuletide Celtic tradition– electric candles flickered joyfully.

"How sweet of Robin to invite us today," Maggie said, unbuckling her seatbelt. "I'm really looking forward to a party!"

"We've earned a bit of fun," Raine laughed companionably. "I'm glad Robin's gathering is early, so I can reap my due from Beau tonight. Maggie, are you still spending the night at Thad's?"

"Yes, I'm looking forward to some much-needed cozy time with him," the sexy redhead answered. "So, you'll have Tara all to yourselves."

"I wish you both a *magickal* night," Aisling giggled.

"And we fancy the same for you," Maggie returned, reaching out to pat the senior Sister on the shoulder.

"Let's get our wine contributions out of the trunk," Aisling reminded.

The opened front door revealed Robin dressed in a witchy Yule gown of green, festooned with red-berry trim at the low-cut bodice. Her green headband, too, was decorated with glossy red berries. "Merry Meet, Sisters, and welcome!"

"Blessed Yule!" As the Sisters trooped inside, they exclaimed over the pine-trimmed parlor mantel; the mistletoe; the lit bayberry, clove, frankincense and myrrh candles; the live Yule tree decorated in the ancient Druid tradition with images of all the things the Keystone Coven wished the waxing year to bring– coins for prosperity, fruits and nuts for success, and pretty charms for love and happiness. Through the open doorway, the dining-room table, laden as a buffet with holiday foods, instantly made their mouths water.

Aisling cried out with glee, "Oh, Robin, the house looks and smells wonderful!"

"Ah, the sights, sounds, and scents of Yule!" Maggie extolled with her crystal laugh.

"Delicious!" Raine remarked, sniffing the air like a hunt-cat.

Whilst the Sleuth Sisters were slipping out of their long, hooded capes, their hostess extended her arms to say, "Let me take your wraps."

They had worn their velvet Yule capes– Raine's was green, Maggie's garnet-red, and Aisling's burnished gold. Beneath, the Sisters' gowns were also velvet, the colors harmonious with their capes– Raine's black with a touch of red and green holly-and-berry trim, Maggie's green, and Aisling's silver. In their hair, the magickal threesome sported medieval-inspired circlets of bright holly and berries.

Almost immediately, Robin's husband Mike approached the new arrivals with a tray holding filled champagne flutes. "Blessed Yule," he greeted.

"Blessed Yule," they echoed merrily.

"I love champagne," Raine enthused, dimpling. "Makes me feel all warm and cozy!"

"Brrrrrr," Aisling teased, flicking a finger over the raven-haired Sister's pert nose, "on a day as frosty as this?" Straightaway, the blonde with the wand headed for the fireplace where the flames snapped and danced welcome to the tune of the medieval music that issued from the Victorian entertainment cabinet in the parlor.

Moonglow and Starlight were passing among the gathering, throughout the open parlor-dining area, with trays of tempting hors d'oeuvres, and the Sleuth Sisters couldn't help but note how happy the pair looked that evening. All the Coven sisters were dressed in festive robes that charmingly bespoke the Yuletide, and the room glittered with the sparkle of lit candles and the enchanted jewelry that adorned the gathered witches.

"Blessed Yule!" they shouted, as the celestial pair advanced toward the Sleuth Sisters.

"Blessed Yule!"

Proffering the appetizers, Moonglow and Starlight beamed, "Thank you, dear Sisters!"

"Try the squash and kale toasts," Starlight suggested with a smile. "Yummy."

Raine set her champagne down on a side table and reached for a toast, popping the small canapé into her mouth. "Mmmm, ditto to that, sister!"

"What are those?" Maggie pointed to what looked like small boats of salad and croutons on endive spears.

"Caesar-salad spears," Moonglow answered. "I highly recommend them. Robin makes them every year. Trust me; they're great if you like anchovy."

"I do." Maggie lifted one of the leafy boats from the tray with a napkin. When she bit into it, her beautiful face mirrored her pleasure. "Yes, indeed," was all she could manage as she polished off the tasty tid-bit.

"Now, what do you recommend for me?" Aisling asked, eyeing the choices with pleasant indecision.

"You like comfort foods," Starlight answered with abrupt truth. "Try the mac-and-cheese minis sprinkled with crumbled bacon. Sister Marie made them. They. Are. Out. Of. This. World!"

Aisling laughed. "You're right about my penchant for comfort foods." She popped one of the cocktail-size creations into her mouth, chewing with delight. "Hecate's crown! That's absolutely scrumptious! I must have another."

"Help yourselves," Moonglow said. "That's what they're here for."

Raine pointed to another savory, asking, "Ooooh, what's *that* little treasure?"

"That is a buckwheat-cheddar blini topped with smoked salmon– a Norwegian appetizer," Starlight answered. "Moonglow made those," she stated with pride. "Try one, but I warn you, you won't be able to stop."

Raine slipped the little canapé into her mouth, anticipating delectable. She was not disappointed!

"Told you," Starlight giggled. "Now," she indicated, "a bagel chip with ricotta, chive puree and prosciutto. We made those together."

As the Sisters were enjoying the hors d'oeuvres, Robin came up to them to say, "I can't stand the suspense a moment longer. Do fill us in on the news. Have you any word on the Pennsylvania marker as yet?"

"No, sister," Raine and Maggie answered together.

"It's much too early, but have no fear, we *will* be awarded that plaque for Witch-Tree Farm and its Witch Tree. Of that, we have *no* doubt." Raine sent her fellow sisters of the moon an emerald twinkle. "No doubt whatsoever."

"I can't help wondering," Robin began, "why Hester placed herself in the middle of the road, when it was *she* who took control of Sam Woods' car. She relinquished control of his car so he could swerve off the road to avoid her and onto the safety of the runaway truck ramp. Why? What was that about?"

"Well," Raine began, "Hester wasn't intending to kill Sam. Deep within the shadowed part of herself, she wanted to punish him, scare the hell out of him, *torture* him, yes, every which-slash-w-i-t-c-h way she could, for what he had done; but it was his own culpability along with his fears that did him in. The Karma he earned is what killed him, and Hester knew the demon would come for him, to collect his immortal soul.

"Shorn of verbiage, the facts are simple. As a man of weak moral fiber, the sonivabitch not only cheated on his wife, he *murdered* her," the Goth gal rumbled, ticking the points off on her ringed fingers, "then he endeavored to make it look like Etta was the killer, and he would have been perfectly content to see her take the rap for his crime. To boot, he was attempting to seduce Sirena into marrying him, so he could inherit the Chambers Construction fortune, on top of the three million-plus he would've gotten for Witch-Tree Farm." After a pensive pause, Raine uttered the thought several were thinking: "Once Sirena's father passed away, he likely would've knocked her off too, to get his hands on the whole pie."

Aisling gave an agreeing nod, reciting Granny McDonough's wise counsel: "Ever mind the rule of three– three times your acts return to thee. This lesson well, thou must learn; thou only get what thou dost earn!" Brightening after a moment, she interlaced her fingers, tipping her hands toward her two cousins. "Let's share Hester Duff's story with the girls, shall we?" she suggested, as she settled into a comfortable chair. "You tell it, Raine. You're the best *raconteur*."

"Yes, tell us!" the Coven ladies urged, each of them pausing in what they were about, for they were all fully aware of the Goth gal's storytelling abilities.

"Everyone get comfy, and I'll do that," Raine answered, always happy to relate a good drama.

"First, let Mike and I refill the glasses," Robin offered. "We'll wait to eat till the Sleuth Sisters have finished speaking. We're all so excited to hear Hester's tale." At that, she and her husband began moving among the sisters, filling their glasses with champagne.

"Gather we witches, young and old, for a glass of the bubbly and a story to be told!" Raine then launched into Hester's saga, as the Colonial sister's husband, Captain Moore, had disclosed in his manuscript. She told it with passion and vigor, rendering the Coven sisters spellbound.

"What a truly magickal legacy!" Robin pronounced when Raine finished. "Thank you, Aisling, Raine, and Maggie, for sharing with us the enchantment of Sister Hester's life! And for solving her mystery, as well as our present-day conundrum!"

Careful not to break their covenants with Chief Mann and Coroner Dr. Wight, the Sleuth Sisters filled the Coven in on how they solved the entangled mysteries, sharing mostly what they'd gleaned from Athena, their crystal ball, as well as what they had gained from visions and their witchy intuitions.

"If you would've seen Sam's terrified face when the lightning lit Hester's name and he looked up to see that huge limb come crashing down on him– there's a vision that will stick with me forever!" Maggie related.

"Great Goddess, bless us!" Verity exclaimed. "I can hardly believe all this! I *do* believe it, but isn't it mind-boggling?!"

When Raine told the girls that Jasper had revealed information to her, they pled to hear it.

"Jasper sent me the telepathic communication that he missed Will and Amanda terribly, and he didn't trust Sam anymore. He sensed evil around him, and though the spirits in the house had the poor dog terrified, he informed me he was keeping away from Sam as much as he could."

"I don't think Sam Woods was always evil," Maggie said after a short silence. "He allowed greed and lust– he lusted after Sirena, but mostly his sin was greed– to lead him into evil. Money can do that to some people. Truth to say– and you had him pegged from the start, Robin– Sam was a *materialistic* person. We discovered, from chatter overheard in his favorite Washingtonville pub, that he always wanted, in his words, 'to be somebody.'"

"Greatness is not measured by money or stature," Aisling said. "It's measured by courage and heart."

"Both of which Sam Woods lacked," Raine muttered.

"He appeared to be a decent person, *at first*; wouldn't you agree?" Maggie asked.

"The chink in Sam's armor was greed." The Goth gal closed her eyes to conjure the killer's face. "The pale, empty eyes, the tight mouth … avarice was there all along." She thought for a moment, reconsidering. "*Vanity* and greed. Sam had a *power*, you know. He was clever, *quite* clever, with women. We learned through our investigation that he had a history of using women to gain his desires. For instance, before he met Amanda, he was living with a successful real estate broker in Twilight Borough, not far from Washingtonville. She footed the bill for many of Sam's expensive tastes."

"Indeed!" Maggie jumped back into the discussion. "His talent fooled his wife and Sirena– for a while, at least– and who knows how many others?! Tricking them with dreams of bliss, whilst he enjoyed the tangible satisfactions of the flesh, I might add." She yielded the floor to Raine, who looked as though she were chomping at the bit to interject something.

"Granny used to say," Raine dimpled, "that no one knows what anyone's marriage is like, except the two people involved– and sometimes one of them doesn't know!"

"I know *that* from experience!" the once-married, always mysterious, Maggie snorted. "But getting back to what I was saying: At the onset, I would not have believed Sam possessed such a secretive, sinister nature. He was excellent at veiling his evil behind that handsome façade of his. I admit, early on, I thought he was a good chap. Often Evil doesn't come with horns and a tail– *but as everything you ever wished for*. Therein was Sam Woods' power over women.

"Oh, and lest we forget to mention to you," the redheaded Sister went on, "Sam didn't want to be burdened with all the time and effort the Witch-Tree property would require." She shifted her glance to Raine and Aisling. "*We* garnered this clue and others from his brainwaves on different occasions. Our thought-harvesting was how we learned that he knew Will was dying of cancer. We picked up fragments of Sam's musings at Will's funeral.

"Anyway, in regard to the farm," Maggie continued, "I remember once his thought was, 'Just what I need– to come home from a full day's work at the lumber company and then have to face all the backbreaking work, time, and money this property will constantly demand and drain from me! And I'll be the one paying for all the upkeep now that Amanda's lost her teaching job!'"

"Sometimes there's no darker place than a person's thoughts, the moonless midnight of the mind– a *killer's* mind," Raine said with conviction. As an empath, I don't just listen to words, I pay attention to tone of voice, subtle facial expressions, especially the eyes, and body movements. I interpret silences. I can hear everything people *don't* say in their silences.

"As for Sam, I think the slug must've always been evil," Raine remarked suddenly. "When I think about how he killed his wife … how he kept stuffing his face, knowing full well that she would soon be gasping her last breath– *cold-blooded and cruel!*" Her ebony brows rushed together in a grimace. "Oh yeah, the evil was in him– *waiting.* Some people are born that way. Sons and daughters of Evil. They're born so that killing doesn't mean a thing to them, not if they can profit by it."

"Shocking. Really quite shocking!" exclaimed Robin, which triggered like-minded comments from the gathered Coven.

"And in our peaceful, sleepy little village!" Undine mused aloud, controlling a shudder.

"The things that go on in a *peaceful,* sleepy little village would surprise the hell out of you!" Raine guffawed. The timbre of her deep voice dipped even lower. "Some of them quite nasty."

"Maggie, you've *too* good a heart. I agree with Raine," Aisling proclaimed judicially. "*Sam was a monster.*"

"A lunatic!" Minerva hollered from the back of the room.

"A pig!" Sea Witch bellowed with disgust.

Several of the Keystone gals tossed in additional remarks.

"As Ian and I were checking out alibis," Aisling picked up the narration, "everything was pointing more and more to Sam. Often the spouse is the culprit when a husband or wife is murdered. I've seen this time and again. We," she looked to Raine and Maggie, "suspected him all along– as did Chief Mann, we were to learn later– though we couldn't let *Sam* know that."

"Didn't Raine and Maggie take a big risk, going to Witch-Tree Farm alone to talk to him without the police?" Astra questioned, turning her wide-eyed gaze on the fore-mentioned Sisters. "He might've killed you both!"

"The biggest risk is not taking any risk," the Sleuth Sisters responded, sharing the concept that, highly concentrated within the magickal bundle of energies they created, to aid them in their quest, was strong protection.

"We had to string Woods along," Raine explained. "Coddle him, so that he wouldn't suspect *our* suspicion of him. For instance, we knew he put the gargoyle, we'd gifted Amanda, out of the house. The evil in him battled that blessed guardian. However, we acted as though we hadn't even noticed it outside."

"Please, let me toss something in here," Moonglow said from across the room. "I want to apologize for my conduct in the past weeks, shooting my mouth off all over town and bringing suspicion down on, not only me, but Starlight and our whole Coven."

*We just got **that** from the chief too,* Aisling said to herself, veiling her thought. *The chief never mentioned it until yesterday, but he suspected the whole Keystone Coven of foul deeds.*

"When our stones turned up missing from the *Samhain* bonfire, it meant trouble ... bad luck," Moonglow was saying, "and that's what we got due to my irresponsible behavior. There are times in life, when we need to stand up for what we believe, and there are times it pays to keep one's own counsel, and I hope this has taught me to know the difference and to balance both. I want you all to know, however, that I am *deeply* sorry."

Starlight reached over to squeeze Moonglow's hand. "Blessed be," she said softly.

"Blessed be!" caroled the others.

"Praise the God and Goddess," Robin added under her breath, sending Aisling a darting sideways glance.

"As we mentioned to Chief Mann," Raine interposed, "there would have been no way to physically prove some of our findings, so it's a good thing we didn't end up having to testify in a court of law."

"Sam got what was coming to him from a Higher Court," Aisling stated with vigor.

The Goth gal grunted her agreement, reflecting for a moment. "But getting back to Jasper, I've learned, over the years, to send telepathic messages from a distance," Raine informed; "so I've let Jasper know that Etta Story, his new owner, is a caring person, and a lonely one, who needs him as much as he needs her. I also let him know that all the scary paranormal activity is over at Witch-Tree Farm. That sort of haunting, as we all know, is when spirits have *unfinished* business at a particular site, and there's no longer any unfinished business at Witch-Tree."

"I have a question," Old Soul Witch probed. "We all remember, I'm sure vividly, your story about the tiger you and Maggie encountered in the wilds when you were children. It was in Nepal, wasn't it? Was that when you first discovered you could communicate with animals?"

Raine gave a quick nod. "In a way, yes. As you know, our parents are archaeologists; and growing up, we accompanied them on numerous digs, all across the globe. Maggie and I were nine the epiphany summer of the tiger in Nepal." Raine reflected for a moment, adding, "The Nepal incident made me realize that I could transfer thoughts to an animal, but I'd already begun to pick up mental images and messages from my animal brothers and sisters; and over the years, I've honed this gift, for which I am truly thankful. For instance–"

"Wait!" Aisling interrupted, raising her hands in the signal for time-out and sparing a grin to Raine. "We'll never get to enjoy Robin's lovely buffet."

"Oh yes we will!" Autumn replied, snapping her fingers. "I've got an idea. How about we all visit the buffet table now; and after we eat, over dessert, Raine can share with us another of her animal experiences. What do you say, ladies?"

"Sounds good to me," Minerva concurred, with the others joining in.

Some time later, Robin stood to ask Raine to narrate her story.

Needing no real encouragement, Raine set her plate down, rose, and running all the images through her mind, began.

"Once when Beau and I were visiting a big-cat sanctuary, here in our Laurel Highlands, that's run by one of our local veterinarians, I was drawn to a particularly beautiful, male black leopard. That's my chief animal totem. Black Leopard constantly reminds me that I am being guided to explore and expand the mysterious secret path of the Shaman.

"Anyway, I noted how *uneasy* this cat was, pacing and looking for all the world like a very unhappy creature. As I stood watching him, he took notice of me and grew quite curious. Within moments, I started receiving images from him of abuse, not in the refuge where he was, but in the place whence he'd come. Furthermore, he told me flat out that he hated his name, Lucifer. He said the name, tantamount to evil, with which his former owner– a muggle to be sure– had burdened him was an *insult* to his spirit. I recognized that this cat had a very old and very wise spirit.

"That same day, I spoke with the veterinarian in charge of the refuge, who told me Lucifer was a very dangerous cat, and that he was at a complete loss as to how to handle him. I answered, 'What he is, is *powerful*, not just in strength, but in his wisdom and knowing. He has, as you are undoubtedly aware, an unfortunate past. He needs understanding and time; and, most of all, he is in dire need of *respect*. Let's begin by assuring him that he is *safe* here, that no one will harm him or demand anything of him now that he's in this sanctuary.

"To cut a long story short, I happened to mention to the leopard, via telepathy, that he harkened me back in time to the big, black cat my granny used to have, the cat whose name was Myrrdyn, the Celtic for Merlin.

"'*That* is the name I want!  I want to be called Merlin,' he told me then.

"The vet immediately changed the cat's foul name to the one the leopard himself entreated through me– *Merlin*.  I continued acting as translator between cat and vet for several weeks; and I am happy to say that, before long, Merlin became a very contented kitty."

"You enchant us!" Robin cried.

Raine's thanks gave way to the Coven sisters' applause. "Blessed be!"

"Blessed be!" Raine answered, exclaiming after a few moments, "Great Goddess! I can't say why, but I just this second got a vision of something– of Robin's witch effigy, with the jack-o'-lantern head, at the *Samhain* fest. Remember how Hester's spirit had enlivened it to warn us that 'Death doth come, the death of three?'"

The Coven answered in a rich mix of replies.

"Hester was right," Aisling said. "First there was Will Granger's death, and it set the wheels in motion for Amanda's murder, followed by Sam's Karma crashing down on him."

"Well, I think we all need to thank our fellow sisters of the moon, the Sleuth Sisters, for what they did to bring about a positive end to this whole Witch-Tree affair," Robin announced, rising from her chair. "Mike, let's make sure everyone's glass is filled!"

The High Priestess and her husband moved about the two adjoining rooms to pour champagne into everyone's flute. When they finished, Robin lifted her glass.

"A collective Thank-You to our beloved Aisling, Raine, and Maggie, who leave sparkle and goodness wherever they go! We sing your praises! Love and Light and all that is Merry and Bright– now and forever!" The High Priestess' glass shot higher, "To the Sleuth Sisters!"

**"To the Sleuth Sisters!!"** the house chorused loudly, with successive expressions of praise.

The McDonough gals looked pleased though a tad embarrassed, as Raine and Maggie turned their rosy faces toward Aisling, who took the cue to respond.

"We recognize the honor you do us, and it's very generous of you; but as our granny– and Buddha– used to say, 'Three things cannot be long hidden, the sun, the moon– *and the truth.*' And we didn't do it alone. We had, as the song goes, a little help … actually more than a little, from family and friends, from YOU, from Chief Mann, from our good Granny's teachings, and our Grantie Merry's powerful crystal ball, Athena, as well as," she sent her cousins a look sated with secrets, "from our other magickal tools."

"Always a team effort!" Raine enthused, lifting her glass with a mien of appreciation. "And *we* salute *all of you!* There's no force equal to that of determined witches!"

"Hear, hear!  We consider ourselves truly– *blessed!*" Maggie finished, her glass raised in acknowledgment.  "Where there is kindness, there is goodness, and where there is goodness, there is always– *magick!*"

The Sisters raised their glasses to the Coven.

"Magick is a gift not all can see.  For those of us who can– blessed are we!" the Sisters chimed in unison.

"Blessed are we," Moonglow echoed, "to know and love the savvy Sleuth Sisters!"

"Hear, hear!!" the others shouted in happy tribute.

**"To the Sleuth Sisters!"** Robin repeated with sudden passion, her glass again held high.

**"Hear!  Hear!!"**

The charmed threesome's thanks were drowned by a burst of applause and cheers, the response wafting and swirling, in and about the entire gathering, to settle over the Sleuth Sisters like a cozy blanket of love.

Almost palpable was the shimmering camaraderie in the elated High Priestess' home.  Within the hearts of the Keystone Coven, as well as in the hearts of those three very special Sisters of the Craft, the love vibration resonated warmly as the energies rose through the gabled roof and up the chimneys, to be released to the enchanting moon-lit sky, in gratitude– to the Goddess.

Postscript: Later that same evening …

Not far from Moonstone Manor, a jubilant spirit floated in ecstasy through the highest limbs of a certain majestic, very old and very special oak tree. Gathered around it were several bright and bouncy orbs, whilst merry laughter drifted through the winter branches glazed with snow– diamond-bright and glittering white.

Synchronously, the Sleuth Sisters, with the Keystone Coven, were just closing their concluding chant at the end of the gathering's festivities. "By the Goddess we are called, witch to witch, heart to heart, merry meet and merry part–

"And merry meet again!"

"When you witch upon a star …"

~ The Sleuth Sisters

# ~ Epilogue ~

Dressed in their black ritual robes, the three Sleuth Sisters, with poppet and Merlin cats, were in their sacred attic space, seated around their amethyst crystal ball, Athena. Each Sister was in a buoyant mood, for the Yuletide was a favorite time o'year for the McDonough gals who were free from their work duties during the Christmas break. The freedom was always such a blessing to the Sisters, and this year there were so many blessings for which to be thankful.

In the giant purple globe, the image that came into focus was none other than Grantie Merry, who was entertaining a festive mood of her own.

"So, we wanted to let you know that we've been granted the marker, thanks in great part to *you*. Witch-Tree Farm with its Witch Tree is now designated an official Pennsylvania historical site," Raine stated with keen satisfaction.

"And yesterday, we drove to Teresa Moore's to return her ancestor's original manuscript to her, along with our heartfelt thanks," Aisling said. "We've found a true friend in Sister Teresa. She's a blessing. As are *you!*"

"We don't meet people by accident," Grantie reminded. "They are meant to cross our paths for a reason."

"Oh," Maggie continued, "and you'll be happy to learn that Etta Story, the Washingtonville Historical Society President we told you about, who is residing in Witch-Tree's farmhouse, has found a real home at long last, *and* she has verily bonded with Will Granger's Airedale, Jasper. As the Bard would say, 'All's well that ends well.'"

"I am so glad you conjured me today, my dear girls!" Grantie exclaimed with the warmth she reserved for those she truly loved.

"We wanted to thank you again for all your help in untangling the Witch-Tree mysteries," Aisling replied, "and get you up-to-date on how everything turned out."

"My pleasure," Merry laughed in a way that matched her joyful soubriquet.

"You never change, Grantie!" Aisling effused.

"Aw," the old woman replied, touched by the compliment, "age has a way of creeping up behind a person and getting under the skin like an imposter. Though, I must admit, I don't think I look my age."

"You don't!" the Sisters spoke at once– and with sincerity.

Their great-aunt smiled. "It's because happiness grows with age, and that's the best beauty secret there is! As I started to tell you, I'm glad to chat today. Your cousin Emerald has finally set a date, *in stone*, for her wedding. It will take place Valentine's Day. You'll be receiving invitations, of course."

"Will it be a muggle wedding or a handfast?" Raine asked.

"It will be a traditional, Celtic handfasting ceremony, and I expect the three of you to attend, so do whatever you need to *now*, to plan ahead for it. The handfast is not the only reason I want you in Salem for Valentine's. I have something, again, that I want to give you, something very special, and so you must come up here in February, for I shan't post such a treasure."

"Oh, what is it?!" Raine implored, clapping her hands at mention of a present.

"Raine," Grantie's old eyes held a trace of enjoyment as well as warmth, "how like a child you can be at times! The gift is to be a *surprise*, so you'll just have to wait. I will say it's more special than anything I've ever given you."

"Well now, this is the second time you've tantalized us with mention of it, so you *have* to give us at least one clue!" Raine insisted.

"My dear," Grantie Merry huffed, "you should know that I don't *have* to do anything. I do what I please. Always have. Always will," she snapped, with more than a hint of tartness.

From Maggie's lap, Cara tittered, covering her mouth with her little, mitt-like hands.

"Oh, Grantie, what could be more special than your gift of Athena or your seaside cottage with its magickal contents you bequeathed us in your will?" Aisling tested, always more diplomatic but just as curious now as Raine, who pretended to pout, though her pretense was convincing! In fact, her face wore such a woebegone expression that Grantie was beginning to soften.

"This gift is among the things in my cottage I have willed to you upon my passing, but I've always believed that sacred items come to us when we're *ready* for them, and *you– one, two, three,*" she cheerily pointed to each of the Sisters, "are ready for this sacred item *now,* you see. Thus, simply put, I want you to *have* it now. It will come in handy in the work you do. I assure you." The centenarian gave a great sigh. "And to be perfectly honest, I simply don't have the energy to use it any longer. Requires a heap o' energy to use it effectively. Yes, it's time to pass it on into good hands, young hands, and what *better* hands than *yours?*"

"Grantie, *please* give us a clue!" Raine entreated, sensing victory. "I know I shan't be able to stand the suspense till Valentine's! *Pretty, pretty ple——ase!*"

With a sparkle in her eyes, the great lady shook her head. "Every witch's heart is a deep ocean of secrets. You mustn't press me to give all my secrets away. I *am* my secrets!"

"*Plea—se,* just one itsy-bitsy clue?" Raine purred, bringing her hands together as if in prayer and ignoring Aisling's sharp elbow in her ribs.

Grantie tilted her face with her upswept froth of white hair in its Victorian-style bun. The Sisters recognized her thinking mode, and they dared not speak.

After a long silence, the McDonough *grande dame* said, with more than a touch of mystery gilding her voice, "It's a very *old,* very *valuable* locket, she whispered. "A bejeweled gold locket with–" She slid to an abrupt stop. "That's enough about the piece– for now."

Clasping her hands together before her mouth, the fingers tapped her lips in a reflective gesture. "And trust me when I tell you it's infused with the very *strongest* magick I have ever encountered. As well you know, I've practiced the Craft my entire life. I wasn't quite four when I began, and I'm now past a hundred." Grantie smiled. "As I told you, it will serve you well."

After a beat, she added, "The locket's magick will be *your* special talent, Raine, just as the crystal ball is Maggie's, and healing and protection spells are Aisling's, though astral projection is another of Aisling's strengths," the *grande dame* rambled; "thus, I believe I'll present you with something quite extraordinary for that too when you come up here for the wedding. See, I *knew* it was a good day for a chat!"

"What does the locket *do*, Grantie?" Raine could not help but whisper in return, for her heart had, indeed, skipped a beat, and their great-aunt's words filled her with wonder and a curiosity that was nearly unbearable.

"You'll have to come up to Salem in February to find out," Grantie Merry replied with utter delight. "'Tis only a few weeks hence. However, I shall grant one more clue– the locket will add a whole new … *dimension;*" she paused, "yes, I think *dimension* might be the proper word, to your lives."

Later, after the Sisters had carefully cleansed and settled Athena into her storage place, with poppet and Merlin cats in tow, they skipped down the attic stairs, chanting softly–

"Still around the corner a new road awaits. Just around the corner– ***another secret gate!***"

# ~About the Author~

Ceane O'Hanlon-Lincoln was born during an April thunderstorm, and she has led a somewhat stormy, rather *whirlwind* existence ever since. A native of southwestern Pennsylvania, Ceane (SHAWN-ee or Shawn) taught high school French until 1985. Already engaged in commercial writing, she immediately began pursuing a career writing both fiction and history.

In the tradition of a great Irish *seanchaí* (storyteller), O'Hanlon-Lincoln has been called by many a "state-of-the-heart" writer.

In 1987, at Robert Redford's Sundance Institute, two of her screenplays made the "top twenty-five," chosen from thousands of nationwide entries. In 1994, she optioned one of those scripts to Kevin Costner; the other screenplay she reworked and adapted, in 2014, to the first of her *Sleuth Sisters Mysteries*, **The Witches' Time-Key,** conceived years ago during a sojourn in Ireland. As Ceane stood on the sacred Hill of Tara, the wind whispered ancient voices— ancient secrets. *O'Hanlon-Lincoln never forgot that ever so mystical experience.*

***Fire Burn and Cauldron Bubble*** is the second of the *Sleuth Sisters Mysteries*, ***The Witch's Silent Scream*** the sexy third. ***Which Witch is Which?*** is the exciting fourth witchy whodunit, ***Which-Way*** the spine-tingling fifth, and ***The Witch Tree*** the sixth adventure in the bewitching series.

Watch for ***The Witch's Secret***, the seventh spellbinding *Sleuth Sisters Mystery*– coming soon.

Ceane has also had a poem published in *Great Poems of Our Time*. Winner of the Editor's Choice Award, "The Man Who Holds the Reins" appears in the fore of her magickal short-story collection ***Autumn Song***– the ultimate witchy-woman read!

William Colvin, a retired Pennsylvania theatre and English teacher, said of her ***Autumn Song***: "The tales rank with those of Rod Serling and the great O. Henry. O'Hanlon-Lincoln is a *master* storyteller."

Robert Matzen, writer/ producer of Paladin Films, said of ***Autumn Song***: "I like the flow of the words, almost like song lyrics. *Very evocative*."

World-renowned singer/ actress Shirley Jones has lauded Ceane with these words: "She is an old friend whose literary work has distinguished her greatly."

In February 2004, O'Hanlon-Lincoln won the prestigious *Athena*, an award presented to professional "women of spirit" on local, national and international levels. The marble, bronze and crystal *Athena* sculpture symbolizes "career excellence and the light that emanates from the recipient."

Soon after the debut of the premier volume of her Pennsylvania history series ***County Chronicles,*** the talented author won a Citation/ Special Recognition Award from the Pennsylvania House of Representatives, followed by a Special Recognition Award from the Senate of Pennsylvania. She has since won *both* awards a *third* time for ***County Chronicles***– the series.

In 2014, Ceane O'Hanlon-Lincoln was ceremoniously inducted into her historic Pennsylvania hometown's Hall of Fame.

Ceane shares Tara, her 1907 Victorian home, with her beloved husband Phillip and their champion Bombay cats, Black Jade and Black Jack O'Lantern.

In addition to creating her own line of jewelry, which she calls Enchanted Elements, her hobbies include travel, nature walks, theatre, film, antiques, and reading "… everything I can on Pennsylvania, American, and Celtic history, legend and lore. In addition– I *love* a good mystery! Historians, in essence, are detectives– we're always connecting the dots!"

~~~

## ~ A message to her readers from *Mistress of Mystery and Magick–* Ceane O'Hanlon-Lincoln ~

"There's a little witch in every woman."

"I write because writing is, to me, like the Craft itself, *empowering*. Writing, as the Craft, is *creation*. When I take up a pen or sit at my computer, I am a goddess, a deity wielding that pen like a faerie godmother waves a wand.

"Via will, clever word-choice and placement, I can arrange symbols and characters to invoke a whole circuitous route of emotions, images, ideas, arm-chair travel– and, yes indeed, even time-travel. A writer can create– *magick*.

"I am often asked where I get my inspiration. The answer is 'From everything and everyone around me.' I love to travel, discover new places, and meet new people. And I have never been shy about talking to people I don't know. I love to talk, so over the years, I've had to train myself to be a good listener. One cannot learn anything new, talking.

"People also ask me if there is any truth to my stories about the Sleuth Sisters. To me, they are very real, though each is my own creation, and since I have always drawn from life when I write, I would have to say that there is a measure of truth in each of their essences– and in each of their witchy adventures."

How much, though, like the author herself– *shall remain a mystery.*

**A Magick Wand Production**

**"Thoughts are magick wands powerful enough
to make anything happen– anything we choose!"**

**Thank you for reading Ceane O'Hanlon-Lincoln's**
***Sleuth Sisters Mysteries.***
**The author invites you to visit her on Facebook,
on her personal page
and on her *Sleuth Sisters Mysteries* page.**

**May your life be replete with—**

*magick!*

"The most beautiful experience we can have is the mysterious.
It is the fundamental emotion that stands at the cradle
of true art and true science."
~ Albert Einstein

*Believe!*